# THE SAPPHIRE SPHINX

## A SCARLET PIMPERNEL RETELLING

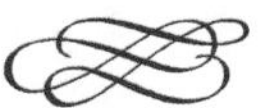

## CLARISSA KAE

CARPE VITAM
~PRESS LLC~

*To my literary and chosen family,*
*you are my talisman*

# ACKNOWLEDGMENTS

This book (and every book ever placed upon a shelf) is never created by just one person. It's the culmination of a spouse shouldering family responsibilities, children shooing authors toward their computers and an incredible community shouting from the sidelines.

I've had my fair share of panicked phone calls and looming deadlines...and an enormous amount of people to thank. Damon, Kaela, Ava, and Isla Belle to start things off (without you, I wouldn't be able to be me). Adam, Connie, Jo, Jesse, Kaylee, Raneé, Jess, Melanie, Esther and the rest of the zoom sprint crew.

I'm grateful for our friendships and the ability to share our stories. Storytelling was, and will always be, a divine calling.

—Clarissa

# CHAPTER 1

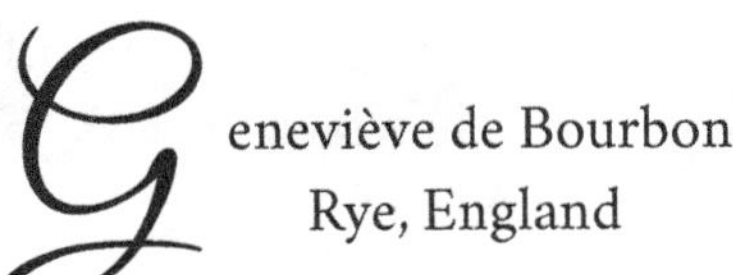

eneviève de Bourbon
Rye, England

Geneviève de Bourbon stood in the middle of her cousin's abandoned nursery with news sheets from around the country spread across the floor. Most of the papers from larger towns were a week old. Living in a sleepy English town made her hobby of tracking spy gossip nearly impossible. She'd already tossed the *Rye Illustrated* to the corner, the articles as useless as ever. Geneviève and half of London already knew of Bonaparte's obsession with a talisman, a gem-encrusted sphinx.

"Are you truly certain?" Her cousin hugged a stack of articles from France. Ever the practical relative, Mary neatly placed the stack on the dresser and bent over the top three London news sheets. "France believes Sir Percy Blakeney is the Scarlet Pimpernel, but he's been quoted at several clubs stating he's staying in England." Mary pointed to the gossip column that had a knack for predicting marriages as well as other juicy facts. "Apparently, his recent marriage has tamed him."

"He's a spy." With a groan, Geneviève went to the nursery window and stared at her uncle and his estate manager walking below into the house. "Sir Blakeney is not supposed to let people know his mind. His whole purpose is to find information, not spread it." She leaned against the glass, her heart heavy. Geneviève should be filled with gratitude that her English cousin was as anxious to help but all Geneviève felt was guilt—laden and ever present.

"We have time yet, Evie," Mary offered quietly behind Geneviève. "Let's focus on what we *do* know instead of what we don't."

"We leave tomorrow—"

Gently pulling Geneviève from the window, Mary smiled. "And we have all night." She waved her arms about. "We've the entire nursery." Her hands smoothed out her skirt, a nervous habit. "Completely undisturbed. Father will be far too busy with the new lambs."

"True," Geneviève said with a little too much force. She *was* grateful her uncle—Mary's father—was preoccupied with his hobby sheep farm to notice their growing obsession with the league of British spies. For Mary, it was a curiosity. For Geneviève—it was so much more.

Mary flattened the map of England and France. She placed one finger on Calais and another on Paris. "We know there's a member of the league leaving Calais. We also know there's a leak, a man who has ties to France *and* England leaving from Calais as well."

Nodding, Geneviève added, "The King's jubilee and Blakeney's wedding pulled everyone to England but Bonaparte's wife is having a birthday bash—"

"Yes." Mary's finger tapped the area labeled *Paris*. "Bonaparte has gathered his captains and armies from Egypt and—"

"Everywhere." The heaviness was back. Geneviève would have to bury her feelings if their little plan was to work. "He's preparing for his next round."

Mary cleared her throat, her hands wringing. "Are you certain, Evie, absolutely certain, you don't want to invite Charles into our confidence?"

Geneviève shook her head. "My brother..." She let the words hang between them. Charles had decided to stay in France even after the revolution had destroyed their family. She'd once thought Charles was being held captive. For years, her brother had stayed silent no matter how many times Geneviève wrote to him. Only after convincing her uncle that Mary and Geneviève were eager to see Paris did Charles respond, inviting them to stay at the family home in Paris. She didn't know what to expect—of her native country or her brother.

Motioning to the Paris news sheets, Mary whispered, "We know Charles is in attendance at Bonaparte's court, but we can't judge him too harshly." She gathered the papers. "If we're to be of any use to the league, we'll have to be among the guilty."

"I'm ready." With a flash of a grin, Geneviève shed the solemn expression. She clasped her hands together and twirled around. "Oh, this is splendid." Keeping her voice high, she pranced about the room. "I do adore your dress, Madame Bonaparte."

Mary clapped with a grin. "Astounding performance."

The facade fell to the floor. If Geneviève was to succeed, her act should not come off as a performance. In truth, she was once as naive and bubbly as her pretend persona. She'd loved and trusted blindly. But Madame Guillotine had changed everything. The French Revolution had destroyed more than her family. Aside from Mary, Geneviève trusted no one.

Late into the evening, Mary and Geneviève emerged from the nursery, the news sheets tucked away. They had dedicated their plan to memory. The beginning was in Calais. They'd stop for a few days in Calais for research on the comings and goings of Englishmen crossing the channel to France. With Geneviève finally old enough to be Mary's chaperone—becoming a spinster at the ripe age of twenty-five had its benefits—they would be free to scour the coastal town for evidence.

They descended the stairs and found a stack of luggage with a black parasol placed on top. An eerie chill swept across Geneviève's neck. Their plan would only succeed if no one knew they planned to join the league of spies—more importantly, Geneviève desperately wanted to restore the monarchy of her childhood. She reached for Mary who'd already begun to groan.

Watching her cousin's face fill with frustration, Geneviève gripped Mary's arm. "Who—"

"Have my lessons been so easily forgotten?" A woman with a severe bun and an ever-grimmer scowl stood at the threshold. Her dress was a drab gray, cut in a fashion that hadn't been seen in at least a decade. Silver hairs stretched out from her temple toward the tight bun. Her skin was deceptively smooth as if she'd not lived or laughed in half a century.

"Miss Agnes." Mary curtseyed and held out an arm to Geneviève. "This is Gen—"

"Geneviève de Bourbon." The woman gave a sharp nod. "I'm aware, Mary. Your uncle informed me of his foolish plan of letting two young, impressionable ladies run amok in France, a country completely devoid of morals—"

"I believe at twenty-five the *ton* no longer calls me young. Or impressionable." Geneviève lifted her chin. The gossips had cleared her of any marital value years before. "And France was a beautiful country once. It will be again."

Miss Agnes narrowed her eyes. She paused a moment before adding, "We leave at first light. It's best for you two to get some sleep." Without another word, she quit the room, her quick steps echoing in her wake.

Mary covered her mouth, her eyes dancing with mirth.

"She's a beast." Geneviève's carefully plotted plan had been dismantled in mere minutes. "There's no way we'll be able to find answers. Not with that woman on our heels."

"Oh, but you've already tamed the beast." Mary gripped her cousin's arm. "I've never seen anyone interrupt my aunt and live to tell the tale."

Geneviève waved away the words. "How else am I to convince the league that I'm an asset if I can't handle a simple Miss Agnes?"

"She does have a weakness." Mary leaned in, her hand cupping her mouth. "She left her post as my lady's companion to become a novelist."

"A novelist?" The severe woman with the parasol could no sooner become a Romantic than Geneviève could swim the channel. Both might be willing, but the Fates would never be that obliging. "I wonder if her stories would be as dry—"

"Oh, Geneviève, Miss Agnes can be convinced to do a variety of improper activities so long as the event can contribute to an intriguing story." Mary's smile fell. "But you'll never be able to act the silly debutante one minute and yourself the next with Miss Agnes around. She can sniff deceit a mile away."

"If the Scarlet Pimpernel—" Geneviève folded her arms and lowered her voice. "If the Sapphire Sphinx can deceive the French, so too can I."

# CHAPTER 2

*L*ord William Cabot
London, England

Plopping onto Sir Percy Blakeney's sofa, Lord William Cabot swatted away his friend's words.

"Cabot…" Blakeney stood, hand rubbing his neck. He paced in the small study, the same room in which he and Cabot pretended to strategize war on their sisters as children. "Cabot, my words were not in jest."

William had spent far too many lazy summers running through the Blakeney corridors to believe him.

"Truly, I am done."

Blakeney was teasing. He must be. As childhood neighbors—and friends—William of all people would know when Blakeney was winding up. With Bonaparte's growing success—and imminent threat to England—neither man could retire. Becoming a spy was the fruition of their childhood dreams. They'd only just begun to accomplish their goals.

"You're not hanging up your capes." William lay back, his hands cradling the back of his head. Blakeney was Britain's greatest spy, the incomparable Scarlet Pimpernel. Blakeney couldn't quit spying any more than he could stop being English. "Tell me what is so urgent that you couldn't wait until after I'd met with Mother."

Sir Percy Blakeney raised his eyebrows. He lowered his voice and said with conviction, "Cabot, I am finished."

William chuckled and tossed Blakeney a look—only to freeze. A severe frown of worry and a furrowed brow looked out of place on Blakeney. Together they'd mounted attacks against horrific odds, but never had Blakeney looked more uncomfortable than in the middle of his ancestral home speaking to his childhood friend. William swallowed the growing lump in his throat, Blakeney's words echoing in his mind, *I am finished.*

An awkward silence fell between them, pulling William to a stand. He felt too awkward on the couch but standing made him feel all the more in the way. As if on que, Blakeney's bride waltzed in with a ruffle of skirts, her face awash in a pretty blush. Blakeney's lips stretched to a crooked smile—setting William on edge. For the first time, William felt like an outsider in the Blakeney home. Every inside joke and wink was between Blakeney and William, but the tenderness William had just witnessed between the newlywed couple had William feeling rather lonely.

He folded his arms, only to unfold them. He began to sit back down but decided against it. Nothing felt right.

Blakeney and William—they were closer than William's own brothers—they didn't keep secrets. They were each other's confidant; there was no goal, no desire they'd not told each other. Granted, Blakeney had broken his vow of swearing off women. The poor bloke had gotten himself married, but no, Blakeney couldn't truly be done with the Scarlet Pimpernel. Blakeney was the reason William had joined the ranks of British spies.

A strange sense of foreboding fell on William's shoulders. The same feeling typically involved a weapon pointed at his chest—or at Blakeney's.

Turning to William, Blakeney flashed his crooked smile, the same look that had melted dozens of eager ladies. "Carry the torch, old boy."

"The torch?" William asked dumbly, the words odd and cumbersome in his mouth.

"It's been an era."

"An era?" William shook his head and side-stepped his oldest friend. Blakeney must be ill, that was the only plausible explanation. "But we've only just begun…"

Blakeney glanced back at his beaming wife on the sofa. They stared at each other, exchanging another tender moment.

William pulled at his cravat, unsure of what to do or say. He'd sworn off women and his rakish past—they *both* had. They'd made a pact. Blakeney had promised his courtship to the little minx would never interfere with his career.

William toyed with his pocket watch. This was not happening. Blakeney could be both, a husband *and* a spy.

"You'll do wonders, Cabot." Blakeney's eyes flicked between his wife and friend. "The league needs you. I'm finished. It's your time to lead the way."

William's mouth fell open, his mind blank. He stood there. Silence gathered around him.

After a moment, Blakeney gently led him out of the study. William said nothing, his brain as useful as the stone steps. At the garden gate, Blakeney clapped William on the back. "It's for the best." He stood waiting while William climbed into the carriage.

William sat back. *Finished.*

Blakeney was done. His days of espionage were over, trading his nights of intrigue for a ginger-haired minx. His timing was horrid.

After years of carefully orchestrated trust, William had further solidified Bonaparte's friendship with a foolish talisman, a jewel-encrusted sphinx. Bonaparte's Egyptian obsession had proved to be his greatest weakness—while matrimony appeared to be Blakeney's.

"Finished…" William rubbed his jaw, the word feeling foreign. *Carry the torch.*

Marriage should take second fiddle to saving their country. Espionage had been, no—*was* everything they'd dreamed it to be as young boys. The fighting. The intrigue. The women—William's rakish smile fell.

The carriage turned down the long drive toward William's ancestral estate, inviting more memories. The moment William had discovered Blakeney's alias—the Scarlet Pimpernel—William had begged, or rather, demanded to follow him into battle. Blakeney had been more than a childhood neighbor. Closer in age than William's own brothers, Blakeney had allowed William to tag along, even during their Eton days. They had created the league, actively gathering apprentice spies into the fold.

With heavy footsteps, William left the carriage. The sound of a rifle had his footmen wincing. Relief fell on William's shoulders. At least parts of his childhood had remained the same.

William circled the home, making his way straight to the elongated side garden. His diminutive mother stood, in the makeshift shooting range, aiming her flintlock rifle at the target. She cocked her head to each side before firing. Had anyone other than Blakeney been their neighbors, his mother's hidden habits would have made every titled tongue wag.

"Ah, William," Lady Asaph handed the rifle over to her footman. His mother waved him over as she pulled off her shooting gloves. "Your sister skipped out on her lessons."

"Not every woman is in need of rifle skills, Mother." The familiarity of his mother's eccentricities warmed him. William had thought his life would skip from one oddity to the next, bypassing old traditions—like getting married and settling down.

Lady Asaph scoffed. "French lesson, William. Why on earth would Catherine be in need of shooting lessons?"

Nodding to the range behind them, William offered, "Shall I point out the obvious or ignore your unorthodox hobby?"

"Oh, William, I wouldn't trust anyone to teach Catherine how to shoot. The gossips would be fluttering about. Myself and possibly your father would be fit for teaching her." The marchioness quickened her pace. For a woman firmly entrenched in the *ton* and all its strident social rules, Lady Asaph refused to give up her independence. "Every accomplished lady should know how to handle a pistol at the very least." She paused for a moment. "I understand the hesitancy with a rifle, the stance can be quite masculine. But a pistol has a feminine flair, don't you think?"

Entering his childhood home, William had stopped listening. They entered the large sitting room just off the sunroom. Straight across from where William stood gave an excellent view of Blakeney's estate. Both men had spent so much of their youth trampling between the houses that a path still cut across the grass. Weeds had begun to fill in parts, but overall the trail still glowed in the midmorning sun. William had assumed their future would be just as intertwined. William's day had begun so full of promise and now it'd turned rather dark.

And lonely.

According to the *ton*, William was unfortunately the third son of the Marquess of Asaph. His rank and singular ability to remain a bachelor made him the prime object of matchmaking mamas, including his own. Lady Asaph's eccentrics only extended to her habit of shooting, nothing else.

Her hand on his arm, she pulled William from his thoughts. "You've come from the Blakeney's residence, haven't you?" She guided William to the sofa. "Come to Almack's tonight."

"Are you shoving salt in my wound already?" Nothing could be worse than rubbing shoulders with eager mothers and desperate daughters.

"If Blakeney can finally grow up and become a husband, so too can you." Lady Asaph arched an eyebrow, daring her son to argue. For such a petite creature, she was truly a force to reckon with. "It was high time he stopped playing at being a spy."

"But, Mother..." William caught the tone in his own voice and winced. Bloody hell. He'd spent the last few years marching along Egypt as Bonaparte's personal guest—pretending to be a scholar instead of a spy. He'd risked life and limb. There was no playing about. This was far more serious than the little game of war William and Blakeney had played as awkward boys. He took a deep breath and made sure his voice fell in a proper register. Secrecy was still of utmost importance. "Please remember that you are supposed to be unaware of our—"

"Psh." She waved away his words. "I'm a mother. There will never be a greater spy than a woman with a child."

"And yet the poor country is left with only bachelors to defend—"

"Ah, so Blakeney has truly left the league. His little time out is permanent." Beaming at her son, Lady Asaph clasped her hands together. "There is hope for you yet."

William pulled on his cravat. He was no closer to becoming a husband than the next poor sop—nor would he entertain the idea while Bonaparte was still bent on conquering the continent. "Perhaps you should focus your efforts on my sister."

His mother made a noise that in any one of lower rank than a countess would have been given the unmannerly name of a snort. As a cowed member of the *ton* had once commented, *Nobody* harrumphs *quite like the Marchioness of Asaph.*

"Just because you're an agent for the league doesn't mean that you can put off settling down forever. Really, William." She took a furtive look around the hall to make sure no servants were in evidence—her sudden concern for his identity gave William a small burst of hope. "You're nearly thirty—"

"Not for a few years."

"Just because you're the Sapphire Sphinx—ridiculous name—doesn't mean you don't have obligations. Responsibilities."

"Saving Europe from a tyrant no longer counts as responsibility?" William lay back on the sofa. He needed to be alone with his thoughts, not be lectured on familial obligations.

"Oh, William. The Asaph title could die out entirely because you couldn't be bothered to spend one little evening at Almack's and meet a suitable lady." She cocked her head to one side, narrowing her blue eyes, blue eyes that were altogether too shrewd for his good. She had been the one to unveil his secret identity. To her credit, she *had* helped from time to time, pretending to lecture him loudly in a carriage while he was sneaking about in a nearby home. Perhaps Britain should retain a league of mothers to battle Bonaparte. There was truly nothing more relentless than the mother of an unmarried child.

"With Blakeney no longer at the helm," William said, hating each word, "I am needed now more than ever. Such is the freedom of being the third son. You've three, no, *four* grandchildren. I sincerely doubt the title is in danger."

His mother frowned. "Accidents do happen. But that's not even to be thought of." A hand on her hip, Lady Asaph began to pace along the expanse of the foyer, bronze silk skirt swishing in time to her steps. "What I meant to point out was that sooner or later, you're going to have to give up playing at espionage."

*Playing* at espionage. He shot his mother a look of both outrage and incredulity. The very same woman had just come in from *playing* at shooting a rifle.

"If Blakeney can scurry back to England, so too can you."

"Blakeney came home because the French discovered he was the Scarlet Pimpernel," William grumbled. Blakeney was supposed to be back in the saddle next month. He'd had the audacity to court his childhood sweetheart. If William's identify were to be revealed—he jerked his head up. "Mother, you wouldn't…"

Lady Asaph paused, a mischievous glint in her eye. "No, I wouldn't." For a moment she gazed dreamily off at an arrangement of flowers in one of the alcoves in the wall. "Such a pity. It would be so effective."

Shaking her head as if to whisk away the temptation, she resumed her brisk progress around the room. "Darling, both your father and I are terribly proud of you. Don't think we don't appreciate that you trusted us enough to confide in us. Look at poor Lady Nehin—she only found out her son was an agent for the War Office after he was captured by that French spy and they started sending her all those nasty ransom notes in French. And he never even had a special name or made it into the illustrated papers." The marchioness indulged in a maternal smirk. "We just want to see you *happy*."

And there it was, the core of practicality underneath his mother's frustrations. William came to her, waiting for her to look him in the eye. "I *am* happy."

Lady Asaph opened her mouth.

William shook his head. "And I am being careful. I promise."

The Marchioness gave another infamous *harrumph,* a terrible attempt at hiding the slight tremor of her lip. She blinked and stepped back. "Have a good time at White's."

"I'm being careful," he repeated.

She nodded and turned away, tugging at William's heart. The poor woman was worried about her son. If she knew the horrors William had seen, Lady Asaph would never let him out of her sight.

He paused halfway out the door and flashed a puzzled look. "How did you know I'm headed to White's?"

In a flash, Lady Asaph's face brightened, her lips stretched to a wide smile. "I'm a mother, darling. We know everything."

# CHAPTER 3

$\mathcal{L}$ord William Cabot
London, England

With Blakeney's words still echoing in his mind, William felt as glum as the weather as he headed down Upper Brook Street towards St. James Street. Only after his thoughts drifted toward his mother did the shadow of smile appear on his face. Lady Asaph could rope William into Almack's faster than France could conquer the continent. The War Office should let his mother loose on France. The country would be far too busy planning weddings; they would never be able to lift a sword against England. Either that or Lady Asaph would have trained the entire French army to have perfect aim and shiny rifles.

"Afternoon, Cabot!"

William absently nodded to an acquaintance in a passing curricle. It was just after five, the hour for flirting while on horseback. There would be a steady stream of fashionable people and carriages clogging the streets as they made their way to Hyde Park. William smiled and nodded by rote, but his mind was already slipping away across the channel to his work in France.

As the youngest boys of their respective families, William and Blakeney had resolved to be heroes. William had charged about the nursery dueling with invisible Frenchmen. Or maybe it came from afternoons playing King Arthur and his Knights of the Round Table in the gardens.

Sent to Eton to learn the classics, William raced through the adventures of Odysseus and Aeneas, earning a reputation as a scholar. Blakeney was a bit too occupied with his discovery of ladies to understand William's obsession, but William was enthralled. He had devoured any and all stories where the hero saved the day. William burned for his own moment when he could set out on his own adventures.

But at graduation, William was forced upon a world of peace and civility. There was little adventure to be had. As the youngest son, William had none of the responsibility of the Asaph title. His father had tried busying an anxious William with estate management, but the steward was annoyingly competent. And William was not.

There was little for William to do but ride about making polite conversation with his tenants and kissing the occasional baby. There was certainly something satisfying about it, but William knew that playing the role of a gentleman farmer would leave him bored and restless.

Until Blakeney had come to save him. With his friend's tutelage, William became a rake of the first order. By the time he was eighteen, the young son of the Marquess of Asaph was a familiar figure in the fashionable gaming dens and bawdy houses of London. He played faro for high stakes and drove his horses too fast and chased ladies with a hungry fervor.

But he was still bored.

And then, just as William had resigned himself to life of empty debauchery, good fortune smiled upon him in the form of the French Revolution. William and Blakeney formed the league. One mission went well and became two, and then three missions until they became absolutely indispensable to the War Office.

"Blakeney," William whispered. The ache opened up, filling with the sudden gloom of losing a dear friend. He shook off the feeling and jogged up the steps and into the familiar club.

The dark wood paneling of White's welcomed William. Instinctively, he began relaxing as he entered the masculine stronghold. The heavy smells of tobacco and spirits hung in the air. Meandering through the first floor, many would-be suitors for his sister made enthusiastic welcoming motions for William to join their tables. He offered a polite nod and kept walking.

"Cabot!" The Honorable Michael Holton flung aside the news sheet he had been reading. He leapt to his feet and pounded William on the back.

"Down, boy." William playfully shrugged off his friend. In a fit of temper, William's sister Catherine had once referred irritably to Michael as an overeager sheepdog. With sandy blond hair flopping into his face and his brown eyes alight with canine eagerness, Michael did bear a striking resemblance to the more amiable version of man's best friend. Their mothers were, in fact, best friends, and pushed their children to maintain the affection.

"How's Blakeney?" Michael asked a touch too brightly.

The easy feeling that had enveloped William a moment ago vanished. "He's finished."

"Finished?" Michael sat back. "The rumors are true, then."

"Rumors?" William had heard nothing about Blakeney hanging up his spying cape.

Michael shrugged. "I'd heard he was to stay domestic. Sniff out the double agent here in England."

Narrowing his eyes, William came closer. "Blakeney had given me the impression he was done. Finished. Forever."

Chuckling, Michael sat back. "Blakeney won't fully retire. Would you?"

"Never."

Michael brushed phantom dirt off his pants while a group of men passed them. Once they were gone, he asked, "When did you get back from London?"

William dropped into his seat next to him, sinking into the worn leather chair. He stretched his long legs comfortably out in front of him. "Late last night. I was with Blakeney first thing this morning." He grinned at his friend. "And now I'm in hiding."

Michael instantly stiffened anxiously. He looked left, then right before leaning forward and hissing, "From whom? Did they follow you here?"

William grinned. "I'm a fugitive from my mother."

Michael relaxed. "You might have said so," he commented crossly. "As you can imagine we're all a bit on edge."

"Sorry, old boy." William smiled as he was handed his favorite brand of Scotch.

Michael accepted a whiskey and leaned back in his chair. "What is it this time? Is she throwing another distant cousin at you?"

"Worse," William said. He took a long swig of Scotch. "Almack's."

Michael grimaced in sympathy. There was a moment of companionable silence as the men, both fashionably turned out in tight tan trousers, contemplated the horror of matchmaking mothers. Michael finished his whiskey and set it down on a low table beside his chair. Taking a more thorough look around the room, he asked William quietly, "How is Paris?"

When Blakeney and William had switched from rescuing aristocrats to gathering secrets, the War Office had wisely pointed out that the best possible way to communicate with William was through young Michael Holton. After all, the two men moved in the same set, shared the same friends, and could frequently be seen reminiscing over the tables at White's. Nobody would find anything suspicious about the two friends in hushed conversation. As an excuse for his frequent calls at Asaph House, Michael had put it about that he was thinking of courting William's sister, Catherine. Despite his mother's wish to have all her children married, William was willing to wait, both for his own marital bliss and that of Catherine's.

William took his own survey of the room, noting the back of a white head poking out over a chair back. He lifted an eyebrow quizzically at Michael who shrugged.

"It's only old man Smith. Deaf as a post and fast asleep to boot."

William nodded. "And his son is one of ours."

"And Paris?"

"Right." William relaxed. "Paris has been…busy."

With a frown, Michael tugged at his cravat.

"Stop that, or you'll have your valet baying for your blood."

Looking down, a sheepish smile crept across Michael's face. He'd rearranged the folds of his cravat from a gentle waterfall to simply falling over.

"Lots of comings and goings from the Tuileries—more than usual," William added. "I'm sending a full report to the office, along with some information compiled by our accidental friend at Bonaparte's Ministry of Police."

"Information?"

William couldn't fight the grin. "A list of all their agents in London. We'll ferret out the little rat who told France who the Scarlet Pimpernel was—*is*." The ache fell around him, dampening the moment. Espionage had been more exciting this morning, with Blakeney still involved.

"Good man." Michael slapped the arm of his chair appreciatively instead. "And your connections to Bonaparte?"

"Better than ever," William said. "The oblivious First Consul has moved a collection of Egyptian artifacts into the palace."

"Including—"

"Yes." Bonaparte had been particularly clinging to an Egyptian artifact. William—as Bonaparte's personal scholar—had conveniently found a jewel-encrusted talisman for him. The moment William handed over the sphinx, he was given the full trust of Napoleon Bonaparte.

"Does he suspect you at all?" Michael's words came in a rushed whisper.

Shaking his head, William wiped his face. He'd been careful to spoon-feed the myth and then commission the sphinx, taking care to age the jewel-encrusted artifact.

While Blakeney had pretended to be a fop, William had bored the French into complacency with long lectures about antiquity. When

Frenchmen demanded to know what he was doing in France and Englishmen reproached him for fraternizing with the enemy, William would gasp, proclaiming, *a scholar is a citizen of the world.*

Bonaparte's decision to invade Egypt had been a disaster for France but a triumph for William. He already had a reputation as a scholar and an antiquarian. Under the cover of scholarly fervor, William had gathered more information about French activities than Egyptian antiquities. With William's reports, the English had been able to destroy the French fleet and strand Bonaparte in Egypt for months—all while he sang the praises of William for finding a sphinx talisman. Bonaparte quickly appointed William his director of Egyptian antiquities. On the return to Paris, William was given two rooms bursting with those same of artifacts and an office in the palace, in the very same wing as the First Consul.

"My office has been moved into the palace." William smiled into his glass. He shouldn't be so smug, but he was rather proud of how the First Consul regarded him.

His jaw open and eyes wide, Michael looked as though he had been handed a pile of Christmas presents in July. "William, this is brilliant. *Brilliant.*" Michael so forgot himself as to raise his voice above a whisper. Quite far above a whisper.

At the far end of the room, old man Smith stirred. "Whaaat? Eh, what?"

"I quite agree," William said loudly. "Wordsworth's poetry is quite brilliant."

Michael cast him a dubious glance. "Wordsworth?" he whispered.

"Mind your volume," William warned.

"If it gets around that I've been reading Wordsworth, I'll be booted out of my clubs. My reputation will be ruined." Michael tugged once more at his cravat.

Meanwhile, Smith had staggered to his feet and done an awkward dance as he tried to catch his balance with his cane. Spotting William across the room, his face darkened to match his faded burgundy waistcoat. "Blasted cheek showing your face here. Have you been consorting with them Frenchies, eh?" He tried to poke at

William with his cane, but his legs gave way. Falling, he shouted in panic.

William jumped to his aid, steadying the man's spindly legs.

Glowering, Smith yanked his arm away and stalked off, mumbling.

Michael was at William's side, his brow furrowed in concern. "Do you get much of that?"

William shrugged off the worry and drained the remainder of his scotch in a single swallow. "Don't be such a ninny, Michael. I prefer Smith's rantings to all those debutantes twittering about the league. Can you imagine what I'd have to put up if the truth got out?"

Michael cocked his head thoughtfully, sending a lock of floppy blond hair tumbling in front of his eyes. "A man could dream…"

"Before you pretend to be the next Blakeney, perhaps you should relay my assignment."

Michael struggled to collect himself and regain the gravity incumbent upon a representative of the War Office. "Your assignment. Bonaparte is using the current peace to call an invasion of England."

William nodded grimly. "He's started growing quiet when I enter the room."

"We know he's struggling with gathering enough funds. We need dates, locations and numbers as quickly as you can get them. We'll have a string of couriers posted from Paris to Calais to relay the information as you find it." Michael's eyes glowed with sporting fervor, a hound on a hunt.

A familiar tingle of anticipation rushed through William—and then a flood of disappointment. This would be the first assignment without Blakeney. "I leave when?"

"Tomorrow." Michael nodded. "Now if Percy was here, the three of us could have a bang-up night of carousing. I guess it'll have to wait until we've foiled old Boney once and for all." He tried to rearrange his cravat and smooth down his hair. "Give Kitty a kiss for me."

William shot him a sharp look. It was bad enough that Michael continued to use Catherine's pet name.

"On the cheek, man, on the cheek." Michael scoffed. "I'd never try anything improper with your sister." Michael pulled on his cravat once before grumbling. He'd somehow made the horrible mess of fabric worse.

William raised an eyebrow at Michael, a skill that had taken several months of practice in front of his mirror when he was twelve but had been a well worth the investment. "At least *I* didn't let my sister dress me up in her petticoat when I was five."

Michael's jaw dropped. "Who told you that?"

"I have my sources." With a sniff, William lifted his chin, a move he'd seen his mother do.

Narrowing his gaze, Michael said, "You can tell your *source* that she's going to have to find someone else to fetch her lemonade at the ball tomorrow night unless she apologizes. You can also tell her that I'll accept either a verbal or written apology as long as it's suitably abject. And I mean *very* abject." He snatched his hat and gloves from a side table. "Oh, stop grinning already. It wasn't that amusing."

William rubbed his chin at though deep in thought. "Tell me, was it a lacy?"

Michael turned on his heel and stomped out of the room, his cheeks aflame like a blushing debutante.

Picking up the news sheet Michael had left behind, William settled back down into a comfortable leather chair. Tomorrow wasn't soon enough.

# CHAPTER 4

Geneviève de Bourbon
Dover, England

Just as the sun began to dip behind the horizon, Geneviève stifled a yawn, grateful Miss Agnes hadn't noticed her unladylike decorum on the bench opposite her. The three of them, Mary, Miss Agnes and Geneviève had spent two days in the carriage traveling to Dover. Their progress slowed as the driver turned down the harbor street. The entire downtown area was lined with hotels and transport buildings. Geneviève craned her neck and searched for the Orchid's Garden, the famed inn and restaurant of the Scarlet Pimpernel. Granted, that little tidbit of information was in the gossip article and not the news section but as far as Geneviève was concerned, facts were facts.

The carriage slammed to a stop as four women walked arm and arm across the street.

"We've lost our moral compass," murmured Miss Agnes with a frown.

Before Geneviève could answer, one of the women turned and laughed, showing the deep cut of her bodice.

Miss Agnes *tsked*. "That is what we will be facing in France."

*France.* Geneviève longed to hear her native tongue. She'd long ago abandoned her accent, moving her mouth to form thoroughly English words. With a sigh, she whispered, *"Tu me masques."*

"Do not mumble." Miss Agnes gripped her parasol. "Speak up."

Panicked, Geneviève glanced at her cousin. Her fluency in French was only of use if no one knew.

"What did you say, Geneviève?"

"Oh, nothing." She waved away the words. "Just something I heard as a child. Probably nothing."

"What was the saying?" Miss Agnes narrowed her eyes. The blasted woman must have seen Geneviève's wide-eyed look.

With a horrific English accent, Geneviève said in French, *"Tu me masques."*

Like a splash of water, Miss Agnes transformed. Her face softened and her eyes looked far off—and then she was back, the severe frown and hard eyes. She cleared her throat, "A literal translation is *you are missing from me.*" She shook her head. "French is a beautiful language but like the people, they are not always logical."

"I am French, Miss Agnes." Geneviève held her head high. "I remember France as loving and warm."

"You are only half-French, Geneviève." Miss Agnes kept her mouth open as if she had more to say but after a moment, returned her gaze to the window.

Mary shrugged silently when Geneviève gave her a questioning look. After what felt like an eternity, the carriage pulled to an easy stop in front of the The Crossing, the largest transport company. Miss Agnes didn't wait for the footman to open the door. She threw open the door, barking orders on where to place the trunks.

"Miss Agnes." Mary scrambled to her aunt's side. "Might we inquire which boat has room before we drag our trunks inside?"

A loud harrumph was all the answer Miss Agnes gave. She rushed inside, leaving Mary and Geneviève with the tired footmen.

With newsboys shouting the headlines, Geneviève paid for a paper while the footmen grunted and unpacked the trunks. Across the top read *Sapphire Sphinx eludes French Ministry of Police, Bonaparte threatens Delaroche.* On the third page, a cartoon had drawn Napoleon Bonaparte clutching a sphinx in one hand, a map of France in the other. Geneviève folded the paper under her arm and tried to envision a spy's perspective of Dover. Would the Sphinx be caught up in organizing his transport or would he be gleaning as much information from the locals? She needed a place to start.

"How do we find this Orchid's Garden?" Leaning on the balls of her shoes, Geneviève tried to peer above the crowd. "It'll take a good half hour for Miss Agnes—"

"No." The driver shook his head. "Miss High And Mighty will have to wait for hours." He pointed to the building. "This one's usually reserved for weeks in advance. You'll need to hire a packet. And I doubt they have any available."

"Splendid." Geneviève gave the confused man a broad smile. She had plenty of time to find the Orchid's Garden.

"And where are you off to?" The footman cackled. "I'm paid to deliver you, not babysit your things."

Geneviève paused. "I beg your—"

"Thank you for your service." Mary smiled, a hand on Geneviève's arm. Waiting until the footmen left, she added, "Don't despair, Evie. Miss Agnes will need to walk down the street to several companies." Her gaze shifted. "Or up the street. We have time and we don't have to lose our belongings."

"But—"

"Practice being a spy."

"Oh, Mary." Geneviève shook off her cousin. "I'm tired of pretending or walking in the woods, my eyes closed. I want to be *doing* something. I need to see with my own eyes. I need to hear with —" Geneviève froze. In the middle of the bustling city was the small sound of a child speaking French. She took a step toward the street and searched.

"What is it?"

Geneviève held up a hand and closed her eyes. The clop of horseshoes on the cobbled stoned streets came first, followed by different English accents punching the air. Try as she might, Geneviève couldn't hear the child. Just as she was about to give up, she heard a man's voice whispering, "*Au revoir*, Blakeney. *Adieu ami.*"

Her eyes shot open. Blakeney. Someone was bidding the Scarlet Pimpernel farewell. She reached for Mary. "Did you hear that?"

"Hear what?"

Whispering, Geneviève repeated, "*Au revoir.*"

Patiently, Mary nodded. "Evie, we're at a harbor." She motioned to the families hugging each other, the men boarding ships or entering hotels.

"But they said Blakeney. That's not just any name."

"Nor would a spy toss out that name for all to hear." Mary smiled at a passing family. "Be patient—"

"We've been promised a private packet." Miss Agnes's shrill voice pieced the air. She burst in between Geneviève and Mary. "I've spoken to the captain personally to make sure we'll be the only occupants." She emphasized *only* with a shake of parasol.

"Wonderful." Geneviève looped her arm in Miss Agnes's—ignoring her shocked look—and said, "I'd love to find the Orchid's Garden. I hear they have—"

Dropping Geneviève's arm, Miss Agness *tsked*. "And miss our boat? Heavens, no. We leave at once."

"I thought the boats were reserved weeks in advance." Geneviève hated the whine in her voice but she could not have Miss Agnes derail her plans.

Miss Agnes stomped her parasol on the steps. "And that is why you and Mary are in need of a chaperone. If you'd been sent here you'd never find yourself in Paris. You'd be…"

Geneviève stopped listening, her ear picking up fragments of French. The male voice. Two men made their way toward the building. One was stocky and balding, the other tall and lithe. The shorter one eyed two women coming his way. His grin was more than appreciative as his gaze went from boots to bosom of the women. The taller one had an air of authority, his swagger and cut of his jacket put him as a gentleman. As he neared, Geneviève thought he whispered, *Adieu ami.*"

# CHAPTER 5

*L*ord William Cabot
Dover, England

Alone in the belly of the small channel boat, William relaxed and sifted through the papers in his bag. In the safety of the dark open room, William could dive into the newest information Michael had given him. William had strategically filtered in pertinent information between scholarly dissertations. Any layman would be bored within a paragraph. There'd been many a Frenchman—or woman—who'd perused his papers with a yawn, teasing William for reading such dull subjects.

The door smacked open with a crack. William whirled toward the entrance, his whole body tensing for trouble. His pistol and knife were under his books. He'd not planned on anyone else being in the small boat. Twenty crowns pressed into the hands of the rather oily-looking captain with another ten promised upon arrival had ensured William's solitude. With a profanity-laced promise, the captain had assured William that the boat would be his alone and would set sail at the next promising gust of wind.

The sound of a door cracking against a wall generally preceded flying chairs or snarled threats, and, if one were really unlucky, the acrid smoke of powder from a pistol.

His pulse racing, William took in the room. The small boat was not ideal for defense. The boat's ceiling was too low for a man to stand and fight properly. And if the bloody boat began swaying—it could lend a whole new aspect to fencing.

The sound of several footsteps descending the steps had William whirling back toward the door. Three figures crowded the base of the stairs—three *feminine* figures. In the place of the burly oafs he had expected, he saw three women in a tight circle. The oldest of the three must be their companion; her bun and tight lip threatened the very existence of mirth.

"This has all the makings of an adventure." The brunette in a narrowly-cut yellow frock appeared to be trying—and failing—to convince the companion of some sort of journey.

William cleared his throat. This was *his* boat, blast it, and no one else had any business being on it, particularly ladies. With Blakeney shackled to the gentler sex, William had no desire to be anywhere near a woman.

The lady in yellow half turned, affording William a momentary view of a pert nose, a determined chin, and one large blue eye. The eye settled briefly on William and just as rapidly dismissed him. With a toss of her mahogany curls, she continued pleading with her assumed chaperone. "The captain said the wind won't turn for hours. We've plenty of time to observe—"

"Miss de Bourbon." The elder woman *tsk*ed. "Inviting chaos is not what I agreed to."

"But how ever can you manage a novel if you've never had an adventure?" The younger lady clasped her hands. "We could just stop in at the Fisherman's Rest for a lemonade. There's nothing untoward or chaotic about a little refreshment."

William *harrumphed*. Loudly.

The young lady, Miss de Bourbon, paid no attention. "And Mary agrees with me, don't you, Mary?" Her tone was the practiced whine of a sniveling debutante. Young ladies learned from the crib how to wrap others around their dainty little fingers. Miss de Bourbon reached for the assumed Mary, her face hidden in the shadow. "Mary and I just want *one* lemonade, Miss Agnes."

William couldn't see the entirety of Miss Agnes's features, but the name suited her demanding presence. She had to be the lady's companion—a severe one at that.

"No one is that thirsty." Miss Agnes apparently lacked both empathy and the drive to drink.

Miss de Bourbon bounced on her feet, like a prizefighter waiting to be let into the ring. The little minx was eager to win the battle— another reason William should avoid the gentler sex.

"I say," William drawled, loudly enough that Michael could have heard him back in London.

That finally got her attention. Miss de Bourbon turned. In full, her face fulfilled the promise of her profile. It wasn't what the French would call a classically beautiful face; her features lacked the sculpted dignity of a marble statue. Instead, her face was a talented engraver's etching, small and decisive. No, William changed his mind, not an etching after all. Her coloring was too vivid for the stark black and white of a print. The deep brown of her hair glimmered with hidden alloys of red gold, life fire shining through a screen of mahogany. Between dark lashes and fair cheeks, her eyes gleamed startlingly blue.

A flicker of frustration crossed her features before smoothing back to the playful face of a spoiled daughter.

True to his aristocratic childhood, William raised a sardonic brow. It was an expression that had been known to make cardsharps fling in their aces and secret agents babble like babes.

With a mischievous glint in her eye, Miss de Bourbon bounded into the room towards him. "You look like you've traveled a great deal. Don't you agree that there's plenty of time to stop off at the inn for a lemonade?"

Before William could suggest that she do just that—preferably lingering over her lemonade until after his boat had sailed—another figure appeared behind her. Miss Agnes. Her frown was more severe than her tone. After many tedious evenings at Almack's, William had discovered two types of chaperone. Both were aging spinsters, but that was all they had in common. The first was the frumpy hen wit. Although, of indeterminate age, the companion would dress in the ruffles of a seventeen-year-old. The companion would twitter and simper when spoken to, read the sappiest sort of novels in her spare time, and generally contrived to accidentally lose her charge at least twice a day. Rogues and seducers loved the first sort of chaperone; she made their endeavors that much easier.

And then there was the other type of chaperone. The grim dragon of a chaperone. The sort who looked like her spine and shoulders were reinforced with marble columns. Chaperone number two would sneer at a flounce or a frizz. She never simpered when she could snarl, and all but chained her charge to her wrist.

Miss Agnes was most definitely the second type, a dragon to her core. Gray hair rigidly pulled back. Mouth pressed into a grim line. The only incongruous note was the cluster of alarmingly white flowers on the top of her otherwise severe gray bonnet.

Despite her bland appearance, hope blossomed. The second type of companion always succumbed to reason. And blessed was the day, William needed a sensible woman—Miss de Bourbon was clearly more interested in lemonade than reason. Miss Agnes would be his savior. William darted a quick glance down at her feet. Underneath the gray hem of her skirt he could just make out two sturdy, thick-soled black boots. Yes, definitely sensible.

William opened his mouth to speak when the tip of a parasol jammed in between his ribs.

Lifting her chin at him, Miss Agnes said, "Who are you, young man, and what are you doing on our boat?"

"I beg your pardon, madam." The words came out somewhat more raggedly than William would have liked. He couldn't sound forceful while he was in pain. The woman's blasted parasol had his side throbbing. "*Your* boat?"

"Why don't Mary and I just pop by the inn while you straighten matters out with this gentleman?" Miss de Bourbon offered brightly.

"You, miss, are staying right here." The dragon managed to reach out and snag Miss de Bourbon's arm while keeping her beady eyes on William. "Yes, *our* boat. That greasy-looking fellow assured us that we should be the only passengers. If you are one of the crew—which, judging from your dress and speech, I assume you are not—go about your duties. If not, kindly depart at once."

While the woman gripped her parasol for presumedly another strike, William edged to the side. Parasols were supposed to be dainty, feminine things, not lethal weapons. "Forgive me, madam, I have been remiss in my social obligations. I am Lord Cabot."

Her frown still firmly on her face, Miss Agnes still looked like she would rather poke him than chat with him. She inclined her head. "I, my lord, am Miss Agnes Wooliston. Allow me to make known to you my two charges, my niece Miss Mary Wooliston"—a girl William had failed to notice moved out from the shadows behind Miss de Bourbon and made her curtsy—"and Miss Geneviève de Bourbon."

The quiet woman, Miss Mary Wooliston, subtly took Geneviève's arm and tried to lead her away. Squeezing the other girl's hand affectionately, Geneviève shook her head and stayed where she was. William was so caught up in this byplay that he completely lost track of what the chaperone was saying until the point of her parasol made another sortie at his waistcoat.

"Have you been attending?"

William had been raised by a woman who could shoot a rifle without so much as a blink. He'd learned rather young that to keep one's head was to be disarmingly honest. "No, Miss Agnes, I fear I was not."

"Hmph. I said we would be pleased if you would take yourself off our boat."

William smiled winningly, while taking care to move himself out of the path of the parasol. "I also paid the captain for the sole use of this ship."

In a shocking surprise, Miss Agnes's face darkened. How that was possible with the woman already possessing a draconic demeanor, William didn't want to know. The woman was undoubtedly more formidable than Bonaparte's army. Had she been a man, she would be indulging in strong language. As it was, given the ominous way she was swinging her parasol, it appeared that she was planning severe bodily harm to the captain, William, or both.

Mary moved forward with the grace and efficiency of a ghost. She put a reassuring hand on the chaperone's arm. "There must have been some mistake," she said soothingly. "I'm sure we can all reach an amiable conclusion."

Miss Agnes looked about as amiable as Medusa and with as much venom in her gaze. "The only possible conclusion is for this gentleman to remove his person from our conveyance."

Watching the chaperone bicker with her charge had been a mildly amusing diversion, but, blast it all, he had real work to do. Important work—saving England work. "Who was here first, madam?"

That argument had failed the Saxons in 1066; it was equally ineffectual with Miss Agnes, who regarded William with all the imperiousness of William the Conqueror. "You, my lord, may have been here first, but we are *ladies*," Miss Agnes responded with a most unladylike scowl. "And there are more of us. Therefore, you will cede your place."

"Why don't we all go to the inn for a nice glass of lemonade and talk it over?" suggested Geneviève hopefully.

"No," both William and Miss Agnes blurted.

With a sniff, Miss Agnes turned to her charges. "We will not be leaving. This gentleman will be the one to remove himself."

# CHAPTER 6

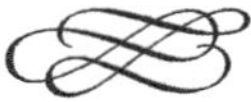

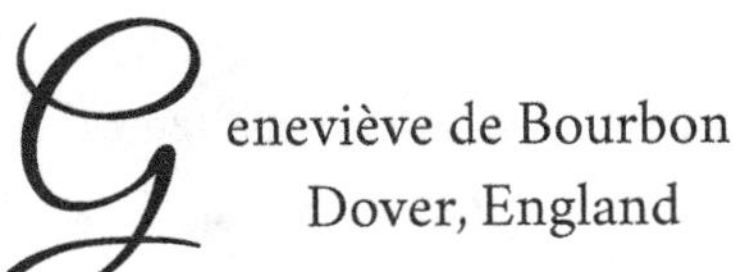

eneviève de Bourbon
Dover, England

Standing back with her arms folded across her chest—highly unladylike, but then, Miss Agnes wasn't looking—Geneviève watched the debacle between Lord Cabot and her chaperon. She was rather impressed with how Miss Agnes wielded a parasol and was rather eager to purchase one herself. From Lord Cabot's wince, the parasol appeared to be an effective weapon. As the two sparred, their barbed sentences ended with incongruous civilities, like protective tips on epées. Geneviève recognized the man as the one on the street hours earlier.

The only question Geneviève wanted answered now was whether either party would notice if she slipped from the boat. She had hoped for a few days in Dover to sniff out the habits of those crossing the channel, either to find the Sapphire Sphinx or the English rat who sold out the Scarlet Pimpernel—if one believed the latest gossips.

Lord Cabot took a step closer to Miss Agnes, close enough that the chaperone had to tip her head back to see him. Miss Agnes was fairly tall for a woman, but Lord William Cabot topped her by nearly half a foot. His blond head loomed over the waving white flowers on her bonnet, gleaming with its own light in the dim cabin. Unlike the men Geneviève had known back in Rye, who still wore their hair clubbed back with a ribbon, Lord Cabot's was cut short in the French style.

Her heart ached. She would be back on her native soil soon. Her hand absently went to her chest.

Lord Cabot carried himself with an air of easy assurance infinitely more convincing than Geneviève's memory of her brother swaggering. From Lord Cabot's highly polished boots to his waistcoat embroidered in a subtle pattern in silver, he was dressed in a casual elegance that made her own countrymen look foppish and overdone. He had evidently anticipated being alone on the boat, his black frock coat tossed over a chair, his waistcoat unbuttoned, and his cravat loosened. Where his collar gaped open, Geneviève could see the strong lines of his throat.

Her cheeks flushed a deep, uncomfortable red as she realized that the cords of his throat had gone still, the room was silent, and Lord Cabot had caught her staring—at him.

Geneviève covered her confusion by saying hastily, "This is absolutely ridiculous! There's no reason at all why anybody should be forced to wait for the next boat. After all, there's plenty of room for all of us." With a sweeping gesture, she indicated the four walls of the room.

"Out of the question," snapped Miss Agnes.

Geneviève shook her dark curls in an unconscious gesture of defiance. "Why?"

"Because," Miss Agnes pronounced witheringly, "you cannot stay the night in the same room as a gentleman."

"Oh." It'd been far too long since Geneviève had taken part in social rules. She'd been holed up in the safety of Rye. She took a quick look at the watch pinned to Miss Agnes's bony chest. From what she could make out, it looked to be just a little past four. Charles's carriage wasn't due to pick them up until the following morning. They could easily stay the night in Calais. Surely it couldn't take all that long to cross such a narrow body of water as the Channel. As long as they reached France before midnight, remaining in the cabin with Lord Cabot couldn't really be counted as spending the night in the same room as a man. If nobody went to bed, it wasn't spending the night. "How long does it take to reach Calais, my lord?"

His hands clenched at his sides, his eyebrow arched. "That depends on the weather." He fumbled with buttoning up his shirt. "Anywhere from two hours to three days."

"Three days?"

"Only in very bad weather," William drawled.

"Oh, it's absolutely lovely outside. Really, what's the harm of sharing the space for an insignificant two hours?" Geneviève could feel Miss Agnes's glare. The woman was becoming more of a hindrance with every passing moment. Geneviève looked around the small group expectantly.

Mary held up her hand for silence. "Listen."

Geneviève cocked her head to the side. She heard the steady slap of waves at the keel of the boat and the scrape of their bags on the wood floor as the motion of the boat made them shift back and forth.

"What am I supposed to hear?" Geneviève asked curiously. "Oh." The boat was en route.

From the disgruntled expression on Lord Cabot's face, he'd reached a similar conclusion. While he wiped his face, Miss Agnes rapped her parasol impatiently on the ground and snapped, "Speak up."

Geneviève glanced from Mary to Lord Cabot for confirmation. "I don't hear the sounds of the people on the dock anymore."

"That's right," Lord Cabot nodded grimly. "We've set sail."

Geneviève's face fell for a moment. Stopping at the inn had ceased to be an option. At least she had the consolation of knowing that the odds of running into the Sapphire Sphinx there had been slim in the extreme. For all she knew, he was in France at this very moment, giving instructions to his band of devoted men or filching documents from under the noses of French officials. But she knew something the English never would. Her life was spared because of a woman and her parents' lives were taken by another. In the shadows of a country, behind the back of each leader, was an army of women eager to keep their family safe.

"There's no point in arguing about it anymore, is there? Two hours and we'll be in France." Geneviève went to the porthole. "Do come look, Mary—don't they look like dolls on the wharf?"

Miss Agnes stayed where she was, standing ramrod straight smack in the center of the room.

"I don't like this any better than you do." Lord Cabot sank down into the chair next to a stack of luggage, his hand waving to Miss Agnes. "But I shall endeavor to stay out of your path if you will keep your charges out of mine."

A wave of guilt washed over Geneviève. She'd not meant to be a bother. Her brother Charles had oft complained of her being in the way. She'd only wanted to ferret out some information before leaving England.

Miss Agnes afforded a grudging nod. "We must hope it doesn't rain," she said tartly, and stalked off to the stairs. Geneviève winced. Her chaperone was more than likely going upstairs to assault an unsuspecting captain with a certain parasol.

# CHAPTER 7

 *L*ord William Cabot
English Channel

Precisely three-quarters of an hour later, the first drops hit the porthole. William was alerted to it by Miss de Bourbon's muttering. She paced with hands wringing. "It can't be raining, it can't be raining, it just can't be raining…"

"Yes, it can." William debated giving up and throwing his papers in the bag. He'd hoped to decipher the rest of Michael's correspondence, but with the woman's nervous energy William could barely think.

The boat swayed suddenly, sending Miss de Bourbon staggering. "I can see that, can't I?" She returned to her mournful vigil by the window. "How much longer do you think the trip will take?"

"My dear girl—"

"Girl?" Miss de Bourbon tossed him a withering look. The little minx could have barely left a governess. She would be a *girl* until a ring was on her finger.

"How much longer do you think the trip will take, *boy?*" Miss de Bourbon folded her arms and stood before William.

"I already told you anywhere from—"

"From two hours to three days." She looked as frustrated as his mother's dog when someone dangled a bone in front of her only to snatch it away. "I was asking for clarification, not repetition."

The Fates must be angry with William. He wouldn't get any work done so long as Miss de Bourbon was tied up in knots. He sighed, offering, "It depends on how bad the storm is."

"How bad—?" A low growl of thunder cut off her words.

"Bad."

A chuckle escaped the woman. By her wide eyes, she appeared to be surprised by the emotion. The sound rang an unexpected note of gaiety in the storm-dimmed chamber. The portholes were too small to let in much light under any circumstances, and with the sun overcast with clouds, only the eerie gray glow of a stormy sky crept into the room. Miss Wooliston had succumbed to sleep on a berth across the room, her embroidery still in her hand, her feet discreetly tucked up under the hem of her gown. Defying the usual laws of nature, Miss Agnes had managed to fall asleep upright in a rickety wooden chair. Even the combined forces of sleep and the rocking motion of the boat failed to relax Miss Agnes's iron spine; she sat as bolt upright asleep as she had while awake.

Circling Miss Wooliston, Miss de Bourbon paused twice her hands at her side. "How can she sleep at a time like this?"

William refused to answer. Sitting in a stiff wooden chair too small for his large frame, an ankle propped against the opposite knee, was already distraction enough. Pretending to be engrossed in his journal was even more so.

The woman began pacing once more, glancing back at her Miss Agnes every few steps. William forced his gaze back to his papers. Watching a lady wrestle with boredom was not his priority. Bonaparte's finances were.

Groaning, Miss de Bourbon left her sleeping friend, returning to the porthole windows. Her yellow skirts made a bright splotch of color in the rapidly darkening cabin as she crossed the room. She paced again—and again—behind William. He tucked the journal closer to him, cutting off her view if she happened to glance over his shoulders.

"What could possibly so fascinating?" Miss de Bourbon hissed.

William could almost feel the pins and needles of her nervous energy as she circled to face him.

"What are you reading?"

William flipped a fat pamphlet over to the other side of the small table for her, keeping his journal closer to him. Antiquarian literature usually worked as well for discouraging inquisitive young ladies as it did French spies.

Her eyes narrowed in the dim light. "The merit of Egyptian myths?" With a delicate finger, she slid the paper closer to him. "By Lord William Cabot of the Royal Egyptian Society?"

With forced pride, William smiled widely. "A wonderful society."

She sat back, her arms folded in a very unladylike fashion--looking very much like William's mother. "I was unaware we had one."

"We do," William said dryly. He didn't have to defend the society. Michael and the War Office had done their duty. There was a board and a War Office for the society. Any man—or lady— could walk in and see William's articles published throughout the office. Granted, he'd never actually written them, but that was beside the point. His cover was iron-clad.

Miss de Bourbon flipped through the pages, tilting the periodical to try to catch the light. "Has there been any progress on the Rosetta Stone?"

"You've heard of the Rosetta Stone?"

She scoffed. "We do get the papers, even in the wilds of Rye."

The last young lady William had delivered his Rosetta Stone soliloquy had asked him if the Rosetta Stone was a new kind of gemstone, and if so, what color was it, and did he think it would look better with her blue silk than sapphires.

"Am I to believe that you are interested in antiquities?" He shouldn't engage with a young chit. Blakeney had made that mistake. William had more pressing things to do, such as plot the Sapphire Sphinx's next escapade. Successful espionage didn't just invent itself.

But more importantly, entering into conversation with young ladies was inevitably a perilous venture. It gave them ideas. It gave them terrifying ideas that involved vows—or worse, leaving the league.

"I don't really know much about antiquities." Miss de Bourbon frowned, her fingers toying with the edge of the pamphlet. "But I love stories. Penelope fooling all of her suitors, Aeneas fighting his way down to the underworld…"

Her tone felt sincere, not flirtatious, but William didn't trust her, not yet. She was still a woman. And women stole good men from doing their duty to God and country.

"I know even less about Egyptian stories." She shrugged, adding, "I think there was Herodotus, but he seemed more like the gossips in the news sheets. Just another sensationalist. Sucking people's brains out through their noses is far worse than anything the *Rye Intelligencer* could write."

With a snap, William closed his false journal. Miss de Bourbon was either a feminine spy meant to carry a coded message, or she was truly the most unusual women he'd ever met. It was clearly the first, as William wouldn't entertain the idea of the latter. Carefully, he said, "Herodotus may have been telling the truth. In the burial chambers of Egyptian tombs, we found canopic jars with the remains of human organs." Waiting, William took in her face, searching for any signs of duplicity.

"We?" Miss de Bourbon arched an eyebrow. Mimicking his earlier tone, she said, "Am I to believe you were in Egypt?"

"Yes, several years ago."

Her eyes widened, her mouth falling open. She dragged the nearby chair to the table and plopped down. "Egypt? And why were you in Egypt?"

Disappointment fell heavy on his shoulders. She *was* an agent. There was no other reason for her sudden interest.

She leaned forward. "Were you there with any other Englishmen?"

"No." Sitting back, William rubbed his chin. If she was an agent, she'd know this.

Her shoulders sagged. "Oh."

Outside, the storm still splattered across the windows and rocked the little boat towards its destination, but William's sole focus was the enigma before him. There was something hidden behind those blue eyes. In the dim light they appeared like blue sapphires, matching the sphinx talisman William had commissioned. There was something more, a depth behind those eyes that drew him in.

"Is there a reason for your interest in Egypt?"

"Just boredom." Miss de Bourbon flicked her hand in the air. The pause in her words belied her casual tone. "Nobody at home talks about anything but sheep or embroidery."

Had William not been searching so intently, he would have missed the tension creeping up her spine and the tightness in her jaw. Miss Geneviève de Bourbon was harboring a secret.

Like a practiced debutante, she tilted her head and sweetly asked, "Do you think it will be fair tomorrow?"

"The weather or your secret?" William kept his face open, a light smile on his lips.

"Secret?" Her mouth formed an *o*. Furrowing her brow, she stared at him. A strange sense of intimacy filled the space between them. The candle flickering a few feet away gave an otherworldly glow to her face. Holding his gaze, she asked, "And what secret am I hiding?"

Leaning on the table, William mirrored her intensity. "Lemonade."

She threw back her head and laughed, the sound joyful, as if all the light in the dim cabin were concentrated in her delicate throat. He did know other intelligent women—Catherine, for one, and a few others of his sister's circle. Bright, intelligent women who were too pretty to be dismissed as bluestockings. He had even, of his own free will, dropped by the drawing room to join them in conversations on one or two occasions, but there was more beyond the surface of Miss de Bourbon.

Perhaps it was the intimacy of darkness, or of the small quarters, but absurdly, he felt quite as comfortable chatting with Geneviève de Bourbon as he ever had with Michael or Adam. Only Michael didn't have immense blue eyes fringed with dark lashes. And Adam certainly didn't possess a slender white neck with tempting indentations over the collar bones. William shook away the thought.

Scooting to the edge of her chair, Miss de Bourbon leaned forward. "I think I found a secret, Lord Cabot. Wasn't Egypt swarming with French soldiers?"

# CHAPTER 8

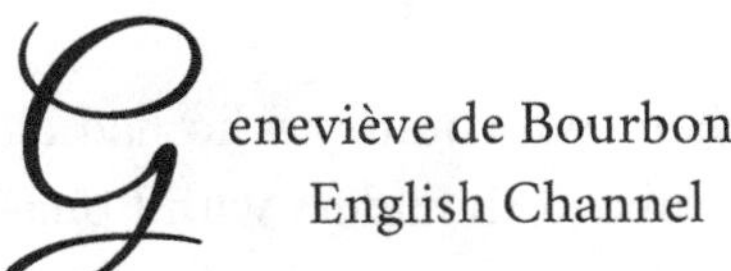

eneviève de Bourbon
English Channel

The steady drum of rain pelting the portholes should have comforted Geneviève instead of increasing her nerves. Hours earlier she'd begged Miss Agnes for a detour for lemonade, a deceitful idea to search for duplicitous Englishmen. She'd no idea that one greedy captain would deliver the very person Geneviève was searching for—an Englishmen who admitted to being entirely too friendly with the French. She searched his face. "Your neck is intact. How ever did you manage to keep your head with so many French soldiers about? Madam Guillotine prefers to separate aristocratic heads from well-bred necks."

"I was with the French." There wasn't a hint or a note of shame in his voice. His brow didn't furrow, nor did his eyes beg for understanding. He sounded more like her uncle rehearsing his upcoming sheep breedings than someone admitting to consorting with the enemy.

"You were with the French." She'd said each word slowly, more for herself than for effect. The words hung in the air. Geneviève had spent years devouring every detail of the Scarlet Pimpernel, living each victory as if she personally was avenging her parents' death. "Were you—did you—could you have been a prisoner of war?"

"No. I went at Bonaparte's invitation, as one of his scholars." Again, nothing. His words weren't laced with guilt. He wasn't hiding —in fact, he appeared to be searching Geneviève's face for something.

Her spine snapped upright. Head up, shoulders back. As she stared at William, her posture locked into a steely rigidity enough to please even Miss Agnes. "You were in Bonaparte's party as one of his officers? You took French coin?"

"Actually"—William lounged back in his chair—"he didn't pay me. I went at my own expense."

Geneviève swallowed hard, an ache opening in her chest. "You went of your own free will."

This was a man, a gentleman from her own country who had all but admitted he was the English rat. He rubbed shoulders with Bonaparte, no—he was the First Consul's scholar. Geneviève had planned to help England and France rid the continent of Bonaparte, not invite one of his agents into conversation.

"You sound horrified, Miss de Bourbon. You must admit, it is the chance of a lifetime for a scholar."

Geneviève's mouth opened but no sound came out. Lord Cabot was right; she *was* horrified. "For an Englishman to accompany his country's enemy, to disregard all duty and honor in the pursuit of scholarship." She rubbed the bridge of her nose. Her own brother had refused to leave France, believing no one should run scared—a feat considering Charles was scared of his own shadow. "You did not want to wait for the English to control Egypt before pursuing your little pyramids?"

"Miss de Bourbon." He reached for her over the table.

Recoiling, her voice rose. "How could any man, any *thinking* man, any *intelligent* man with any amount of feeling ignore all that a cruel nation had done for something as trivial as scholarship frivolity?"

"Miss—"

Geneviève held up her hand. "So many... so many slaughtered by their own people. How could you disregard all of that for the sake of a few tombs? It is a slight to his county and a slight to mankind."

But, if she was being quite honest, what stung most wasn't the slight to mankind, but the sense of betrayal his words caused. He had been witty and interesting and charming. It was utterly ridiculous. She had known the man all of two hours. One couldn't really claim betrayal after two hours' acquaintance. Even so, in those two hours, it wasn't as though he had lied and claimed to have fought for the English and then let slip by accident that he had been with the French.

The gleam in his green eyes that had been good-natured became sinister. Even the dark hues of his clothing went from elegant to dangerous, the sleek pelt of a panther on the prowl. He was probably quite practiced at gulling the unwary into liking and trusting him. His casual attire and familiarity in travel meant he was well-versed in journeying back and forth to France.

Across the table, William raised an eyebrow at her in silent inquiry. The gesture made Geneviève want to whack him over the head with his Egyptian pamphlet.

Geneviève struggled for words to voice her revulsion. "Scholarship is all very well and good, but after what the French did—while England, your own country, was at war with them."

"*Your* own country." His lips quirked up.

Warmth filled her cheeks. Blast it all, she was blushing. She'd not meant to let that little fact slip. "England. I simply meant England."

"I wasn't in the French army." William held up a finger. "I merely traveled with them."

Geneviève shook her head. She wasn't an innocent school girl. "Egypt was a military action first and a scholarly expedition second. You can't claim not to have known—I'm sure even the wild Americans knew."

"Priorities, my dear, priorities." William folded his hands on the small table. "You are behaving as if you've just discovered nine dismembered wives in a cupboard in my bedchamber."

"That would be a considerable improvement."

A flicker of annoyance crossed his face. She was breaking through his facade. He brushed an imaginary speck of lint off his sleeve but the vein on his neck ticking belied his rising frustration. "I chose to concentrate on the scholarly aspects."

She lowered her voice in a husky whisper. "You chose to ignore the thousands of innocent people slaughtered on the guillotine."

"What," he asked languidly, like a vapid London fop, "has the guillotine to do with my researches?"

Geneviève stood with a snap, her blood filling with fury. This man, if he could even be called human, was consumed with selfish callousness. Even her hen-witted brother had more character in his sniveling spine.

Pointing a finger at him, her voice shook. "That army was led by the same people who slaughtered thousands of their compatriots in cold blood. The ground of the Place de la Guillotine was still red with the blood of the murdered when you went to Egypt. By your very presence, you condoned their villainy."

He smiled with a devilish glint in his eye. Lord Cabot possessed the sandy blond hair of a rake and the broad shoulders of a man in authority. "I quite agree, dear girl."

"Girl? Surely you are not daft enough or blind enough to realize I am not a mere girl." Her heart pounded in her chest, pulsing with indignation. "What the French did was reprehensible—"

"Did." He held up a finger. "Not doing, *did*. They stopped killing off their aristocrats several years ago."

Recoiling, Geneviève covered her mouth. How could a person be so callous, so selfish—as if those aristocrats were strangers, nothing more than dead fish thrown over the side of a boat. Her parents were living, breathing humans. Not forgotten points in history. "Why bother with the prisons, Lord Cabot? A murderer is not a killer until after he has killed. It's in the past, why bother arresting the poor sop?" Straightening her spine, she forced her face to relax. She lifted her chin. "The predator does not simply abandon hunting because it's in the past—"

"My dear—"

"Do not patronize me, my lord," she hissed. "The fact remains that Bonaparte profited off the backs of good people, honest men and women—" her voice cracked. She swallowed the rising fury. For once, she wished for Mary's calm demeanor. "And you, an Englishman, profited as well. You danced with the devil to fill your scholarly pride."

His jaw tightened for a moment. Quick as it came, the whisper of frustration was gone. "You are bound for Calais."

Geneviève blinked. "By Jove, you *are* daft."

"If I profited off Bonaparte by Egypt, my dear, what are you doing on a boat bound for France?"

"How dare—"

"Please, enlighten me on your definition of guilt by association— that is what you were referencing, weren't you?" Picking up his journal, he began thumbing through the pages. "Oh, my darling, would you mind terribly reading my notes? I have been recently accused of being too blind to see."

Geneviève growled like a wounded animal and braced herself against the table. "You insufferable dandiprat—"

He motioned to her torso. "And that dress you're wearing."

Geneviève's hands flew automatically to her bodice.

"Isn't that the French style? The revolutionary style? If associating with the revolutionaries is a hanging crime, what about aping their fashions?" He *tsk*ed with a shake of his head. "For being up in arms about the French, you seem to embrace—"

Smacking the table, Geneviève winced. She cast a glance at Miss Agnes. Counting to five, Geneviève slowed her breathing. She would not let a traitorous Englishman goad her into a heated temper. She'd endured worse than this fop of a man. "You know nothing, Lord Cabot. You know nothing of what France endured, what hardships were caused. You are nothing but a spoiled Englishman."

"And what, pray tell, could a lady teach men about the world?" William looked up from toying idly with the lace on his cuffs.

Fighting tears, Geneviève shook her head, refusing to answer. Sweeping her skits away as though from something infected, she resumed her post by the porthole, her back to Lord Cabot. She would find this league of spies and she would right the wrongs Bonaparte had done. She was Lady Geneviève de Bourbon descended from ancient French royalty—by Jove, she would stop at nothing.

# CHAPTER 9

ord William Cabot
English Channel

The boat rocked with the fervor of an angry storm. In the corner of the room, William pounded the nearly flat pillow under his head. His attention did nothing for his comfort. Tossing and turning on the meager blankets, each movement added another log to his rising temper. He'd given the cot to the blasted women. Miss Geneviève de Bourbon was filled to the brim with self-righteous judgement. William punched the pillow again. He had no illusions that his pounding would render the pillow comfortable, but punching something made him feel better, and he couldn't very well punch Geneviève. She'd pricked his conscious which was absurd. William had nothing to feel guilty about. He was sacrificing everything for the good of his country, unlike the spoiled little minx.

After her little rant, William had kept punctiliously to his side of the cabin. There might as well have been a line drawn across the scarred wooden floor. Miss Agnes had woken with a start and insisted on raising a literal barrier down the center of the room.

"I will not have you share a bedchamber with a person of the opposite sex," she'd declared to her charges, and gone off to badger the captain for spare sailcloth. The captain had refused to be badgered. Not to be thwarted, Miss Agnes had commandeered William's cloak. Strung up along the center of the room with Miss Agnes's, Geneviève's, and Mary's cloaks, it made a rather uneven but passable partition.

Unfortunately, it did nothing to keep out the image of Geneviève's furious face.

William pummeled his pillow again. So, the lady had condemned him for hobnobbing with the French. He had thought he was used to that by now. Old Smith wasn't the only one to have taken issue with William's activities. Over the past few years, William had run the gamut of disapproval, from snide remarks hissed behind his back to outright lectures delivered to his face. But he'd never spent a night awake, abusing his pillow, after being reproved.

"You are a prize fool," he whispered to the dark corner. He should be delighted to have rid himself of the tedious company of a simpering young chit. Usually, he had to employ every ounce of his ingenuity to be rid of them. But to be fair, Geneviève's company hadn't been all that tedious and she hadn't simpered. She had read Herodotus. No matter how many classics the girl had perused, young ladies were a liability that an intrepid spy could not afford. William had learned that lesson well years ago—and had been reminded of mere weeks before. Blakeney might be able to walk away from this life, but espionage was a calling William wouldn't ignore.

Paris was the last place William needed an English debutante clinging to him. He couldn't ferret out Napoleon's plan for invasion *and* court the young miss, especially now. William had been waiting for this assignment for years—the entire War Office had been waiting for signals that Bonaparte was trying to invade England. It was one of the few countries the First Consul hadn't gotten around to yet. Italy, the Netherlands, Austria, all had fallen. England had the advantage of a watery moat, but how long could it hold out against Bonaparte's tactical brilliance?

Another punch at the pillow for good measure. William was a

Cabot. His ancestry was English for centuries. He was and would forever be English down to his bone.

And yet, Miss de Bourbon's haunted eyes and severe frown chased away his sleep. There was a depth to her hurt which made little sense to him. She was nothing but a young miss wanting to run around Paris on holiday.

William had, after all, behaved very badly indeed. And it was compounded by the fact that Miss de Bourbon had had the right of it. Maybe a little naïve, a little too self-righteous, but essentially right. Hell, had their positions been reversed, he would have said the same himself. In a more logical, less emotional fashion, of course. In return, he had been not only ungentlemanly, but downright unkind.

Damnation, he didn't have time for this. England still needed to be saved, and he couldn't save England unless he got some *sleep*. William dragged his blanket up around his ears and prepared to settle down for a much-needed rest.

The boat groaned a complaint and William's blanket was as thin and flat as the pillow. Even with the emaciated cloth pulled halfway over his head, William's trained ear heard the soft thud of someone swinging her legs out of bed. And then, close on the heels of the previous noise, a series of slow, soft footfalls. It had to be Miss de Bourbon, thought William resignedly. Neither the chaperone nor the other lady looked the sort who would wander about after hours. Poking his head out of the nest of blanket which smelled regretfully like its last occupant—someone who obviously took a very dim view of bathing—William heard a thud and a muffled cry. Ah, he wisely concluded, someone stubbed her toe. The footfalls resumed with a slight limp. William's lips twitched into a grin in the darkness.

The grin disappeared as the midnight prowler slipped out the door of the cabin and closed it behind herself with a cautious click. William sat bolt upright in bed, no longer the least bit amused. Of all the damn fool things to do. The little ninny should have realized that the deck would be teeming with rough men. If she happened across a drunken sailor at this time of night—he cursed and scrambled to his feet.

William paused in a half-crouch. She was certainly none of his responsibility. She had made it more than clear that she wanted nothing to do with him. And that was all very well and good since he wanted nothing to do with her either, and she could bloody well take care of herself.

William flung himself back on the floor with enough force to bang his head against the wall. Hard. Maybe it was the bump on his head affecting his judgement, but as he rubbed his aching cranium, William began to have disturbing images of Miss de Bourbon alone on deck. Leaning over the railing to stare at a star, slipping, and tumbling into the hungry waters. Or being backed into a corner by a drunken sailor with nobody to hear her scream.

With one leap, William was back on his feet and three-quarters of the way to the door.

# CHAPTER 10

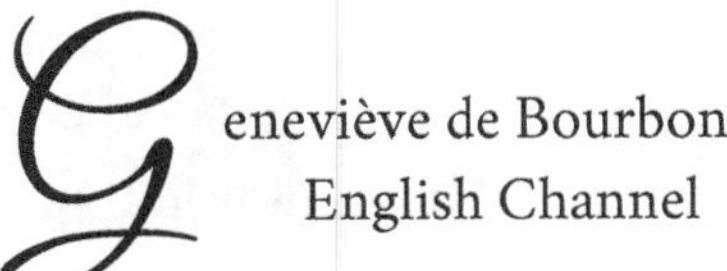

Geneviève de Bourbon
English Channel

Creeping up the short stairs, Geneviève gave up on sleep. She had left her slippers untouched on the floor; bare feet would make less noise. Feeling her way carefully in the dark along the partition, she moved with hopefully the silent grace of an experienced spy. Geneviève paused by the doorframe and listened again. All was still. The storm had spent itself several hours ago and the calm water lapped gently at the boat. Lifting her skirts, Geneviève tiptoed up the stairs to the deck.

With all the portholes closed, the air in the cabin below had grown heavy and dusty, but worst of all, it was stuffed with the rasping of Miss Agnes's snores. The gentle rocking of the ship should have put Geneviève to sleep. It had put Mary to sleep. When Geneviève had pulled herself up and peeked over the edge of the bed—which she had at least four times—she could see Mary in the berth above her, the blankets over her lightly rising and falling with her regular breaths. But Geneviève remained hideously, uncomfortably awake.

For hours, Geneviève had flopped back onto her back. She'd tried counting sheep, but all that did was bring back memories of Rye. Rye, which had seemed so detestable for the last decade or so, took on a far more attractive aspect in retrospect. There was the blue and white room she shared with Mary, the back staircase she had sneaked down so many times, her favorite climbing tree in the orchard.

It had all seemed quite simple back in Rye. They would stop off at the Orchid's Garden for a glass of lemonade, and Mary would distract Miss Agnes while Geneviève pretend to use the facilities. Geneviève would have a great deal of trouble finding the necessary room and would have to linger about the common room of the inn, glancing about as if searching for the correct door, and looking vague. In the process, she would be able to drift in the direction of two men having an intent conversation—for there were *always* two men having an intent conversation in her plans— Geneviève would overhear one whisper to the other in anxious tones something that would clearly mark him as the Sapphire Sphinx or the Scarlet Pimpernel. She would have settled for a passing comment of Sir Blakeney's recent wedding.

But that hadn't happened.

The whole idea of her helping the English, or any other country, defy Napoleon had fallen rather flat, much like the lazy water below after the storm. Geneviève would love to saddle Miss Agnes with the lion's share of the blame. For a woman supposedly writing an invigorating novel, Miss Agnes was decidedly against adventures. The woman was void of creativity. There was little doubt her novels would be as rigid and painful as the blasted parasol.

On the deck of the boat, the wind caressed Geneviève's cheeks. The weather had certainly humbled Geneviève's plans. If she'd only been more forceful, perhaps she would be in an inn somewhere, or better yet, on the cusp of becoming a member of the league. Not stuck in a boat with a traitorous Englishman.

The niggling doubt crept in. Geneviève could very well be dragging her cousin—and in all respects, Miss Agnes—across the Channel on a fool's errand.

The dark night pressed in on Geneviève like a physical force. Gripping her shawl tighter around her shoulders, she felt a rush of something, a feeling not forceful enough to be rage but not bright enough for hope. She held out her arms, her hands trembling. She'd left the sweltering blackness of the cabin below and Miss Agnes's muffled snores. And there it was, the familiarity smacked her chest. The emotion washed over her with a snap. *Grief.* The twisting and rushing and churning of grief, the wax and wane of both hope and sorrow.

Geneviève breathed in the cool night air hoping the sea could cleanse her mind. Her eyes accustomed to the darkness, Geneviève made her way carefully to the edge of the deck and rested her arms on the railing. After the musty air of the cabin, even the bouquet of tar and damp wood that rose from the deck smelled of freedom to Geneviève. The moon, hidden behind the clouds, threaded the sky with delicate silver strands. Their supernatural glow reminded Geneviève of the three Fates of Greek myth, spinning peoples' destinies on their spindles. For a moment, alone on the moonlit deck, she had a fancy that if she looked long and hard enough, she would be able to distinguish her own thread, disentangle it from the rest, and follow its glistening length to her destiny.

"Silly." Geneviève shook her head at herself. After all, she already knew her destiny. She didn't need to search in the clouds to discern it. She would track down the Sapphire Sphinx, make herself an indispensable member of his league, and, of course, restore the monarchy. It would take more than one treacherous scholar with mocking green eyes to discourage her.

Geneviève leaned against the railing. Over a decade ago, she was too small to even touch the railing when she'd been sent to England. She had only the vaguest recollections of that journey, some of them involving her favorite doll and sweet treats. The feeling of being left behind was the one souvenir Geneviève had yet to give up. She'd wanted her brother to come with her or even her mother. Living with her cousin and uncle was supposed to be for a month, maybe a year at most. She couldn't remember her mother's face or her father's laugh. In her mind, both parents stood on the wharf, waving at her. But time had given Geneviève an extra serving of distrust—for others and for her memories.

Peering into the mist, she could almost see her family smiling, beckoning her home. If she took a deep breath, she could pretend to inhale her mother's lavender perfume.

"I'll make it right. I promise," she whispered to the night and squeezed her eyes shut. She tried to conjure up the Sapphire Sphinx—her favorite daydream, the one where he pressed her hand in his and begged for her help—but the image was as flat as an amateur painting. And the Sapphire Sphinx's voice kept taking on the inflections of Lord William Cabot.

Soft footfalls fell on the deck behind her. The moment vanished abruptly into the silvery night. The spell was broken. Gripping the railing, Geneviève refused to turn around. Only one person would come searching for her. Miss Agnes had chased away her sleep, the snores just as intrusive as intruding on this intimate moment. Frustration turned to anger. Geneviève wanted a moment, a minute of solitude. Miss Agnes would reprimand her for being alone and list every one of society's rules that Geneviève violated.

A familiar male voice whispered, "You shouldn't be out here."

# CHAPTER 11

*L*ord William Cabot
English Channel

With her hands leaving the railing, Miss de Bourbon shrieked and spun around. Her mouth fell open, a knowing look coming across her face.

"You were expecting someone else?" Sneaking a glance, William rubbed his jaw. He'd rushed up the stairs out of concern while this little minx was expecting other company.

"Miss Agnes, if you must know." She folded her arms and looked behind William.

"You shouldn't be out here," he repeated.

Leaning back against the railing for support, she snapped, "And you shouldn't sneak up on people."

Scowling, William came closer. The blasted woman was either alarmingly naive or belatedly stupid. He couldn't decide which was worse. "You shouldn't lean on the railing like that. These ships are seldom in good repair."

"Save your lecture for—" Geneviève staggered back as the rail wobbled.

He slid next to her, putting an arm behind her to steady her. The last thing William needed was for a young miss to go overboard and derail his mission.

Geneviève recoiled from his touch. "I thank you for your warning, but I am quite all right." She left him at the railing, walking towards the front of the boat.

"You'll get splinters." He shouldn't follow, but despite his annoyance he was born a gentleman.

Geneviève ignored him. Poised on the prow of the ship, shoulders back, chin set, she looked like a particularly fierce figurehead. She was obviously trying quite hard to ignore him.

Narrowing his eyes, William stared at her unabashedly, watching the way the moonlight made her skin glow white against her dark hair. When he'd first spotted her on the deck, her face was tilted to the night sky, an angelic glow about her.

Shaking his head, William held out his arm. "Come below."

Her back stiffened. "No."

"It isn't safe."

Hold out her arms, she turned to face him. "The storm has moved on. I'm quite alright." Geneviève sat herself down on the damp deck and circled her knees with her arms.

*Blast.* William sat down beside her. He couldn't bloody well leave her alone. "There's more dangers than the weather."

Geneviève looked at him in surprise. "You'll stain your trousers."

"Stain my trousers?" William scowled. Only he would waste precious time with a hen-witted woman.

"You're a gentleman." Her tone was hard. "You can't risk getting brown streaks on your little trousers." She motioned to his legs. "Can you think of the horror?" She shuttered dramatically. "Grass stains. Rust stains."

"Do not fret, I've ruined plenty of trousers." He smirked into the night. "But no one has ruined more gloves than my mother. Gun powder can stain something fierce."

"Gun powder?" Geneviève chuckled, her frame relaxing against the railing.

"What of your skirt?" Keeping his tone light, William wanted to hear her laugh again.

She leaned back and kicked out her feet. "Every one of my skirts has grass stains." Pointing to her elbow, Miss de Bourbon smiled wide, her eyes sparkling. "I've scraped my elbow and broke this arm when I was a girl. Climbing trees was a fascination I couldn't give up." In a snap, her face fell.

William playfully pushed his shoulder into hers. "Climbing trees is a goal for everyone, no matter the age."

Her hands went to her lap. "I've heard it's unladylike."

"So is shooting a rifle, but my mother refuses to give up her daily practice."

"You jest."

"I'd be more afraid of being on the deck alone than a stain on your skirt." William slid off the railing to his feet, offering her his hand. "Let's go back inside."

Geneviève batted at his outstretched hand. "No."

*Blast.* Rubbing the bridge of his nose, William counted to five. She was reminding him more of a toddler than a debutante. "Miss de Bourbon, you cannot remain out here alone."

"I am not a child." She clenched her fists at her sides.

"This might be your first adventure out of the nursery—"

"Do not patronize me, Lord Cabot. I am well into my twenties and deemed *on the shelf* by—"

"Oh." William swallowed the surprise. He'd pegged her wide-eyed wonder as an innocent debutante. He waved away her words and began again. "Someone might come upon you in the darkness."

"Someone already *has.*" Miss de Bourbon hugged herself.

"I came out here to see that you were safe." Groaning, William swallowed a string of curses. He would have had more luck convincing a toddler to march into bed than Miss de Bourbon. Another reason William would run from matrimony.

"Other than being accosted by a traitorous Englishman, I am clearly safe."

"What?" William snapped. He'd been patient. He'd done his duty but by Jove, this woman was impossible. "Good night, Miss de Bourbon. Enjoy your lonely sojourn on the deck. If any sailors come after you, don't scream for me."

William turned sharply on his heel and stalked off towards the stairs. Two yards away, he stopped and marched right back.

Miss de Bourbon sniffed and covered her face in her hands.

Shaking his head at her, who was watching him with a growing confusion, William said, "No. Sorry."

"No?"

"No." William lowered himself back down next to her. "I can't just leave you here. Unfortunately for both of us, I was raised with a sense of honor—"

She grunted at *honor*.

Clenching his jaw, he continued, "Honor that precludes leaving a young lady alone in the middle of the night with a crew of ruffians. If you persist in remaining outside, I shall have to remain, too. Besides it's easier for me to stay here with you now than when you start screaming."

"I wouldn't scream."

"Let's not put it to the test, shall we? Carry on with whatever you were thinking about. You'll scarcely know I'm here." As if to prove his point, William swiveled his head and gazed ostentatiously off at the ocean.

"I was hoping to be alone with my thoughts."

He whispered, "Quiet as a mouse. I'm not here."

"Alone, Lord Cabot. Perhaps you've spent too much time with the French to understand English, but *alone* means by oneself."

He refused to be baited. He repeated in his mind, *I'm a gentleman... I'm a gentleman...* William could hear her uneven breathing and heat rising from her body in the chilliness of the night.

"Please go to downstairs." Her voice cracked. "I can smell your citrus cologne."

The emotion in her words affected him more than it should. Guilt crept in. William should have been more patient. Had his sister been upset, he would have teased Catherine out of her mood. He blurted,

"You're not on the shelf."

Miss de Bourbon's head snapped up.

William groaned. He'd only wanted to distract her. "You said you were on the shelf and you're not. I thought you were fresh from the nursery. But you're clearly not as you said *well into your twenties*." Scooting closer, he tried again. He'd lost his mind somehow. "I was twenty-five when I was in Egypt—"

"Please, stop."

"I apologize, Miss de Bourbon." Under cover of the darkness, he shifted his weight to face her. "Let us start again." He took a deep breath. "What brings you to France?"

She scooted backwards.

William put out a hand. "Retract your claws. I'm scarred enough from this afternoon. Can we cry a truce at least for the night?"

Some of the wariness crept out of Miss de Bourbon's stance. "You can be England and I'll be France before the Revolution," she offered.

"Sorry. I'm afraid you're stuck with the present."

"Only if you stay on your own side of the Channel, then." She indicated the sliver of deck that separated them.

"What would you do if I tried to invade?" William wiggled his eyebrows in mock flirtation.

"I'd call out the heavy artillery." She motioned to the hatch leading down the cabin.

"I'm sorry. You can't pass off a Miss Agnes as a brace of guns. Not allowed. And I assure you, chaperones are not an acceptable weapon in modern warfare. Dragons, maybe, but not lady companions."

Miss de Bourbon shrugged. "Why not? They both breathe fire."

"Touché."

She cradled her chin between her hands. "You don't have to stay up, Lord Cabot. Truly."

"I cannot—"

"I know, I know." Shrugging, she added, "Your honor."

Silence stretched between them with only the water lapping against the boat. Perhaps it was the heaviness of his mission or the quiet of the night, but a strange feeling of intimacy washed over the boat.

"Miss de Bourbon?" He came closer. "What brings you to France?"

"Oh." Her voice broke once more.

"Is it that much of a secret?" William teased. He felt an urgency to keep her mood light.

"No, no, of course not." She rocked back and forth, her words coming in hesitant bursts. "It's quite dull really. I'm going to live with my brother in Paris."

William clapped his hands together. "How dare he? Does he know he's living among the enemy?"

Miss de Bourbon stumbled to her feet, catching her skirt on her bare toes and clutching the railing to steady herself. She towered over him. "My brother is half French. I am half French. Is there anything else you wanted to know, or may I go back to the cabin?"

William took her hand and tugged her back down. Shame filled him. "If your brother's in France and you were in England, where are you parents?"

"They suffered the embrace of Madame Guillotine," she said tersely.

Still holding her hand, William squeezed it lightly, for comfort. He'd behaved badly. "I am sorry. So sorry."

"They had a rare union. A love match, you see."

Oddly enough—William did see. His own parents had married for love, and just as Miss de Bourbon had said, it was a rare union between aristocrats to marry for love. His parents had stayed in love, rather distressingly so. He'd been forced to witness his parents holding hands under the table. Not to mention all the times William had accidentally stumbled upon his parents kissing in corridors. But for all the faces he'd made and the occasional inarticulate noise indicating extreme disgust, William secretly thought it was rather comforting. Even sweet the way his indomitable mother would blush and flutter at a whispered comment from his father. His dignified father would bolt abruptly out of debates in the House of Lords just to take tea with his mother.

It wasn't until he'd hit the London social scene as a rakehell, fresh from the innocence of Eton, that William had realized how unusual it was, that sort of connection his parents enjoyed. Until then, he had naively assumed that all married couples were like that, holding hands under the breakfast table and kissing in corridors. But then he saw married men in brothels and received scented solicitations from married women. In all of his meanderings from ballroom to ballroom, William had seen perhaps one couple in ten who shared some sort of affection, one couple in a hundred truly in love. And he had realized, for the first time, that what his parents had was something wonderful and rare, and that he himself could never stoop to settle for anything less.

And Miss de Bourbon must have seen the same, and have it wrenched away.

"I'm sorry," he said softly.

"You didn't wield the ax." The moon had gone behind a cloud, leaving her face in shadow, no glimmer of light to reveal her thoughts.

"If I had known, I wouldn't have baited you. I didn't realize you had a personal interest." He didn't know if it was the shame or the night but somehow it seemed the most natural thing in the world that he would take her free hand in his own, and even more natural that he was leaning towards her and she towards him.

# CHAPTER 12

Geneviève de Bourbon
English Channel

Their joined hands formed a bridge across the deck, the moon casting an intimate glow. Geneviève couldn't tell if he were pulling or she was. There no longer seemed to be a place where her arms ended and his began. And what did it matter if there were? Geneviève closed her eyes and felt his warm breath on her lips.

*Crack.*

The piece of railing Geneviève had been leaning upon earlier detached itself from the deck and tumbled into the water. Suddenly, Geneviève's hands were her own again. Blinking dazedly as she opened her eyes, she saw that their own personal Channel was back in place between them and that William had his own hands planted firmly on the deck on either side of him. It was enough to make her think she had imagined those past few moments, if she still hadn't been able to feel the tingliness left by William's breath on her lips.

"The captain should see to getting that repaired." William's voice was the slightest touch unsteady. "I'll say something to him in the morning."

Geneviève nodded. For once in her life—and such occasions were rare indeed—she couldn't think of anything to say. She'd pretended her parents were on the wharf, had she gone so far as pretending to kiss Lord Cabot?

Geneviève bit down on her lower lip and squirmed on the hard deck. Planning the restoration of the monarchy was so much easier than dealing with the aftermath of the almost-kiss. She should be concentrating entirely on her, not agonizing over a man of dubious morals. Even if that man did have cheekbones to make sculptor weep. Geneviève went back to gnawing her lower lip. She wiped her brow and began pacing.

"What is your brother's name?" Lord Cabot asked.

"Charles," Geneviève replied absently. "He's several years older than me." She winced. Lord Cabot didn't need to know, nor did he care about her brother.

"Charles." He sat upright, his back stiff. "Charles de Bourbon, the son of Eduoard de Bourbon?"

"Why are you surprised?" They shared the same last name. "What are you playing at?"

Lord Cabot's eyes were wide. He shook his head then rubbed his neck, only to stare back at her. "Charles de Bourbon is your *brother*?"

"Yes—"

"You look nothing like each other." He stretched out his arms.

Mirroring him, she asked, "What are you saying?"

Lord Cabot dropped his arms, his mouth open and eyebrows raised. "Charles de Bourbon is French. Very French."

Geneviève winced. Lord Cabot didn't need to repeat the French part. She'd thought they had moved past their earlier argument. "Yes." She swallowed the frustration. "You know him, then?"

"A bit." He'd clenched his jaw.

"A bit?" She could feel the lie. She'd not seen her brother in over a decade and the few memories she had were of a quiet boy in the shadows. But a shy boy would not make someone like Lord Cabot nervous. "I've not heard from him in years. My uncle says he's well-liked in France." The lie came a little too easy. She'd overheard her uncle complain to a neighbor about his French nephew the fop, that he was the laughingstock of the court. And that was the hope she clung to. If her brother was an outsider of Bonparte's inner circle, then he was loyal to the monarchy.

Lord Cabot drummed his fingers against the deck. "He doesn't look like you."

"You mentioned that." There was something delightful in watching the man fret. She tapped her foot impatiently. "We did when we younger. My mother's family is tall and fair. Stately."

"He's fair."

A memory crept up on her. She was thrown back in time to her father—she couldn't see his face, but Geneviève knew it was him. He lifted her on his shoulders so Geneviève could grab for the stars. He had even given her a tiny little diamond bracelet—a string of stars, he had sworn, gathered while she was asleep in the nursery.

"My father promised, when I was old enough, that he would lift me into the night sky so that I could string myself a necklace. A necklace of stars." Geneviève blinked back tears and stared longingly into the sky.

There were no stars tonight.

But there was one very silent man beside her, watching her closely, and Geneviève plummeted abruptly into the present, like Icarus falling from the sky, shaken and a little abashed.

What had possessed her to reveal so much? Her memories of Mama and Papa were her own, her treasured cache, more precious than any number of necklaces of stars. She spoke of them to no one, not even to Mary, who was the sister of her heart, her one confidante, and the person who knew her better than anyone in the world. Yet it had slipped out when speaking to Lord Cabot.

Obviously, her wits had been addled by the almost-kiss and the moonlight. People did silly things by moonlight. It didn't matter that the moon had gone behind the clouds quite some time ago; it was still there, affecting her actions, even if she couldn't see it.

Though there was also something about Lord Cabot. Something that made it quite easy and natural to confide in him. Something she couldn't blame on the moon. Something that made Geneviève feel vulnerable, and she wasn't at all sure she liked it.

Geneviève broke the fragile silence by saying with forced bravado, "Why are *you* going to France?"

"I'm the First Consul's director of Egyptian antiquities."

Geneviève blinked. "The First Consul—*Bonaparte*—you're his director of antiquities?"

"After we returned from Egypt, the First Consul invited me to—"

"You weren't sorry at all, were you?" Her heart sank. She shouldn't care. He was a stranger. One with a horrible morals and traitorous tendencies. But if Bonaparte could convince an Englishman to be in France's royal court, what hope did Geneviève have? Her last name had once meant something to France, the very reason revolutionist had targeted them. Her father had tried—and failed—to help the reformation. So many families broken and blood spilled all for an Englishman to run around with the greatest enemy France and the world had ever known, Napoleon Bonaparte. "You were saying what you felt, and you weren't sorry. You've no idea the pain—no idea the—"

"Geneviève, I—" He reached for her hands, but she backed away, wiping her hands furiously on her skirt as though to exorcise his touch.

"We are not nearly acquainted enough to be so informal nor will we ever be."

He offered a stiff bow. "I apologize, Miss de Bourbon."

"I don't understand." She wiped an angry tear off her cheek. "You've been with the French all along. You never left. You've been with *them* the whole time. If you stayed with them, you can't have thought that what they did was so terrible. Why pretend to be sympathetic when you weren't? I'm such a fool to think someone like you would under—"

"You're not a fool, Geneviève—"

"Don't you dare tell me I'm not a fool. Don't you dare presume to tell me anything, ever again." Pacing, she wrung her hands, angry that her emotions had taken over. She needed to breathe. She could not bloody well become a spy if she lashed out so easily.

Once again, Lord Cabot stared at her, mouth open and eyes wide. His expression only fueled her frustration.

Geneviève groaned, pausing for a moment in her tirade. "I told you about my *parents.*"

He grabbed the railing and yanked himself to his feet. "What has that got to do with anything?"

"Nothing. *Nothing.*" Geneviève waved her arms wildly. "It has nothing to do with the fact that you are a rogue and a cad and a bounder and a traitor to your country and—"

"Oh, am I?" Lord Cabot advanced with the stealthy prowl of a panther, his voice a low purr more threatening than any growl. "Define treachery, Miss de Bourbon."

Geneviève noticed the dangerous light in Lord Cabot's green eyes, but somehow the jade glare only fueled her own rising anger. Rather than backing away, she stomped forward to meet him. "Treachery," she declared furiously, tipping her head back till her upturned nose practically brushed his chin, "is when a man willfully allies with the enemies of his country."

Geneviève took a half step back, not from intimidation—never that—but because her neck hurt. Blast the advantage of height. It was unfair that he should be able to look down his nose at her in such a supercilious way. If his physique were to mirror his character, why, he should be a nasty, shriveled, twisted gnome of a man. Not a towering golden Adonis designed to lead innocent females into almost-kisses. The injustice of it rendered Geneviève even angrier.

"Treachery," repeated Geneviève shrilly, "is when an unscrupulous man deceives innocent young ladies into believes he is a—a person of sense and sensibility. When all the while—"

"Innocent?" roared Lord Cabot. "Innocent. You're the one who's always picking fights with me. You call yourself innocent. *I* was innocently discussing Egyptology this afternoon, when you hauled off and started abusing my character."

"That might be because *you're* the one in the employ of Bonaparte."

"At least I don't go about throwing stones at other people's glass houses."

"Oh no, you'd just guillotine them, wouldn't you?"

Lord Cabot grabbed Geneviève by the shoulders. "You are absurd."

"Don't touch me." Geneviève backed away from him, seething. "Don't speak to me and don't you dare follow me."

"It's about time you decide to be sensible and go downstairs." William murmured, walking after her.

"I thought I told you not to follow me."

"Do you expect me to sleep on the deck?" William inquired acidly.

"You could sleep on the floor of the ocean," Geneviève muttered and started down the short flight of stairs.

He poked her in the shoulder blades. "What was that you said?"

Geneviève's hands clenched into fists at her sides as she kept walking. "I said I'm not speaking to you."

"Oh, that's logical," drawled Lord Cabot.

One hand on the door of the cabin, Geneviève gave an agitated hop and then winced. This man brought out her inner toddler. Lifting her chin, she straightened her spine. "Just leave me alone. Stay on your side of the room and leave me alone."

"Your wish is my command." Lord Cabot bowed mockingly and disappeared without a sound behind the wall of cloaks.

# CHAPTER 13

*L*ord William Cabot
Calais, France

William could feel the anger radiating from Miss de Bourbon—or Geneviève— from behind the partition. There was something delightful about aggravating her. Her eyes were expressive, quickly tossing and turning from joy to anger. She might have banned him from speaking with her, but he really wouldn't mind spending time with her—William paused misstep. He shook the idea from him. No matter how much he might enjoy riling Miss de Bourbon's nerves, he couldn't. England couldn't afford another leader of the league to leave, and matrimony was a death sentence to an espionage career.

Besides that, William just didn't have the time to spend. He'd already wasted previous hours on the trip across the channel. He couldn't waste a minute more. Not if he wanted to discover Bonaparte's invasion plans before French troops set foot on English soil. Nobody knew better than William how quickly Bonaparte could move—the Italians, and the Austrians, and the Dutch could vouch for Bonaparte's military prowess. Geneviève was spirited but nothing but a distraction.

*Geneviève.* Smiling, he massaged his pillow. There was comfort in knowing Geneviève was just a few yards away, seething. Blast it all, she was the most intriguing woman he'd ever stumbled across. She was probably dreaming of chucking him into the Channel.

The hours passed and humor turned to dread. He had dismissed a ridiculous voice in his head, which sounded alarmingly like his sister, informing William that his behavior was that of a child.

*She started it,* William mouthed, feeling worse. Devil take it, he had sunk to the level of arguing with people who weren't even there. If he continued like this, he'd be more fit for Bedlam than espionage.

He needed rules or a list to keep himself in check. Miss Geneviève de Bourbon wasn't just any lady from England. Last year, Charles de Bourbon had become a man of interest for his frequent trips to England. Little holidays that Geneviève appeared to be unaware of. She spoke as if she'd not seen Charles in a while, but the man was either a smuggler or the double agent working for both countries. William would hand over a fortune to watch Geneviève verbally assault her brother if she discovered his secrets. She'd been more than willing to thrash William when he was a simple stranger. He swallowed hard. A stranger he needed to stay.

At the first sign of morning, William huddled near the window for reading light. *Monsiuer Delaroche* were the first two words deciphered. No surprise. Delaroche was Bonaparte's current Ministry of Police and kept a list of potential problems, forever trying to sniff out the rat in the French court. Depending on Delaroche's mood, William would be added and dropped at will. After all, an Englishman could not be trusted.

William paused. The next part of the message—he checked it twice—Delaroche had added Sir Percy Blakeney's wife to his list.

His stomach churning, William felt a growing dread. Blakeney's determination to leave the league had felt sudden, but perhaps Blakeney had already known his young bride would become a target.

The next section gave William a bit of hope. Bonaparte was displeased with Delaroche's inability to capture any spies. Apparently the First Consul threatened to replace the Ministry.

William had read the French papers. They were convinced—rightfully so—that the Sapphire had to be an Englishman just like the Scarlet Pimpernel and not a traitorous Frenchman. William had thought his childhood with Blakeney would become common knowledge, but so far only his friendship with Michael was public. There'd even been a satire or two poking fun at Delaroche's incompetence until the First Consul had the theatre shut down.

The women stirred and William quickly packed up his things. Try as he might, he couldn't get Miss de Bourbon to meet his gaze. Nor could he get the woman to look in his general direction. The dragon of a chaperone gave one-word answers while Mary was just as polite as she was the day before.

Miss Agnes positioned herself directly in William's line of vision for the remaining hours. The moment the boat sidled up to the harbor, the women grabbed their things and left. Relief should have welcomed William, the women had been a distraction, but he'd not seen two waiting carriages, only his. If William's sister was arriving on either side of the channel, he'd have a carriage—and extra footmen—ready for her. Tea and other items weren't the only products smuggled. A lady could disappear in a blink of an eye.

In the weak, early morning light, the wharf was almost eerily deserted. Only one carriage had braved the dawn chill, a battered black carriage with a broken sidelamp and starbursts of mud along its sides. It didn't bear a crest, nor did it seem it'd borne an occupant in some time. He spotted his carriage coming down the street, his crest on full display.

Perched on the harbor, William fiddled with his bags, buying time while he watched the women. Their heads swiveled back and forth, glancing nervously up and down the street. There was still no sign of a carriage bearing the de Bourbon crest. The dock at Calais lacked the bustle and flurry of Dover, the very reason smugglers loved this harbor.

As William's carriage neared, Miss de Bourbon tugged her shawl tighter as three men in rough work clothes trotted up and down the gangplank, heaving assorted boxes and bundles into the carriage. She bounced on the balls of her shoes as four black horses trotted into view, followed by William's sleek black carriage. The coachmen rose on his box and gave an unservile halloo in a decidedly English voice. "Lord Cabot!"

Miss de Bourbon's gaze snapped to William's, her eyes narrowing. "Of course your carriage arrives on time. We can't have French scholars waiting in the elements."

Her tone was deceptively bright, her eyes the only indication she wished William a dire fate.

"Hullo, Gideon." William left his perch and strode over to his carriage. "Have a nice drive?"

"As nice as can be had on them damned French roads, milord— begging your pardon, ladies," Gideon hastily added, as Miss Agnes's loud sniff of reproach alerted the coachman to the presence of three rather disheveled female persons on the wharf. "All pits and potholes, they are," he earnestly explained to Miss Agnes.

Miss Agnes sniffed again.

Gideon shrugged and turned his back on the old harpy. "When do I get to drive on good English roads again, milord?"

Miss de Bourbon stiffened and lifted her chin.

"When Bonaparte donates his collection of antiquities to the British Museum," William said dryly. The words came out by rote—he and Gideon had been through the same routine conversation several times before. William held out a hand to the women, catching her gaze. She scowled violently.

It would have been quite an effective scowl if the wind hadn't blown her curls into her face. William couldn't stop the grin as Miss de Bourbon pawed clumps of hair out of her mouth.

He, of course, didn't feel one way or the other about the girl. She was just a chance acquaintance, and if she happened to dislike him, that was her own affair. He scarcely knew her.

He did, however, know Charles de Bourbon. De Bourbon seemed to think nothing of leaving his female relations stranded in Calais. William could easily imagine de Bourbon being distracted by an inconsequential fitting for the latest style of breeches or too lazy to be bothered by anything other than himself.

*Blast it all.* William couldn't leave these poor women at the docks. He didn't like to think of three gently bred young ladies being stranded by the wharf. Certainly, there were inns in Calais, but they catered to a very different sort of clientele. No doubt there was at least one respectable establishment, but docks, as William knew far too well from his peregrinations back and forth across the Channel, tended to attract the most unsavory sort of riffraff. With that deadly parasol of hers, Miss Agnes made a formidable guard—whoever picked her to look after Miss de Bourbon and Miss Wooliston had known what they were about—the thought of his sister Catherine stranded for a week in Calais had his jaw clenched. There was nothing for it but to take the women back to Paris with him.

# CHAPTER 14

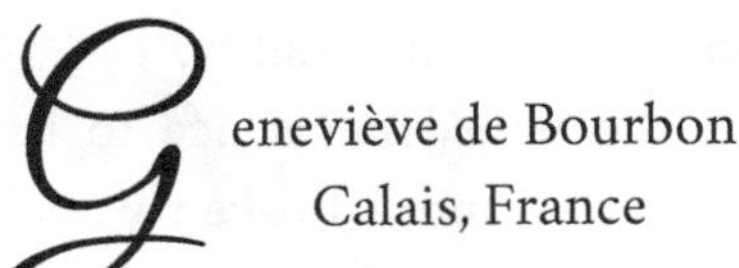

Geneviève de Bourbon
Calais, France

Standing on the quiet docks of Calais between her cousin and chaperone, Geneviève fought the shiver of fear. The harbor was eerily silent, the result of a storm Geneviève assumed. For months she'd dreamt of this moment. She'd naively expected to dive into a sea of English spies and French henchman. With nothing but her wit, she was to be the monarch's savior.

But with the wind pawing at her hair and no sign of her family's carriage, a harsh reality shook her by the shoulders. She blinked back the tears of frustration. Geneviève had been so determined, so convinced she alone was needed in France to right the wrongs of the last decade.

To add a measure of insulting salt to her wounded pride, Lord Cabot stood just behind her, chatting cheerily to his coachman. His stylish black carriage was just a few meters from where she huddled next to Mary. Lord Cabot hadn't been forgotten by his brother. He didn't have old ghosts to avenge or any moral compass directing him forward.

As if he'd heard Geneviève's thoughts, Lord Cabot walked closer. Catching his eye, she looked away. Her cheeks went warm, adding another level of frustration. "Insufferable man."

Mary looped her arm in hers, whispering, "Evie, I really wish you would tell me what happened between you and—"

Geneviève gave a subtle shake of her head.

Casually swinging his hat in one hand, Lord Cabot strolled toward Miss Agnes. "Madam, your carriage seems to have been delayed. May I be so bold as to offer the use of mine?"

*Oh no.* Geneviève drew herself to her full five feet and three inches and set her chin. "That really won't be necessary. I'm sure Charles's coach will arrive any minute now. There are dozens of reasons why it might have been delayed. Broken wheels or bandits…"

Miss Agnes and Lord Cabot, on either side, were looking down at her with frighteningly similar expressions of polite incredulity.

Narrowing her eyes at Lord Cabot, she willed her voice to be commanding. "I'm sure there *must* be bandits, and a broken wheel could happen to anyone."

Lord Cabot tilted his head and in voice meant for a small child said, "Perhaps you're right."

Geneviève took a deep breath and resisted the urge to stamp her foot. Preferably on Lord Cabot's. "At any rate, when Charles's carriage does arrive—which it *will*—it would be dreadfully rude of us not to have waited for it, after he's put his coachman to so much trouble. And what if the coachman thinks we haven't arrived yet and stays to wait for us? Why, the poor man could be stranded here for days."

"Your concern for your brother's coachman does you credit, Miss de Bourbon," Lord Cabot commented dryly, with a wry twist of the lips that suggested he knew it was not Charles's coachman who troubled her, "but, at present, *you* seem to be the one stranded, not he."

Geneviève squared her shoulders for further argument, but Miss Agnes prevented her with a commanding thump of her parasol. "I will have no more argument from you, Miss de Bourbon. Your brother's coach was to have been here this morning. It was not. The storm set us back, but the coach should have been waiting. Therefore, we are accepting Lord Cabot's kind offer, and I trust that you brother's coachman, should he appear, shall have the basic sense to return to Paris. Is that understood? My lord, you may instruct your man to load our baggage."

"Miss Agnes, I am yours to command." He bowed with far too much flourish. "Miss de Bourbon, the opportunity to extend our acquaintance, as I am sure you will agree, is an unexpected delight."

"Indeed." Geneviève tossed back at him adding a dose of skepticism.

And he laughed. The fool actually laughed.

Filled with rage, Geneviève stalked off to the side of the dock as William's coachman joined two sailors in loading all of their trunks onto the top of the carriage.

Mary slipped an arm through Geneviève's. "It *is* very good of him."

"It gives the appearance of goodness." Geneviève stole a glance at William, who was speaking gravely to Miss Agnes. "All the better to hide a thoroughly black soul."

Mary's pale brows drew together in concern. "What did he do to make you feel so about him?" Lowering her voice, she added, "He didn't behave improperly to you?"

"No," Geneviève said, her voice gruff and her hands clenching. Groaning, she felt even crosser than before. The memory of the almost-kiss—had it even been an almost-kiss?—danced mockingly at the edge of memory, taunting her with her own foolishness. Good heavens, had she truly lost her mind? That was the only reason she'd even considered kissing such a base rogue. It had to be. Geneviève wasn't sure whether she was more irate with Lord Cabot for charming her into liking him or with herself for allowing herself to be charmed when she ought to have known better. But more than Lord Cabot, Geneviève had betrayed herself. The gentleman was at traitor to his native country and in kissing—or almost kissing—Lord Cabot, Geneviève had duped herself.

Mary was still watching her expectantly. Mary, Geneviève decided, could not be told of the almost-kiss.

"No," Geneviève repeated. "He did not cross a line with me, but he was or rather *is* improper. His principles are offensive."

"Evie—"

"Can you believe that the man is employed by Bonaparte? An Englishman, a member of the peerage, galivanting across Egypt and now France. How could anyone with any sort of moral compass work for that—"

"It might be well not to judge him too hastily," Mary interjected as Geneviève's voice rose dangerously above the slapping of the waves.

"Trust me, it's a *very* well-considered judgement."

Holding up a finger to her lips, Mary whispered, "You've known him all of a day."

"A day? An hour is too long." Geneviève watched the last of the trunks be loaded onto the carriage, her heart sinking. "Oh blast, I was hoping Charles's coach would appear before we had to leave with *him*."

Lord Cabot came to them, a wicked grin on his face. He greeted each girl with a deep bow as they fell in beside Miss Agnes. The fool could don the facade of civility and charm when he wanted. Her darkest suspicions were confirmed when Lord Cabot followed up his bows with, "Good morning, Miss Wooliston, Miss de Bourbon. I trust you slept well on the boat?" He spoke lightly, his gaze resting impersonally on Mary and Geneviève in turn.

"Quite well, thank you," said Mary.

Geneviève glowered. "I was kept awake by the sound of someone stamping about on deck."

Lord Cabot smiled blandly and kept up the lie. "It's well you didn't go up to investigate. You never know what rough sorts you might encounter on a Dover packet."

"I believe I have a fair idea, my lord."

Mary's bonneted head swiveled from one to the other. She gave Geneviève a hard look from under the straw brim. "There's something you're not telling me," she whispered.

"Later," Geneviève hissed back.

Lord Cabot regarded them with the same infuriatingly benign

look of condescension men assume when women whisper in front of them.

Miss Agnes rapped her parasol against the ground like an exasperated orchestra conductor. "Are we to stand here wasting the day or shall we depart? Sir?" Grabbing Lord Cabot's outstretched arm, she climbed regally into the carriage. Murmuring her thanks to Lord Cabot, Mary followed, taking the seat beside Miss Agnes.

Pointedly avoiding resting her hand on Lord Cabot's arm, Geneviève peered into the interior of the carriage. *Drat.* She would have to sit next to Lord Cabot.

Geneviève wedged herself into the very farthest corner of the bench. The gentleman gave her a somewhat sardonic look as he settled down on his side. The carriage jostled into movement.

Lord Cabot leaned towards Geneviève. "It's not catching, you know."

Geneviève opened her mouth to retort, but Miss Agnes's eye was upon her like a falcon sighting its prey. With as much dignity as she could muster, Geneviève turned her back on him and stared out the window.

Geneviève stared out the window for quite some time. She stared out the window until there was no sign of the coast in sight. She stared out the window until her neck ached. After an hour, she began to wonder if she would ever be able to move her head again. Beside her, Lord Cabot was conversing with Mary in low, pleasant tones. "Compared with the works of Mozart, Herr Beethoven…" Mary was saying earnestly. Next to Geneviève, his voice rumbled in reply, but it was fading… fading… fading… Geneviève only had time to think, confusedly, how odd that his voice should be so pleasant when he was so very unpleasant himself, before she fell asleep.

# CHAPTER 15

$\mathcal{L}$ord William Cabot
Paris, France

Miss de Bourbon slept through a debate on the merits of new Romantic music. Leaning precariously across the coach, Miss Wooliston tucked a shawl around her cousin's sleeping form.

"I'll do it," William volunteered as Mary tottered on the edge of her seat. He reached for the shawl, and Mary handed it to him gratefully before sliding back against the velvet squabs. William's coachman tended to display his feelings for the French by lurching violently into every pothole he could find, which meant that the coach was swaying from side to side with greater force than the boat in last night's storm.

William toppled back into his own seat more hastily than intended and turned toward Miss de Bourbon. She had fallen asleep curled up against the window, one hand under her cheek, and her back rather pointedly towards William. With her booted feet dangling an inch or two off the floor, she looked quite tiny and fragile.

Stifling a laugh, William tilted his head. Miss de Bourbon hadn't seemed all that little when she was snapping at him. She never stayed still or silent long enough for one to notice her petite frame.

When she was awake, Miss de Bourbon exuded enough energy for the entire French army, and packed just as furious of a punch. A smile stretched on his lips. He had the memory of Miss Agnes's assault on his ribs. Perhaps the chaperone had taught her charges to attack in the same way. Miss de Bourbon had enough sharpness in her words. Her anger amused him, and, for the life of him, he couldn't seem to muster up a decent spurt of indignation. Instead, he found himself squelching down an entirely inappropriate feeling of fondness.

There was only a few hours left of her company. The fact that Miss de Bourbon was related to Mr. Charles de Bourbon might be a tad inconvenient, as the fool spent far too much time at Tuileries with the First Consul. With any luck, she'd avoid him like the plague. And William could get back to his mission.

Miss de Bourbon mumbled something and flopped over into William's shoulder. Her breath came steady. He waited for her to spring away in horror, but she nuzzled against the fine wool of William's coat. Instinctively, William's arm rose to wrap around her shoulders. It was, of course, just a reflex reaction. He snuck a quick, guilty look at Miss Agnes. Thankfully, the dragon was deep in a book and didn't seem to notice her charge snuggled up against a gentleman.

William clamped his arm to his side. He had no desire to find himself on the pointy end of Miss Agnes's parasol for improper advances. And how much more infuriating it would be to earn a punctured kidney for half-unconscious improper advances to a girl who wouldn't give him a civil word if she were awake. This version of Miss de Bourbon was rather pleasant, curled up against him soft and warm. He sniffed. She smelled like lavender water. William sniffed again.

*Thump.* Miss Agnes's book slammed shut.

William's head jerked up with enough force to make him dizzy.

"Could you kindly contrive to breathe in a more decorous fashion?" Miss Agnes admonished. "I have known sheepdogs with more genteel respiratory habits. Miss de Bourbon!"

Miss de Bourbon had begun to stir next to William and seemed to be trying very hard to lodge her nose permanently in a fold of his coat.

"What sheep?" murmured Miss de Bourbon into William's collarbone. "I detest sheep."

A sound suspiciously like a chuckle emerged from Mary. Miss Agnes reached for her parasol. William prepared to dodge, but this time Miss Agnes's instrument of torture had another victim at its tip. One well-placed poke in the ribs, and Miss de Bourbon's eyes fluttered open. "What?"

"You are to remove yourself from Lord Cabot *at once.*"

Her words had far more effect on Miss de Bourbon than the point of the parasol; Miss de Bourbon looked down at William's coat, up at his face, and recoiled with such force that she nearly rebounded off the wall of the coach. "I… did I… oh goodness, I never intended…"

William plucked a curling brown hair from the wool of his jacket. Holding it out towards Miss de Bourbon, he said gravely, "I believe this belongs to you."

"Keep it." Miss de Bourbon was busy wedging herself back into the far corner of the seat.

"Most obliged."

Miss de Bourbon looked at him skeptically through bleary eyes and leaned her head against the side of the coach. In front of them, Miss Agnes had resumed reading intently. Miss de Bourbon squinted at the letters on the spine.

"You're reading *The Mysteries of Udolpho.*"

"How very clever of you, Miss de Bourbon." Miss Agnes turned a page.

"I didn't think you cared for—that is, I didn't know you read those type of novels."

"I don't." Miss Agnes looked up over the top of the volume that gave the lie to her statement. "There was nothing else to read in the carriage and not all of us care to sleep in public." Looking much more cheerful once she had made her jab at Miss de Bourbon, Miss Agnes continued. "The style of the book is quite arresting, but I find the heroine entirely unsympathetic. Swooning solves nothing."

"You should write your own," suggested William. Miss de Bourbon's and William's eyes met in a moment of pure amusement. "For the purpose of edifying young females, of course."

"I intent to," Miss Agnes snapped back.

Miss de Bourbon started to return William's grin when she quickly frowned and hunched down in her seat. Abruptly, she turned her head and stared out the window.

The coachman had slowed down to a pace little faster than a walk. The narrow streets would permit nothing faster. Most were missing cobblestones; water and refuse ran in streams down the center of the street, and Miss Agnes had to duck back as a rivulet of filth poured from one window to join the much below. People scurried back and forth through the refuse, occasionally stopping to curse at the carriage. Miss de Bourbon added more colloquialism to her rapidly growing collection.

"How very French." Miss Agnes conspicuously held a handkerchief to her nose.

"It's not all like this, is it, my lord?" Mary asked William in tones of such polite distress that William laughed.

"Your cousin's house is in a far nicer neighborhood, I assure you, but yes, much of Paris is in a sorry state. Bonaparte has grand plans to rebuild, but he hasn't had the time to put his schemes into practice."

Miss de Bourbon murmured, "Too busy conquering the world?"

Smiling as brightly as he could pretend, William said, "I'm sure he would be flattered by your summation."

Miss de Bourbon flushed brilliantly and returned to her window.

Making a sharp turn that nearly sent Miss Agnes's parasol into William's ribs, the carriage clattered into the stone courtyard of the ancient home of de Bourbon—and stopped abruptly. The drive was blocked by a shabby black carriage; mud splattered its sides, and a shattered lamp hung drunkenly on the side nearer to Miss de Bourbon. Several men were occupied in unloading large brown paper packages tied up with string.

"Why have we stopped?" demanded Miss Agnes.

"A coach is blocking the door." Miss de Bourbon poked her head back out.

William opened the windows and called to his coachman, "Mr. Preston, could you please ask them to let us pass? Tell them the vicomte's sister has arrived."

The coachman puffed out his chest. With great enthusiasm, he shouted out in his ungrammatical French that they were all to clear out as the lady of the house had arrived.

One of the workers paused to shout back that there was not a lady of the house.

"There is now," Preston shot back. "Just who do you think that there lady is if she ain't the lady of the 'ouse?"

The worker made an extremely rude suggestion in French. Miss de Bourbon's eyes crinkled as if she understood, but then blinked, asking, "What did he say?"

"He voiced his disbelief as to your identity." William refused to translate exactly.

Preston, red-faced with fury, retorted with an inventive blend of French and English invective.

"Really!" Shouted Miss Agnes, who had apparently caught the English half.

"Really, indeed," echoed William, looking quite impressed. That one comment about the reproductive habits of goats had been quite original.

"This is ridiculous." Miss de Bourbon rubbed the bridge of her nose. "This is my family's home."

"I quite agree." Miss Agnes thumped her parasol. "To refer to an innocent creature in such salacious way—"

"No. Not that. This." Miss de Bourbon's arm gesture encompassed the stalled carriage, the courtyard, and almost clipped William's chin. He eyed Miss de Bourbon speculatively. She didn't pause or even seem to notice. "It's ridiculous to remain mewed up in the carriage when we're here already. Why on earth can't we just walk to the door? That's why we have legs, for heaven's sake. I'm going to find Charles."

And with that, Miss de Bourbon unlatched her carriage door and prepared to hop out.

Only to be unceremoniously hauled back into the carriage by the scruff of her skirt.

"Oh no, you don't," said William, making up in firmness what he lacked in originality. "You are not going out there."

It was hard to glare at someone when he still had his fist wound in the back of one's skirt. Miss de Bourbon yanked irritably away and twisted to face William. "Why not?"

William raised a sardonic eyebrow and indicated the courtyard where two other men in varying states of dirt and undress had joined the first in exchanging less than witty repartee with Preston.

Narrowing her gaze, Miss de Bourbon eyed the men, her shoulders began slumping. "We can't just sit here."

"I agree. I'll go." There was something about her furrowed brow that gave William a surge of pride. "I'm the only one who knows what your brother looks like."

"I can recognize my own brother," Miss de Bourbon muttered.

It was at that point a portly Charles de Bourbon came from the house, his arms waving. With too much lace on his cuffs, his arm movement was exaggerated. The poor sop began chastising the workers in the courtyard in rapid French, demanding to know the cause of the delay.

William swung out of the carriage and yelled from the top step. "De Bourbon!"

Charles raised his head. Like William, his hair had been cut short in the classical style made popular by the Revolution, but this man had a pair of fuzzy sideburns crawling down his face towards his chin. They stretched so far down his face that they touched the absurdly high points of his shirt collar. It was a wonder that Charles was able to turn his head to look at William at all; his shirt points stretched up to his cheeks, and his chin was entirely buried by an exuberant cravat. The new look made William pause. In his profession, changing an appearance usually meant the person was hiding something. William had done the same when he went undercover. Granted, William typically donned a fake beard and a black mask when sneaking in the night, but something was going on at the de Bourbon estate.

A voice emerged from the folds of the cravat. "Cabot? What are you doing here?"

William didn't glance back in the carriage. Hopefully, Miss de Bourbon didn't hear her brother. "I'm delivering your sister, de Bourbon. You seem to have misplaced her."

"My sister?"

Miss de Bourbon stumbled a bit on the uneven cobblestones as she landed, but by dint waving her arms about managed to keep herself upright. "The last time I saw you, you were just a gawky boy. You… used to be tall."

Charles's face—or what William could make of it—vacillated between bewilderment and horror.

Grabbing her skirts in both hands, Miss de Bourbon dashed at her brother. "Charles. It's me, Geneviève. I've finally come home."

Charles's mouth fell open. "You weren't supposed to arrive until tomorrow."

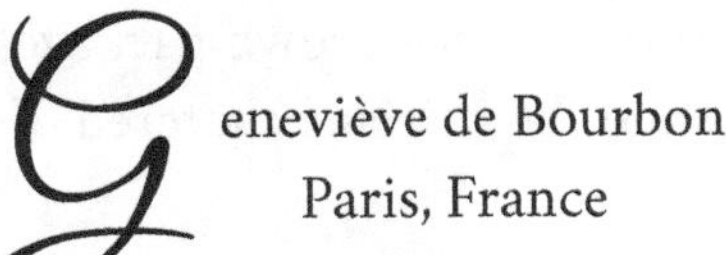

enevière de Bourbon
Paris, France

On the edge of the courtyard, Geneviève stood, blinking back the rising emotion. She'd not been here in years. Her last memories were filled with fear. She'd hoped, she'd prayed her brother would have met her at the dock. Or at least remembered that she was coming. The man only loosely resembled her brother, the only indication was the location and voice. She lifted her chin and stamped her disappointment down. "You thought I was to arrive tomorrow?" Her stomach twisted. She tried to ignore the enormous parcels and men going back and forth from the house. "That would explain why your coach wasn't there. I was so sure we'd told you we would arrive today—"

"We did," said Miss Agnes coldly.

"—but we're here now. Charles, I am so glad to see you again." Geneviève threw her arms impulsively around her brother.

Charles patted her rather awkwardly on the back. "Likewise, I'm sure."

Tucking her face, she retreated. The family in her memory hugged each other. Loved each other. Willing her voice to be steady, she said,

"This is our cousin Mary, who is one of the cleverest, most wonderful people you will ever meet." Geneviève tugged Charles across the courtyard towards the carriage. "Mary, this is Charles."

Charles murmured his greetings through the lace-edged handkerchief he had pressed to his nose.

"Are we to sit here all day?" demanded an imperious voice from the carriage.

"Oh, and that's Miss Agnes Wooliston, our great aunt and our chaperone. Miss Agnes, do come down and meet my brother, Charles."

"I am waiting," pronounced Miss Agnes, "for the carriage to deliver us to the house." Her disembodied voice emerged from the carriage with all the solemnity and terror of the Delphic Oracle.

"Of course, of course." Charles scurried across the courtyard and muttered something to the waiting servants. The last brown packages made their way hurriedly into the house and the carriage clattered off through the gates.

"That's a lot of parcels, de Bourbon." Lord Cabot furrowed his brow.

Pulling at his cravat, Charles blurted, "I've been redecorating the west wing—finally time to get rid of all that musty stuff my parents left, don't you think? Anyway, it requires a lot of draperies. That's what those were, you know. Draperies." Charles rubbed his lace handkerchief across his perspiring forehead.

"The musty stuff?" Geneviève retreated. She'd spent years yearning for something, anything of her past. She'd wanted to see her parents' room, to live within the same walls as her ancestors. She'd wanted to be home. "You haven't changed everything, have you?"

Lord Cabot's carriage pulled up to the door, the coachman scrambling about.

"Redecorating takes some time, you know. Mama's room hasn't changed a bit. You can use it as your own if you like."

"Really?" Her voice cracked.

"Well, yes, if you like." Charles's tone sounded more confused than generous.

Lord Cabot helped Mary and Miss Agnes down from the carriage. He'd become stiff and almost distance since greeting Charles and to be honest, Geneviève was grateful. Lord Cabot leaving was much safer. He was far, far too distracting. With only a tip of his hat, the man disappeared into his carriage.

Having spent the whole day avoiding him—or as much as one could avoid someone sitting next to one in the confines of a coach—Geneviève was utterly unprepared for the wave of disappointment that swept over her as she watched Lord Cabot flee into his carriage and rapidly clatter out of the courtyard.

Gradually, Geneviève realized that Charles was trying to steer her inside, jabbering away all the while. "So nice of Cabot to bring you—watch that step there—I trust you had a good journey?"

Geneviève pushed all thoughts of Lord Cabot away as she entered the house. She'd imagined it much lighter, much happier than the old, dark foyer. Her brother had been alone all this time. Her heart softened. She gave her brother's arm a quick, affectionate squeeze. "Thank you so much for inviting us, Charles. I've been wanting to come home for the longest time and, oh—"

Gone was the elegantly appointed foyer of her youth. Only the seeping marble staircase remained the same. The tapestries and gilded mirrors had been stripped from the walls, the Louis XV tables from their posts on either side of the stairs, and the classical statues from their niches.

"Isn't it splendid?" Charles's waistcoat threatened to explode as he puffed out his chest with pride.

"Ostentatious might be the better word," Miss Agnes commented sharply.

"It's… it's…" Geneviève groped for words.

Charles beamed, at ease for the first time since Geneviève had arrived. "*Retour d'Egypte* is all the rage," he said complacently.

"Is that a sarcophagus?" Geneviève pointed to the corner of the room. Imitation obelisks flanked the entry to the east wing and mock sphinxes guarded the staircase. She was grateful Lord Cabot had not entered their home. For the better part of a night, Geneviève had regaled against his quest for antiquities while Charles had been guilty of the same. She stared incredulously about her. "Do we have to answer the sphinx's riddle before we can go upstairs to bed?"

Charles looked blank. "Are you tired?"

Ignoring his question, she asked, "Are the new draperies also Egyptian in theme?"

"New draperies? Um, no." Charles stiffened again. He waddled over to one of his faux sphinxes and began absently stroking tis stone head. "About Mama's room…"

"It was so thoughtful of you to offer it to me."

Charles tugged uncomfortably at his immense cravat. "It might be best to wait a week or two before you move to Mama's room. The west wing's rather a mess. Lots of dust and, uh, rats. Yes, definitely rats. So, um, you might not want to go into the west wing at all. Dangerous. And dirty. Very dirty," Charles stammered.

Geneviève's stifled the rising suspicion. "If you think it's unsafe…"

"Oh, it is!" Charles beamed. He was entirely too eager for her *not* to stay in her mother's room. "The maid will show you to your rooms—bring you dinner on a tray—theater engagement—must go—good evening." Charles shouted for servants, aimed two kisses in the general direction of Geneviève's cheeks, nearly toppled himself over bowing hastily towards Mary and Miss Agnes, and fled in the direction of the west wing.

"Most odd," commented Miss Agnes.

"Most," Geneviève whispered. She would have to inspect the west wing at the first opportunity. A fear crept up her spine. She had come to France to help restore the monarchy, but she wasn't quite ready to toss over her brother. Not when she'd waited so long to be home.

Only a few hours later, Miss Agnes, *The Maid of Orleans* firmly tucked under one arm, announced she was having an early night and closed the door behind her with an emphatic clap.

From her bedroom door, Geneviève paused and considered her route. The home had been built, like so many houses of the seventeenth century, in a square around a central courtyard with the wings sticking out in front just enough to create the small cobblestone drive they had come through. As long as she could see the greenery of the front garden through the windows to her left, there was no way she could possibly get lost. Geneviève's own bedroom was on the bit that jutted out to form the stone entryway. Turning, she retraced her steps along the corridor towards the back of the house, past Mary's and Miss Agnes's rooms, past the closed doors of guest bedrooms, and past a narrow servants' stair.

After an age, the hallway finally turned, leading her into what should be the north wing. A half-open door revealed a large suite that could only be Charles's valet. The servant hummed a bawdy ballad as he brushed his master's frock coats. Geneviève tiptoed past very, very quickly into more closed doors.

When she was a child, she'd remembered the house as large, but she'd not realized just how enormous it truly was. She had counted at least fifteen bedrooms and still hadn't reached the west wing. But at bedroom seventeen, the hallway just stopped. Geneviève put her hands on her hips and advanced on the wall. The simpering shepherdesses on a large tapestry to her left shook their crooks at her and laughed at her perturbation. Geneviève disregarded them and stared at the plain red wall ahead of her. There had to be another wing there. Bearing in mind Charles's valet down the hall, she tapped lightly at the red wallpaper. Ouch. Geneviève nursed her bruised knuckles. The wall was decidedly solid. In fact, she was quite sure that had been stone under the red wallpaper.

Geneviève wandered back to the window overlooking the central courtyard. To her right, there was most definitely another set of windows. One was so close that she could probably climb from her current post onto the sill of the other. She'd envisioned moments like this, but her racing pulse had her questioning her mind. The courtyard below was elegant and flowering, but the shrubbery was not substantial enough to break a fall. There had to be an easier way in.

On the other side of the hall, the turn had occurred right after the window. Geneviève gave the immense tapestry another look. The rococo splendor of gazebos and gardens and lovers was really quite out of step with the cool classicism of the rest of the hallway. The red paper with its frieze on the top was designed to suggest Pompeii and ancient pottery. Or had she remembered that wrong? Perhaps she should have enlisted Lord Cabot's help on antiquities—the thought made her pause. Was her brother in league with Cabot? She shook the thought. The few paintings scattered along the wall were classical scenes in the style of David, all bold colors, strong lines, and not a garden, gazebo, or lover among the lot.

They appeared to be a random collection from medieval to eighteenth century. All hung side by side—and rather clumsily at that, now that she knew what to look for—as if to hide something. Geneviève burrowed in the dusty fabric, searching for an opening, but fell behind the tapestry into a room.

Geneviève stumbled into her parents' suite, dizzy with memory. There were no dust sheets. Under a gray film of disuse, everything had been left exactly as it was fifteen years before when she had departed for England, leaving Charles and Papa behind. Her mother's writing case lay open on her escritoire, the ink dry and caked at the bottom of the well. In her father's dressing room, Papa's wigs were still perched in a row on their stands. Geneviève fought off waves of recollection. Any moment now, Mama would scoop her up, and—

Geneviève could understand why Charles had closed off their parents' rooms.

Steeling herself, she followed the small spiral staircase down from her father's study to the floor below. The boards creaked slightly under her slippers, but they held her weight. She was in what had once been the library, before the Revolution had intervened. The dusty books called to her—through the grim, Geneviève could see the works of Homer in Greek, and a whole shelf of Latin works in elegantly tooled bindings. They could only have been Papa's, Papa who used to snuggle her in his lap in Mama's sitting room and tell her fabulous tales of centaurs and heroes and maidens turned into trees.

Geneviève wiped her damp cheeks and hurried into the next room. Papa's books would have to wait for another time; now, her mission was to explore the west wing before Charles returned.

She found herself in the ballroom. All of the furniture, a series of elegant couches and chairs, was pushed to the sides of the room, clearing the center of the floor for dancing. The immense room stretched most of the length of the wing and had a series of French doors opening onto the flowering courtyard on one side. At least, Geneviève *assumed* they opened onto the courtyard. The glass was opaque with fifteen years' filth. Squinting in the darkness, cobwebs draped candle sconces like lace, and spiders swayed inside their creations to the tunes of music only they could hear. At the very end of the room was a little raised area, which the musicians must once have occupied. It still contained a harpsichord, a harp—and a pile of brown paper packages.

Geneviève crossed the room at a run, slipping and skidding on the parquet floor.

Those were the mysterious packages. And there were others too: big wooden crates of all sizes stacked against the wall, next to more and of the floppy paper parcels. Geneviève's imagination thundered away like post-horses pounding down the Calais road. Draperies—that's what Charles had said they were, but no, they must be disguises for the League of the Sapphire Sphinx.

She ached to rip into the paper, but she forced herself to painstakingly unpick the knot of one of the packages. Finally, the last strand gave way and the parcel fell open in Geneviève's lap.

It was white muslin.

Geneviève stared stupidly at the cloth flowing over the dusty lap of her dress. It was nothing but yards and yards of white India muslin.

Geneviève scrabbled through the material. There was nothing hidden within the India muslin except more of the same fabric.

Disappointed and perplexed, Geneviève settled back on her heels before rushing to the wooden boxes, tugging at the lid. Three splinters and one lost fingernail later, the crate remained obdurate. Whoever had hammered the lid shut had not stinted on nails.

"Drat!" Geneviève pounded the crate with her foot. The contents made an interesting swishing noise.

Intrigued, Geneviève knelt on the ground, grabbed the crate, and tried to shake. It was too heavy for her to do more than rock it slightly, but she could hear whatever was inside shifting. Something fine, like a leaf or a powder.

Gunpowder.

Geneviève staggered to her feet, clutching the lid of the crate. There had to be something she could use to pry that lid off, a stick or a poker. Or, maybe, if she knocked the crate over, she could jar the lid off. That struck Geneviève as infinitely preferable to leaving the crate to search for a poker. Kneeling, Geneviève wedged her fingers under the edge of the crate, ignoring the abrasion of wood against her palms. She heaved. The box tottered right back into place. Gritting her teeth, Geneviève wiggled her fingers back under the box and heaved again.

The box toppled over on to the parquet floor with a tremendous crash. Lid intact.

Hands on her hips, Geneviève stared at the crate. She would have to find a poker.

That was when Geneviève heard the sound. It was half a breath, half a groan. Like the sigh of a spirit in torment. Geneviève tottered towards the edge of the ballroom. It was most likely wind she had heard. A house of this age nearly always had drafts. Or rats. Charles had spoken of rats. Geneviève didn't like to think of herself as squeamish, but she could definitely do without vermin. Pulling her skirts close to her ankles, she peered along the floorboards on either side of the room.

Someone had left a boot dangling off the edge of a sofa with a leg still inside it.

On a sofa by the wall, lay a sleeping man with a bloody bandage wrapped around his brow.

# CHAPTER 17

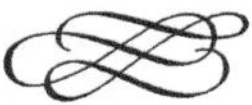

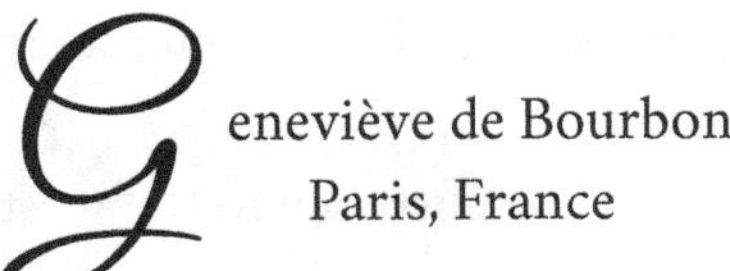

eneviève de Bourbon
Paris, France

Racing into Mary's room without knocking, Geneviève slammed the door behind her and slid against the doorframe. "You'll never believe what I found."

"Two kittens, three skeletons—" Mary turned a page "—and a ghost?"

"A wounded man."

Mary dropped the heavy tome she had been reading from her lap. "A servant with a scratched finger does not count as a wounded man."

Geneviève pursed her lips. "He had a bandage wrapped around his head, and—do you have smelling salts?"

"I do have smelling salts, but come now, what are you thinking?" Mary put her book down on the coverlet next to her.

"I need to wake him up to question him—oh, we don't have time for this. We have to go back to the west wing."

"It doesn't sound as if he'll be going anywhere," said Mary mildly, searching in her reticule. She held up a small, green glass vial. "What were you planning to ask him?"

Practically dancing with impatience, Geneviève yanked her cousin out the door. "Where the Sapphire Sphinx is, of course."

"What makes you think your man would know the Sphinx?"

"There has to be a shorter wait to the west wing. If we go down the front stairs and to our right..." Geneviève started towards the stairs.

Mary caught her hand. "If we walk, we'll be less conspicuous."

They descended the stairs at a snail's pace. Geneviève dug her fingernails into her palms with impatience. At the base of the stairs, she glanced about. No servants. The candles were still lit in the foyer, and nobody seemed to be about. To their left lay the rooms of the east wing, to their right, a seemingly dead end.

Her pulse raced. She'd dreamed of this moment. With every step, she felt her heart lift. She was where she was supposed to be, doing what she was meant to do. Her only regret was that her parents were not here to see it.

Geneviève searched for another tapestry. The entrance to the west wing was as clearly marked as if someone had slapped a sign on it with a tapestry depicting another Greek tragedy. As the entrance downstairs was more prominent than the one upstairs, Charles had taken an extra precaution. In front of the tapestry, he had placed a bust of Cleopatra on a marble pedestal.

Tense with excitement, Geneviève pointed towards Cleopatra. "There. That's the entrance."

Mary picked up a small candelabrum from a marble chest. "Shall we?"

Together, they lifted the heavy tapestry high enough to clear the candles and slipped underneath. They found themselves in an antechamber with gilded walls and dainty chairs that looked as though they would collapse if anyone so much as looked at them. The antechamber led into a music room, complete with an ancient pianoforte, painted. Geneviève hurried Mary onwards into the ballroom. Their vision was entirely blocked by piles and piles of brown paper packages.

Mary stopped at the same box Geneviève had.

"There wasn't anything interesting in them," she whispered as skirted around the piles. "Just muslin."

"What an odd place to keep muslin."

"Maybe they ran out of space in the airing cupboard. My wounded man is just down there, on the sofa." Geneviève took the candelabrum from Mary and hurried forward. "I couldn't get the lids off the crates, but I think—" Geneviève broke off as she brandished the flames above the sofa to illuminate—nothing.

"Where is he?" Geneviève waved the candles about, peering under the sofa, running to the next sofa and the next. "I know he was right there. He was fast asleep."

"Geneviève…"

She whirled around to face Mary, flames swirling with her in a diabolical sort of halo. "Please, please, don't tell me I just have imagined him, Mary. I *know* I saw him."

Mary said gravely, "Bring the candle over here."

Complying, Geneviève followed Mary's gaze. Against the faded white silk of the couch was a streak of fresh blood.

Mary experimentally reached out a finger. "He can't have been moved more than a few minutes ago. It's still wet."

"But who moved him?" Geneviève swiveled with the candle as though the person responsible might be hiding in the corners of the room. "And where?"

"They likely took him through the French doors, possibly into the courtyard?" Mary kept her tone even, her words measured.

Geneviève raced to the nearest door. For being so old, it opened without a squeak.

"It's been newly oiled," commented Mary under her breath.

Thrusting the candles at Mary, Geneviève dashed down a shallow flight of three steps and out into the garden while Mary examined the doors. It hadn't rained recently this far into France. The ground wasn't damp enough to hold footprints, nor was there mud to track along the stone paths. And there were doors into the east wing, the north wing, the west wing. Far too many options. The man could have been carried through any one of them. Geneviève prowled the perimeter of the garden, peering through door after door. Unlike the windows and French doors to the west wing, the ones to the east and north were well-scrubbed. Geneviève peered in turn into two drawing rooms, another music room, a breakfast room, and an immense state dining room that took up a large portion of the north wing.

"Geneviève," Mary whispered at her shoulder. the candles in her hand cast eerie shadows on the stone of the balustrade. "Come, I want to show you something."

"They must have taken him out through one of these rooms."

"And then downstairs through the servants' quarters? I think you may have lost your wounded man." They were making their way around the garden back to the ballroom doors. Mary paused next to an armless statue of Hercules. "None of this explains why he was lying in the ballroom. What kind of wound was it?"

Geneviève gestured to her head. "I'm not sure exactly where on the head. It was bandaged, but there seemed to be some sort of gash on the left side of his head. At least, I think so. That's where the blood was on the bandage."

"Could he have simply hit his head on something while unloading those packages from the carriage?"

"Then why all the subterfuge? Why hide him in the ballroom and then whisk him away again?" A breeze whipped Geneviève's dark curls into her face. Fear tried to surface but an excitement she'd never felt hummed in her veins.

"He could have felt better and left."

The warmth had departed with the sun, and Geneviève shuddered in the twilight chill, feeling the evening breeze pierce the thin fabric of her frock. "Do you really believe that?"

Mary leaned briefly against Hercules, her lips pursed. After a moment she straightened. "No, I can't. I'll show you why."

Geneviève hurried with her cousin back to the ballroom, where Mary paused just within the entrance.

"Yes?" Geneviève prompted Mary, trying to keep the urgency from her voice. The temptation to shake her cousin's shoulders was rising by the second.

"Look at this." Mary indicated the door.

"It's dirty?"

"That's just it. It's too dirty. It looks like someone deliberately took garden dirt and smeared it along the glass. See? Here and here? It's too thick and too uniform to be merely dust and age. It's as if—"

"—someone didn't want anyone seeing in." Geneviève clasped her hands together. *This* was why she was needed in France.

Mary quickly moved the candles aside as Geneviève leaned in to peer at the dirt on the doors, her short curls swinging recklessly close to the flames.

Mary nodded. "That's just it. But why? What does Charles have to hide?"

Geneviève shut the door with a decisive click and beamed at her cousin. "Don't you see? It's proof that he's in league with the Sapphire Sphinx."

# CHAPTER 18

Lord William Cabot
Paris, France

William swung down from his carriage in the courtyard of his modest bachelor residence, only five bedrooms and a small staff of ten servants, not counting his valet, cook, and coachman.

As he walked inside, Adam stood in his living room, leaning against the wall. His slender frame was outfitted in a newly fashioned waistcoat and shirtsleeves. With shocking clarity, William realized how vulnerable his espionage career was. Blakeney leaving was a void but if Adam left, William would quickly become a sitting duck for the Ministry of Police. Adam had been by William's side as a friend so subtle and silent that France paid the man no attention. Not even Delaroche gave the man a second glance, completely unaware of Adam's indispensable position as William's right hand man.

"It's good to be back." William pulled off his hat.

"After your dangerous mission into the heart of London society?" Adam smiled softly. "Escaping the matchmaking clutches of your mother is quite the fete."

"She sends her love."

"And Michael?" Adam grinned. "Does he still hold a candle for me?"

Chuckling, William let the warmth of old friendship wash over him. "He's still not forgiven you for Eton."

"He's not learned that the quiet ones are the most dangerous." Adam shrugged. "Just as you've yet to learn your mother will shackle you to a wife."

William raked his fingers through his hair. "I only just made it out of there alive."

In mock solemnity, Adam clasped his hands together and sent a pleading gaze to the ceiling. "Dear Gods of Egypt, tell Cabot dying is not the way to avoid marriage."

Rolling his eyes, William pulled his friend into his study just as his butler appeared. "Gideon, can you see if cook has anything to eat?"

"As you wish, my lord." Gideon hobbled off to the kitchen.

"He does make a convincing octogenarian." William was surprised Gideon kept up the act when all three men knew the truth. "If I didn't know better, *I* would be fooled."

Instead of answering, Adam darted into the study and emerged shuffling a stack of papers. "You're not the only one he's fooled. I gave him last Saturday off, thinking he would wash the gray out of his hair, possibly do the rounds of the taverns. Instead, he pulled up a chair before the kitchen fire, threw an afghan around his shoulders, and complained about his lumbago."

The two friends exchanged looks of mingled amusement and distress.

"Good butlers are hard to find." William shrugged. In truth, his butler's playacting helped keep William and his fellow spies safe.

"Unfortunately for him, Gideon will be with you for a great many decades to come."

"That's the last time we accept an out-of-work actor into the League."

Adam arched an eyebrow. "It could have been worse—he could have had delusions of being Shakespeare and acting out scenes from Macbeth—"

"He would have fit right in with the members of the Council of Five Hundred," William commented wryly, referring to the legislative body set up by the revolutionaries attempting to imitate classical models of government.

William shook his head sadly. "They read too many classics; such men are dangerous. At any rate, I prefer Gideon's current delusion. I take it, as matters stand, that he hasn't lost all track of why he's really here?"

"If anything, he's entered into it with even more gusto since he decided that he really is an eighty-year-old butler. He plays cards with Delaroche's butler every Wednesday—apparently they exchange remedies for their rheumatism and complain about the poor quality of employers nowadays," Adam added with a twinkle in his eye. "And he's been carrying on a rather odd and informative flirtation with one of the upstairs maids at the Tuileries."

"Odd?" William sniffed hopefully as he entered the dining room, but comestibles had not preceded them.

"He attained her good graces by complimenting her special formula for silver polish. They then proceeded to the intimacies of cleaning crystal."

"Good God." William began rifling through the stack of correspondence that had accumulated in his absence. "To each his own, I suppose."

The pile Adam had brought him contained typical letters, reports from his estate manager, invitations to balls, and perfumed letters from Bonaparte's eager sister Pauline. Pauline had been trying to entice William since he had returned from Egypt, and the amount of perfume she poured on her letters increased with each failed attempt. She must have become desperate with the amount of perfume wafting from the table.

Signaling to a footman to fetch the claret decanter, Adam lowered his voice, "How was it, truly. How was London, how was Blakeney?"

*Blakeney.* Bracing himself on the table, William felt the strange flutter of grief. This was his first true mission without Blakeney. Both men had veered off to separate areas for the same mission, always reuniting at the end. But now there was no eventual regroup.

Adam cleared his throat. "You look like you're in need of a restorative."

William abandoned his letters and flung himself into a chair across from Adam. "Mother must have dragged me to every major gathering. If there was an affair of over two hundred people, I was there. I attended enough musicals to render me tone deaf, if not deaf in actuality. I—"

"No more, please," Adam shook his head. "I refuse to believe that it could have all been that bad."

"Oh, really?" William raised one brow. He shot his friend a swift, sideways glance. "A good many ladies asked after you."

"And?" Adam's voice was studiedly unconcerned.

"I told a certain lady you had taken up with a Frenchwoman of ill repute and were currently expecting your third illegitimate child. By the way, you're hoping for a girl this time."

Adam choked on his claret. "You didn't. I'm sure I would have heard from my mother by now if you had."

William tipped his chair back with a sigh of pure regret. "No, I didn't."

"How are you with Blakeney and him not..." Adam looked away, displaying a deep interest in the arrangement of silver on the sideboard behind William.

"Fine." The lie came easy. William's throat went dry.

Silence filled the room. For decades William ran between his childhood friends and his Eton. He'd assumed the easy cadence between all his friends would never stop, but with Blakeney settling down with a wife, William felt the noose of obligations. Defending king and country had felt superior to any other responsibility, so why did he feel as if he was at the tail end of a fox hunt, alone and without purpose?

Adam cleared his throat again. "There were a number of interesting developments while you were away."

"What sort of developments?" William leaned across the table.

Espionage was a safer, more comfortable topic. "I hear there's changes in store at the Ministry of Police."

"Napoleon's insolent brother-in-law has been making mistake after mistake in trying to find funding."

"It's true then." William waited for the surge, the rush of excitement at gathering information.

"Ol' Boney is broke." After another sip, Adam slid the glass away from him on the table. "If the rumors are true that he wants to invade England, he needs cash. Munitions aren't cheap. Soldiers need supplies."

"Bonaparte is supposed to crack down on smugglers, confiscating their treasurers." William leaned back in his chair. "It would take him years to gather enough merchandise to fund a war. Our connection in Calais—"

"The innkeeper? He's noticed an unusual amount of activity over the past few months. The serving wench at the Orchid's Garden saw a group of men transferring a series of large packages from a Channel packet to an unmarked carriage and taking off down the road towards Paris."

"Could it be just the usual smuggling activity? There was an absurd amount of parcels delivered at de Bourbon's home." William nodded his thanks as the footman set a bowl of potato and leek soup down before him. At this point in the conversation he should be feel like a hound eager to bounce off after a fox. Of course, he had better make jolly sure first that it was a fox and not just a rabbit or a bunch of waving leaves. Ever since war had broken out between England and France, the smugglers of both countries had done a brisk trade, hauling French brandies and silks to England and returning laden with English goods. There had been one or two occasions in the past where William had gone haring off into the night, convinced he was on the trail of French agents carrying valuable intelligence to England, only to wind up with a boat full of disgruntled French smugglers and ten-year-old brandy.

"There is that," Adam conceded. "But Gideon heard the Ministry of Police has been very quietly detailing men to guard shipments of something coming in from Switzerland. He wasn't sure what, and he didn't know when—at least not yet—but he did say that it was top priority, whatever it was."

"That sounds vague." William had chased far too many dead ends to take the account seriously. "You have someone watching the major roads and waterways?"

Furrowing his brow, Adam said, "Yes, in addition to another three cases of brandy in the cellar, we also have a few leads. Whatever these shipments are, Edward Taunton is up to his neck in it."

"Edward Taunton." William wiped his face. "Are you sure?" They'd chased after the slippery smuggler for years.

"He's not just a smuggler, Cabot." Adam rubbed the bridge of his nose. "He's our man, he has to be. He's the most consistent in traveling between countries. He'd sell his own soul for the perfect price. He must be—he *has* to be the spy who revealed Blakeney to the French."

Hope bubbled in William's chest. If he could twist the reveal of Scarlet Pimpernel, then Blakeney could be tempted to return. Blakeney had left because someone had told the world of the man behind the mask, but if Taunton could be convinced to change his story, the Scarlet Pimpernel might just appearance once more.

While Taunton claimed a relation with a distinguished English family through his father, it was a poorly kept secret that he had been raised by his French mother in circumstances that could hardly be called respectable. Having wrangled his father's family into buying him a commission in the English army, he had promptly deserted in the midst of battle and decamped to the French. He was a man easily bought.

"Taunton has been frequenting the docks," Adam continued. "I've had our boys watching him. We've noticed a pattern. Every few days, someone will come to his lodgings with a note, and then he hares off in a carriage to the waterfront."

"With no other gentleman?" William tapped his finger on the edge of the table. Taunton wasn't clever enough to maneuver this well.

"He always takes an unmarked black coach and four—"

"I thought he only had that flashy curricle of his." William made sure to put his soup spoon down before speaking. "That hideous bright red thing."

"It wouldn't be all that bad if it weren't for the color," Adam added wistfully.

"Taunton?" William prompted. "Save your love of curricles and phaetons for your trip to England."

"Right." Adam smiled ruefully. "The use of the carriage heightened our suspicions. We traced it to a livery stable not far from Taunton's lodgings."

"The curricle would be too noticeable." William had seen a similar carriage at the docks, but it'd looked abandoned. "What does he do once at the docks?"

"I followed Taunton—"

"You're not a spy—"

Adam waved away William's concern. "I was disguised as a sailor. He went to a rather disreputable tavern. It was quite a good thing that I was wearing a hook."

"And there I was with the debutantes while you were having all the fun." William mimicked Adam's earlier mock prayer, hands folded and eyes on the ceiling.

"Calling it *fun* might be stretching matters a bit. While I was otherwise occupied with retaining my skin in one piece, I did notice Taunton engage in conversation with a bunch of ruffians and then slip into a back room. When he didn't return, I left the establishment just in time to see Taunton and his men finish loading the carriage with a number of brown paper packages."

"I saw a large number of brown parcels at de Bourbon's. What was in the packages?"

Adam rolled his eyes. "If we knew that, I wouldn't still be having him followed. But you're correct, at least some of the shipments have made their way to the Hotel de Bourbon."

"De Bourbon..." His sister couldn't know of Charles's activities. She was ready to throttle William for just accompanying Bonaparte.

"The little toady man, hanging about the Tuileries." Adam lifted his chin. "You've met him." A grin spread across his face. "On many occasions."

Carefully, William spoke, making sure to keep his tone even. His friend needed little encouragement if a woman was involved. "It's just a devilish coincidence. I shared a boat—and a carriage—with de Bourbon's sister and cousin."

"His sister?"

William abruptly pushed away his glass. "Yes."

"What a great stroke of luck. Could you use the acquaintance with the sister to discover more about de Bourbon's activities?"

"That," William said grimly, "is not an option."

Adam eyed him, the grin growing. "You don't need to propose to the girl. Just flirt with her a bit. Take her for a drive, call on her at home, use her as an entrée into the house."

"Miss de Bourbon is not an option." William twisted in his chair and stared at the door. "What the devil is keeping supper?"

Adam leaned across the table. "Ah, I see."

"No." William shook his head. "There's nothing to see."

William was about to deliver a baleful look in lieu of a response when he was saved by the arrival of the footman bearing a large platter of something covered with a sauce. William leaned forward and speared what looked like it might once have been part of a chicken.

"Have some," William suggested to Adam, ever so subtly diverting the conversation to culinary appreciation.

"Thank you." Undiverted, Adam continued, "Tell me more about your Miss de Bourbon."

"Leaving aside the fact that she is by no means *my* Miss de Bourbon"—William ignored the sardonic stare coming from across the table—"the girl is as complete an opposite to her brother as you can imagine. She was raised in England, somewhere out in the countryside. She's read Homer in the original Greek—"

"This *is* serious," murmured Adam. "Is she comely?"

"Comely?"

"You know, nice hair, nice eyes…"

"She doesn't look like her brother, if that's what you're asking," William bit out.

Adam slapped the table. "But if you're taken with her, that's wonderful." His lips twitched. "You can court her *and* investigate her brother at the same time."

William gave the napkin he had just listed to his lips an irritable twitch. "No, I cannot. First of all, she hates me."

"That's quick work. How did get her to hate you in all of one day?"

"It was a day and a half."

Something between a snort and a snicker escaped Adam's lips.

"Easy for you to laugh." Once upon a time, William had been a rake. Now he apparently angered instead of seduced women.

"No arguing with that," chuckled Adam. "No, really, what did you do?"

William plant his elbows on the polished wood of the table. "I told her I worked for Bonaparte."

"And that was all?"

William's lips quirked. "She's rather passionate on the subject of the Revolution."

"Then why is she returning to France? She's aware Bonaparte is—"

"I know, I know."

"And you won't tell her—"

"No!" William pushed back from the table so hard that the legs of his chair nearly splintered.

"You could let me finish a sentence once in a while, you know," Adam said mildly.

"Sorry," William muttered.

"I'm not suggesting you go shouting your identity to every comely young lady who wanders your way. But if this one is special, wouldn't it be better to take the chance of confiding in her—in a limited way," he added hastily, "than risk losing her? If she's so fanatical about the Revolution, it seems rather unlikely that she would betray you."

William pressed his lips together. "You sound like my mother."

"Since I like your mother, I'll take that as a compliment, and not as the insult for which it was intended." Adam leaned both elbows on the table. "You've not abandoned the league if you find a woman. Serving king and country takes many forms."

"Even if Geneviève—"

"So that's her name."

"*Miss de Bourbon.* If Miss de Bourbon makes an accidental comment—in strictest secrecy, because, of course, these things are always passed along in strictest secrecy," William spat out, "to her cousin Mary, Mary's a discreet sort of girl; she might not repeat it. But the house is teeming with servants. Even if they don't have a bloody lady's maid in the room with them, there's bound to be a footman lurking somewhere about. And then there's de Bourbon himself, who may or may not be on Bonaparte's payroll, but who would do anything to ingratiate himself to him. How long would the league last if my identity were to become known to him? I give it the time it would take for him to call his carriage and waddle his way to the consul's study." William raised his wineglass in an ironic salute. "Farewell, Sapphire Sphinx."

"That's only the very worst case."

William's lips twisted in a humorless smile. "Isn't that what we ought to plan for then? I can't risk it, Adam. Not with Blakeney gone. Even if there weren't other impediments, I couldn't risk it. Too many people depend on me."

Adam looked at him steadily, a friend of too long standing to be daunted by either irony or idealism. "You know what Michael would tell you if he were here. He'd say, *you're being too bloody noble.* And, in this instance, he'd be right."

Breaking Adam's gaze, William lounged back in his chair and changed the subject. "Did anything else thrilling transpire while I was away? Like Delaroche choking on a chicken bone?"

Adam pushed aside the remains of his own cold chicken. "Delaroche, I regret to inform you, is still alive and kicking. I must say, the man does have an instinct for theater. He strode into the Tuileries the other day and informed Bonaparte that, as the Sapphire Sphinx hadn't struck for over a fortnight, it was clear that he, Delaroche, had scared him away."

"That will never do," William drawled. He rocked back and forth in his chair, a devilish gleam creeping into his emerald eyes. "After all, it would be deuced unkind of us to let the man continue to entertain these delusions, wouldn't you say?"

Adam hunched forward, his own eyes taking on an answering sheen. "What do you think one might do to disabuse him of these unhealthy fantasies?"

"Well…" William toyed with the stem of his wineglass, admiring the way the candlelight struck crimson glints off the dark liquid. "One might raid his secret files, but one has done that already, so what's the fun in that?"

"Or," Adam mused, getting into the spirit of the game, "one might leave mocking notes on his pillow, but—"

"One has done that already, too," William concluded sadly. "Does Delaroche have any files we haven't looked at yet?"

Adam shook his head. "No. I'd say you made a rather thorough job of that. How about rescuing someone from prison? We haven't done that in a while, and it's sure to infuriate Delaroche."

William rocked upright so fast that he banged into the table, setting dishes and cutlery jumping. "I knew I kept you around for a reason."

Adam grimaced. "You flatter me."

"What of Bastille? We could tamper with their supply train again."

"The moldy bread and moldier water?"

"Don't forget the occasional rat as a treat on holidays. I'm sure the French consider it a great delicacy. Like frogs, or cow's brains."

Adam groaned. "No wonder they had a revolution. They were probably all suffering from chronic indigestion."

"There may be something in that theory." William pushed back from the table and stood. "But let's save writing your *History of the Causes of the French Revolution* for another night. We have far more diverting activities ahead of us…"

# CHAPTER 19

ord William Cabot
    Paris, France

William regarded the assemblage in the Yellow Salon of the Tuileries Palace with a yawn. Not terribly much, it seemed, had change in his absence. William resisted the urge to tug at his carefully arranged neckcloth; the room was uncomfortably warm with the heat of too many bodies and too many candles. Scantily clad women drifted from cluster to cluster like moths flitting from lamp to lamp—only, William noted with some amusement, unlike the insects, the ladies stayed as far away as possible from the telling light of the flames. Bonaparte's wife, Josephine, had draped the candle sconces and mirrors in gauze, but even the gentle light betrayed cheeks layered with rouge.

A burst of raucous laughter sounded from across the room. Over the curled and turbaned heads of the crowd, William trained his quizzing glass on the source of the sound. Ah, Taunton. Between his long, curly sideburns, Taunton's face was flushed with heat and drink. He had one arm propped against the mantelpiece; the other gesturing to some story he was weaving. William considered wandering over to investigate, but from the sound of the guffaws wafting from the fire-place, Taunton was telling jokes, not deep secrets.

William let his quizzing glass trail about the room. The usual gossip, the usual flirtations, the usual crowd of underdressed women and overdressed men. It was enough to make one understand why the French were always moaning on and on about *ennui.* He'd never met a culture steeped in supposed boredom.

"Who are those provincials with de Bourbon?" Bonaparte's cousin, Denon elbowed William in his ribs. "The two young ones are not ill-favored, but those *clothes.*"

The cousin, who had headed the scholars in Egypt, and was at present in charge of setting up Bonaparte's new museum in the Louvre Palace, had very decided ideas about aesthetics, especially regarding women.

As for the sort of woman William preferred—following Denon's gaze, William sighted Geneviève de Bourbon, one gloved hand lightly resting on her brother's arm. William's *ennui* evaporated in an instant. With some amusement, William noted that Geneviève fidgeted like a horse at the start of the Derby, straining to see around her brother into the crowded salon. Did the minx know she was in the court of her enemy? She appeared curious, not judgmental. The anger she'd wielded against William was nowhere to be seen.

De Bourbon had paused in the doorway exchanging pleasantries with a group of pretty young ladies, and Miss de Bourbon—*Geneviève* —was not weathering the delay well. As William watched, Miss Wooliston, standing behind Geneviève with Miss Agnes, leaned forward and whispered something in Geneviève's ear, to which she responded with a quick, rueful smile. William started to smile back at her, even though the look had not been intended for him.

*Geneviève.* Her name felt like a caress in his mind. The thought had William reeling. He couldn't be so cavalier with his mind. He needed to steel himself. Geneviève must be nothing more than Miss de Bourbon to him. And yet, her presence in the room had a vibrancy to every color and an alertness to his mind he'd not felt before.

"They should hand all young women from the provinces a fashion plate and march them to the dressmaker before they let them into the Tuileries," Bonaparte's cousin said.

"These have the handicap of being from England." William would never argue fashion with a Frenchman.

"Ah, that explains it." The man stared unabashedly at both young ladies. "Those heavy fabrics, those boxy styles, they are so sadly English. As charity to them, we ought to send a boatload of dress-makers across the Channel."

William wouldn't have called Miss de Bourbon's form boxy. True, her dress didn't hug her frame like those of the French ladies, who wore their filmy dresses with only a single slip, dampened to make the fabric cling to their legs. More than one woman had caught her death of cold by doing so in winter, but Frenchwomen seemed to agree that style was worth the risk of death. Miss de Bourbon's dress fell grace-fully from its high waist, lightly skimming her hips, merely hinting at the feminine form beneath. Next to the plain white lawn worn by the other women, the satin of her dress glimmered in the candlelight like snow seen by moonlight.

"Put them in French clothes and they will still be English women," William commented admiringly.

Misunderstanding, the man shook his head. "So sad."

De Bourbon had finished introducing his sister to another gentleman and was beginning to make his way through the crowd towards Josephine Bonaparte, who sat like a queen in a state towards the back of the room.

The man droned on as William's gaze kept drifting to Miss de Bourbon. The distance from across the room buffered him, letting his eyes linger on her face for longer than he should have.

Joy, surprise and curiosity flittered across her face as her brother introduced her to one of Marie Antoinette's former ladies-in-waiting. Edward Taunton came forward and folded into an elaborate bow. She blinked incredulously at his gold-embroidered peacock-blue coat and giggled something to Miss Wooliston under cover of her fan that made serene Miss Wooliston's eyes water with suppressed laughter. Miss de Bourbon's lip gave a perceptible curl as she made her curtsy to the Ministry of Police, Paul Delaroche. He brooded in the light-hearted assembly like a raven amidst a gathering of doves. And then—finally—Miss de Bourbon's eyes lighted on William.

She tripped over the hem of her dress.

It was just a small stumble, not enough for anyone else to mark, but enough for William to be oddly pleased. Well, one did like to have one's presence noted. Miss de Bourbon quickly regained her balance and continued walking with her head tilted to prevent William from entering her line of vision. So she didn't intend to acknowledge the acquaintance, did she?

Bonaparte's cousin elbowed William. "You know these English-women, no?"

"No. I mean, yes, I do know them. We shared the boat over from Dover two days ago. One is de Bourbon's sister, the other his cousin, and the dragon with the purple plumage is their chaperone."

"*Une femme formidable,*" hissed Denon, eyeing Miss Agnes's plumage with considerable alarm. "These English—their women are lacking of all the social graces. They do not realize that flirtation is an art. The boredom you must have endured upon that ship."

"Not at all. You do these ladies an injustice." Just because Miss de Bourbon bore him a grudge didn't mean *he* had to be uncivil. "Miss de Bourbon—the small, dark-haired one—is surprisingly well-read. She has some very original observations about the relations between the Greeks and the Egyptians."

The man squinted at Miss de Bourbon's back through his quizzing glass. "Ah, a—how do you call them—a bluestocking?"

"Geneviève is not a bluestocking."

"Geneviève?"

William coughed into his hand. "I'm not sure what to call her, but bluestocking isn't correct."

"An Original, perhaps?" The man peered through his quizzing glass at Miss de Bourbon for an uncomfortable amount of time.

"An Original." William couldn't repress a smile as he remembered Geneviève's comments on metaphorical cannibalism and the French Revolution. "Assuredly."

# CHAPTER 20

Geneviève de Bourbon
Paris, France

Under an ornate ceiling and gilded columns, Geneviève waded among the crush of people paying their respects to Madam Bonaparte. Twice she'd caught Lord Cabot's gaze. She kept her posture straight and her chin lifted, refusing to back down from their silent duel. Her boot caught on her hem. Perhaps it was a one sided—and all in her head—duel, but she would act the part. In less than two days, Lord Cabot had made her feel irrational. Out of control. She was Geneviève de Bourbon, and very much *in* control. She'd spent years preparing for this moment.

Mary whispered, "How long do you intend to keep your head at that angle?"

Without turning her head, Geneviève asked, "Is he still looking at me?"

"You're being ridiculous, Geneviève."

"He annoys me." Even to her own ears, Geneviève sounded like a child. And for some reason, she laid the blame at Lord Cabot's feet.

"And if you pretend not to see him, you don't have to talk to him?"

"Exactly."

"It is not polite to whisper," whispered Miss Agnes.

Geneviève rolled her eyes behind her fan. Her neck ached from her stiff posture. She'd come in search of the Sphinx, or at least a hint of who he was.

Since their arrival, she had eavesdropped on ten conversations with great stealth and skill. As a result, she now knew exactly how deep a certain Murat fellow was in debt to his tailor, where to find the best kid gloves in Paris, and that a Rochefort lady, whomever that might be, was supposedly engaging in illicit amorous relations with her footman, or maybe her groom. Unless the energetic Rochefort somehow knew the identity of the Sapphire Sphinx and could be blackmailed, Geneviève really didn't see how any of this information could be the slightest bit useful.

As for the Sapphire Sphinx himself, Geneviève had dismissed most of the guests as far too French. Unless the Sapphire's very name was an indication of his nationality. So far, she had met only two men of English extraction. One, a Mr. Whittlesby, with hair and sleeves both flowing in romantic disorder, had taken one look at Mary, flung himself prostrate at her blue slippers, and composed an on-the-spot ode to *the pulchritudinous princess of the azure toes*. Mercifully, Miss Agnes stepped hard on the poet's hand, cutting him off with a squeak in the middle of his second stanza. True, it could all be a spy persona, but he had a level of desperation that didn't mark him as a spy. Geneviève frowned behind her fan.

Her second candidate, Mr. Edward Taunton, was, like his name, only half English, and his bright regimentals were as off putting in their own way as Mr. Whittlesby's rumpled white linen. But there was a certain bold gleam to Mr. Taunton's blue eyes that might bespeak a man of action hidden under all that gold braid.

The crush of people pushed Geneviève and her small audience toward Josephine Bonaparte. The woman half rose from her chair and nodded in acknowledgment. There was something familiar about her. She smiled very sweetly, pausing at Geneviève, and said in French, "I knew your dear mother before the Revolution. She was such a lovely woman. When she discovered I loved roses, she sent me some cuttings I'd been longing to add to my garden. You shall have to come someday to see my little garden at Malmaison, which wouldn't be nearly so nice as it is but for your darling mama."

Mme Bonaparte spoke French with a lilting Creole accent that settled on its hearers with the benevolent warmth of island sunshine. Under her diamond diadem, her large hazel eyes gleamed with kindness.

Holding her breath, Geneviève tugged on an old memory. She wondered if this Josephine was the same woman who'd lost her husband by the same brutes who killed Geneviève's parents. Geneviève longed to curl up at her feet like a small child and beg for tales of her family. But she couldn't sacrifice all of her plans for a moment of nostalgia. If Mme Bonaparte—and thus all of the court—knew that she spoke French, half of her utility to the Sapphire Sphinx would be lost.

Geneviève forced a puzzled look onto her face and said in broken, school girl French. "Remembering the French I am not. The esteemed is speaking the English maybe?"

An expression of mild distress crossed Mme Bonaparte's pleasant face. From the corner of her eye, Geneviève could see Charles turning bright red with horror. "I beg your pardon for my sister, your excellence."

A pretty blonde girl leaned over the back of Mme Bonaparte's chair and said, "There's no need for apologies, M. de Bourbon!" Switching to English as poor as Geneviève's French, she said carefully, "Mama desire to tell you zat she was 'aving zee acquaintance of your mama."

Charles, looking for all the world as though he wished the polish parquet floor to part and swallow him up, performed hasty introductions, presenting the blonde girl as Hortense de Beauharnais Bonaparte, Mme Bonaparte's daughter by her first marriage, now married herself to Napoleon's younger brother, Louis. Miss Agnes stamped heavily on Charles's foot, and he finally introduced Miss Agnes and Mary as well.

"I must to you beg pardon for my English abominable," Hortense said with a self-deprecating wave of her fan. "My stepfather he was liking of my tutor so I 'ave lacked for lessons."

"Your English isn't bad at all," Mary reassured her. "It's much better than my French, I assure."

"Yes, you do yourself far too little credit." While Charles waxed lyrical in showering the First Consul's stepdaughter with compliments on her linguistic abilities, Geneviève found herself seized by the most brilliant of plans. A plan that would secure her access to the palace on a regular basis.

"I would be happy to teach you English," she blurted.

Hortense looked so delighted and grateful that Geneviève almost felt guilty for her subterfuge. Almost.

"Would you really?"

"Of course, she will." Charles's face bore the expression of a man who has sighted the promised land after an uncomfortable session with brimstone and pitchforks. His sudden squeeze of Geneviève's hand informed her that she was back in her brother's good graces. "The de Bourbons are always happy to be of service to the First Consul and his family. When would you like her to begin?"

Had Charles always been such a deplorable toady?

With some mutual expressions of gratitude, much bad English from Hortense, and some even worse French from Geneviève, they settled upon the following afternoon for the first lesson. Charles bowed himself out of the presence of the Bonaparte ladies to chat with some acquaintances. The poor coward appeared to be nothing like Geneviève's father. Or herself. She'd thought for a brief moment that he was in league with the Sphinx, but now the room seemed to spin. The urge to rush back to Mme Bonaparte and beg for stories of her parents threatened to break her spirit.

A throat cleared behind her. She spun around. A strong, sun-browned throat she had once seen tantalizingly displayed by an open collar and loosened cravat. The skin on her arms prickled and her neck ached with the pressure of not turning to look. Oh, blast the man, couldn't he have even left her a moment to gloat over her good fortune?

"William," on Hortense's lips, the name was soft and exotic, *Weelum*. She demanded of him in French. "When did you return?"

Lord Cabot bowed over Mme Bonparte's hand before kissing her daughter's. "I returned Monday night."

"And you have not called until now. *Cad.* Is he not a beast, Mama, to have deprived us of his company for so long? Eugene will be disappointed to have missed you—he is off at the theater tonight."

Geneviève was about to back quietly away, when Hortense laid one gloved hand gently on Geneviève's arm. "There is a lovely countrywoman of yours to whom I would like to introduce you." Beaming, Hortense tilted her head in Geneviève's direction, and drew Geneviève forward. Geneviève tried not to balk visibly under Lord Cabot's knowing eye. "Mlle de Bourbon, I would like to you make zee acquaintance of Lord William Cabot."

"We've already met," Geneviève said hastily.

"You 'ave?" Obviously intrigued, Hortense looked at Lord Cabot from under her eyelashes.

"Don't matchmake, Hortense, it's a beastly habit," Lord Cabot advised in French. In English, he said to Geneviève, "If Hortense will spare you, I would like to introduce you to the director of the Egyptian expedition of the *scholarly* bit."

"I caught your meaning, my lord. You needn't belabor it." Geneviève narrowed her eyes at William over the lace fringe of her fan. Fans were truly wonderfully useful items.

"Geneviève." Miss Agnes's feathers shook reprovingly.

A mischief glint appeared in Lord Cabot's eyes. "Because I thought you would enjoy discussing the classics with him."

"I would think my efforts would have little to recommend them to scholars so widely traveled." Geneviève snapped her fan closed.

Amusement tugged at his lips. "Oh, I would say—"

"Josephine." A bellow shook the candles in their sconces.

Unconsciously, Geneviève grabbed Lord Cabot's arm, looking

about anxiously for the source of the roar. About the room, people went on chatting as before.

"Steady there." Lord Cabot patted the delicate hand clutching the material of his coat. "It's just the First Consul."

Snatching her hand away as though she'd been burned, Geneviève snapped, "You would know."

"Josephine!" The dreadful noise repeated itself, cutting any further remarks. Out of an adjoining room charged a blur of red velvet, closely followed by the scurrying form of a young man. Geneviève sidestepped just in time, swaying on her slippers to avoid topping into Lord Cabot.

The red velvet came to an abrupt stop beside Mme Bonaparte's chair. "Oh. Visitors."

Once still, the red velvet resolved into a man of slightly less than medium height, clad in a long red velvet coach with breeches that must once have been white, but which now bore assorted stains that proclaimed as clearly as a menu what the wearer had eaten for supper. He pulled his hand from his pocket and Geneviève fought the gasp. In his palm was the beloved jewel-encrusted sphinx. The London papers hadn't invented fiction. Napoleon Bonaparte had a good luck charm. Although, Geneviève thought it a little ironic that his talisman not only contained sapphires but was in the shape of a sphinx. The First Consul was holding —quite literally—his enemy spy in his hand, the Sapphire Sphinx.

"I do wish you wouldn't shout so, Bonaparte." Mme Bonaparte lifted one white hand and touched him gently on the cheek.

Bonaparte slipped the sphinx back in his pocket. He grabbed her hand and planted and a resounding kiss on the palm. "How else am I to make myself heard?" Affectionately tweaking one of her curls, he demanded, "Well? Who is it tonight?"

"We have some visitors from England, sir," his stepdaughter responded. "I should like to present..." Hortense began listing their names. Bonaparte stood, legs slightly apart, eyes hooded with apparent boredom, and one arm thrust into the opposite side of his jacket, as though in a sling.

Bonaparte inclined his head, looked down at his wife and demanded, "Are we done yet?"

*Thwap.*

Everyone within earshot jumped at the sound of Miss Agnes's reticule connecting with Bonaparte's arm. "Sir. Take that hand out of your jacket. It is rude *and* it ruins your posture. A man of your diminutive stature needs to stand up straight."

Something suspiciously like a chuckle emerged from Lord Cabot's lips, but when Geneviève glanced sharply up at him, his expression was studiedly bland.

A dangerous hush fell over the room. Flirtations in the far corners of the room were abandoned. Business deals were dropped. The non-English speakers among the assemblage tugged at the sleeves of those who had the language, and instant translations were whispered about the room—suitably embellished of course.

"It's an assassination attempt," A woman next to Geneviève cried dramatically, swooning back into the arms of an officer who looked as though he didn't quite know what to do with her, but would really be happiest just dropping her.

"No, it's not, it's just Miss Agnes," Geneviève tried to explain. When she'd objected to a chaperone she never anticipated chaos as the reason.

Miss Agnes advanced on Bonaparte, backing him up so that he was nearly sitting on Josephine's lap. "While we are speaking sir, this habit you have of barging into other people's countries without invitation—it is most rude. I will not have it. You should apologize to the Italians and the Dutch at the first opportunity."

"Zey invited me." Bonaparte explained indignantly.

Miss Agnes cast Bonaparte the severe look of a governess listening to substandard excuses from a wayward child. "That may well be," she pronounced in a tone that implied she thought it highly unlikely. "But your behavior upon entering their country was inexcusable. If you were to be invited to someone's home for a weekend, sirrah, would you reorganize their domestic arrangements and seize the artwork from their walls? Would *you* countenance any guest who behaved so? I thought not."

"So much for the Peace of Amiens," Geneviève started to whisper to Mary, but Mary was no longer beside her. She thought, vaguely, that Mary had still been about when Lord Cabot had intruded onto the scene, but after that her attention had been so filled by the presence of Lord Cabot that she couldn't swear with any certainty to anything else at all. Geneviève slanted her eyes to the right, seeking a furtive glimpse of a strong arm in a superfine coat. Instead, Geneviève found herself eyeing a puffed sleeve. No longer furtive, Geneviève twisted to look at the spot that Lord Cabot had been occupying beside her before the hullabaloo with Miss Agnes erupted.

Lord Cabot had evaporated.

Geneviève tried to peer around the room, but the fascinated circle of bodies around Bonaparte and Miss Agnes was several people deep, and it seemed that Bonaparte had a penchant for employing very tall officers. Geneviève found herself staring straight into several gold-bedecked uniform coats. She would need a stepladder to see over them. Worming her way out of the crow, Geneviève stepped on four different toes, smelled several different perfumes at close range, got tangled up with one ornamental sword and almost tumbled over as she finally broke free.

Beyond the human wall, the rest of the room appeared deserted. To Geneviève's right, a woman had a man backed into the corner and was running a finger suggestively down his cheek. Some people have no shame, thought Geneviève. On the other side of the room—Geneviève's eyes scooted back to the first corner.

Being caressed in plain view of anyone who cared to look, in Mme Bonaparte's salon, was none other than the infamous turncoat, Lord William Cabot.

*Good heavens.* A woman was caressing Lord Cabot's ear—in public. Transfixed, Geneviève backed up a couple of steps on her soft slippers. A candle sconce was placed just about their heads, so Geneviève could view the scene and its actors with hideous clarity. The woman wore a white lawn gown so diaphanous that the light went right through it, revealing the decided absence of any slip at all, wetted or otherwise. Her dark hair fell in smooth curls from a circlet of pearls high on top of her head, one particularly long curl calling attention to the fact that the woman's dress had practically no bodice, unless one were willing to count a brief scrap of lace bristling two inches above the high waist. She was incredibly, undeniably beautiful.

Geneviève hated her on sight.

Charles had pointed the woman out to her earlier. Geneviève racked her memory as the woman slid on hand into the shining gold waves of William's hair. Pauline. That was it. Bonaparte's younger sister, Pauline Leclerc. Her affairs were as legendary as her beauty. Geneviève wasn't supposed to know such things, but she had read the gossip sheets assiduously for years. When it came to France, the English papers had few qualms about reporting scandal at its most scandalous, without even the protective veil of a euphemism.

Watching Pauline twine herself sensuously around Lord Cabot had Geneviève smoothing down the opaque material of her skit, aware for the first time that her own frock had been designed by a rural modiste in Rye, working of fashion papers several months old. Geneviève's hand went up to her own very modest scooped neckline, toying with the charm that hung in the hollow of her throat. Next to Pauline's diamonds, the little gold locket on a silk ribbon around her neck must look a trumpery affair, a child's trinket. Geneviève suddenly felt very young and very gauche, a little girl spying on an adult party.

Of course Lord Cabot would dally with such a crass strumpet. Two people with no morals. They served each other right.

Mary pulled at her sleeve. "Geneviève."

"Did you see that?" Her finger shook with indignation. At every turn, Lord Cabot was self-serving, from his scholarly pursuits and-- she shook the thought. She wasn't quite sure how to describe the type of pursuit he was behaving in at the moment.

Mary looked from William and Pauline to Geneviève. "He doesn't look like he's enjoying her attentions. Geneviève, Charles—"

"If he's not enjoying her embrace, why doesn't he move?"

"Perhaps because she has him backed against the wall. Geneviève you must—"

"That's no—"

"Charles is engaged in an extremely suspect conversation and I think you ought to go list *at once,*" Mary whispered in one long breath, before her cousin could interrupt yet again.

Geneviève's mind cleared at once. "What?"

"Charles and Taunton," Mary whispered urgently. "<u>They</u> slipped out while everyone was distracted by Miss Agnes."

Her body snapped to attention and she dashed for the door with Mary at her side.

Geneviève pressed her ear against the convenient gap afforded by a keyhole. The ancient locks had been designed with aesthetics in mind, not security. The keyholes were ornate and enormous. Geneviève could hear every word said, unmuffled by the wood of the door. Unfortunately, not terribly much had been said so far. Charles had rambled on and on about the high favor in which he was held by the consular family.

Charles dragging Taunton off in private just to gloat made little sense. Yet Mary had been so sure their conversation was suspect, and Mary wasn't one to succumb to fancy.

Geneviève's neck was beginning to ache form tilting her head at an unnatural angle and the ornate brass ornamentation of the keyhole pricked against her ear. She thought she heard someone behind her. She spun around but saw only Mary.

Had it not been for that wounded man in the ballroom, Geneviève would have been convinced her brother was merely one of the many boring men in creation. But there *was* that wounded man. Charles could be speaking in code but the sound of boots pacing impatiently up and down the parquet floor in the next room indicated Taunton found Charles's monologue equally grating.

Of all the men she had met that evening, Taunton *was* the most likely candidate to be the Sapphire Sphinx.

The steady rhythm of Taunton's steps came to an abrupt stop. So did Charles's monologue.

"Enough pleasantries. Have you squealed, de Bourbon?"

Charles's voice was oddly muffled as he gasped, "How could you think—no, never."

"Good." The word was nearly obscured by a thud, as though someone had dropped something heavy.

The Sapphire Sphinx. He *must* be the Sapphire Sphinx. Geneviève was too excited for completely sentences, her thoughts exploding in fragments.

"Tonight then?" Charles asked breathlessly.

*Tonight.* Geneviève mouthed excitedly to Mary. She pressed her ear hard to the crack in the door.

"Might as well," drawled Taunton. "No sense waiting."

"You could drive back with us and we could say we were retiring to my study for some port and cards and—"

"I know where to find you, de Bourbon."

"Right." Charles subsided.

"Though I must say"—Geneviève heard the boots begin to click again—"I wouldn't mind sharing a carriage with that sister of yours."

The footsteps rapidly neared the door. There was no time to dwell on the last, highly interesting comment, or await its sequel. Geneviève abandoned her keyhole and made anxious waving motions at Mary. The two of them scurried for cover behind a pair of over-sized gilded chairs. Crouched behind the furniture, Geneviève felt a bit like a child. If either man brought a candle or came close, the chairs would do little to hide them. Geneviève squeezed back more firmly into her corner. If caught, they would just have to brazen it out. They could say they'd gone looking for Charles because Miss Agnes was making a scene. That would prompt Charles to rush toward the chaos.

The door swung open, nearly careening into Geneviève's chair. Covering her mouth, Geneviève kept herself from flinching.

"Sir." Even in the dark, Charles looked like a halibut. "That is my sister you are discussing."

Taunton crossed the antechamber in three long strides, Charles puffing behind. "Your point?" And the door slammed behind the two men. Clip-clap, shuffle, shuffle... Taunton's decisive tread and Charles's shuffling gait receded along the marble gallery.

Mary's head poked out, turtlelike, from behind the back of her chair. "Geneviève," she whispered, "I don't like that man."

Geneviève placed a finger on her lips.

"Unless they tiptoed back, I think we're safe."

Geneviève bounced up, and gave an extra little hop of glee, just for good measure. "Isn't this exciting, Mary? What absolute luck. And if you hadn't followed Charles, we'd never have—"

Mary was clearly not listening, because she broke in with a worried, "That Mr. Taunton is no gentleman."

Geneviève glanced up from brushing dark smudges of dust off the satin of her dress. White was no color for a spy. "But, Mary, he *must* be the Sapphire Sphinx. Who else could it be?"

"That doesn't ,make him a gentleman. And we don't know he's the Sapphire Sphinx."

"Oh, *Mary.*" Before she gave way to pique, Geneviève recalled that her cousin hadn't had the benefit of the keyhole. In tones that rapidly escalated from a whisper, she hastily repeated the conversation she had overheard. Standing, she added, "I'll just hide in Charles's study and eavesdrop on their conversation. Obviously, they couldn't talk here with all of these revolutionaries about, but tonight I need only to get to Charles's study before he does."

"We're so close, Mary." She crowed. "I can't believe we've already found the Sapphire Sphinx."

"Nor can I," Mary said darkly.

# CHAPTER 21

*L*ord William Cabot
Paris, France

After extracting himself from Pauline's pretend advances, William chased after Charles de Bourbon and Edward Taunton. He couldn't participate in Pauline's desperate attempt to make her beau jealous. After searching, William had given up until listening to Miss de Bourbon and her cousin discussing their theories on Taunton being the Sapphire Sphinx. If only the Ministry of Police was so easily persuaded. Miss de Bourbon had just made the case against William confiding in any lady of his dual persona. Plain and simple, Adam was wrong. There was no rush of righteous indignation. Only a growing sense of loneliness.

With a heaviness he'd not felt since Blakeney's home, William prepared for the rendezvous. He paused outside the window of Charles de Bourbon's study, tugging the hood of his black cloak further down around his face. He always felt deucedly silly in this getup. Black breeches, black shirt, black cloak, black mask. It was the sort of outfit worn by pretentious highwaymen with names like the Romeo of the Night.

If the black weren't so bloody useful for blending into the night, William would have been much happier carrying out his missions in buff breeches. To add insult to injury, the mask tickled the bridge of his nose.

William set his mask straight and eased open the library window. The drapes had been left open, and unless de Bourbon were lying on the floor in the dark—an image which boggled William's mind—the study was clearly deserted. He would have time to do a little scouting and hide himself properly before de Bourbon and Taunton met. If William had timed it right, it should be roughly a quarter to twelve. From what he knew of de Bourbon, he was just the sort of hackneyed individual who was bound to hold any clandestine meeting just at the stroke of midnight. Hell, if de Bourbon were a spy, he would probably *enjoy* wearing all black.

An instinct for dramatic flair was one thing de Bourbon had in common with his sister. Grasping the windowsill in both hands, William hoisted himself up and into the room, just managing not to get his legs tangled in his cloak. He wobbled a bit as he landed on the squishy cushions of the window seat, hopping down onto the floor rather more rapidly than he had intended.

Taking in the room, William noted the recessed windows with their thick velvet drapes that would be his line of retreat if he heard footsteps in the hall. A desk, a small table bearing a brandy decanter, a standing globe—the furnishings of the room, while expensive, were few. Not having a bookshelf made the study feel awkward. Unused. The only reading matter of any kind apparent in Charles de Bourbon's study was a pile of well-thumbed fashion papers featuring the latest in waistcoats. The man was obsessed with his appearance.

The obvious place to look would be the desk. But this desk was a spindly affair, little more than glorified table, with room for only one narrow drawer. De Bourbon might not be the quickest frog in the pond, but even he couldn't possibly be dim enough to store evidence of illicit activities in his desk.

The Ministry of Police stored his most sensitive files in his desk—or, rather, *had* stored his most sensitive files in his desk. Smiling,

William was rather proud of Delaroche's change in storing information.

De Bourbon had hung paintings above his desk and above the table on the far side of the room. Both gleamed with newness. There had been no time for dust to colonize the curlicues in the gilded frames, nor were the surfaces of the paintings themselves dulled by sunlight or grime. In most of his investigations, William followed the rule that anything conspicuously new was automatically suspect. Trust de Bourbon to be different. Everything in the study was conspicuously new. The desk, with brass sphinxes' heads inlaid into the wood of the legs, couldn't be more than a year old, and the small table bearing the decanter was clearly from the same craftsman. Even the mantelpiece on the fireplace was a recent addition.

In fact, in the entire room, the only object not new, fashionable, and, to William's mind, unpardonably ugly was the globe standing in the corner of the room, between the table and the window. There had been just such a globe in the library at Asaph Hall when William was young. Due to William's habit as a beastly eight-year-old of spinning the globe as fast as he could make it go for the joy of seeing the countries blur into multicolored blogs, the Asaph Hall library globe was no more. An overly eager spin had left it airborne and out the window, unceremoniously ending its existence by bouncing into an ornamental fountain. William had been confined to paper maps for years —but the glee of his eight-year-old self returned as he neared the globe.

Wrapping his fingers around the contours of the globe, William lifted it up off its stand and shook it—the swishing sound of paper rasped inside. He shook it again. Rather a lot of paper, by the sound.

His fingers probed for the catch, and he had just found a suspicious bump somewhere along the equator when William heard a bump of an entirely different kind. And a nose that sounded curiously like the word *ouch.*

William stood very still, weighing his options. That might not have been an *ouch* at all. It might have been a squeaky floorboard, or a mouse. Yet, if there were even the slightest chance of it being a human voice, the sensible thing to do was to dive out the window and make his escape.

"Oh," a feminine voice whispered.

In French, William asked, "Who's there?"

In the same language, a familiar woman spoke, "Don't worry, it's just me. Ouch."

"Just me?"

The small figure of Miss de Bourbon wriggled its way out from under the desk. First a dark head and then a pair of shoulders slithered partway out. "Oh, blast, my hem's caught." The head disappeared again under the desk.

Too incredulous even to be angry, William stalked over to the desk, grabbed a pair of slim forearms, and pulled. There was a slight tearing sound, and out popped a rather disheveled Miss Geneviève de Bourbon.

"You're here." She inhaled sharply. "In the flesh. In my brother's study." Tilting her head, she motioned from his head to his boots. "Well, not much flesh as you're covered in black."

"And you know who I am?" William forced his tone to be even. He was on the tip of chuckling at the minx.

"I'd thought my sojourn would go unrewarded. But you're here." Rocking on her heels, Miss de Bourbon was positively beaming. "You might call yourself the Sapphire Sphinx, but I know you as the savior of royalists. The scourge of the French."

"French." William straightened. Every word she'd said was in French.

Miss de Bourbon shook out her skirts and flashed him a smile that dazzled even through the moonlit darkness of the study.

He continued, making sure to speak only in French, "May I inquire as to what you were doing under that desk?

"Waiting for you," Miss de Bourbon said brightly, as if that were all the explanation that was needed. "You *are* the Sapphire Sphinx, aren't you?"

"Don't you think it would be rather foolish of me to answer that question?" And even more daft for William to stay in the study.

"Only if you fear that I might have the secret police stashed away behind the curtains." Impulsively, Miss de Bourbon grabbed one of his gloved hands and led him to the closed curtains of the other window and flung them open. She twirled to face him. "See? No Delaroche. You're perfectly safe."

Standing far closer to Geneviève than propriety would have ever allowed, in her brother's darkened, deserted study, William had his doubts about that statement. It would be so easy to lean just the slightest bit forward, to brush that unruly curl out of her eye, to cup her face with his hands—William pulled back, away from Miss de Bourbon. If he couldn't make her leave, he would feign departure and lurk under the windowsill.

"You're not planning to leave. I've been under that desk for ages waiting to speak to you." Her eyes took him in as she positioned herself directly in the path of his escape. "I want to help you."

"*Help* me?" The woman had lost her mind.

"Please, if we are to work with each other, call me Geneviève."

Shaking his head, he retreated. William couldn't afford to be trapped by a young maiden. Nor could the Sapphire Sphinx.

"Yes." She lifted her chin. "I have an entrée into the palace. I'll be giving Bonaparte's daughter English lessons. No one except you knows I can speak French, so they'll talk freely in front of me and I can overhear all sorts of useful things. I'm not squeamish and I'm excellent at disguises and—"

"No." The Sapphire stalked rapidly towards the window. "It's out of the question."

"Why?" Geneviève—Miss de Bourbon—darted after him. "Do you not trust me? At least give me a trial. Let me do something to prove myself. If I fail, I'll go away, I promise. You'll never hear from me again."

William paused, arrested by the echoes of his own voice nearly a decade ago. He had stood there in Blakeney's study, pleading with him, begging him, promising anything at all for the chance to go on just one mission.

A thought pierced through. Blakeney's wife was on Delaroche's list, as was the rest of her family. William's face hardened. He had only been a little older than Geneviève at the time, but he rode, he boxed, he fenced and damn it, he wasn't a tiny female who could be flung over the shoulder of the first lout who happened along. She had cousins and a brother in France. She was in far more danger than William ever was.

"Wouldn't you be happier practicing your embroidery?"

"Embroidery?" She balked. "Embroidery? Do you have any idea how many years I've studied the comings and goings of every ship, every gentleman crossing the channel?. Embroidery?" Her voice rise with each word.

"Or you could always take up an instrument." William tried to herd Geneviève towards the door. "Why don't you go see if there's a harp in the music room?"

"Are you trying to fob me off?"

There didn't seem to be any point in denying it. "Yes."

Geneviève planted her hands on her hips. "I came to France for the express purpose of joining your league. This isn't some silly whim. Unlike *some* people, who flit about the continent and consort with the enemy..."

*Like Lord William Cabot.* The words hung in the air between them.

*Like me*, William specified with an inward smile. There was a bit of relief that he'd gotten under her skin.

"...I take the plight of France very seriously, and I intend to do something about it."

"An unusual interest for an English debutante."

"Most English debutantes," Geneviève explained with a flick of her hand, "don't have a father who died on the guillotine. I do. And I intend to make sure his death does not go unavenged."

Heavy silence stretched between him. Dozens of excuses and reason flitted through his mind like aimless arrows. He should cut her off and leave her be, but her defiant stance softened his.

"Your father might consider it a greater tribute for his daughter to live long and happily. A spy cannot hope for either."

"My parents were robbed of long and happy life by the Revolution."

"All the more reason for you to aspire to both."

"How could I live long and happily knowing that their murderers prosper?" Geneviève's hands clenched into passionate fists, her lips in a delightful scorn. She might have been going for intimidating, but the effect had her looking like a kitten pretending to be a lion. "I have spent my entire life in training for this moment. You can't shoo me away with platitudes about living a happy life." Geneviève took a deep breath and brushed phantom dirt off her skirt. "All I ask is one chance. Is that so unreasonable?"

"Yes. It is." William seized Geneviève by the shoulders and marched her over to the mirror over the fireplace. "You"—he pointed at her reflection in the glass—"are a lady."

"That's not exactly an original observation." Geneviève squirmed out of his grasp. "And besides, I really don't see what that has to do with the matter at hand. I—"

"It has everything to do with the matter at hand." This woman was becoming more ridiculous by the moment. She and every other lady was being protected by the league. Their job was to protect the innocent, to defend their country, not send innocent ladies to the den of French beasts. "You have no idea of the risk you'd be putting yourself into."

"No more than you do every time you undertake a mission. I understand the danger. And I'm not worried."

William pumped his hands into tight fists. Her flippant attitude was dangerous, not just for herself, but for every spy that came into contact with her. "You shouldn't even be here now. It can only be termed criminally idiotic of you to be alone, in the dark, with a man whose identity is entirely unknown to you. Or with any man, for that matter."

"But your identity *is* known to me. You're the Sapphire Sphinx. And if it's propriety that you're worried about, who is there to see us? As long as no one knows you're here, my reputation is perfectly safe. And *I'm* certainly not telling."

Groaning, William forced himself to breathe evenly. There'd be plenty of plans gone awry but so far this mission was proving to be the most frustrating. "Your naiveté is terrifying."

"I am not naïve," she said stiffly. "Unless it's naïve to weigh all the evidence and come to a reasonable conclusion. I've read about everything you've done. *Everything.* You've always been the very soul of honor. Why would you do so much good for so many people only to behave ill towards me? Is that naïve?"

"Yes," he said sharply. "And what proof do you have that I even am the Sapphire Sphinx? I could be a bloody highwayman for all you know."

"I felt your ring."

"You what?"

"I felt your ring. When I took your hand, when you first came in. I could feel the shape of the sphynx engraved on your signet ring through your glove. After all," she added smugly, "there was no other way I could be sure it was you. I am not quite so naïve as you think."

"Oh." The little minx had a point. He'd not realized she'd even checked his hand. "The ring could be stolen from my earlier mission tonight."

"It so happens to be the very signet left for discovery every time the Sphinx strikes?" She stepped closer, her voice lowering. "In the very same manner that the Scarlet Pimpernel claimed his missions with a certain flower?"

"Geneviève—Miss de Bourbon." He would not be so informal with this wily of a woman. "I could be a smuggler. A thief. A great many things. And—"

"Would a smuggler or thief stand about talking to me in French?" Geneviève batted her eyes innocently. "There is more within me than you give me credit for. Admit it, I've already passed your initial thought."

William could solve this little problem by making her despise him. He'd done the same on the boat with one comment about his adventures in Egypt. He could mock her ambitions, belittle her abilities, dwell crudely upon her physical attributes. Within ten minutes, rather than begging him to stay, Geneviève would be pushing the Sapphire Sphinx headfirst out the window with a boot in his back for good measure. All he had to do was make her hate him.

"Miss de Bourbon—"

"Geneviève." She rocked back on her heels. "It doesn't matter what excuse or strategy you try to employ, I will be of service to the league. If that means I am to knock upon every door in Paris, so be it."

"Minx," he said with a groan.

The china clock on the mantelpiece rocked on its base, the high pitch chimes ringing out the door.

Geneviève froze.

"Midnight," William said grimly. *Blast.* If his suspicions were right, de Bourbon could be here any moment.

The last chime of the clock was still reverberating through the room when it was replaced by a very different sort of sound. An uneven series of clumps and thuds filtered softly through the closed French doors. Just on time, William thought dourly, listening to the footfalls on the flagstones of the courtyard. Not only Charles de Bourbon, by the sound of it, but a whole series of booted feet.

Damn. He couldn't allow himself to be found here. Even if de Bourbon wasn't an agent for Bonaparte, William's presence in his study, at midnight, in the company of his sister, would be bloody hard to explain.

Swift action was required. So William acted, swiftly.

Grabbing Geneviève's arm, William pulled her with him behind the curtains of the window seat.

# CHAPTER 22

Geneviève de Bourbon
Paris, France

Without an explanation, the masked man pulled and pushed Geneviève behind the curtain. She fell back with a thud against the man's chest. Not just any stranger, *the* Sapphire Sphinx. He hadn't admitted the fact, but there was only one explanation. No other man would be dressed in black with a sphinx signet ring in the middle of the night. Geneviève struggled to catch her breath and her balance. She had lost her footing entirely when the man hauled her behind the curtain, but no matter how she tried to get her bearings, she wound up on top of him, sprawled across his chest.

"Sh," he whispered.

Geneviève hadn't said a word, but with her head against his chest she could hear his heart beating in rapid staccato. That made two of them, as her own pulse was racing. The linen of his shirt pressed warmly against her cheek, lightly scented with the clean, spicy tang of orange peel. Geneviève pushed against an uncomfortably hard cushion to lever herself up off the Sapphire Sphinx.

He groaned, and the cushion shifted beneath her hand in a most uncushionlike fashion. She froze. It wasn't a cushion but the Sapphire Sphinx's thigh. Geneviève snatched her hand away with a speed that would have done Miss Agnes proud.

Losing her balance, Geneviève tumbled back against the Sapphire. "Off," grunted the man.

"Sorry," Geneviève mouthed and then groaned. The back of her head was facing the Sapphire; he couldn't see her lips. She fought the rising frustration. She was meant to assist the spy, not accidentally accost him.

From the corridor, a growing chorus of men's voices became louder. Not just one voice, but several. Grabbing the end of the window seat for balance, Geneviève moved away from the Sapphire. The man emitted a sort of muffled groan. Geneviève winced, mouthing another unseen apology.

Outside, someone dropped something, a crash with the sound of wood splintering followed by rough voices and loud cursing. Geneviève strained to hear. Two men appeared to be quarreling with one sounding very much like Lord Cabot's English coachman from the week before.

Geneviève cast a quick sideways glance at the man on the window seat beside her. Between his mask, hood and the oversized cloak, there was little of his face revealed. She wouldn't be able to read any emotions from what she could see. A thought wiggled in—if the Sapphire Sphinx planned to meet Charles, why was the spy hiding behind the curtains with her? The Sapphire should have shoved her behind the curtains and gone on to his rendezvous with Charles on his own.

Closing her eyes, she concentrated her senses on the noises coming from the courtyard. Fragmented voices shifted and blended into each other. Against the blur of voices, another thud resounded through the night.

A new voice broke in. "Careful with that, you fools."

Geneviève's eyes flew open. "It's Charles," she whispered to the Sapphire.

He pressed a gloved finger to his lips. She opened her mouth—he placed the finger on her lips.

Geneviève's eyes flew to the Sapphire Sphinx's face. Her breath stilled as she realized that through the slits of his mask, his gaze was riveted on her mouth. For a moment, time slowed. Geneviève's world narrowed to his intent eyes, and the pressure of his finger against her lips.

He brushed his finger back and forth along her lower lip. Without thinking, she leaned forward as he traced his way along the curves of her mouth to her upper lip.

Curling the fingers of her left hand around the edge of the window seat, Geneviève tried to still her racing pulse. Aside from the occasional hug from Mary, Geneviève had not been touched affectionately by anyone in years. She'd not realized how utterly alone and starved for emotional crumbs she'd become.

A quick memory of the feeling Lord Cabot had caused on the boat flashed through her mind, but the Sapphire's hand moving from her lips to her hair blotted out any thought of anything else. His fingers slid up through her curls, gently curving her face towards his as they knelt, facing each other, under the wide velvet window seat.

Shutting her eyes, Geneviève held her breath. His fingers combed through the strands of her hair, his other hand stroking warm and firm down her back. His arms tightened around her, pulling Geneviève against him, her chest pressing against his. She lifted her hands to his head, fingers on the mask. He jumped back, sending Geneviève tumbling.

"Is that what you're after?" His voice was dangerously low. "To have a look at my face? To tell the world who the Sapphire Sphinx is?"

"No, I was caught up—" she paused, realizing his admission. "You *are* him, aren't you?"

Without answering, he scrambled to a stand. He ran a hand over his cap and muttered, "Damnation. They're gone."

"Who are you hiding from?" A rising doubt crept in. Twice Geneviève was alone with a man and experienced an almost-kiss. There had to be a reason, even if the almost-embrace was a distraction.

"I wouldn't answer that—"

"If you'll utilize my brother to restore the monarchy, why not his sister?"

Peering in the room, he cursed again. "I missed them. Completely."

"There's thousands more who are scared of Bonaparte. Who want the monarchy restored." Geneviève hadn't been in the country long enough to know for certain, but she couldn't be the only Frenchwoman mourning the France of her childhood. "What can I do?"

The Sapphire spun around, his gaze on the courtyard below. He unlatched the window and paused, as if just realizing she'd spoken.

Lifting her chin, she said loud enough to make him nervous. "How do you plan on restoring the monarchy?"

"Restoring the monarchy?" In the dim light of the moon, his eyes were clearly confused. "How can you employ yourself or any lady to a ridiculous and dangerous task? You cannot be a spy. You cannot assist —" He shook his head and in English said, "Monarchy? The goal of England is to prevent an invasion. Not restore the monarchy. Geneviève—"

Gasping, she covered her mouth. "Your voice. I *do* know you."

"I'm a spy." He shrugged but the concern in his voice belied his nervousness. He'd made a mistake. "That is more than you should know."

Geneviève grabbed his cloak in both hands. "Do I know you from the Tuileries reception? From England?"

"Till we meet again, Geneviève." In one polished movement, he swung himself over the windowsill and scrambled down to the courtyard below.

Geneviève leaned out the window after him. For the first time since she'd left the small town of Rye, she felt a burst of hope. *The Sapphire Sphinx.* She'd met him, but more importantly, the Sapphire knew *her.*

Gathering her skirts tougher, she bunched them above her knees and leaned over the sill. There was a ten or twelve foot drop. If only she were dressed as the Sapphire and didn't have to wrestle with skirts. Twice she attempted to climb out but could only get one leg over before trying over again. With one deep fortifying breath, Geneviève bravely positioned herself on the edge of the windowsill, allowed herself one last clutch at the sides of the window, closed her eyes, and jumped.

She landed with a jarring thud, stumbled, and sprinted towards the edge of the house. Rounding the corner of the east wing, Geneviève caught the faintest sight of fabric swishing around the front of the house, just outside of the courtyard.

Geneviève grabbed the wall as she wove around the corner and skidded to an abrupt stop, just before the iron gates standing guard to the courtyard. The gates had been closed after their return from the Tuileries, Geneviève was sure of it. They shouldn't be open in the dead of night. The gates had to be twelve feet tall, and were, as Geneviève knew from watching the grooms struggling with them earlier that day, heavy enough to require the efforts of two men to move. Not exactly the sort of door one might accidentally leave ajar. If Charles had opened them to let the Sapphire in, the man wouldn't be hiding and escaping through a window.

Geneviève tiptoed cautiously towards the courtyard.

It was quite a different thing approaching the gates on foot, rather than sailing through them ensconced on the raised seat of a carriage. The gate in front of Geneviève reared forbiddingly into the air. The ornamental *fleurs de lys* that adorned the upper curve of the gate so charmingly in daylight bristled like the spears of a veritable regiment of sentries.

Flattening herself against the wall, Geneviève turned to peer through the bars. The elaborate ironwork of the gates, leaves and flowers and curlicues twining so closely together that they almost formed a solid barrier, hid her from the view of anyone within—or at least she hoped it did. Geneviève twisted her head at an uncomfortable angle so she could look through the two-inch gap between a flower and a leaf.

A plain dark coach, horses moving restlessly, was preparing to leave the courtyard. Geneviève couldn't discern the features of the coachman perched on the box in the front; he wore a shapeless hat, and a long muffler had been wound round his face. On the lip of the coach, speaking softly to her brother, stood none other than Edward Taunton in a long black cloak.

Gesturing to Charles with one black-gloved hand, he swung into the coach. Black gloves, black cloak—the only thing missing was the cap and mask covering his face. Confusion swept over her—the Sapphire Sphinx was Edward Taunton.

# CHAPTER 23

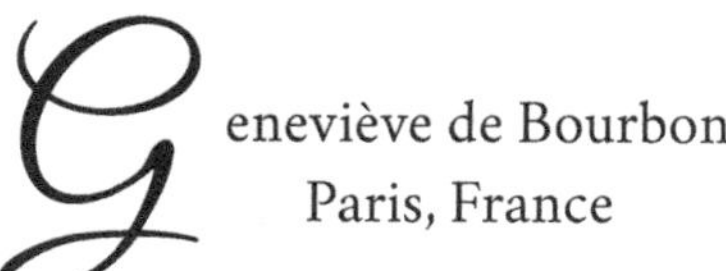

Geneviève de Bourbon
Paris, France

Circling the house, Geneviève tried to find an open window. It was more than skirts that kept her from scaling the stone walls to her brother's study. The night air had her hands shivering.

*Taunton.* Geneviève rolled the name through her mind and found she tried to anglicize the surname. No matter how she pronounced it or punctuated it, Taunton just didn't sound like the sort of name this Sapphire Sphinx ought to have.

But no other man would be dressed in black and leaving the estate. The evidence was overwhelming even if Taunton's conversation with her brother hadn't been enough to prove his identity. Seeing him climbing into his carriage wearing a long black cloak of the same sort that Geneviève had been in such intimate contact with only solidified her theory. Two men in black cloaks roaming about her brother's house in the dead of night strained the imagination, and that Taunton would be leaving from the front of the house just after the Sapphire Sphinx set off in that direction was enough of a coincidence to settle the debate. Her stomach twisted into knots. Her body refused to believe the man who'd threaded his hands through her hair was Taunton.

Another walk around the house and her brother was back in his study, a candle lit in the room. She crept along the wall and tried the servant door—sighing gratefully when it opened.

Back in her room, she lit a candle by the bed and changed out of her soiled clothes. In the quivering point of light, she stuck her shoes in the crate, pulled on a clean white linen, night rail, brushed her hair fifty times, laid on the covers, and blew out a candle.

But sleep escaped her.

She couldn't sleep on her side or on her back, and she couldn't sleep rolled into a ball with her arms around the knees. She'd met *The Sapphire Sphinx*. For years she'd dreamed of dashing about solving mysteries on the continent—her heart sank. Restoring the monarchy had always been her primary goal. A rock of disappointment rolled around inside of her. She'd envisioned joining forces and bringing about the France of yesteryear. But the Sapphire admitted to not caring about the monarchy.

At two o'clock, flat on her stomach with her head at the footboard and her feet picking the pillow, Geneviève replayed her conversation with the Sapphire Sphinx in a slightly improved version.

At three o'clock Geneviève had rolled the covers into a little ball at the foot of the bed and was wondering whether the Sapphire Sphinx had just kissed her—or at least *almost* kissed her to get her stop bothering him.

By four o'clock, Geneviève had been reduced to pulling little tufts off the coverlet.

At nearly ten in the morning, it had taken the combined efforts of Mary and Miss Agnes to drag Geneviève out of bed in time for her first English lesson for Bonaparte. Charles shuffled uncomfortably across the seat in his carriage.

The silence fell between them, awkward and heavy. Geneviève needed to know about his relationship with the Taunton—and if the man was truly the Sapphire Sphinx. "Charles—"

"You'll need to be on your best behavior, Geneviève." He frowned and pulled at his oversized sleeves.

She bit back a retort, uneasy with him calling her Geneviève instead of Evie. A simple name had her feeling alone in the city of her birth. Charles cleared his throat and squirmed once more. He was more of a stranger than a relative. They no longer looked alike. Trying again, she said, "Do you miss—"

"You've lost all your French." He *tsk*ed and shuffled his weight again.

His words had her blinking back emotion. And then a flood of disappointment. She couldn't become a spy if she was choking on tears with her brother. She needed to be strong. And subtle.

Geneviève steadied her courage as the carriage drew up before the Tuileries, decanting her and Charles into the courtyard. A bored-looking sentry waved them into the palace.

At the entryway, Charles grabbed her elbow. "I'll meet you here in two hours."

Before she could respond, he scuttled off down the corridor on his own errand. She had another half an hour—according to the elaborate clock on the wall—before she met Hortense. From the rugs to the tapestries, Tuileries held the standard on pomp and circumstance. Her mother had spoken of the grandeur of Tuileries and her heartbreak during the revolution. Geneviève didn't understand how the same people who hated the monarchy and the wealth of the aristocracy could welcome Bonaparte and the excess surrounding him.

Tuileries by day was quite a different prospect than the Tuileries by night. Last night, the rooms were bedecked with orange blossoms and arrangements of roses and filled with heavy perfumes worn by guests. Not even the odd crumpled petal remained. All had been swept away by efficient servants, leading in their wake the less pleasant scent of ammonia and lye.

Last night there had been grenadiers standing stiffly at attention. At least Bonaparte made no attempt to hide the source of his power.

Geneviève passed servants lugging pails of water like soldiers leaving their ships and a pale young man in an ill-fitting frock coat with ink-stained fingers, most likely someone's secretary. She turned to follow him but spotted a familiar frock coat in the next room. It was undeniably her brother; no one else would wear gold lace in that quantity, collar and cuffs, but his voice held a very uncharacteristic air of authority as he spoke in a rapid whisper.

She strained for a glimpse of his companion. Her pulse raced at the prospect of encountering the Sapphire Sphinx again, and she leaned further forward around the doorframe. All she could make out was a hand and a bit of black sleeve. Charles's garish cuffs blocked Geneviève's view, but the man appeared to be holding paper. A note of some kind.

For several minutes, she stared and repositioned, but Charles and his companion had disappeared. He had whisked his padded shoulders and lacy ruffles out of her path faster than the Sapphire Sphinx leaping through a study window. Wringing her hands, Geneviève needed to corner her brother and get some answers.

Part of her hoped Charles's foppish attitude was a facade. If she could pin him down and get some information—he might tell her, as he frequently had when they were small children, to mind her own business. In fact, it seemed more than likely that was just what Charles would do. He had never been amenable to sharing.

Geneviève should probably keep an air of ignorance—and spy on her brother whenever the opportunity arose. She would have to consult with Mary—

"Disgrace!" someone bellowed.

Geneviève stopped abruptly, shocked out of her reverie. She spun around. No one. She was alone in yet another of the little antechambers that separated the grander areas of the palace. The noise had emerged from the door towards which she had been thoughtlessly wandering, a door that stood slightly ajar, as though someone had just entered.

"You are a disgrace!" the bellower repeated, with, if possible, an increase in volume. And spite.

Geneviève was considering edging her way back out of the anteroom, when another much softer voice interposed, "But Napoleon, I—"

Geneviève's breath caught in her throat. While not exactly a meeting with the Sapphire, the conversation held promise for the eavesdropper. Perhaps a scandal that she could convey back to the English news sheets? Lifting her muslin skirts in both hands, she tiptoed her way into the space between the door and the wall.

"Leclerc only dead for a year!"

*Leclerc.* The name might mean little in terms of international espionage, but Geneviève pressed her ear against the hinges of the door hard enough to leave a permanent dent. The last time she had spotted Pauline Bonaparte Leclerc, the shameless woman had cornered Lord Cabot in the salon. Lord Cabot's amours meant nothing to her, nothing at all. It was just that *any* scandal that might be damaging to the Bonaparte clan could be helpful to her cause. She repeated the thought twice, but neither time felt right.

Through the gap in the door, Geneviève could hear the clomping of boots on the parquet floor as Bonaparte raged about the room. "You cannot be out of mourning."

"Napoleon, I cut off all my hair and placed it in his coffin."

The smack of a palm hitting wood. "Hair grows back. It already has. And you—chasing anything with trousers."

Geneviève waited eagerly for a reference to Lord Cabot and that scandalous scene in the salon.

"My Minister of Police complained that you pinched him in an inappropriate place. Again."

"Oh, but, Napoleon, it wasn't an inappropriate place," Pauline reassured him eagerly. "It was in my sitting room."

Geneviève eyed the wood of the door with incredulous disgust. Either Pauline Leclerc was one of the most truly addlepated people she had ever encountered or wickedly clever.

"What was he doing there?" Bonaparte roared.

"I had to have someone check for spies," Pauline answered innocently.

*Crash.* Bonaparte had hurled something against the wall.

Geneviève squinted against the hinges. Ah, an inkwell, judging from the large black splotch adorning the wallpaper. For a moment, Geneviève was grateful for the distance she felt toward Charles. Her brother didn't meddle in her affairs, nefarious or otherwise. Charles wouldn't be caught asking Geneviève about an amour.

"Don't be angry with me, Napoleon," Pauline whined. "It's just that I am so bored—"

"Bored? Bored! Find a hobby." His voice grew with each word. "Go shopping—"

"You can't begrudge me my innocent little amusements—"

"Your innocent amusements are an international scandal. What do I have to do? Send you to a nunnery?"

An excellent solution. Geneviève would have seconded the idea had she been a legitimate part of the conversation rather than an eavesdropper.

"How can you"—*sniff*—"be so unkind? All I want"—*sniff*—"is a little happiness."

"All *I* want is my family not to embarrass me."

"This is Josephine's doing, isn't it? She's poisoned your mind against me."

Geneviève had been decidedly right in like the First Consul's wife. Josephine was clearly a woman of good taste and sound judgement—except in marrying Bonaparte.

With a dangerous tone, Bonaparte said, "Hold your tongue."

"If that's what you want, I'll just leave. You'll never have to see me again." The sound of chair legs scraping against wood was followed by Pauline sobbing her way out of the room.

Geneviève cringed back against the wall, fearing both disclosure and the impact of the door, but Pauline slipped easily through the gap—nobody in the throes of distress should be that graceful, thought Geneviève critically—bawling into her handkerchief all the while.

"Pauline, don't cry." Bonaparte charged out of the room after his sister. "Pauline!"

The door slammed open. Fortunately, Bonaparte's shouts drowned out Geneviève's involuntary *oomph* as the heavy wood whacked the air from her lungs.

Once Geneviève had flexed her shoulders and shaken out her arms and felt more like an ironed bedsheet, she tiptoed around to peek into the room that Bonaparte and his sister had recently vacated.

Geneviève's eye took in, one by one, a wall with a large ink splotch, an iron staircase that looked a bit like an ink splotch itself against the pale wall, and a carpet marred by yet more ink splotches. By far the most interesting feature of the room was a desk, piled with stacks of papers, and surrounded by enough broken quills to re-feather a plump goose.

Bonaparte had left his study empty.

Smiling, she wished the Sapphire could see her now. With a quick glance either way to make sure no one else was about, she rushed into Bonaparte's study.

Geneviève picked her way across the broken quills and balled-up bits of paper on the floor. She really mustn't disturb anything and arouse suspicion. If he returned, she could claim to be lost and looking for Hortense. Geneviève practiced looking innocent and mildly daft as she made for the desk. Widen the eyes, drop the lower lip—if worse came to worst, cry. From that last interview, Geneviève had gleaned a crucial piece of intelligence. Bonaparte had a soft touch for crying women.

In the center of the desk lay a piece of paper covered with writing, as well as an unintended design of ink dots splattered by the abandoned quilt that lay next to it. Bonaparte must have been working on this when his sister disturbed him.

Another glance about the room and Geneviève snatched it.

"Article 818. The husband may, without the concurrence of his wife, claim a distribution of objects moveable or immovable fallen to her and which come into community..."

She paused, the paper shaking in her hand. Bonaparte can't truly believe in a law like this. She defied any future husband who would try to claim a distribution of her objects moveable or otherwise without her concurrence—but worse, this law didn't aid her investigation. Unless Bonaparte's plan for conquering England was to contract a marriage between the two countries and then claim that as husband, France was entitled to all of England's objects, movable and immovable.

Replacing the document, she found a fragment of classical pottery serving as a paperweight for a sheaf of papers. At any other time, Geneviève would have been intrigued by the artifact; keen on her mission, she went straight for the documents, which were folded and roughly bound together with a piece of string. Carefully, Geneviève eased the letter on the top of the pile. Ten thousand francs. Geneviève squinted at the writing. It was a bill from Josephine's mantua-maker for a white lawn gown embroidered with gold thread. Geneviève yanked out the next paper from the pile, which turned out, unsurprisingly, to be an invoice for the matching slippers. Recklessly, Geneviève shook out all of the papers, and began to thumb through them. She flipped past bills for cashmere shawls, for diamond bracelets, for shipments of rose cuttings, for more pairs of slippers and gloves and fans than Geneviève could imagine using in a decade of continuous parties. There wasn't a clandestine note or a suspicious purchase among the lot.

Unless the documents were a code. Perhaps what was meant by slippers was really rifles—different colors could refer to different types. Geneviève snatched back the documents she had dropped in disgust seconds before. Perhaps by looking at them more closely she would find a key to the code.

On second glance, it became quite clear that the bills were indeed bills. The only thing revealed by looking at them more closely was that Geneviève's imagination was more effective than her spying. And that Josephine, for all her charm, was a prodigious spendthrift. The English papers delighted in carrying tales of Josephine's extravagances and Bonaparte's infuriated reaction. It was rumored—in the *Spectator,* not the *Rye Intelligencer*—that Josephine had already bankrupted the French treasurer with her uncontrollable wardrobe.

Scowling, Geneviève bundled the folded papers back into their string. Marvelous. She had stumbled into Bonaparte's abandoned study in the spying opportunity of a lifetime and discovered marital discord.

Geneviève rested her hands on her hips and glared at the desk. Really, there had to be something more informative among the clutter. She returned to rifling halfheartedly through Bonaparte's desk. Perhaps the Sapphire Sphinx had been right to run off in a huff. It had certainly been naïve to believe that a man clever enough to take over the rule of a turbulent country, cutting out numerous competitors at home and conquering a slew of countries abroad along the way, would be dim enough to leave his plans for invasion of England in plain sight upon his desk.

She vowed that by the time she emerged from this room, she would have something to report to the Sapphire, something that would make his eyes widen with admiration and his jaw drop.

Geneviève's gaze drifted up around the walls, searching for secret caches. That painting on the far wall could conceal a safe of some kind. And over there, by the window, that long dark line might be a relic of another inkpot that had perished for its country, or it might indicate a break of some kind in the wallpaper. Geneviève planted both her hands on the desk and leaned forward for a better look.

A quick prick hit her finger. Peering on the desk, she shook her head. A simple paper cut. The sharp edge that had sliced her finger poked out from underneath the blotter. Grabbing the edge with her uninjured left hand, Geneviève yanked it free. Another bill. The series of numbers marching across the page gave credence to that theory, but the signature at the bottom was Delaroche's. Rereading, the numbers were categorized into *ships of muslin, rifles of rubies* and *boots of leather.* With a shock, the answer came. This wasn't a bill for Josephine's muslin and gems. The Minister of Police had sent Bonaparte calculations for the cost of the Army.

Geneviève's first impulse was to stuff the paper into her bodice and flee. She went so far as to poise the paper over her neckline, but it would create a lump under the thin fabric of her dress and Bonaparte was sure to notice its absence. She would just have to memorize it. Two thousand four hundred ships, Geneviève repeated to herself, and one hundred and seventy-five thousand men. Geneviève felt a swell of indignation that had nothing to do with proving herself to the Sapphire Sphinx or the ills done to the monarchy. Her overactive imagination had presented her with an image of 175,000 Frenchmen marching grimly through her uncle's peaceful meadows, trampling his fields and kicking his sheep.

The treasury, Delaroche wrote, could not support such an expense. No wonder, thought Geneviève, glancing at the pile of bills she had plunked back down on the desk in irritation moments before. The next time Geneviève saw Mme Bonaparte, she would be sure to bring her attention to the necessity of owning at least three diamond tiaras.

At the bottom, Delaroche noted he'd secured funds from the Swiss. Geneviève scowled at the letter. *Secured.* Bonaparte didn't secure anything. He demanded, threatened. The money, in gold, was to be transported by coach from Switzerland to Paris in just over a week to what Delaroche had said was *a safe place.*

Without money, Bonaparte's invasion of England would be thwarted. The discontented masses would rise against him. And the monarchy would be restored. Geneviève grinned as she stuck the letter carefully back under the blotter. Not bad work for a girl fresh from Rye.

Geneviève ran from the study. She needed to notify the Sapphire Sphinx and—Geneviève collided at high speed with someone entering the anteroom from the other direction. Her head was still spinning as a pair of capable hands righted her, and a warm chuckle sounded somewhere above her ear. "What an original way to make your presence felt."

# CHAPTER 24

Geneviève de Bourbon
Paris, France

"My Lord!" Geneviève hastily stepped back, this time banging into a bust of Julius Caesar that wobbled ominously on its marble pedestal. Geneviève adjusted the bust before he could take a leap off his stand.

"Had you known it was me you would have taken care to run into poor Julius instead?" Lord Cabot supplied with a smile of such conspiratorial goodwill that Geneviève nearly reeled back into poor Julius once more.

"Something like that," admitted Geneviève weakly. Clearly, she was still slightly dazed from her two collisions.

Geneviève felt behind her to make sure she wasn't going to back into anything else. With Lord Cabot in it, the anteroom shrank to nothing. The tall figure in tight buff breeches and a pale blue jacket filled Geneviève's line of vision. Sunshine from a window above encircled his head with a deceptive halo. A man who'd abandoned his country should never be given a halo or anything heroic. Lord Cabot was the last man in the world who deserved any celebration.

"You just missed Mme Leclerc," blurted Geneviève.

"Pauline?" Lord Cabot frowned in a way that could indicate either confusion or displeasure. "Oh, no, was she looking for me?"

Nodding toward the other end of the corridor, she said, "That way."

"Oh." He raised his eyebrows but didn't charge off after Mme Leclerc. Instead, Lord Cabot leaned lazily against the paneled wall as though he had no other purpose in the world but to stand in a little anteroom with Geneviève. There was a familiarity in the way he looked at her.

Sidestepping, Geneviève asked, "Don't you want to go that way?"

With a wry smile, Lord Cabot shook his head. "No."

She searched his handsome face. She would have thought that he would be in more of a hurry to run off after his paramour. On second thought, maybe that wasn't all that surprising. Look how rapidly he had gone from flirting with Geneviève to dallying with Mme Leclerc. Just the way he had flitted off to join the French in Egypt when his very own country was at war with them. Faithless cad.

Geneviève's feelings towards Pauline Leclerc rapidly spiraled from animosity to pity. That poor, gullible woman had clearly been as thoroughly taken in by the glib charm of the perfidious Lord Cabot as had Geneviève herself. The woman might wear dresses with as much substance as cobwebs, and her intellectual capacities might be even flimsier, but still, she deserved better than to be treated like that.

"You ought to," said Geneviève hotly.

"Ought to what?"

"Go after Mme Leclerc." Narrowing her eyes, Geneviève pointed toward the corridor.

"Is this an attempt to free yourself of my presence?" He stepped closer.

"No." Geneviève wouldn't be caught alone in the corridor or anywhere with Lord Cabot's charm. She would figure out a way to leave without offending Bonaparte's favorite pet.

"No, you don't want to be rid of my presence?"

Holding up a hand, Geneviève said, "Ridding myself of your presence was not my intention—"

He grabbed her hand. "Delighted to hear it."

Geneviève pulled her hand from his. "I was hoping to induce you to behave with some consideration—"

"By leaving you alone as quickly as possible?"

"No." Geneviève scowled at him. She needed to leave and without this cad becoming suspicious. She wouldn't become another Mme Leclerc. "No. I mean no offense. I'm just eager to leave."

Tilting his head, Lord Cabot paused. "Let's back up a step, shall we? You want me to go after her?"

"The decent thing to do is go after Mme Leclerc and make things right with her."

Blinking, Lord Cabot ran a hand through his hair. "Make things right?"

"How can you be so callous?" Like a fool, Geneviève had nearly kissed this man in a boat—and almost kissed the Sapphire Sphinx. Mme Leclerc was Bonaparte's sister, a lady unable to refuse. Geneviève would have been tossed aside without another thought.

"You don't mean to say that you thought that Pauline and I—no."

"I saw the two of you together last night, in Mme Bonaparte's salon. Do you deny it?"

A grin crept across his face, mischief glinting in Lord Cabot's eyes. "What man wouldn't want to be seen by Pauline? She is, after all, an exceptionally beautiful woman, don't you agree?"

Geneviève nodded woodenly.

"With exceptionally fine eyes," he added devilishly. "The sort of eyes a man can lose himself in."

Geneviève's head jerked up and down by a fraction of an inch.

Lord Cabot lowered his voice and leaned forward conspiratorially. "And exceptionally little conversation."

Geneviève gaped.

Moving back a step, Lord Cabot waved a nonchalant hand. "She has very little to say about the Rosetta Stone, and absolutely no interest in Homer."

Geneviève leaned back against the wall, feeling completely thrown off balance. For the life of her, she couldn't remember why she had brought up Mme Leclerc in the first place.

"Geneviève," said Lord Cabot softly, "There is not, nor was there ever, anything between me and Pauline."

"Other than her dress," muttered Geneviève.

She hadn't meant the comment to be heard but Lord Cabot's hearing was unfairly sharp. He gasped with laughter. As he laughed, his green eyes crinkled at the corners, glinting with flecks of gold like leaves touched by the sun.

"While I must confess that the only person I was looking for was Bonaparte—"

She jabbed a thumb over her shoulder. "He also went that way."

"I am delighted to have stumbled across you," Lord Cabot continued with a grin.

"I can't imagine why."

He *tsked*. "Can't you?"

"You needed to discuss Homer with someone?" Geneviève suggested tartly, flinging out the first unromantic image that came to mind.

"Close enough. I was planning to send you a note, inviting you to come see my antiquities tomorrow."

Something about the way William said *my antiquities* as proud as a schoolboy with a particularly smashing toad to show off made Geneviève want to smile despite herself. They weren't really his antiquities; they belonged to Bonaparte, who had collected them in the course of leading the armies of the Revolution. No right-minded Englishman would admit to having anything to do with those antiquities. And no right-minded Englishwoman would have anything to do with Lord Cabot, Geneviève reminded herself sternly. Teasing green eyes or no.

"That will not be possible," she said coldly.

Lord Cabot's eyes lingered knowingly on her face. "No blood guilt can pass to you from a few harmless objects."

Geneviève lifted her nose in the air as though she hadn't the slightest notion of what he was talking about.

"Think about it," he continued softly. "These statues and jewels and fragile bits of humanity were buried deep in the earth centuries before the world ever heard of Bonaparte. The relics of a civilization that was old while France was still covered in forest, and London a mere gathering of mud huts."

His words cast a spell in the midafternoon quiet of the room, evoking images of shimmering sands and scurrying men in white robes and black-haired women keening their grief in elaborate burial chambers. His voice calmed something inside her.

"Tomorrow afternoon, then. Your cousin and chaperone are, of course, included in the invitation." He grinned. "Miss Agnes might like a mummy case for use in her horrid novel."

"I haven't accepted."

"But you want to."

*Blast.* The insufferable man was absolutely right; no matter her feelings for him, she longed to see hieroglyphs carved into stone and ornaments that might once have dazzled the eyes of Marc Antony. Miss Agnes wasn't the only one with an interest in adventures.

"Why hesitate?" Lord Cabot pressed his advantage. "You're not afraid, are you?"

"Of what?"

"Of ancient curses? Of enjoying my company?"

Since that was precisely what terrified Geneviève, she bristled indignantly. "Of course not. Tomorrow afternoon, you said?"

"Two o'clock, perhaps? The artifacts are lodged in a wing of the Tuileries, until we move them into the Louvre. Ask any sentry to show you the way," Lord Cabot directed, with a smile that struck Geneviève as uncomfortably close to a smirk.

"You don't have any apples to offer while you're at it, do you?" she asked sourly.

"Satan tempting Eve in the garden? Not a terribly flattering role for me, is it? And you're overdressed for the part."

Geneviève's blush rivaled the hue of the dangerous fruit they had been discussing. "Might I ask a favor, my lord?"

"A phoenix feather from the farthest deserts of Arabia? The head of a dragon on a bejeweled platter?"

"Nothing quite that complicated," replied Geneviève, marveling once again at the chameleon quality of the man beside her. How could anyone be so utterly infuriating at one moment and equally charming the next? Untrustworthy, she reminded herself. Mercurial. Changeable. "A dragon's head wouldn't be much use to me just now, unless it could offer me directions."

Lord Cabot crooked an arm. "Tell me where you need to be, and I'll escort you."

Geneviève tentatively rested her hand on the soft blue fabric of his coat. "That's quite a generous offer when you don't know where I'm going."

"Ten leagues beyond the wide world's end?" Lord Cabot gave a lazy grin.

"Methinks it is no journey." Geneviève matched the quotation triumphantly and was rewarded by the admiring light that flamed in Lord Cabot's eyes. "No, not nearly that far—at least, I hope not. This place does seem large enough to house a couple of continents. I was looking for Hortense Bonaparte's chambers."

The statement was close enough to the truth, and Lord Cabot accepted it without a murmur of disbelief. "You're in the right place," he informed her, steering her back into Bonaparte's study. "That little staircase will take you right up to Josephine's chambers, and Hortense's are next door."

"Thank you." Geneviève lifted one foot to the first step.

"Think nothing of it." Lord Cabot leaned an arm on the newel of the stair. Even with Geneviève a step up, he still smiled down at her. "It wasn't much of a journey. I owe you nine leagues at least."

"Bring me a phoenix feather, and we'll cancel the debt. Good day, my lord, and thank you for the directions." Geneviève lifted her skirt and ascended another step.

"You'll have to accept a mummy case or two instead." Lord Cabot's voice arrested Geneviève mid-step. Letting her skirt fall, she turned, only to discover that his smile was even more devastating when faced eye to eye. Or lip to lip, as the case might be. Geneviève swallowed hard.

"Why were you so eager for me to visit?" she asked suspiciously.

"Because," Lord Cabot furrowed his brow, "I think I like you."

And then he smiled and bowed as if the last statement hadn't made Geneviève's jaw drop till it practically hit the bottom stair, and with a bland, "Good day, Miss de Bourbon."

He took his leave before Geneviève could retrieve her jaw and her faculties of speech.

"And good day to you too," she muttered as she flounced up the stairs. *I think I like you.* What on earth had the man meant? Geneviève shook her head. She didn't care. That was a luxury should would not partake in. Her mission did not hinge on Lord Cabot's affection. It made no difference.

Geneviève stopped short on the upper landing and lifted her chin. She had more important things to worry about. She collared one of the young pages who seemed to do nothing but loiter about the corridors waiting to carry messages, clandestine or otherwise.

Which was why, when Geneviève hissed, "Can you take a message for me?" the page gave her a look that questioned her mental capacities.

"Yes, miss."

"Can you keep it secret?"

Another look, this time compounded with wounded dignity. Geneviève was sinking in the page's estimation by the moment. "Of course, miss."

"Oh, good." Leaning forward, Geneviève whispered, "Tell him I must see him urgently. Don't forget. *Urgently.* Because I have something terribly important I have to tell him, and he'll know what it is, after our conversation last night. I'll meet him at the Luxembourg Gardens at midnight. And don't forget—*urgently.*"

The page looked understandably confused. "Tell who, miss?"

Geneviève refrained from banging her hand against her head in extreme self-disgust. Just because she had let Lord Cabot rattle her.

"Edward Taunton," she said, pressing a coin from her reticule into the boy's hand. "Make sure to deliver my message solely to the ears of Edward Taunton. And don't forget—"

"I know," said the boy, with the world-weary air of one who had heard it all before. "Urgently."

# CHAPTER 25

*L*ord William Cabot
Paris, France

Shaking his head, William wandered back out of Bonaparte's study and through the anteroom, which suddenly seemed much darker without the cheerful yellow of Geneviève's dress. He wondered if she held a memory of their almost-kiss last night as he did.

It was ludicrous. He had kissed dozens of women in his time. He'd not actually kissed Geneviève, nor should he. England needed the Sapphire Sphinx, not a lovesick puppy. He needed to focus, not become distracted by a young miss in muslin.

Back in his rakehell days, all it had taken was a smile across a ballroom, a nod of the head towards a garden, a note passed surreptitiously from gloved hand to gloved hand. So easy. But Blakeney was gone—his one note to a lady's hand had turned into matrimony. He'd fallen in love and left the fate of England to William.

He could easily arrange another assignation with Geneviève, but she welcomed his arms as the Sapphire Sphinx. Therein lay the rub. The Sapphire Sphinx and Lord Cabot unanimously concurred that Geneviève was to have nothing more to do with the former. She had curtailed his inspection of de Bourbon's study, just as he had gotten to the good part, the mysterious cache of papers in the globe. True, for all he knew the globe might contain nothing more exciting than de Bourbon's billets-doux. Or it might contain papers vital to the defense of England. As if that weren't enough, he had arrived just in time to see villainous-looking rascals trailing out into the night and had heard de Bourbon bidding Taunton an uninformative farewell.

He probably should have tailed Taunton home. William exercised the *probably.* No doubt about it, the responsible thing to do, was to follow Taunton. Instead, the Sapphire Sphinx had lurked in the bushes outside the Hotel de Bourbon, making sure that one Miss Geneviève de Bourbon made it safely inside.

One night's work—William sternly pulled his mind back to the matter at hand. One night's work could be accounted lost with good grace. To lose another night's work verged on irresponsibility. Geneviève wouldn't be Geneviève if she didn't keep pestering him for his identity and a place in the League. From the moment they'd met, she'd been clear. Her heart was on saving France, and Lord Cabot was everything Geneviève detested.

As he had trudged back home last night through the dark and smelly streets of Paris, he'd decided that the Sapphire Sphinx was to avoid Miss Geneviève de Bourbon as though she were Delaroche himself—but Lord Cabot could call on Miss de Bourbon. She would never succumb to the English gentleman. He was free to tease and flirt with abandon.

After all, William reasoned with himself, as long as he confined his calls to non-spying hours, his tenuous relationship with Geneviève could be kept separate from his work.

The challenge to charm Geneviève into liking him gave an extra lift in each step. She might have almost kissed the Sapphire Sphinx last night, but William had once been a notorious rake. Nothing could be more diverting than hugging that porcupine of a lady. Of course, it would be even better if it was William she was thinking about, not the spy.

All he had to do was dispel her lingering anxieties about his character. William paused next to a painting by David. That might be too difficult a feat without revealing his secret identity. Too much effort. Far better to try to seduce Geneviève out of her scruples. *That* was a plan worthy of the master strategist who had saved scads of French noblemen from the guillotine.

With that out of the way, William could once more concentrate on sallying forth and doing his bit to defend England against old Boney by drinking French brandy and winning at cards.

William dropped in on a record breaking four salons and card parties between eight and eleven o'clock. At one, he eavesdropped on conversations under the cover of music; at another, he elicited information over cards. At yet another, he rifled through his host's desk while a poet declaimed in a room across the hall. It would have been five parties had he not spotted Pauline Leclerc as he entered the fifth salon. Grabbing his hat and gloves back from the astonished maid, he disappeared.

Just after eleven, William was dropped off at his final destination— another friend of Bonaparte—and told his coachman he'd find his own way home. As his carriage pulled away, William settled his hat more firmly on his head, gave his gloves one last tug, pasted on a social smile, and ascended the steps to the front door. He was let in by a maid, who took his hat and cloak and pointed him upstairs. William made his way up the marble staircase, skirting around a young dandy clinging to the banister who was already clearly the worse for drink. William feared for the next guest to pass below the staircase.

Reaching the landing, William considered his options. To his right, food had already been laid out in the supper room, and a cadre of devoted gallants were making up plates for their beloveds of the moment.

William spotted his hostess in the crush and nodded to her. She waved her fan at him with more enthusiasm than decorum, a combination of the late hour and generous drink. These parties teemed with young adventurers, aging flirts, and hardened roués, all barely clinging to the fringes of society.

Down the hall, the crowd in the card room was thinner than usual.

William wandered through the room, murmuring polite inconsequentialities to acquaintances, and declining the offer of a rubber of whist from Mme Tallien. Under fashionably languid lids, William's green eyes darted ahead of him across the room. Paul Barras, a former head of state, sat over solitaire at a table near the door. He would be of no use. William likewise dismissed a gaggle of giggling women in hideous striped turbans. But near the fireplace was one of the rats from last night.

"Taunton, old chap," William drawled. "Not having much luck at cards tonight, I see. Murat." William nodded to the Consul's brother-in-law, who was listing in his chair at an angle that declared that the snifter of brandy before him was by no means his first.

Taunton kicked a char at William. "Care to try your luck, Cabot?"

"Jolly good of you." William dropped lazily into the little gilded chair.

Taunton rose and stretched, swaying only a bit in the process. "Think nothing of it. I'm off as soon as I win some of my blunt back. Got an assignation with a hot piece of baggage."

William yanked his chair up to the table. "How much does she cost?"

Taunton guffawed, baring large white teeth. "This one's free. Makes a nice change, eh?"

William politely bared his teeth in response, but since his interest in Taunton's romantic affairs was about on par with his desire to learn about the finer points of taxonomy, he quickly turned the topic of conversation to a more promising avenue.

Slinking into the chair, he asked Taunton, "Any chance you're thinking of selling that curricle of yours?"

"What?" Taunton pounded the table. "Sell the Chariot of Love? It would send the ladies of Paris into mourning."

"And their cuckolded husbands would throw a fête." William brushed phantom dirt off his trousers.

Smug, Taunton smiled. "Tonight's lucky lady doesn't have a husband. Just a—"

"I ask," William interrupted. Nothing could entice a nausea like a

Taunton conquest tale. "I have a friend who's looking for a carriage, and I know he admires yours."

"Who wouldn't?" Taunton stretched out his legs.

William wondered how they managed to support the weight of such a massive ego. "I've advised him that a closed carriage would be far more useful. What do you think?"

Taunton snorted. "If you're an old lady. Women go mad for a nice little curricle. I can tell you about the time—"

"Curricles are very well for a spin about the park, but what about longer trips, or conveying packages? There's simply not enough privacy or room." William motioned to the deck of cards. "Who's dealing?"

"Me." Taunton grabbed the deck and began shuffling with the case of a practiced gamester. "What's your game, Cabot? Commerce? Euchre? *Vingt-et-un?*"

"Whatever you were playing." He gave a casual wave. "So, you'd recommend the curricle, would you? What about midnight assignations and that sort of thing?"

Taunton flipped three cards William's way. "It's easy enough to hire a coach."

"Do you have any recommendations?"

"There's a little man in the rue St. Jacques," Taunton said easily, kicking back and looking at his cards. "Has a plain carriage and doesn't ask too many questions, if you know what I mean."

"I'll remember that," replied William, with an amused smile. A little man on the rue St. Jacques. He would send Adam down tomorrow to make inquiries. William mentally ticked off item one on his list. "How far does he let you take it?"

"I've been as far as Calais and back." Taunton frowned and dealt himself another card.

"Did you have family visiting from England?" William inquired pleasantly.

"No, I—" Taunton's mouth snapped abruptly shut.

Forcing a loud laugh, William mimicked Taunton's earlier slapping of the table. "Say no more. Say no more." He held up a hand. "The lady's reputation must be protected. I understand. Pass the decanter, would you?"

Shoulders relaxing, Taunton shoved the crystal decanter across the table. William raised it in a comradely gesture before pulling out the stopper and pouring some of the amber contents into a glass. Damn. Taunton wasn't drunk enough to spill his secrets.

"To nameless ladies." William hoisted his brandy in the air.

"I'll drink to that." Taunton downed the contents of his glass and reached across William for the decanter.

"Nameless ladiesh," slurred Murat from a corner.

Now there was a man who was drunk enough to be of use.

"You've been at peace too long, Murat," William said cheerfully. "It's weakened your head for drink. Better work on that or they'll take away your commission."

"Him?" Taunton jabbed a finger at Murat, who was listing rocking about like a boat caught in a storm. "There's some perks to being the First Consul's brother-in-law, eh, Murat? Even if you do have to put up with his sister."

Murat blinked. "More brandy?"

William helpfully leaned across the table and refilled Murat's glass. "Your miss giving you a hard time?"

"Thash a'ri'." Murat gestured expansively, sending half the contest of his glass sloshing over onto the walls. "Goin' away shoon."

"You're leaving soon?" Quick as he could, William supplied the poor sop with another glass of brandy.

"Caroline wouldn't take no. Told him I needed a big—" Murat hiccupped and glanced around the table confused, as if he'd just discovered where he was.

"Leave it to Caroline to bully Bonaparte." Taunton chuckled and took another swig. Caroline possessed the face of an angel and the ruthless ambition of her brother Napoleon.

Nodding slowly, Murat shrugged. "Could be next month." Another sloppy shrug. "Could be next year."

"What could be next month?" William asked softly, keeping his voice too low for Taunton to overhear.

"I'm to be a general in the new—" Murat leaned over and wretched on the rug—and William's boots.

These were the moments when William envied Michael his clean, quiet desk job at the War Office. The poor man was nervous to be a general and Bonaparte was waiting for something, a key that could take a month or a year.

"Be ri' back," Murat announced, reeling off, hopefully to find a change of linen.

"Another glass of brandy and you'll be right as rain!" Taunton shouted after him.

"Perhaps we might relocate to another table?" William breathed through his mouth, but nothing helped the stench.

"All right with me." Taunton shrugged. "I'm leaving in ten minutes. The girl will be waiting for me at midnight. I might keep her waiting a few minutes—the suspense always makes 'em more eager—"

"How about this table?" William had no desire to hear any more of Taunton's romantic advice. Before Taunton could continue with his plans for the evening, William hastily complimented his jacket.

"I'll give you the name of my tailor," Taunton offered generously.

William would rather face a firing squad than wear a peacock-blue frock coat with gold facings and cameo buttons, but flattery was the doorway to information. "You're pretty chummy with de Bourbon."

Taunton grunted in response.

"Couldn't you persuade him to patronize your tailor? Or at least one who isn't color-blind? It's deuced hard on the eyes for the rest of us."

"Nature didn't give him much to work with." Taunton snagged the brandy bottle and glasses from their old table, just as Murat wove his way back, minus his soiled cravat and waistcoat.

William feigned confusion. "I had thought you were friends."

Taunton shrugged, evading the implied question. "Who wouldn't be his friend with such a toothsome sister?"

William fought back the urge to stop Taunton's words with a fist. William had, admittedly, entertained much the same thought himself, but the gleam in Taunton's eye reminded William of a stalking panther.

"The cousin is reputed to be the beauty of the family." William felt a twinge of guilt at dangling Mary to the wolves.

"Not my type. I like 'em little and cuddly, not cold and statuesque. Maybe you scholars lust after statues, but not me."

William would relish thrashing Taunton and fervently hoped he was involved in shady business on behalf of Bonaparte. Taunton begun enumerating Geneviève's physical attributes, complete with grotesque gestures. Clutching the crystal decanter, William could easily launch the heavy object into Taunton's head, but he still had little idea on Taunton's true connection with de Bourbon and would be decidedly less likely to find out if he bludgeoned Taunton senseless.

Holding up a hand, William protested, "You don't want to make the lady you're meeting tonight jealous."

"No danger of that." Slapping his brandy balloon onto the table, Taunton doubled over with laughter at a private joke. "Make her jealous—ha—no danger of that at all."

"Why not?"

Taunton grinned wolfishly at William. "Because tonight's lucky lady *is* Geneviève de Bourbon."

# CHAPTER 26

Lord William Cabot
Paris, France

William saw blood—or rather red. Every shade of red imaginable, but mostly Taunton's blood. He saw himself driving his fist repeatedly into Taunton's face. It took all of his considerable strength of will not to turn that vision into a reality.

Clenching his fists under the table, William forced his face to relax. "Miss de Bourbon?"

"Some men have all the luck." Murat drawled.

"It ain't luck; it's my handsome face." Taunton hauled his friend up by the collar and deposited him back on the seat of his chair. "Met the girl for five minutes last night, and already she can't wait for a little tête-à-tête with me."

That wasn't the way William remembered it. Clearly, there was some mistake. Taunton must have invented the assignation to impress his friends. Or he was meeting some other woman and had her confused with Geneviève. There had to be a simple explanation.

Through painfully tight lips, William got out, "What did she do? Accost you in your chambers after the party?"

168

"Nah." Taunton flung a card on the discard pile. "She sent an urgent message. An *urgent message?*" Taunton guffawed again. "She wants me badly."

"Nobody sends me meshages like tha' anymore." Murat's eyes drooped like a sad puppy.

"An *urgent* message, you say?" William leaned back in his chair and scratched his head. With any luck, no one would notice the tightening of his jaw.

"That's women for you." Taunton tossed back another snifter of brandy. "Says she must see me *urgently*, because she had something *terribly important* to tell me. Said I'd know what it was about after our conversation last night." He laughed, his eyes greedy. "As if any fool couldn't figure out what the girl wants."

"What about her brother?" William blurted out.

"What about him?"

Waving a hand in the air, William asked, "Won't he object to his sister arranging assignations with you?"

"De Bourbon?" Taunton threw back his head and laughed.

Eying the fool, William hoped the weight of it would cause him to overbalance, perhaps knocking himself out on a handy piece of furniture. There was a sharp edge of a card table right there—but Taunton's luck was in and William's was out. Taunton's head snapped back to center without Taunton so much as wobbling. "De Bourbon? He knows better than to come up stuffy about this."

That was taking French nonchalance too far, decided William. Not to mention that de Bourbon was half -English, and thus should bloody well know better.

"But it's his *sister*." William pushed to a stand. "Rather a nasty trick to play on a friend, seducing his sister."

Taunton shrugged. "De Bourbon owes me. Good night, gentlemen."

"Do you need a ride?" William spoke rapidly as Taunton began to move towards the door. "If you're willing to wait a moment, I'll send for my coach. I can drop you off on my way home."

*And make good and sure you never make it to your assignation, William* thought grimly. Many accidents could happen along the way. His English coachman, not knowing the streets of Paris well, might get lost, and drive about in circles for hours. Long enough for Geneviève to think herself abandoned and leave in a fit of pique. Or the carriage might encounter a fatal pothole. Or Taunton might pass out from drink, with a little help from his newfound friend.

"Very decent of you, Cabot." Taunton, who had paused for one glorious moment, set one foot in front of the other. "But it's a short walk."

"Are you sure?" Feigning concern, William put an arm over Taunton's shoulder. "Where are you meeting her?"

"The Luxembourg Gardens." Taunton grinned and shrugged off William's arm. "Women and their romantic notions. I'd have preferred a bed."

A quick ride with William and Taunton wouldn't be able to walk, let alone seduce a woman. William would have preferred to smash his fist right into Taunton's smug mouth. Instead, he forced himself to bid Taunton a pleasant good night. He contemplated giving him a little shove down the marble stair, but too many potential witnesses were milling about.

As he snatched back his gloves and hat from the maid at the foot of the stairs, William contemplated racing ahead of Taunton, lying in wait and knocking him down from behind. The streets of Paris abounded with footpads. That gold watch chain of Taunton's shouted *grab me* to any nearby thief. Taunton would be out cold, Geneviève would be safe, and no one would be the wiser.

Except William had no idea which route Taunton planned to take. He'd lurk there in an alleyway by a street Taunton might never walk past while Taunton forced himself upon Geneviève in the Luxembourg Gardens. *Geneviève.* She'd been full of wit and substance—how on earth did she seek out Taunton?

Bounding down the steps after Taunton, William saw him strolling towards the Seine, towards the bridge that separated them from the Luxembourg and Geneviève. William momentarily considered alerting de Bourbon to his sister's peril, and just as quickly dismissed the idea. Even if he were to find de Bourbon at home, even if Taunton were wrong about de Bourbon's indifference, he didn't like to think what might have befallen Geneviève by the time he had wrenched de Bourbon out of a chair and shoved him into his coach.

There was only one thing to do. William rapidly changed course and headed for home. He stormed through the front hall of his house, capsizing a small table and knocking a picture askew. Charging into his study, he flopped to his knees and began flinging books from the bottom shelf of his bookcase—all the while cursing Geneviève.

Only a naïve woman would send an urgent message to rendezvous with a strange man in the middle of the night. This was another reason Geneviève should never help the league and why William should never be allowed near a lady. Geneviève's chaperone, Miss Agnes, would have tackled her with the parasol. Even Mary, her cousin, should have shouted some sense at her. Geneviève was anything but invincible. When William found her, he'd shake her till she couldn't stand. And then he'd lock her into a room with a hundred locks so she couldn't send any more urgent notes to disgusting men setting up ridiculous meetings at obscene hours of the night.

Seizing on a fold of black cloth, he yanked his cape out of its hiding place. No time to change his breeches; the cape would have to hide the tan cloth, and at least his boots were black up to the knee. The mask followed the cape, and William was up and running, mask dangling from his hand.

Adam walked into the room and with one look at William said, "What is wrong? By Jove, you've gone mad."

"Can't talk." Lord Cabot bounded down the stairs of his town home.

Seconds later, William sprinted in the direction of the Luxembourg Gardens and his damsel in distress. His resolution for the Sapphire Sphinx to avoid Geneviève de Bourbon had lasted less than a day.

# CHAPTER 27

G eneviève de Bourbon
Paris, France

Geneviève shoved back her hood. Unfortunately, the removal of the draped fabric did little to improve her vision. She had the hooded cloak, the sturdy boots and the urgent information, but she had forgotten a lantern. She did know she was in the Luxembourg Gardens. But beyond that, Geneviève was at a loss. One shrub looked very much like another in the darkness.

"Ah, there you are." Taunton's low voice carried down the long alley of trees. The large space distorted his voice, thickened it, made it sound unnervingly different than it had the night before. He was speaking English instead of French, but something else felt off. He emerged just around the bend. "I've been looking for you."

Taunton's booted feet echoed on the flagstone path as he closed the distance between them, moonlight glinting off the gold embroidery on his coat. He wore the rich frock coat she had seen the night at the Tuileries, and his curly head was hatless. Geneviève fought down the sense of unease steadily rising like the fog around her. She'd assumed he'd arrive in all black like he'd done at her house.

"I'm sorry," Geneviève said, her own voice tinny to her ears. "I got a bit lost."

"You can make it up to me." Taunton took her by the shoulders and pulled her close. "Like this."

His hands and his voice felt different. She'd nearly kissed the man last night and had thought the Sapphire Sphinx was taller. Gentler. Shutting her eyes, Geneviève rested her cheek against his chest and froze.

He smelled wrong.

Geneviève rapidly pulled back, eyes wide with alarm. In that brief moment she had been pressed to his jacket, she had smelled tobacco, brandy, and leather. No citrus cologne.

"Don't be such a tease." Taunton reached for her.

Geneviève narrowly evaded his grasp. He couldn't be the Sapphire Sphinx. That man was limber and able to scale down from her brother's study.

"You know you want me." Taunton captured one of Geneviève's hands and reeled her in.

Damp lips descended on her own. Geneviève found her protests being displaced by a large tongue forging between her teeth. Gagging, Geneviève shoved hard against Taunton's chest. The hard metal of Taunton's watch fob scraped against her palms, but Geneviève scarcely felt the pain as she strained against him. One last jab in his middle and he stumbled back.

Geneviève wiped her lips with the back of her hand. Taunton's eyes narrowed dangerously.

"You seem to have the wrong idea. I mean, I didn't invite you here to kiss you. I want to *talk* to you—talk to you about... Charles's birthday."

"About Charles's birthday." Taunton's voice dripped disbelief.

Geneviève couldn't blame him. She scarcely believed herself. "I've been away so long that I scarcely know what he likes anymore, and I wanted to throw him a splendid birthday celebration as a thank you for bringing me out here." Geneviève backed up towards the line of trees. Her heart pounded in her chest. *Fool.* She was nothing more than a fool. Her first attempt to help, truly help the league, and she'd entangled herself with a cad.

Biting her lip, Geneviève tried again. "I apologize for the confusion. You have every right to be angry. I didn't mean to bring you out here under false pretenses. Really. I'm truly very sorry."

Her apology seemed to have touched a chord in Taunton.

Geneviève let out a sigh of relief. "Thank you for being so understanding."

Taunton sidled towards her, and an arm snaked out, grabbing Geneviève around the waist. "There's no need to be shy," he crooned. "Come on now. You can tell me what you really want."

"You. Don't. Seem. To Understand." Geneviève gasped out the words as she pushed against Taunton.

His grip tightened around her and his mouth moved moistly against her ear. "Oh, I understand all right. You're just afraid to ask for it."

Taunton's tongue flicked against her ear; he was holding her so tightly her arms were pinned between them, the skin of her forearms scratching against the embroidery of his coat. Panic spread from her chest down her arms. Her legs began shaking. Taunton's mouth kept moving, following hers, trying to invade her lips.

Geneviève twisted her head to the side, struggling desperately to free her arms from Taunton. She could hear the peaceful chirping of birds and the murmur of water in ironic counterpoint to the rasp of Taunton's harsh breath in her ear.

"You don't understand," she panted again.

Taunton's head followed hers.

Geneviève's neck ached with the strain of pulling away. She needed to push him away long enough to make him listen to reason and understand that there had been a mistake. Wet lips trailed across Geneviève's cheek. Yanking an arm free, Geneviève shoved against Taunton's face with all her strength.

*Crunch.*

She succeeded far better than she had imagined.

Taunton howled, releasing Geneviève. "You've broken my nose."

Geneviève stared in horrified fascination at the dark liquid dripping through Taunton's fingers. With his left hand, he yanked frantically at his cravat until the knot came undone, wadding the fabric up against his nose.

Geneviève gasped. "I'm sorry."

Taunton's pale eyes met hers over the crumpled cloth. With a low growl and a murderous glint in his eyes, he flung the cloth aside and advanced on Geneviève.

One yard, two feet. Taunton was steadily closing the distance between. "You're going to pay for this."

Geneviève set her arms the way she had seen her cousin Ned do when he was boxing with the stableboy. "I swear to you I will break something else."

"That will cost you," Taunton warned.

His hands swallowed Geneviève's. He forced her arms around her back. Her mind blanked. No one had ever treated her roughly or grabbed her in anger. Panic stole her thoughts.

The pain in her shoulders snapped her out of her stupor. Geneviève pushed back with all her might, straining to keep his arms from closing around, but years of lifting books in her uncle's library had done little to prepare her for a contest of strength. Her breath rasped in her throat. Another layer of panic. She couldn't scream for help.

Blood from Taunton's nose dripped down onto Geneviève's cheek, and she gasped and wrenched her head away. The movement was all Taunton needed to consolidate his victory. With a final burst of force, he twisted her arms behind her back, pinning them together with one large hand. Geneviève jerked against his grasp, arching away from him as far as she could, but he yanked her back against him. His fingers grasped her wrists as tightly as though they had been bound with a dozen sailor's knots.

"My brother will call you out for this," hissed Geneviève.

Taunton tugged her curls, hard. "Your bother couldn't shoot a slug."

Geneviève's nostrils flared. "You value yourself too highly."

"Why, you little—"

Geneviève's sturdy boot slammed down on Taunton's. The hard, square heel ground down into the leather with a marvelous crackling nose. Taunton roared in pain. Twisting her wrists, Geneviève pulled free from Taunton's loosened grasp. *Blast.* Taunton's hands were already grabbing for her, pulling at her dress as she tried to run. She should have broken his fingers, not his toes. She heard the unpleasant sound of rending cloth, but Taunton still held firm. Any moment now, Taunton's other hand would shoot out and it would start all over again.

*No.* She wouldn't stand for it. Geneviève whirled and swung at Taunton's face with her right fist. Her knuckles grazed the underside of Taunton's chin and plunged into empty air.

Taunton tumbled to the ground at her feet with a crash like the fall of Goliath.

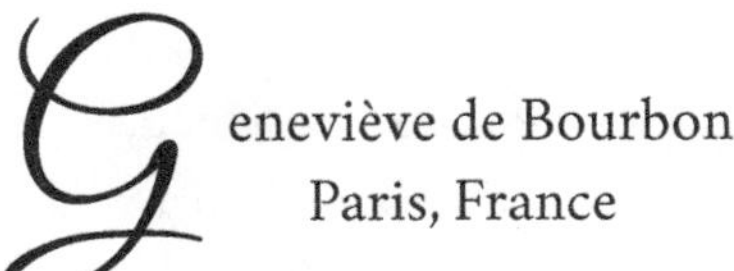

eneviève de Bourbon
Paris, France

Still struggling to catch her breath, Geneviève stared in confusion at Taunton's fallen body. She really hadn't thought she had hit him that hard. And then she heard it. The sound of another person's breathing, from where Taunton had stood. Geneviève looked up abruptly, just as a shadowy figure bounded over Taunton's body. "Did he hurt you?"

Geneviève blinked. "The Sapphire Sphynx." Her voice cracked. She glanced from the crumpled figure on the ground to the hooded spy in front of her. Dumbly, she said, "You're not Taunton."

"You thought I was *Taunton?*" Standing over Taunton, the Sphinx seethed. "That's—did he hurt you?"

"No." Her mind was dizzying and her pulse raced, but no, she wasn't truly hurt. Staring at the Sapphire Sphinx, she felt small. And childlike.

Where Taunton was bulky, the Sapphire had a graceful, slender strength. One broad-fingered hand lay on the ground hear Geneviève's foot, brown hair sprouting around the knuckles. So very different from the long-fingered hands in black leather gloves clenched at the Sapphire's sides. Even Taunton's teeth seemed larger and coarser than the Sapphire's. Granted, she'd only see him in her brother's dim study and—if she was being honest—had worshipped the spy from afar for years.

Pointing to the man, the Sapphire said, "This, *this* is why you cannot help."

Stumbling back, Geneviève felt a growing pressure in her chest and blinked back against the tears. She was not some innocent school girl. The fall of Bonaparte meant more to her than this indignant spy.

"Do you know what Taunton was going to do with you? Do you?"

"Would it have been more to your liking if it was behind a curtain? In a relative's study?" The words came before Geneviève could stop them. "This—" she mimicked him and pointed at Taunton. "*This* is happened because you wouldn't tell me your name. How was I to know that Taunton—"

At the sound of his name, Taunton stirred and moaned. The Sapphire crossed over to him in one quick stride and administered a brisk, brutal kick to Taunton's gut.

Geneviève winced. "Wasn't that a little… unnecessary?"

"Do you want him waking up?" Anger came rolling off his frame. "I thought not. You'd better hope that his brains are addled enough that he won't remember any of tonight's events."

Geneviève recoiled away from both men. Her arms throbbed where Taunton had grabbed her. She could still feel his slobbering mouth on hers. Geneviève wrapped her arms around her stomach and wondered what the Sapphire would say if she was sick all over his shiny black boots.

"I'll be going home now."

"I'm not done with you yet." The spy crossed his arms over his chest and regarded Geneviève with asperity.

A bath. That was what she needed. She'd scrub out her mouth with tooth powder while the servants drew her a long, painfully hot bath.

"You've no right to preach at me again."

"I do not preach. Stop looking at me like that."

"Like what?"

"Like—" He groaned and let his head fall back, as if he plead to the moon for help. "Do you have no sense at all of the danger you were in?"

Geneviève, folding her arms across her chest to hide the shaking, said evenly, "This would never have happened if you had told me who you were."

"Who told you to go looking for me?"

"I had urgent news and had no idea if you were ever going to deign to contact me. Or continue on being the hypocrite—"

"Hypocrite?"

"You are, in fact, the someone who puts himself in danger, but are lecturing—"

"I run to rescue you—"

Geneviève forced her shoulders down and her chin up. She would never be able to help the league if he thought her weak. "I didn't need rescuing."

"So you were having a peaceful little chat with Taunton when I approached? You left the house alone, unchaperoned, unguarded at midnight of all idiotic times. You're lucky that Taunton was the only one who attacked you. Footpads, pick pockets—"

"Stop." Her voice broke the word in two. She wasn't a complete fool. She'd crossed a line. "I… I…" A tear fell. Then another.

"I'm sorry. I'm sorry, I shouldn't have…I'm sorry." The Sapphire circled Taunton's body and pulled Geneviève toward him.

She fell into his chest, her hands gripping his jacket. Warmth covered her. Another tear. She wiped it away, angry that she was crying instead of staying strong. "I'm not weak."

"I didn't say you were weak, Geneviève." He cupped her chin. "I said you were foolish."

She stiffened.

Smiling, he brought against his chest, a hand in her hair. "I shouldn't be holding you. But by Jove, I almost lost you."

His voice—the tone—sounded far too familiar. He'd not spoken a word in French, only English. She peered up at him. "How did you know I was here?"

"Taunton was bragging at the salon of your urgent message. I was there to get information, and I can only be boring and scholarly for so long when…"

Geneviève stopped hearing him. *Scholarly.* There was only one man who would wear *scholarly* as a badge of courage. Lord William Cabot. Her mind jogged about, tying each little clue and memory together. Lord Cabot was in Egypt with Bonaparte during the great French failure. The Sapphire had known Genevieve's given name and was familiar with her—as if they'd met before. She glanced back at Taunton. She'd made the mistake of assuming she knew the Sapphire's identity.

"For most of my life, I've wanted justice," Geneviève blurted out. "I wanted nothing more than to help the league. I devoured everything about the Scarlet Pimpernel. I kept waiting for that moment, for the time I could return to France."

The Sapphire's mouth fell open. He must have been in the middle of speaking and appeared to be confused.

"Who are you?" She stepped closer. The temptation to pull off his mask and cap grew with each passing second.

"I cannot tell you that, Geneviève."

"But you know who I am."

"I'm a spy—"

"You're English."

"Gen—"

She held up a hand. "I'll go home now."

"Wait."

Shaking her head, Geneviève started walking. She was nothing more than a school girl. Her heart and head were confused. She didn't know up from down.

He circled her and reached for her hand. "I'm sorry."

She blew passed him.

He tried again. "I think I like you, but I cannot—"

"You think you like me?" Geneviève rubbed the bridge of her nose.

*I think I like you.* Lord Cabot had said the same thing yesterday in the corridor of the Tuileries. "You spent one moment behind a curtain. Sir Sapphire Sphinx, you don't know me."

In one large step, he covered the ground between them. He cupped her chin, and despite her frustration she leaned into his touch. She briefly closed her eyes and felt the rush of safety.

He brought his forehead to hers. "I know your heart is true, and that more than anything you want to give France it's glory again." He kissed her forehead. "I know you can't tolerate a turncoat or anyone hinting at betraying his country." Brushing his lips against hers, he whispered, "I know that despite everything, I should run far away from you. But I found myself running toward you."

Taunton moaned again and the Sapphire jumped from her. "I need to move him."

She stood, her mind reeling. Lord Cabot *had* to be the Sapphire, but his distrust stung. The hurt grew as he grimly circled the fallen form of Taunton

"If he has any recollection of tonight's activities, he'll make the link between me and the Sapphire Sphinx." He swooped down on Taunton's recumbent body and began sniffing at Taunton's waistcoat. "He reeks of brandy. We can dump him behind a tavern. He'll fit right in with the other drunks passed out in the gutter."

*We.* Geneviève was included in his plan. Hope blossomed as she joined the Sapphire in peering down at Taunton's collapsed form, stretched out on the dirt, arms limp, hands limp. Being so near made Geneviève's flesh crawl. She took some comfort in the crooked angle of his nose.

The Sapphire—or rather, Lord Cabot—had begun hauling the man's limp torso upright, long sleeves protecting his arms from the scratchy gold braid on Taunton's jacket. Watching anxiously to make sure Taunton's eyes didn't roll open, Geneviève took a tentative hold of Taunton's boots.

They set off in silence down the path, between a row of silent trees, the Sapphire Sphinx backing up with long strides that took two of Geneviève's shorter steps to match.

Geneviève determinedly turned her thoughts to the quandary of filching the Swiss gold out from under the noses of Bonaparte's agents. And if she jumped nervously when a man with gold embroidery on his cloak swaggered past them into the gardens, the Sapphire Sphinx made no comment. Geneviève glanced swiftly at the burden hanging between them, just to make sure Taunton was still there, unconscious, limp and harmless. Momentarily reassured, she returned to considering the benefits and drawbacks of gunpowder, though she still flinched every time the leaves around them rustled with the passage of a human body.

Much to Geneviève's relief, the gardens finally gave way to the busy streets of the Latin Quarter. Shouts and laughter spilled form brightly lit tavern windows, making Geneviève blink at the sudden glare and gasp at the sour reek of spilled spirits.

A group of students pounded out a bawdy ballad in Latin on the street across from them while a group of sailors across the way were doing their best to out-sing the students with an equally bawdy sea chanty. Just in front of them a man reeled through a door into the street, nearly barreling into the Sapphire Sphinx before collapsing in the gutter.

No one gave Cabot and Geneviève a second look.

Geneviève could only conclude that hooded men and disheveled women bearing unconscious bodies weren't as unusual an occurrence as one would suppose.

Speaking softly under the cover of all of the merriment going on about them, the Sapphire Sphinx leaned across Taunton's unconscious body and murmured to Geneviève, "Once we dispose of our cargo in a manner befitting him, I'll take you home."

"Cargo," Geneviève repeated and tried to breathe through her mouth.

"This looks like a promising ally." He peered into a cul-de-sac between two noisy taverns. One man already occupied part of the gutter, arms flung wide, and one boot missing. "Let's drop him right over there."

Geneviève held her tongue. Now wasn't the best time to relay

Bonaparte's plans for invading England. Certainly not over the body of a member of Bonaparte's military, unconscious though he certainly seemed to be.

She hastily let go of Taunton's feet as the Sapphire unceremoniously dumped Taunton into a liquid that Geneviève hoped was spilled wine. Taunton's body landed with a satisfying thump.

Brushing his hands together with the air of a man who considers a job well done, Lord Cabot took one last look at the crumpled figure in the gutter. Taunton had begun snoring noisily, his mouth flopping open. His gaudy coat was smeared with dirt and mottled with blood. Between the state of his attire and his coarse expression, he looked like nothing more than a servant who had gone brawling in his master's clothes. All he needed to complete the scene was an empty bottle in his limp hand.

William glowered at the fallen body. "How could you think I was Taunton?"

"Vanity, thy name is man?"

"Objecting to being compared to *that*"—the Sapphire jerked a finger over his shoulder at Taunton as he took Geneviève by the arm and steered her towards the river—"is not vanity. It's simple self-respect."

"He was in my brother's courtyard, wearing a black cloak just like yours. What else was I to think?" Geneviève watched his face, the little that was uncovered, to find a moment of recollection, a moment where Cabot would realize Geneviève knows his secret.

"It does make a certain amount of sense."

They trudged down stone steps onto a pier to wait for one of the small boats that ferried passengers along the Seine for a fee. The Sapphire eyed her. "Though why you couldn't tell the difference—"

"I had only met him once, and briefly, at that. And when I found the information—"

"The information—" his eyes narrowed. "The information that was so vitally important that you had to set up an assignation in the middle of the night?"

Geneviève cast a sideling glance. "And now I am suddenly helpful?"

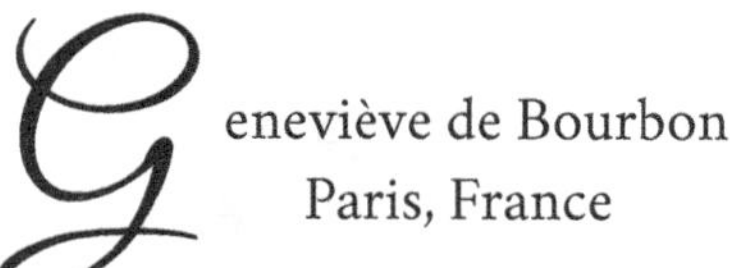

enevière de Bourbon
Paris, France

Dripping with sarcasm, the Sphinx placed a hand on his hip and said, "You are a beacon of helpfulness."

"Bonaparte's plans." She folded her arms. Her information *would* be a beacon of helpfulness, and hopefully, the beginning of his trust. "They were under his blotter on his desk."

The spy shook his head, his hand falling to the side. "You were in Bonaparte's study."

The memory came rushing back. Geneviève had run out of the study and straight into the Sapphire. The final link was there. There was no more doubt, no more guessing—Geneviève knew without a shadow of a doubt that Lord Cabot was very much *the* Sapphire Sphinx.

"He plans to land a force of one hundred seventy thousand men with twenty-four hundred ships," Geneviève whispered. "But Josephine has emptied the treasury, so he can't do it until gold enough to finance the expedition arrives."

"So that's what Murat had been talking about. Nothing could be done until the gold arrived." He began pacing in front of her. "After six years of close contact with the Bonapartes, six years of listening to Bonaparte rant about his wife's extravagance—he's broke?"

"From what I read—" Geneviève grabbed his arm, excitement dancing on her skin. "He's arranged for a loan from Swiss bankers. Not that Bonaparte would ever pay it back, but the money is due to come in by carriage at the end of the month. If we can just—"

"Intercept the gold before it reaches Bonaparte." The Sapphire continued for her, grinning broadly. "We can stop the invasion of England—"

"Topple the government." Geneviève bit her lip. "If the gold doesn't arrive—"

"How many men will be guarding it?"

"The letter didn't say," Geneviève admitted. "Delaroche just wrote that it would be heavily guarded, whatever that means."

"Stealth, rather than force," he muttered, resuming his pacing.

"What about a smaller version of the Trojan Horse?"

"A smaller what?"

Geneviève offered, "In Greek mythology, the Trojan Horse was a—"

The Sapphire shook his head. "You want to intercept the Swiss gold with a small wooden horse?"

"Not exactly." Geneviève climbed up on the dock and let her legs back and forth. "Send a delivery of barrels to the warehouse—barrels of something they might want—and when they haul them inside, we can leap out and seize the gold."

Ruefully, he shook his head. "What if they don't stop to pick up the barrels? If they're Delaroche's men, they'll be under strict orders. We could probably float by in a trunk with *huge treasure in here* painted in foot high letters across the top, and they wouldn't so much as glance at us."

"Drat." Geneviève wrung her hands. "If the Trojan Horse idea doesn't work, maybe Mary and I could pretend to be dancing girls looking for work, and—"

"No."

"You don't like that either?"

"I loathe, revile, and detest that idea," the spy replied blandly. "Next?"

"We can set the warehouse on fire," Geneviève added with a firm nod as if the case was settled.

He stopped his pacing and knelt beside Geneviève's makeshift pedestal. "Do you mean to try to burn down the building around the gold?"

"What we could do is start a small fire that will let off a lot of smoke—there must be some way to do that—and someone could start shouting *fire*. With any luck, the guards would panic, and leap out of the building. And even if they didn't, they would be so preoccupied with putting out the blaze that we could slip inside during the confusion and make off with the gold."

"The gold will be heavy." The pacing began again.

"We set the fire, bash them over the head during the confusion, and *then* make off with the gold?"

He stopped, a finger in the air. "You might have something there. We'd have to find out how the men in the warehouse were to be dressed. My guess is they won't be in uniform. They'll more likely be disguised as workmen. If my chaps can slip in and blend with the guards..."

The Sapphire hopped to his feet, nearly colliding with Geneviève's chin. "Wait, how do we know which warehouse it will be? We can't go up and down the streets setting fire to every warehouse we see."

Geneviève gave a little bounce on her perch. "And we don't have to. On the very bottom of Bonaparte's paper was written the address of a warehouse on the rue Julius. A bit arrogant, don't you think?"

The Sapphire's lips twisted wryly. "They picked the street for the name of the Roman emperor who conquered Britain? Clever. Very clever."

"But not clever enough for us." Geneviève's outstretched hands and eager smile issued an irresistible invitation to the Sapphire to join in her exultation.

She laughed delightedly as he bypassed her outstretched hands, and, seizing her around the waist, whirled her in a triumphant circle. Geneviève felt the muscles of his shoulders move under her hands, the folds of his cloak swirl about her own legs, and tilted back her head with the dizzying joy of it all. It was better than a fair, better than a play, better than any daydream she had ever devised.

The Sapphire's arms tightened around her as he completed one last whirl. Geneviève's body brushed slowly along the length of his as he lowered her to the ground. Her wits seemed to have been shaken away while the spy was spinning her in circles. After all, she should be thinking about defeating Bonaparte, not about the shocking intimacy of the Sapphire's cloak entangled with her skirts. Some witty comment was in order but the warmth of the Sapphire's body against hers made wit well-nigh impossible.

With the uncomfortable feeling that somehow she was losing the thread of the conversation entirely, Geneviève dragged herself back to the matter at hand. "Where shall we meet to storm the warehouse?"

The Sapphire Sphinx blinked. "We?"

Geneviève nodded vehemently. "Of course. I can dress up as a workman. What do you think?"

"You waiting for a ride?" A boatman called out, punctuating his words by spitting into the water.

"Yes," the Sapphire replied, giving the boatman their destination, and hastily hustling Geneviève on board.

One of Geneviève's boots caught on the hem of her dress as the spy helped her over the rim of the boat. She pitched forward, making the boat rock back and forth while the boatman cursed loudly. Leaping lightly into the boat, the Sapphire caught her before she had done more than stumble.

"Tourists," the boatman muttered, pushing off from the quay.

The Sapphire steadied Geneviève and helped her down onto the bench. In her stumble, Geneviève had released her iron grip on her cloak. Cabot's grin turned to a frown. "Your dress is torn," he said harshly, his arm tightening around her shoulders.

Geneviève hastily pulled the edges back together, her face clouding. Her bodice was intact, covering the vital bits, but her reputation and future could be destroyed if caught. "That must have happened when I pulled away from Taunton. I thought I heard—"

"I should have hit him harder."

Something in his tone, an intense anger underlying the seeming calm, made Geneviève's eyes fly to his face. He *was* angry. It burned from the stern cast of his lips to his narrowed eyes. But there was something more, something deeper, something that warmed Geneviève deep down. "I think you hit him more than hard enough. And I might have broken his nose, which I think is a rather more than fair return for some torn fabric, don't you?"

The Sapphire failed to answer. For a moment, Geneviève was worried that he had been struck ill. His eyes were slightly glazed and crossed. Alarmed, Geneviève searched for the telltale signs of fever. His forehead didn't seem to be particularly flushed, but his breathing was certainly coming faster.

"Are you all right?"

"I shouldn't have tried to kiss you." He inhaled sharply and placed his forehead on hers. "I'm no better than Taunton."

She started to chuckle. "Which time? You tried to kiss me…"

He shifted, his lips nearly touching hers. A thrill swept up her spine. He stiffened, as if realizing they'd almost kissed again. She leaned forward, brushing her lips against his. His arms tightened. The soft brushing of lips turned hungry in an instant.

His mouth opened eagerly, his hands in her hair. She wrapped her arms tighter around him. Pressing up against him, she kissed him as he had been kissing her. A warmth filled her—a feeling of home, of longing, cradled her.

"We're outside," he panted, tearing his mouth from Geneviève's. He gave a pointed look at the boatman who appeared to be ignorant of their embrace.

Geneviève smiled dreamily up at him, lifting a hand to run it along his cheekbones down to his lips. "I know. Have you ever seen so many stars?"

"Shall I fetch you a necklace of them?" he asked tenderly.

Geneviève's hand stilled on the Sapphire's cheek. She drew in a sharp breath. "A necklace of stars," she repeated, her voice unsteady. Lord Cabot had said the same thing to her on the boat weeks earlier. She'd shared with him an intimate memory of her father. And now they shared a kiss. She had spent years believing the only way to heal the ache in her heart was to storm France and restore the monarchy. But here, under the stars, she felt a shift. Perhaps, Geneviève needed to stop searching for the warmth of her childhood—and start searching for the love she'd once felt. "A necklace of stars," she repeated once more.

His brow furrowed. "Is something wrong?"

Her glazed eyes snapped back into focus, filling with joy. "No. Everything's absolutely right."

# CHAPTER 30

*L*ord William Cabot
Paris, France

Reason returned to William with the force of a blow. The air between them crackled like a storm about to ignite. Something had changed. He retraced the night in his mind. Somehow, Geneviève had become soft. The light in her eyes was far too warm, too familiar. Try as he might, he'd lost his head every time she was near. Deep within him, William also felt relief. There was something about Geneviève that drew him to her. He could not quit the blue-eyed brunette if he tried. The thought sent a jolt through him.

William hauled himself up onto the bench and plunged his hands over the side, letting the cold water awaken his senses. Since hearing Taunton brag about Geneviève, William had lost his way, her safety his only desire. He would have stuck his head over the edge, too, but he wasn't at all sure what might be lurking in the water, and he wouldn't put it past that boatman to help the rest of him into the river.

He hadn't been thinking. That was the problem.

As cold water and equally chilly thoughts began to clear the haze from William's brain, he realized that he'd risked the entire French operation. Taunton could easily link him to Geneviève and now the Sapphire Sphinx.

Leaning over, he helped Geneviève up from the floor, trying not to look too closely at her pink cheeks and shining eyes. He tried once more to remember what he'd done or said to warrant the dreamy look in her eye.

"That was wonderful." She sighed.

William dropped a few coins in the man's calloused hand, so consumed with his revelry it took him a moment to realize that Geneviève was attempting to climb out of the boat on her own, teetering back and forth with one foot on the edge, and looking in imminent danger of toppling into the water at any moment.

William handed Geneviève out of the boat and tried not to notice the way her fingers lingered on his arm or the glowing smile she cast up at him from under her too-large hood.

Something else niggled at the back of William's mind, something to do with the Swiss gold. A chill that had nothing to do with the night air engulfed William. Based on Adam's reports and the evidence of his own eyes, de Bourbon was up to something that involved the transport of mysterious packages. He spent that part of his day not occupied by his tailor lurking about the Tuileries. It took no great leap of intelligence to jump from there to the conclusion that de Bourbon was up to his neck in the affair of the Swiss gold. And Geneviève was his sister, mysteriously summoned back to France just as Napoleon commenced his plans for the invasion of England. What better way to entrap the Sapphire Sphinx? Provide him some intelligence, discover his plans—and summon Delaroche. It would be a sure way to Bonaparte's favor for de Bourbon and his sister.

William's eyes slid sideways towards her, down to the little hand resting so trustingly on his arm, and he swore silently.

Nobody could be that good an actress. Her reactions to her parents' deaths could have been feigned—but if so, she ought to be at Drury Lane. Every one of William's instincts, well-honed over a decade of outwitting the French, screamed her innocence.

But he couldn't take that chance. There was too much at risk. The dozen men needed in the assault on the coach bearing the Swiss gold each had a family back in England. Adam would insist on going along. Adam, who was one of the few men William could unreservedly call friend.

He had to end it with her—whatever *it* was. When this mission was all over, when the invasion of England was thwarted, he could court her like the proper lady she was. But not until then.

They came upon de Bourbon's drive. William checked for an open window, his hood hiding all but the tip of his nose from Geneviève's view. As they drew to a halt outside an unlatched first-floor window, Geneviève turned to face him, gazing up at the masked face revealed beneath his hood.

"Thank you," she whispered. "Thank you for rescuing me and thank you even more for everything else."

Rising on tiptoes, Geneviève leaned toward him—he jumped back, leaving her to nearly topple.

"I'm sorry," he blurted. "None of this should have happened."

Geneviève took a step forward and rested a hand on the his chest. "Don't be sorry," she said with conviction, "I'm sorry to have dragged you into a fight with Taunton, but I can't regret anything."

He shook his head. "Don't, Geneviève."

Under her fingers, his chest was heavy with guilt. Geneviève should hate him. He'd kissed her and flirted with abandon only to keep himself out of reach.

"Are you worried that the praise will go to your head?" she teased.

He redirected his gaze somewhere to the left of her shoulder. "I'm serious, Geneviève."

"So am I." Her eyes shone in the moonlight, her smile wide and bright.

"Geneviève, we can't see each other anymore."

Pulling back, she stared at him. "What do you mean? You mean we shouldn't go on meeting like *this*? It *would* be much nicer to meet by daylight, to see your face when you speak."

"I mean just what I said."

Her shoulders drooped and her face fell. "You don't want to see me anymore?"

He nodded slowly, the look in her eye twisting his heart.

"You don't like me." Her brow furrowed, confusion settling in. "You lied."

"That's not it." Taking Geneviève's hand, which still rested forgotten against his heart, he gently returned it to her side. "I'm sorry, Geneviève. I wish it could be some other way."

"*What* other way?" she demanded. "You're talking in riddles. Why can't you see me again?"

His jaw tightened, and he gazed out into the air over Geneviève's shoulder as though the answer might be lurking somewhere in those selfsame stars. Awkwardly, he admitted, "It's the mission."

"Oh." She inhaled sharply. "And my information wasn't helpful enough?"

"Yes—no." Lowering his hooded head to look at her, he pronounced with finality, "I can't let infatuation get in the way of the mission."

"Infatuation," Geneviève repeated, her eyes begging him, willing him to take back the word. "Is that what you feel for me? Infatuation?"

A dreadful, frozen silence followed. The nightingales stopped chirping. The wind stopped blowing. The moon was as stiff and brittle as Geneviève.

"That's one way of describing it."

"Thank you," Geneviève said tightly, "for being honest."

"It's not—I don't want you to think—*damn*." He cursed.

"Good night." Geneviève nodded stiffly and as if tears might start. "Thank you for seeing me home. You can leave now."

Only he didn't.

He took a step towards her, his entire body taut with tension that made his cloak rustle. He leaned forward on the balls of his feet, and the muscles in his throat worked at the growing lump. "Geneviève, I—" he paused.

She blinked, eagerness in her eyes.

His weight shifted back to his heels, and his body and face stilled again. "I'll help you up over the window."

Geneviève planted her elbows on the windowsill. "I'll be quite all right on my own, thank you."

"No, you won't." He brightened at her stubbornness. There was comfort in her strong will. The fire that had dawn him in was still there. He'd not broken her. "I saw you trying to make your way inside last night."

"Do not touch me." She struggled until William placed a hand under her bottom and boosted her over the windowsill, as unromantic as though he were heaving a sack of grain into a wagon. One rough push and he withdrew his hand.

"Good night, Geneviève," he said softly to the night. When he no longer heard movement he added, "I'll make it up to you soon. Trust me."

As he slunk around the side of the house, William reminded himself that it would be pure lunacy to spring back and apologize. This was for the best. And if he kept telling himself that over and over maybe he would be able to wipe out the distressing image of Geneviève's frozen face. Far better that Geneviève be unhappy than good men die, William rationalized loftily. Only, this time, the noble sentiment fell rather flat. William writhed with an uncomfortable combination of guilt.

The league needed to get their hands on that gold quickly, because he didn't think he could take much more of this. William had one last errand. He counted windows until he found the one he wanted. No light gleamed from behind the heavy draperies. Smiling silently to himself, the sleek smile of the panther on the prowl, William hauled himself over the edge of the window and into the empty room. *Déjà vu*, he thought as he jumped lightly down from the velvet-upholstered window seat. Only this time there was no Geneviève waiting for him beneath the desk.

At least, he hoped not.

Just to be safe—since one really never knew with Geneviève—William took a quick peek under the desk. No, no Geneviève. William reminded himself that he should be experiencing relief, not disappointment.

Making his way to the globe, William took up where he had left off the night before. His fingers felt for that telltale crack along the equator, easing towards the tiny bump that must be—

William smirked as the two halves sprang open. The catch.

His smirk disappeared as his mouth dropped open in shock. What in the blazes? Plunging his hand into the rounded base, he ran it back and forth and around. He felt along the top of the glove to see if something might be glued to the inside. He stuck his head in so far that his nose bashed into the bottom. Clutching his wounded appendage, William staggered back and slammed the globe shut.

Someone else had gotten there first.

# CHAPTER 31

Geneviève de Bourbon
Paris, France

"Good morning, slugabed." Mary's voice came from somewhere close at hand. Geneviève rolled over, the covers still bunched up around her shoulders, as Mary continued, with the unconscious condemnation of the naturally early riser, "It's past eleven already. You've lost half the day."

"No great loss," Geneviève murmured. Despite the comfort of the familiar dialogue, a sense of malaise weighed heavily over her. Her eyes felt scratchy under their lids and the back of her throat ached as though with the onset of the grippe. Memories of the night before began to return slowly, in patches. Taunton on the ground. All the stars shining at her. The Sapphire Sphinx kissing her—oh. Geneviève squeezed her eyes even more tightly shut. As if shutting her eyes could block out the memory of the sapphire saying, *we can't see each other anymore.*

"I brought you a chocolate," Mary offered in her level voice, always patient and calm. Instead of comfort it only brought annoyance. "And I have something to tell you."

Geneviève slowly pushed the covers back from her chin and blinked blearily at Mary in her Grecian-style gown, her hair in a knot at the back of her head, a pile of papers in one hand, and a fluted chocolate pot in the other. Mary looked a bit like a minor classical deity. Geneviève envied her cousin's serenity.

"I thought that would coax you out," Mary said with some satisfaction. But her tone changed as she took in Geneviève's reddened eyes. "Are you all right?"

Her cousin's love, concern, and hot chocolate——made tears prick in Geneviève's eyes.

Mary put down her papers, tugged the pillow away, and handed a reasonably dry-eyed Geneviève a porcelain cup of lukewarm chocolate.

"What happened last night?" Mary asked, settling herself down on the bed in the hollow next to Geneviève's hip. Her skits blended with the sheets, white on white. "I stopped by after I heard your door click shut, but you were lying so still I couldn't bear to disturb you. Did you speak to your Sapphire Sphinx?"

"I think we may have to restore the monarchy without the Sapphire Sphinx," Geneviève said, her eyes on her cup of chocolate. She looked up at Mary with a false, strained smile. "That will give us much more freedom of movement, don't you think?"

Mary watched the contortions of Geneviève's lips with alarm. "What's wrong, Geneviève?"

"Nothing's wrong. The Sapphire Sphinx and I just realized we had different..." Depths of emotion? Different ideas of the value of a kiss? Geneviève pressed her lips together tightly. "Objectives," she finished brightly. "He wants to stop the invasion of England, and I want to restore the crown. That's all." *And I know his identity.*

"The two aren't necessarily incompatible."

The Sapphire Sphinx—or Lord Cabot—seemed to think so. He found her a distracting infatuation, incompatible with stopping the invasion of England. Incompatible with *him.*

The rich chocolate tasted like acid in Geneviève's mouth.

"Who needs the Sapphire Sphinx?" declared Geneviève, hauling herself up on her elbows. Just because he's—" *handsome, charming, witty, tender,* her mind supplied—"had more experience doesn't mean he's indispensable. We'll do just as well on our own."

An ache fell on Geneviève. *On our own.* Maybe she could pretend she had never found him, never believed she fell for him, had lost nothing but daydreams.

"Something happened last night with the Sapphire Sphinx. Was he uncouth?" Mary asked darkly. "Did he hurt you?"

"No, nothing like that. He just—"

"Just what?" prompted Mary, a deadly hint of steel in her gray eyes.

"It's complicated."

Mary refilled Geneviève's cup of chocolate and handed it back to her. "It can't be that complicated."

So Geneviève explained. She told her about the meeting in the study, the fracas in the gardens—Geneviève rapidly hurried through that bit, as Mary's face darkened in a way that foretold lectures to come—and the dreadful walk home.

Mary listened thoughtfully. "I'm not sure this means what you think it means."

Geneviève plucked listlessly at an embroidered lily on the edge of her eiderdown. "I'll never see him again, and that's all there is to it."

"Geneviève, you can't just—"

"Romance would get in the way of my mission, anyway. It already has."

"Birds of a feather," muttered Mary. "That sounds a great deal like—"

"When you woke me up, you said you had something to tell me?" Geneviève cut in.

Mary retrieved her tidy stack of papers. "It will keep till later. We're to go to the Tuileries at four, and I have some little odds and ends I want to tie up before then."

Geneviève buried her head again in her pillow. "I'd forgotten. Lord Cabot's antiquities." For the first time, doubt crept in. She was sure, so certain last night that Lord Cabot was the Sapphire Sphinx, but she'd also thought the Sphinx held a *tindre* for her. She'd been wrong on the latter.

Her spirits were still low hours later as Miss Agnes shepherded them into the Tuileries to keep their appointment with Lord Cabot. Geneviève derived less than the usual enjoyment from watching Miss Agnes make loud demands in English and poke the baffled guards with her parasol. An entourage of three footmen, all clutching their sides in pain, eventually escorted them to Lord Cabot's office.

The room was smaller than Geneviève had anticipated. Or maybe it merely seemed small due to the clutter of objects that filled the room. Long tables ran down both sides and the center of the room, their surfaces covered by vases, pottery and fragments of jewelry. Crates, lined up one after another, formed a solid block beneath the tables and rose in tottery piles at the corners of the room. At the very end of the room sat Lord Cabot, nearly hidden behind a stack of immense, leather-bound ledgers. He was, Geneviève saw as they moved further into the room, squinting at a shard of pottery, the quill in his other hand poised over a page already half-filled with tidy script.

And he wasn't fully clothed.

Geneviève didn't mean to stare, but Lord Cabot's jacket was slung over the back of his chair, his waistcoat hung open, and the linen of his shirt was so very fine. The healthy sheen of skin showed through the white fabric. Geneviève watched, fascinated, as the sleeve bunched and pulled against the sleek muscles of his arm as he reached over to dip his quill in the inkwell. Her eyes traveled up the length of his arm to the loosened knot of his cravat, the pulse moving in the hollow of his bare throat.

"Hrrrmph." Miss Agnes cleared her throat forcefully enough to create a hurricane three counties away.

"I do beg your pardon." Lord Cabot grabbed for his jacket. "I hadn't expected you for another quarter hour yet. Welcome." He ushered them into the room, turning his devastating smile in special welcome upon Geneviève.

"When were you in Egypt?" asked Miss Agnes in her peremptory way, saving Geneviève form having to say anything at all.

"I went over in ninety-eight with Bonaparte's expedition and returned later that year," Lord Cabot said, not meeting Geneviève's eye.

She rocked on her heels. Geneviève had spent considerable time yelling at Lord Cabot over his Egyptian adventures. Perhaps Lord Cabot *wasn't* the Sapphire Sphinx. It made little sense to announce the end of their meeting the night before she was to arrive.

Miss Agnes continued, "You were in Egypt when Blakeney destroyed the French fleet?"

"Yes." Lord Cabot hastily picked up a necklace from one of the long tables lining the sides of the room. "This is a necklace made of faience, which is—"

"Where were you?" Like the dragon she was, Miss Agnes was determined to steer this conversation to help her novel and tolerated nothing else.

The necklace dangled in the air in front of Geneviève, shades of dusty red and blue, as Lord Cabot turned to cock a confused eyebrow at Miss Agnes. "Where was I when?"

"Never mind." Miss Agnes waved an imperious hand. "It doesn't signify."

Mary stepped in to rescue him. "What's this, my lord?" she asked, indicating a piece of stone, engraved with what looked to be little squiggles and pictures, which stood propped against the wall.

"We think that might be a funeral stela," explained Lord Cabot, running a finger fondly along the carvings. "See the pictures up top? That's the pharaoh in the middle, giving offerings to a god—that's the chap with Horus, on his right. His queen with the tall hat stands on his left."

"Who was she?" asked Geneviève, moving to stand next to him, drawn in despite herself.

"We don't know," Lord Cabot admitted, grinning boyishly down at her. "Would you like to hazard a guess? Perhaps a princess from a faraway land, brought overseas from her home."

"Shipwrecked on the coast of Egypt," Geneviève added. She couldn't help joining in. "Like the heroine of a Shakespeare play. Forced to disguise herself as a boy, until her innate nobility shines through her humble robes. She catches the eye of the pharaoh—"

"And they live happily ever after," finished Lord Cabot.

"I wonder what really happened to her," Geneviève said, eyes scanning the unreadable symbols in front of her. It reminded her of the first time she had looked at the Greek letters on the page of one Papa's books, how it seemed impossible that the strangely configured strokes of ink could resolve themselves into the love of Ariadne and the treachery of Theseus. Amazing how many stories dwelled on men repudiating the women who loved them. Theseus and Ariadne, Jason and Medea, Aeneas and Dido. Too bad she hadn't learned her lesson well enough from her storybooks.

"You don't think she lived happily ever after?" Lord Cabot asked softly, his fingers brushing past Geneviève's as she traced the contours of a small bird.

"That's an ending for books, not for people."

"What are books about, if not people?" His gaze was intent, as if he were drinking her in.

Geneviève backed away from the force of Lord Cabot's gaze. "Why don't you ask Miss Agnes?" she suggested. "She can tell you all about the characters in her horrid novel, I'm sure."

Lord Cabot didn't so much as glance at Miss Agnes. His green gaze narrowed even more intently on Geneviève. What was it about his voice, his presence, his talk of happy endings that was making her so nervous? Geneviève felt a slight flush rising in her cheeks at the sight of Lord Cabot's tapering fingers stroking the stone tablet, caressing the contours of the carvings. She focused her eyes on Lord Cabot's face. She could see the little crinkles at the corners of his eyes, the gold tips of his lashes, the slight dusting of pale hairs across the bridge of his nose.

"Asaph," announced Miss Agnes out of nowhere.

Lord Cabot started and banged his head against the stela. Geneviève let out the breath she'd been holding in a giggle.

"The Cabot Marquesses of Asaph of Asaph Hall. In Kent, unless I mistake myself," Miss Agnes continued.

Rubbing the bump on his head, William smiled ruefully at Miss Agnes. "You know your *Peerage's* well."

Miss Agnes sniffed. "Young man, I live in the countryside, not the wilds of America. We are not entirely cut off from the civilized world."

"My apologies."

"When I made my debut, I knew my peerage better than any girl in London. I could identify the crest on a carriage from five streets away. The Asaph estates are adjoined by those of the Blakeneys, are they not?"

"Does that mean you know the Scarlet Pimpernel?" Geneviève asked. Suspicion whirled around her like a gentle breeze.

Lord Cabot's face stilled for a moment, his face expressionless. Geneviève blinked and it was gone. Lord Cabot was now smiling, all affability, at Miss Agnes as he replied, "Yes, I spent much of my youth raiding the Blakeney kitchens. Would you like to see a mummy?" he added. "It might prove a useful device in your novel."

He took Miss Agnes's bony arm, and steered her down the center of the room, away from Geneviève. Geneviève hurried after them. "What is the Scarlet Pimpernel like?"

"Blakeney is a splendid chap," Lord Cabot said warmly. "He never even scolded me for picking all the plums out of his plum pudding."

Geneviève smiled, trying to read his face.

Lord Cabot smiled back. They smiled together. How could this be the same man, the spy, who told Geneviève they could not see each other again. It was quite definitely a *moment.*

It was, alas, only a momentary moment. Miss Agnes spoiled it by banging her parasol against the flagstones of the floor.

"We trespassed on your hospitality long enough." Miss Agnes shook off his arm and grabbed Geneviève's. "I have learned all I desired about Egyptian antiquities. Come along, Mary, Geneviève. Don't dawdle. I'm sure Lord Cabot has much to do."

"I'll see you to your coach," Lord Cabot offered, as Miss Agnes chivied her charges forward with the tip of her parasol.

This Miss Agnes graciously permitted. Lord Cabot regaled Geneviève with tales of his childhood exploits and Sir Percy Blakeney's benevolence all the way through the palace. Geneviève, enthralled, quietly noticed that all of his stories stopped at least a year before Sir Percy became the Scarlet Pimpernel. She countered with her own tales of training to be a member of the Pimpernel's band, all of the midnight escapes from her nursery, and costumes filched from the scullery or her uncle's wardrobe.

"Don't forget the time you tried to train the sheep to stampede at the sound of a whistle," chimed in Mary.

Lord Cabot arched a quizzical eyebrow at Geneviève.

"I thought they might be useful in an attack," Geneviève protested, lips twitching with suppressed laughter. "After all, we didn't have any cavalry at hand, so I had to make do with what we had."

"Tell me," he said, lowering his voice in a tone of mock confidentiality, "did you actually try to *ride* the sheep?"

Geneviève flushed, looking, one might say, somewhat sheepish.

"Waving a wooden sword and shouting battle cries." Mary giggled behind a delicate hand.

"I was only eight." Geneviève held out her hands in defense.

Mary pulled on her arm. "Yes, but you were twelve when you set your hair on fire."

"Let me guess," Lord Cabot ventured, grinning at Geneviève. "You were experimenting with gunpowder to blow up the Bastille."

"Actually," Geneviève corrected him loftily, "I was applying ashes to my hair to see if they would make me look convincingly aged and gray-haired. The only problem was that I didn't stamp out all of the embers quite thoroughly enough. Uncle Bertrand wouldn't let me have any gunpowder," she added wistfully as they stepped outside.

Lord Cabot flung back his head and guffawed. The courtyard of the Tuileries rang with his laughter as he escorted the three ladies to Charles's carriage. He made his bows to Miss Agnes and Mary, handing them into the carriage. Finally, Geneviève stood alone before the open door.

His voice lowered to an intimate murmur that made the skin on Geneviève's arm prickle, and ought to have caused her chaperone to drag her away at once. "Stay away from gunpowder," he cautioned, bowing over Geneviève's hand. With a quick, mischievous glance into the carriage to make sure Miss Agnes was occupied in conversation with Mary, Lord Cabot flipped Geneviève's hand over, and pressed a lingering kiss on the sensitive skin of her palm.

Geneviève's shocked gaze flew from her palm to Lord Cabot's laughing eyes. She stared at him, her confusion palpable on her face. In the fraught moment before she turned to climb up into the carriage, he ran his thumb in an intimate caress over her palm. And then he winked. He told *her* to stay away from gunpowder?

# CHAPTER 32

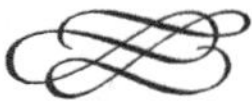

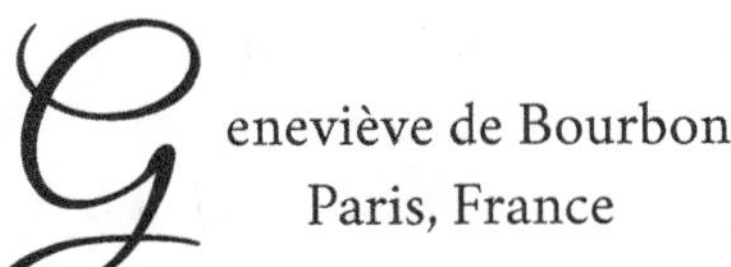

enevière de Bourbon
Paris, France

Geneviève stumbled into the carriage in a state of confusion. Confusion seemed to be her normal state nowadays. Geneviève tried to remember what it felt like to feel sure of herself, her plans, her opinions and the people around her, and failed miserably. First, there had been the Sapphire Sphinx, who had baffled her by seeming to care for her then repudiating her. And now Lord Cabot. Lord Cabot, who, whenever she thought she had him pegged—as a charming antiquarian, as an evil abettor of the French, as the lover of Pauline Leclerc— did something to confuse her. And now the combination—or possible combination, of the two men being one.

Maybe, thought Geneviève, her hands pressed tightly together in her lap, she was just too easily charmed. It said something rather unpleasant about the shallowness of her own character that she could fancy herself in love with the Sapphire Sphinx one day and be fascinated by Lord Cabot the next. She had been so sure of her feelings for the Sapphire. And of his for her. *I think I like you.*

Both men spoke of a necklace of stars like her father's promise.

Both phrases fluttered in circles around her head.

She had never told the Sapphire Sphinx about her father's promise; she had never even told him about her parents' death. Only one person in France knew about her childhood memory. One person who had grown up next door to Percy Blakeney, who had been in Egypt when Bonaparte's fleet was destroyed. One person who had been sporting tight tan trousers the previous afternoon. One person who always wore citrus-scented cologne.

And the one person who told her they couldn't see each other. With one final flourish, Geneviève sank into the facts. Over and over again she argued with herself—without a doubt, Lord Cabot *had* to be the Sapphire Sphinx. Her heart broke at the thought.

"That cad," Geneviève breathed.

Mary broke off midsentence in her conversation with Miss Agnes and touched Geneviève's hand. "Are you feeling quite all right?"

Oblivious to Mary, to Miss Agnes, to discretion, Geneviève jerked her hand away and slammed it back down against the seat. "That utter sniveling *cad*."

"Geneviève? Would you like to tell me what's wrong?" Wide eyed, Mary hovered from a safe distance, lest Geneviève strike out again. Geneviève could have told her she was safe. The only person Geneviève wanted to hit, again and again and again, was several yards back in the Tuileries, but in the moment, Geneviève wasn't capable of uttering anything quite that coherent.

"Cad… disgusting…" Geneviève's arms flailed wildly.

Mary scooted a little farther back on the seat and looked anxiously at Miss Agnes. "Should we?"

Miss Agnes, however, was smiling quite unconcernedly, if slightly maliciously, at Geneviève. "You certainly took your time figuring it out. Why else would a man be traveling about with the First Consul. Did it truly take me spelling his childhood—"

"You knew?" Geneviève's eyebrows flew up till they nearly reached her hairline. "All this time, you knew? And you didn't tell me?"

Mary looked brightly from Geneviève's agitated face to Miss Agnes's smug one. "Oh, are you talking about Lord Cabot being the

Sapphire Sphinx—Evie, I'd thought you knew but just didn't want to believe it."

"Oh." Geneviève flung herself face-first into the seat cushions.

"Oh, Evie, I'm sorry. I thought that's what you understood from last night's meeting," said Mary apologetically, wrenching a corner of her skirt out from under Geneviève's head.

"Wonderful," sputtered Geneviève, lifting a flushed face from the bench. "Just wonderful. I couldn't be certain last night because why on earth would he tell me we can't see each other again but invite me over to his house."

"At least the First Consul doesn't know yet," volunteered Mary. "Nor does the Ministry of Police."

"Yes, but they haven't been kissing him," cried Geneviève.

"I take that to mean that you have?" Miss Agnes's beady eyes fixed on Geneviève like a vulture sighting prey.

"Not exactly," Geneviève lied quickly.

"I will refrain from comment on your reckless disregard for your reputation." Miss Agnes's voice scraped across Geneviève's raw nerves like talons clawing flesh. "Your morals I leave to your conscience. Since what is done cannot be undone, it remains only to take what little good one can from this unfortunate episode."

"You mean that now I've learned my lesson and know never to kiss anyone ever again?"

Miss Agnes impaled Geneviève on a look of utter contempt. "Kindly contrive not to be more absurd than the good Lord made you. No. I require a full description of the kiss or kisses for incorporation into my novel."

The world and everyone in it had gone mad. That was the only explanation that Geneviève could come up with. Lord Cabot, Bonaparte's antiquarian, was absolutely the Sapphire Sphinx. Miss Agnes, rather than scolding her for improper behavior, wanted to use the experience in a book.

Bewilderment momentarily distracted her from Lord Cabot's deception. But only for a moment. "How could he be so *cruel?*" she whispered, her eyes clouded.

"Why don't you go to him and tell him you know who he is?" suggested Mary.

Geneviève shook her head so vehemently that her loose curls whipped across the end of Mary's nose. "You don't understand, Mary. I want to make him *suffer*."

Miss Agnes emitted a cracking noise that might have been a laugh. "Ah. Young love."

Geneviève scowled at her. "What in heaven's name are you talking about?"

"You shouldn't take heaven's name in vain, missy. You might want to go there someday." Miss Agnes smirked.

Geneviève simmered.

Finally, Miss Agnes rolled her eyes and huffed. "It's quite simple. You wouldn't hate him so much unless you loved him. Hmm. I like that. Maybe I'll use it in my book."

"At least *someone* benefits from this farce."

"Don't take that tone with me, young lady. I'm on your side in this. You needn't goggle your eyes at me. The young man played with your affections in a most inappropriate way and deserves whatever punishment you choose to mete out." Miss Agnes considered for a moment before adding, "Excluding physical mutilation. One must acknowledge the bounds of decency."

Geneviève gave a laugh that sounded suspiciously like a sob.

"How do you intend to wreak your revenge?" Miss Agnes asked briskly.

Geneviève plunged with relief into her favorite distraction. Planning. Planning almost anything was a dependable remedy for weepiness. Planning ways to wreak devastation, vengeance, and mayhem upon the guilty golden head of Lord William Cabot was even better. Geneviève rubbed her eyes clear and set to work.

The ideal revenge would be to serve back to him the bitter brew of his own devising. Perhaps she could appear at his chambers in disguise, heavily veiled in black, and convince him that she was a secret agent sent by the War Office. Or, even better, she could be a French agent defecting to the English. He wouldn't see her face, and she would speak in a heavy accent—a Provencal dialect, perhaps, southern and exotic, with echoes of the troubadours and courts of love—so he wouldn't recognize her voice. And once he was terribly, painfully in love with her, she could repudiate him on a dark midnight, and leave him standing broken beside his own Taunton. An eye for an eye, a tooth for a tooth, and a deception for a deception. Justice in its purest form.

The plan was perfect.

And entirely impracticable. There was nothing to guarantee that she could make him love her. Besides, one yank of her veils and the whole plan would be undone. Geneviève sank back into thought. What mattered most to him was his blasted mission.

"I'll beat him to the Swiss gold. I'll show the Sapphire Sphinx that he isn't the only one who can thwart Bonaparte." Geneviève grimaced. She'd only confided that information to Mary, not Miss Agnes.

To her credit, Miss Agnes leveled an appraising gaze at Geneviève. "I thought there might be some mettle in you."

Both Mary and Geneviève stared openmouthed at Miss Agnes.

"Was that a compliment?" whispered Geneviève to Mary.

"It sounded like one," Mary agreed, eyes wide.

"Don't allow it to go to your head," Miss Agnes interrupted dryly. "I spoke solely of potential. You may yet prove the contrary."

"Thank you," said Geneviève.

"I like this plan much better than tormenting Lord Cabot." Mary leaned forward on the seat.

"Oh, I still intend to do that, too." Geneviève nodded, she was absolutely bent on that part of the plan. "Miss Agnes's right. He broke the do-unto-others rule, and now he's going to get his just deserts. It's too bad *I* can't pretend to be two people, just to show him what it feels like."

"Let's not go into that again." Mary held up a hand. "How shall we intercept the gold?"

"We already had a plan." Geneviève's lips twisted in a rueful grimace as she relayed the plan she and the Sapphire Sphinx had contrived the night before. Miss Agnes listened intently. "If that is the plan the Sapphire Sphinx intends to employ, we must find another one."

"We don't have enough people for it." Mary folded her hands primly in her lap. The woman was ever-practical. "The Sapphire Sphinx has a league; we just have us. Not that we aren't formidable," she added hastily, with a glance at Miss Agnes.

"Why shouldn't we be a league?" demanded Miss Agnes.

"That's it. Geneviève—" Mary's mouth was a round *o* of amusement. Speechless with mirth, she rocked back against the seat, one hand pressed to her chest, the other held out to her cousin.

"Out with it," snapped Miss Agnes.

"The Talisman," gasped Mary.

Miss Agnes's narrowed eye and clenched jaw looked at Mary as though she was considering transporting the young lady to Bedlam.

"The Talisman?" Genevieve hoped her tone came across curious.

Mary leaned closer to Geneviève. "Before the Sapphire Sphinx appeared, we were going to be our own league, and call it—"

"Napoleon's Talisman." The beginnings of a smile tugged at Geneviève's lips. "We liked it better than the League of Flowers."

"Shall we?" asked Mary breathlessly, a faint pink flush rising in her pale cheeks. "Shall we become the Talisman? Bonaparte believes his success comes from a jewel-encrusted artifact. What if we, a group of women, are the secret to the league's success?"

"Oh, Mary." Geneviève launched herself across the seat to hug her cousin. "I would like nothing better. We'll make Bonaparte quail at the very sight of his own Talisman."

# CHAPTER 33

*L*ord William Cabot
Paris, France

William bounded joyously up the steps of his town house, flinging open the front door without waiting for Gideon to get there first. All the way home, he had savored the memory of Geneviève's face as he had kissed her hand good-bye. He had lingered happily over the confused pleasure in her eyes as he whistled through the Tuileries garden, and he had grinned over her slightly parted lips as he evaded the slops a brawny maid tossed from an upper window.

He opened the entryway door and paused. The front hall table wasn't there. Or if it was, he couldn't see it. His foyer was entirely filled with piles of bandboxes and his—"Mother?" William blinked once, then twice. His mother was still there.

"Oh, hello, darling." His mother waved a hand at him in greeting before returning to harassing his butler. "Now let's get this straight. Those two hatboxes go in the front bedroom, and the large trunk goes in—"

Gideon emitted one of his theatrical groans. William envied him that.

"Mother?"

"Yes, dear?" His mother thrust another hatbox on the pile Gideon was already holding. "Oh, do stop whining. You have the build of a man half your age."

"He is half his age," William said dryly. "Mother, what are you doing here?"

He'd meant the question to come out calmly, but his voice reverted to somewhere preadolescent on the last word.

"Oh, how silly of me." Gideon took advantage of Lady Asaph's momentary distraction to scuttle behind the pile of luggage. The marchioness beamed at her son. "We came to help you of course."

William's head reeled and he sat down rather abruptly on a huge trunk. By the size of it, his mother had packed a full silver service, two wardrobes, and perhaps a footman or two.

William tackled the most pressing question first. "What do you mean by we?"

"They were here a moment ago." His mother peered at the mountain of baggage as though expecting half of *Britain's Beloved Peerage* to pop out. "I suppose Adam must have taken them into the drawing room. Your father is here, of course. It's been so long since he and I have been to Paris together." The marchioness smiled mistily. "You came along after our last trip to Paris, dear."

"Mother." William sighed, the room became significantly warmer.

Lady Asaph pointed to the stairs. "Catherine's here too. A little continental polish will be just the thing to set her off for her next season."

Lady Asaph might have said more, but her words were abruptly truncated by the cacophony of several loud thumps, an ear-curdling shriek of rage and a hearty masculine yelp.

William frowned. "That does not sound like Catherine."

"Well, no. We also brought along—"

"Hullo, William!" Michael bounded around the pile of boxes, pushing a floppy lock of blond hair out of his eyes. "Why does your butler hate me?"

"He hates everyone." William turned to his mother. "Is there anyone else you brought who you'd like to warn me about? Great-aunt Hyacinth? The underfootman from Asaph House?"

"Always happy to see you, too, old chap." Michael whacked William on the shoulder. "Stop grousing and come along. Adam's got tea and crumpets for all of us in the drawing room."

William scowled at the back of Michael's head as he followed him into the drawing room.

Catherine stood on tiptoe to press a quick kiss to William's cheek. "I'm sorry, William," she whispered. "I know I should have tried to stop them."

"Thanks, Kitty." William squeezed his sister's shoulders.

"But, well, I rather wanted to see Paris, so…" Catherine shrugged apologetically.

"Thanks," William repeated dourly. "Thanks a lot."

Kitty covered her mouth with her hand and retreated to her chair. "Sorry."

"Is that picture crooked?" Lady Asaph bounced into the room behind William and moved the simpering Watteau shepherdess above the settee a fraction to the left. "Really, William, I don't understand how you young men manage to live in such a state of chaos. Dirty cravats under the settee, empty brandy glasses on the table, and is that a piece of cheese under Catherine's chair?"

With a swish of petticoats, Catherine expeditiously relocated to the settee.

Lady Asaph shook her head and straightened another picture. "I'll talk to the maids after we've had our tea."

"I'm assuming you haven't come all this way to supervise my housekeeping."

"That would be silly, wouldn't it?" replied Lady Asaph tartly. "Oh, do sit down, William. You're making me dizzy prowling about in circles like that. It's like watching one of the lions in the Tower."

William felt a great deal of sympathy for the Tower menagerie as he flung himself into a chair, which, of course, promptly skidded back a good six inches. His mother watched him indulgently. *Empathy* for the animals in the Tower might be more like it. William loved his mother—he would be the last to deny that fact. She was the very paragon of a mother, and he was awfully glad he had been born to her and not some other woman and so on and so on and so on. But at the age of twenty-seven, he deserved a certain amount of privacy. He was sure he had to be the only agent operating in France—or England or Russia or the farthest wilds of the Americas—whose mother showed up at random on his doorstep. It wasn't right.

His mother adjusted another portrait. "As soon as you left, I started thinking—"

"They do that, you know." William's father said from the safety of his chair.

Lady Asaph swatted him, a gesture more symbolic than practical, as the marquess was seated a good three feet out of range. "As I was saying," she continued, with a pointed look at her spouse, "after some thought, your father and I decided that your mission would go much faster if we came over and helped you."

William swung around to glare at his father. Making little pointing gestures at his wife, Lord Asaph affected an expression of innocence. William wasn't fooled. His father had been angling to be involved in his missions for years. Hell, he was worse than his mother. William looked hard at Lord Asaph. Being a peer of the realm, a man of dignity and substance, master of four estates and hundreds of dependents, Lord Asaph did not blush or squirm. He did, however, discover a sudden deep interest in the folds of his cravat.

William rubbed the bridge of his nose. "Mother—"

Just when he thought nothing worse could happen, just as he was about to tackle the catastrophe at hand, another disaster erupted.

Michael leaped from his chair next to Adam and hooted, "William's in love."

All activity in the room drew to an abrupt close. Adam's teacup halted guiltily in between the table and his mouth. Catherine dropped her biscuit. His mother stopped straightening the pictures on the walls. His father looked up from his cravat.

"In love?" Lady Asaph opened her mouth in a delighted *o*. "Oh, William."

"Michael, blast you. I am not in—" William emitted a strangled noise.

His mother tugged at his arm. "Darling, how wonderful! Who is she?"

William shrugged away. "But I just said—"

Michael nodded sagely, a great, big infuriating grin spreading across his face. "Yes. Clearly a victim of Cupid's amorous dar—you know, throwing that cushion at me just proves my point. What do you say, Catherine?"

"Catherine," William pronounced chillingly, "is not going to say anything at all. Not if she doesn't want to be bodily lifted onto the next packet for Dover."

Catherine's mouth snapped shut.

Michael, too large to lift, was less easily silenced.

"I, for one, want to meet this paragon," Michael announced. He donned a lovesick look, doe-eyed and lips pouted, and strummed a chord on an invisible lute. "Does she have a balcony under which we might stand and call for her? Oh, Geneviève, Geneviève, wherefore art thou—"

"Not long for this earth," William uttered through clenched teeth.

Michael retrieved his hand from its languishing position on his brow. "Is that any way to speak of your beloved?"

"I was speaking of you."

"Why, William, I never knew you cared."

"Do be quiet, Michael." Catherine stood and *accidentally* stepped on Michael's foot in passing with a force that ensured that the only noises emerging from his mouth were inarticulate ones indicating pain. "We'll never get anything sensible out of William if you don't stop provoking him."

His large hands closing around Catherine's waist, Michael lifted her off his foot and set her down firmly on the settee. "But what's the fun of sensible?"

"Michael does have a point," mused Lady Asaph.

Five heads twisted sharply her way. Or, rather, six heads, if one counted Gideon, who was listening outside the half-open door.

"My dear." The marquess said mildly, "I have known you longer than anyone else in the room, and I must say that you have always struck me as a supremely sensible woman. I would rather object to your altering your character at this late date."

"Thank you, darling." Lady Asaph blew a kiss to her husband. "I'm rather fond of your character, too. But I was referring to Michael's suggestion that we meet this Geneviève. If we were to call on her after dinner—"

"It is too late to call." William pulled at his cravat. He would be the only agent convicted of killing his family. Or dying of complete and utter embarrassment.

"Don't be ridiculous," his mother replied blithely. "We're in France. They don't keep proper hours here."

William turned in silent appeal to Lord Asaph.

"Don't look at me." His father stretched out his legs. "I've learned when not to get in the way of your mother."

"Thank you, darling." Lady Asaph beamed. "That's one of the things I love about you."

"I'll accompany you, Lady Asaph," Michael offered angelically.

"Nobody asked you," snapped William.

"Is that any way to treat your dearest friend?"

"Don't you mean my *former* dearest friend?" William glared at him.

Holding up his hands in mock innocence, Michael added, "Don't yell at me. Yell at Adam. He's the one who told me about Geneviève."

"If Michael gets to go, I get to go, too." Catherine folded her arms and lifted her chin. "After all, *he's* not even family. If Geneviève's going to be my sister, I ought to get first crack at meeting her."

"Before you reserve the chapel," William drawled, in an obnoxious London man-about-town voice, "there are a few things that ought to be made clear."

"Darling, you aren't afraid we'll embarrass you, are you? I promise, we'll be on our best behavior, even your father." The marchioness wrinkled her nose playfully at the marquess.

"Mother." Running a hand down his face, William sighed. His family had no idea of the danger they'd put themselves—and the entire mission in. And now Geneviève. He'd *just* convinced her to stop involving herself in the mission. Granted, he didn't do that as Lord Cabot, but as the Sphinx.

# CHAPTER 34

Geneviève de Bourbon
Paris, France

"Where is she? Where is the little witch?" Nostrils flaring, Edward Taunton burst lopsided through the door of the dining room where the de Bourbons were partaking of supper. His angry blue eyes lit on Geneviève. "You!" he bellowed, limping down the length of the table.

"Sir!" Miss Agnes's voice stopped Taunton dead in his tracks. "What is the meaning of this intrusion?"

"Her." Taunton pointed at Geneviève, all but frothing at the mouth. "Her!"

"She," Miss Agnes corrected primly.

"Yes *her!*" Taunton's lip curled in a manner that made Geneviève wish to find some pressing reason to adjourn. Preferably with the door locked behind her. Her arms ached with the memory of Taunton's painful grip. She wouldn't let him touch her again. She'd break her wineglass over his head and ward him off with the fragments. She'd break his other toe—no, that would require an unpleasant proximity.

Miss Agnes sighed. "No, Mr. Taunton. Not her, *she*. Did your father's family teach you no English grammar? Or has life in the army whittled away at your verbal skills until you are capable of nothing save the occasional incorrect monosyllable?"

"Grammar," repeated Taunton, with a nasty look in his eye that Geneviève feared had little to do with English. One beefy finger pointed straight at Geneviève. "I'll show you grammar."

Geneviève shot up in her place. "And I accuse you of behavior unbecoming to a gentleman, and I demand you leave my house at once."

"I think I'll leave," murmured Charles, heaving his bulk out of his chair.

"Sit," Miss Agnes commanded.

Charles sat.

So—unexpectedly—did Edward Taunton.

"I've always been very good at dealing with dogs," commented Miss Agnes.

Edward Taunton promptly stood back up.

Miss Agnes lifted an eyebrow. "Some need more training than others."

Taunton ignored her and started again towards Geneviève. "What do you mean *your* house? It's *his* house, and he'll do as I say or suffer the consequences, right, de Bourbon?"

"Um…" Charles, having been forbidden to leave the table, seemed to be attempting to cram himself under it.

With a steady and soft voice, Mary said, "Why don't you take a seat, Mr. Taunton, and I'm sure we can get this all sorted out."

Intent on his prey, Taunton paid Mary no more mind than the candlesticks at the table, or the silent footmen by the sideboard.

"I'm so glad you stopped by, Mr. Taunton." Mary stood, her hands clasped in front of her. "I've been wanting to ask you about the tea and the India muslin."

Taunton stopped dead two chairs away from Geneviève, his eyes and tongue bulging like those of a dog whose owner had yanked too abruptly on the leash.

"India muslin," he croaked.

"And tea." Mary placed a finger in the air. Geneviève could have sworn she saw a glint of amusement in her cousin's eye, but Mary's demeanor was as self-contained as ever and her voice was devoid of any hint of mockery. "Tell me," she asked, in a tone that contained only innocent inquiry, "do the authorities know of your import business?"

Images shifted in Geneviève's head into a complete whole. The strange packages in the ballroom that Geneviève had hoped might contain supplies for the Sapphire but hadn't. The dirt-blackened doors and windows of the west wing. Now that Mary had put the pieces together, it was as patently obvious as Taunton's guilty fury. Charles had never had anything to do with the Sapphire. Nor had Taunton.

Her brother and Taunton were smugglers.

Taunton's eyes darted from side to side, landing on Charles. Turning an alarming shade of green, Charles shook his head violently.

"The wounded man?" Geneviève felt strangely out of place. Years ago, she'd begged Mary to join her in future adventures. She never thought Mary would lead the charge.

"A customs official," replied Mary, her gaze never wavering from Taunton. "How much did you pay him to forget that little incident, Mr. Taunton?"

"I don't know what you're talking about." Taunton stomped across the room to loom over Mary.

"Really? And I suppose my cousin doesn't know anything either." Mary glanced at Charles, who was still shaking not only his head but the rest of his portly body as well. His cravat quivered with agitation. Mary sighed. "I suppose there is nothing for it but to ask the authorities to settle my curiosity over the tea and muslin in the ballroom. The *British* tea and muslin."

Taunton's broken nose turned bright red with rage. "You wouldn't dare."

Her voice still as soft and inviting, Mary said, "You, Mr. Taunton, are not in a position to make terms."

"You can't prove anything." Small flecks of saliva spattered in the air as Taunton blustered. "The ballroom's empty. You don't have any proof."

"I fear, Mr. Taunton, that you are mistaken on that score. You see" —Mary smiled, a gentle cure of the lips that held the entire room silent—"I do have proof. I have your records and your correspondence. I found them secreted in a hollow globe in my cousin's study. Your own pen tells against you."

Taunton's large hands flexed dangerously. Mary didn't so much as flinch.

"Touch Miss de Bourbon again," Mary warned, her voice as steely as her spine, "in anger, in lust, or even in greeting, and those papers go directly to the authorities."

The tense silence was broken by the dry sound of Miss Agnes clapping. And then the room dissolved into madness. With a roar, Taunton flung himself at Charles. Charles pleaded and shrieked and babbled. Taunton's hands closed around his throat, turning his protests to gurgles. China crashed into fragments against the parquet floor. Geneviève ran and hugged Mary. The footmen wisely snuck out the door while no one was looking. Miss Agnes whacked the back of Taunton's head with her soupspoon, calling him an insolent son of a rabid dog.

And the butler cleared his throat.

"*Ahem!*" He had to try several times before the room stilled, raising his voice to a level that would have rendered a man of lesser vocal capacities mute for a month. Miss Agnes paused with her spoon raised about Taunton's head. Taunton stopped with his fingers digging into Charles's vocal cords. And Charles stayed just as he was, his tongue hanging slightly out, pop-eyed with terror.

The butler proffered a card on a silver tray to Charles. Miss Agnes snatched it on his behalf.

"Lord and Lady Asaph would like to pay their respects," the butler intoned, his gaze fixed somewhere above the bizarre tableau created by his master, Taunton, and Miss Agnes.

"Put them in the green salon," instructed Miss Agnes, since Charles seemed incapable of speech. To be fair, Taunton's hands were still locked about his throat. "And you." She dealt Taunton another smart whack with a now-dented silver soupspoon. "Stop throttling Mr. de Bourbon and take your leave at once."

Taunton was shooed. With an eloquent sneer at Mary and Geneviève, who stood with their arms about each other's waists for support, he sauntered out the door after the butler.

"One can only hope he will not encounter the Asaphs." Miss Agnes dropped her soupspoon into her bowl with a clatter.

Asaph. The name sounded familiar, but Geneviève was too busy making sure Taunton's retreating back kept retreating to give it any thought. "When did you find out about the smuggling?" she whispered to Mary.

"Last night," Mary whispered back. "I was going to tell you this morning, but—why are we whispering?"

"I don't know." Geneviève shrugged helplessly. "It just seemed the thing to do."

"Come along, girls." Miss Agnes propelled them out of the dining room. "We don't want to keep our guests waiting."

"I'm surprised you're taking this so calmly," Mary hissed to Geneviève as they approached the threshold of the green salon.

"Well, I was a little worried, but you dealt with him splendidly."

Mary looked at her confused. "Oh, do you mean Taunton? I was talking about"—the footman, walking before them with a candelabrum, flung open the doors of the green salon—"Lord Cabot," Mary finished weakly.

Geneviève's mouth opened but no sound emerged.

Lord Cabot leaned nonchalantly against the mummy case, his arms crossed over his chest. At Geneviève's entrance, he uncrossed his arms and smiled with a depth of welcome that made Geneviève's stomach do more flip-flops than an entire troupe of acrobats at a village fair.

Those lips, curved into a devastating smile, were the ones that had delivered quite the blow.

Asaph. Geneviève would have whacked her head with the heel of her hand if too many people hadn't been looking on. That's what she got for reading Latin and Greek when she should have been memorizing *Britain's Beloved Peerage*. As Miss Agnes had so helpfully pointed out that afternoon, the Cabot family bore the Asaph title.

A petite woman in a green and blue gown was poking interestedly into a funeral urn, while the somewhat taller brunette beside her protested, "But Mama, do you really want to know what's in there?"

As Geneviève and Mary approached, Mary keeping a hand on Geneviève's arm for moral support, both looked up. Dropping the lid of the urn, the woman in green swept forward with a warm smile distressingly like William's. "I do hope we're not intruding. I was all agog to meet our dear William's traveling companions. You must be Miss de Bourbon?"

The brunette waved enthusiastically over her mother's head. "Since we're introducing ourselves, I'm Catherine. You know Catherine? Kitty? The little sister? Didn't William tell you about me?"

Next to Catherine, a broad-shouldered man in a crumpled cravat rolled his eyes. "Surely he must have mentioned me, the best friend?" he simpered, in obvious imitation of Catherine's enthusiastic greeting. "You know, the best friend? Michael?"

Geneviève saw murder written in the brunette's hazel eyes.

"You can be so juvenile sometimes, Michael."

"The next packet to Dover, Catherine," William warned in awful tones.

Catherine's mouth snapped shut. She even refrained from responding in kind when Michael stuck out his tongue at her.

"They were just fed," Lady Asaph explained apologetically.

"Young man." Miss Agnes pounded her parasol against the floor. "Kindly replace that object in your mouth."

Michael's tongue disappeared behind his lips with the speed of an army retreating into a castle and yanking down the portcullis.

"How splendid." Lady Asaph bustled forward, laying a friendly hand on Miss Agnes's bony arm. "You *must* tell me how you do it. And who you are."

Miss Agnes, with an angle to her chin that amply portrayed her disapproval of the impropriety of the proceedings, even if the cause of the mayhem was a marchioness, made herself known to Lady Asaph, and presented Mary and Charles, the latter still a bit purple about the throat and bulging in the eyes.

Lady Asaph ignored the disapproval emanating from Miss Agnes and beamed directly at Geneviève. "I still haven't introduced myself, have I? I am Lady Asaph, and this"—a wave of an emerald-laden hand at the silver-haired man looking on with amusement a few feet away —"is Asaph, and that's—oh, well, you know, Catherine." Catherine dimpled. "And the ill-behaved young man with the unkept hair—"

Michael hand went anxiously to his head. Catherine smirked.

"—is the Honorable Michael Holton. Let's see, you all know William already. Have I forgotten anyone?"

The brunette, otherwise known as *you know, Catherine,* twined her arm through Lady Asaph's. "You left out Adam again."

"Adam, darling." Lady Asaph let out a cry of distress and held out a hand to a quiet young man standing near William. "I didn't mean to neglect you."

"He's used to it by now," Catherine explained in an aside to Geneviève.

"That"—Lady Asaph leveled a quelling glance at her daughter— "was unkind. Adam is just so much better-behaved than the rest of you that it's easy to forget he's there."

"Was that a compliment?" Michael inquired of Adam.

"Do you see what I mean?" sighed Lady Asaph to Geneviève.

Geneviève, utterly bewildered by the entire Asaph invasion, did the only thing she could do. She smiled. She was rather thankful for Lady Asaph's cheerful volubility. It saved her from having to speak to Lord Cabot. By keeping her eyes fixed on Lady Asaph and Catherine, she could almost pretend he wasn't there. Almost. The more she told herself not to look, the more her eyes strayed towards him.

She'd sworn to berate him and beat him in the quest to tackle the Swiss gold, but she'd not expected to be welcomed by his family in her own home. She couldn't scream or throw things; that would certainly alert Lord Cabot to her newfound knowledge of his double life. Tormenting him had seemed like such a splendid idea in the carriage, but Lord Cabot's presence turned simple things complicated. Revenge, for example. Such a nice, simple idea. But whenever Lord Cabot smiled at her over his mother's head, Geneviève wanted to smile back.

Maybe that wasn't such a dreadful idea, Geneviève rationalized. After all, she did need to lull him into a false sense of security before she meted out her revenge. She would flirt with him, repudiate him, and then best him at espionage. It was all part of the plan.

After much altercation, Lady Asaph finally got around to introducing Adamrey, Second Viscount Pinchingdale, Eighth Baron Snipe.

"So many titles, so little Adam," sighed Michael, stretching to emphasize his two-inch advantage over the Viscount.

"So much brawn, so little brain," countered Catherine.

Michael rolled his eyes. "Who beat whom at draughts last week?"

"Who underhandedly caused a diversion by bumping into the board?"

Michael assumed an angelic expression. "I don't know what you could possibly be referring to. I would never do anything so low as to knock over the board and rearrange the pieces."

"William never cheats at draughts," Lady Asaph whispered to Geneviève. Lady Asaph winked an unspoken permission for familiarity.

*William.* Warmth spread across Geneviève's chest. William, not Lord Cabot.

"No, only at croquet," Michael put in sarcastically. "Or did that ball just move two wickets all by itself?"

"You," drawled Lord Cabot, strolling forward to join the little group around Lady Asaph, "are merely sore because I sent your ball flying into the blackberry brambles."

"Thorns all over my favorite breeches." Michael motioned to his legs.

Catherine covered her mouth. "*That's* what became of those."

"Did you think Michael had suddenly discovered good taste?" William grinned.

"I don't know why I put up with this family," Michael muttered.

"Because we feed you." Catherine playfully elbowed him.

"Thanks, Kitty." Michael ruffled her hair. "I would never have figured that out on my own."

"He's like one those stray dogs that follows you home," Catherine continued, warming to her theme, "and once you've given him a meal, keeps scratching on the kitchen door, and looking up at you with big mournful eyes."

"All *right*, Kitty," said Michael.

"Madness only runs in part of my family," William said softly to Geneviève. "My brother is quite sane, I assure you. And Michael isn't related at all."

"Third cousin twice removed." Michael pouted.

"By marriage," William corrected, his eyes not leaving Geneviève's. "I trust you had a pleasant afternoon?"

Geneviève had spent the remainder of the afternoon on her stomach on her bed, contemplating the relative merits of boiling him in oil as opposed to hanging him by his feet and hitting him with a spiked stick.

"Yes. Quite." Geneviève belatedly remembered that she was supposed to be flirting with him, and added, "I *especially* enjoyed the antiquities."

"Ah, so you like antiquities." Lady Asaph broke in, with a significant look at William. "How splendid, do tell me more."

Within ten minutes, Lady Asaph had deftly extracted the information that Geneviève had been born in France, raised in Rye, and didn't much care for turnips.

Catherine burst in. "Has Mother told you yet about the time William tried to tear up the floor of the gazebo with a pickax?"

* * *

"Miss de Bourbon." William pulled at his cravat, a growing annoyance in his eyes. "The statues in the courtyard appear to be exceptionally fine. Would you do me the honor of showing them to me?"

Geneviève's skin tingled with excitement at the invitation. Every sensible instinct in her body told her to decline. But there were certainly more than enough people about to chaperone them, Geneviève persuaded her sensible side. This was a perfect opportunity to put her plans for revenge into practice—what could be more romantic than a moonlit garden—and she'd be a fool not to leap at it.

"Yes, I'd like that," Geneviève responded with scarcely a moment's hesitation.

"—blood spurting everywhere. Wait, what did you say, dear?"

"I asked Miss de Bourbon if she would take a turn in the courtyard with me. She said yes. And I would like to make clear that I barely scratched his hand."

"The courtyard." Lady Asaph beamed. "What a good idea. I mean, you shall have to be chaperoned, of course. Catherine, darling, why don't you go with them."

"How can I *be* a chaperone when I *have* a chaperone?" Catherine protested.

Tapping her foot in impatience, Lady Asaph whispered something in Catherine's ear. "Oh, right." Catherine waggled her eyebrows meaningfully at her mother.

"Shall we?" William extended an arm to Geneviève.

Brother and sister exchanged a long look as they exited through the French doors onto the balcony. Catherine yawned ostentatiously and collapsed onto a stone bench. "It has been an awfully long day. I'll just sit down here and watch the stars, if you don't mind terribly."

Geneviève prayed she wasn't blushing as she caught William mouthing *thank you* to his sister.

Tucking Geneviève's arm more firmly through his, William led her down the three shallow steps into the moonlit garden.

# CHAPTER 35

Lord William Cabot
Paris, France

Geneviève cast about for something to say as they wandered towards the center of the courtyard.

William—no, she needed to think of him as Lord Cabot. He kept pace with her on the walkway. Geneviève forced herself to look up from her contemplation of four sets of toes and face her nemesis. Something about the angle of his head as he glanced down at her was so like the Sapphire Sphinx that it made Geneviève's heart contract. She forced a fixed smile onto her lips in the face of his quizzical gaze. Of course he looked like the Sapphire Sphinx. The blasted man *was* the Sapphire Sphinx. Geneviève hoped the crunching of gravel underfoot sufficiently masked the gritting of her teeth.

"Did you really duel with hedges?" asked Geneviève. She was strong, Geneviève reminded herself.

"Only because my father told me that they were dragons," Lord Cabot responded, with a grin that could melt stone. He waved his left hand in the direction of the shadowy clumps of shrubbery. "I assure you, your brother's garden is safe from me."

"A little hacking with a sword looks like it might do some of these plants good," Geneviève commented, stooping to touch a leaf on an overgrown rosebush. "Ouch!"

"Prickly things, aren't they?" Lord Cabot took the hand Geneviève was flapping about and turned it over to examine the pricked pad of her finger. His fingers burned against her wrist and palm.

"They have to protect themselves somehow." Geneviève wrenched her hand away.

"You sound like you empathize."

"My Aunt Abigail is a great cultivator of roses." Geneviève evaded the implied question and Lord Cabot's amused gaze, turning from the rosebush to wander along a small graveled path. She was doing quite well, she congratulated herself. She was keeping the conversation light, and his touch hadn't affected her at all. Or at least not that much. Oh, heavens, she hoped he hadn't felt the way her pulse was racing in her wrist.

"Perhaps I should speak to her about the removal of some thorns."

Forget touch. The hideous man didn't even need to touch her to send shivers down her spine.

"Shouldn't we look at some statues?" Geneviève suggested breathlessly. "After all, that is what you told your mother."

"Oh, that. I am sorry about inflicting my family on you like this."

Just because he sounded like a chastened schoolboy didn't mean she should feel sympathy for him, Geneviève told herself. It didn't change the way he had played with her affections. Bluebeard had probably had a mother, too.

"I think they're lovely," Geneviève said stoutly, and meant it.

"Most of the time," Lord Cabot replied wryly, glancing back to the balcony where Catherine was sitting with her head ostentatiously tilted up towards the night sky, "I would agree with you."

"You are lucky to have them."

Lord Cabot glanced down at her with too much understanding in his green eyes. "I am sorry about your parents. Truly sorry."

Geneviève shrugged uncomfortably. "We don't need to revisit that."

"But I think we do." William stopped as they rounded an over-grown bush and reached for Geneviève's hand. "We started off badly on the boat and I want to fix it."

"There's no need." Geneviève hastily shifted her hand out of reach. "You've been more than kind. Having us to see your antiquities, for example," she continued a little too brightly. "That was terribly, um, kind of you. So now that's all settled."

Clearly it wasn't. Lord Cabot moved closer. "What can I do to convince you I'm not an evil traitor?"

The bush prickled through the thin fabric of Geneviève's frock. When, she wondered indignantly, had she lost control of the conversation? She was supposed to flirt with him, he was supposed to fawn besottedly, and she was supposed to crush his hopes under her dainty slippered heel. Not *this*. His tangy cologne filled her nostrils, blotting out the scents of the garden, assaulting her with memory, weakening her with desire.

"I'm convinced," Geneviève blurted. He was so close that the ends of the starched fabric practically tickled the end of her nose. One more step and his knees would brush against hers.

The cravat receded. "Good."

Geneviève let herself look up. It wasn't one of her wiser decisions.

"I wouldn't want you to think ill of me," he said softly. His words stroked her like a gentle breeze. His hand moved to brush a lock of hair off her cheek. Slowly. Gently. His green eyes sought hers in a lingering caress as his head tilted towards hers.

"No." Geneviève yanked her head back so violently that her hair tangled in the branches of a bush. Her blue eyes were wide with panic. "No. I—I can't. I just can't."

Lord Cabot took a step back, hands in his pockets. "Why not?" he asked neutrally. "Do you still dislike me that much?"

Dislike. Oh goodness. What an inadequate term. She wanted to take him by the shoulders and shake him until his teeth rattled and then kiss him till they were both gasping, and he asked her if she *disliked* him? Geneviève hadn't the slightest notion what exactly she felt towards him—the English language didn't contain words enough to encapsulate the blizzard of emotions storming through her—but it certainly wasn't dislike.

"No," she croaked. "I don't dislike you."

Lord Cabot's face relaxed almost imperceptibly. "Then why…"

She could tell him the truth, Geneviève thought madly. She could call him to account for his actions and give him the chance to explain himself. She drank in the features of his face—the straight slope of his nose, the watchful green eyes, the clean angles of cheekbones and jaw. The Sapphire Sphinx unmasked.

The bracing memory of his deceit stiffened Geneviève's resolve to make him suffer as much as possible.

Casting her eyes to the side, she declared, with all the conviction she could force into it, "I love another."

His face paled, his eyes went wide only to narrow. "Who is he?"

"Please don't ask me that." Hugging herself, she offered, "I must keep his identity a secret."

Realization crossed his features. His shoulders sagged. "Tell me more about your perfect love."

"I never said he was perfect."

"He's not?" Lord Cabot sounded offended.

She stopped herself from sighing. Lord Cabot appeared to be jealous of the Sapphire Sphinx. The temptation to stomp like a toddler and shout at him grew with each passing moment. Forcing herself to relax, she batted her eyes. "You heard Miss Agnes. There's no such thing as a perfect man."

"What's wrong with him?" He came closer.

"He didn't trust me as he should." She glared at him.

Lord Cabot's mouth shut into a very tight line.

Geneviève was watching him closely. "Were you about to say something?"

Lord Cabot shrugged. "Merely that your secret love, whoever he may be, is a very lucky man. Shall we return to the others?"

The walk back across the garden was considerably quicker than the stroll out. Geneviève had to scurry to keep up with his brisk strides. Maybe it had to do with being out of breath, but victory didn't leave nearly as sweet a taste in Geneviève's mouth as she had anticipated. If he had ever really cared, he would never have given up that easily. Clearly, thought Geneviève savagely, she hadn't even been an infatuation.

Catherine looked up eagerly as Lord Cabot and Geneviève hove into view. "Did you have a nice—" she began but the phrase trailed off as she caught sight of her brother's stony face.

"I'll leave you here to get acquainted." Lord Cabot all but shook Geneviève's fingers off his arm, executed a bow in her general direction, and plunged through the French doors into the drawing room.

"What happened?" Catherine extended her arms to Geneviève. "Shall I skewer him until he apologize. He can be quite the bear. I've loads of embarrassing stories for ammunition."

"Oh, not him. The Sapphire Sphinx. He's the problem."

Catherine arched an eyebrow—she knew. Geneviève sighed. Of course his sister knew. She plopped onto the bench, her pride at her feet and divulged the events of the last month.

At long last, Catherine reached for Geneviève. "I'm so sorry. That's appalling. How could he let you think he was two people?" Catherine glowered in the direction of her brother.

"I feel an idiot for not having realized. If I hadn't been so convinced that he was utterly under Bonaparte's thumb…"

"It is a wonderful idea, isn't it?" Catherine covered her mouth. "But he *still* should have told you."

"What hurts the most is that he didn't trust me enough to tell me." Geneviève groaned. "Just now, when I told him I loved another, he could have made amends by simply saying—"

"It's me, or something like that." Catherine nodded.

Geneviève grinned despite herself.

"Oh no. That would have been far too easy. He's an absolute dear, and a wonderful brother, but he *is* a boy." Catherine shook her head in irritation. "He has delusions of authority. They all do. He thinks he always knows what's best for everyone and how to organize their lives."

"That's exactly the problem." Geneviève waved her hands about.

"He needs to be shown that he can't always organize everything for everyone."

Catherine looked gratified. "Oh, absolutely."

"Something must be done."

"I couldn't agree more." Catherine nodded emphatically. "They need to be taken down a peg or two occasionally. For the good of womankind."

Mary came outside, a hand on Geneviève's shoulder. "Geneviève, are you going to tell her?"

"Do you have a plan already? Oh, please tell." Catherine swished her long hair out of her face and leaned forward imploringly. "I won't utter a word."

# CHAPTER 36

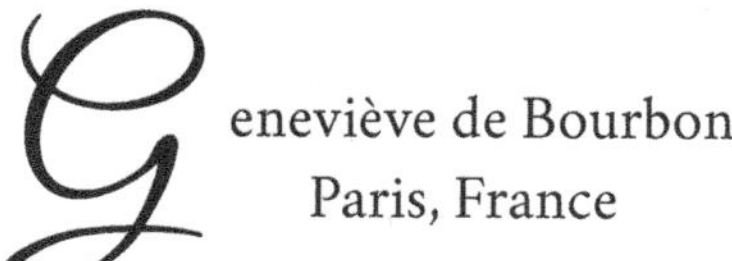

eneviève de Bourbon
Paris, France

Unbeknownst to either the Ministry of Police or the Sapphire Sphinx, in a large townhouse on the other side of the city, the three women at Hotel de Bourbon formed the Talisman Committee.

Considerable thought was expended as to how the illustrious career of the Talisman ought to begin. Miss Agnes, under whose high-necked bodice lurked the sort of bloodthirsty spirit that accounted watching gladiators being gored by lions as rather good fun, would be satisfied with nothing less than running through a Frenchman and hanging him by his feet from the blade of the guillotine.

Mary, after a startled look at Miss Agnes, suggested filching some files from Delaroche's office, a plan which was instantly voted down by both of the others. Geneviève dismissed it as insufficiently daring, Miss Agnes as boringly bloodless. Geneviève's plan A, that they sneak into the Temple prison in cunning disguises and liberate some deserving prisoners, was met with equal scorn. As were plan B, plan C, and even plan D, which involved dressing up in the clothes of the previous decade, dusting themselves all over with flour, and flitting about Bonaparte's bedside as the ghosts of murdered aristocrats.

"We don't have to do anything too spectacular," Mary pointed out, her hands outstretched between Geneviève and Miss Agnes. "After all, this is merely a calling card. Something to make the Minister of Police aware that he has a new adversary."

"A *better* adversary." Miss Agnes sniffed.

"Since our real mission is the retrieval of the Swiss gold," Mary continued, "Shouldn't we keep it simple?"

Geneviève sat bolt upright on the settee, blue eyes gleaming with mischief. "Why don't we sneak into his bedchamber and leave a note and a toy version of his Talisman on his pillow?"

Miss Agnes's thin lips, which had begun to move automatically into their sneer position, relaxed into speculation instead.

"I like it." Mary's voice rose at the end as if she was surprised by Geneviève's good idea.

Tapping her foot, Geneviève added, "We could leave a note saying we're responsible for the disappearance of the Swiss gold? We could leave it at the warehouse."

The idea passed the Committee of the Talisman by unanimous vote. It all seemed an excellent idea at the time, with even Miss Agnes deigning a rare nod of approval. Mary, the Talisman with the neatest handwriting, drew up the note to Delaroche. Miss Agnes then procured their costumes, a task accomplished with one quick raid on the grooms' quarters. Discovering the best time to enter Delaroche's lodgings was left to Geneviève, who struck up a conversation with Delaroche's groom as she waited for the de Bourbon carriage to be brought around after an evening party at the Tuileries. If he was nonplussed at being addressed by a lady, the groom failed to show it. He proved surprisingly helpful in apprising her of his master's schedule, repeating several times that Delaroche had an engagement outside of Paris on the evening of the thirtieth. Geneviève ought to have been pleased that it had been so easy. But by the time two days had passed, Geneviève found herself wishing she had been assigned something a little more, well, active. Something that would keep her mind off Lord Cabot.

This latter task wasn't in the least helped by the fact that Lady Asaph had enthusiastically adopted both Mary and Geneviève, and persisted, with significant sidelong glances at Geneviève, in relating many adorable tales of William's youth. Geneviève tried not to listen too eagerly but couldn't help herself. She could just see a miniature William jauntily leveling a sword at a yew bush, and from there it was only a short step to picturing the very devastatingly adult William facing off against Taunton.

If she was being honest with herself, it wasn't just in the presence of William's family members that memories plagued her. They leaped into her head when she was plotting with Miss Agnes, flitted in front of her when she was brushing her hair at her mirror, and positively taunted her as she lay unsleeping in bed. It was utterly infuriating to be sitting at the breakfast table, staring at the remains of a brioche, and to hear the whisper of the Sapphire Sphinx's voice in her ear and feel the brush of his hand across her cheek. And Geneviève's heart leaped painfully into her throat every time she saw a black cloak swishing down the street.

Why couldn't he leave her alone? Oh, but there was the rub—Lord Cabot, and his alter ego, the Sapphire Sphinx, *were* leaving her alone. When she and Mary called on Lady Asaph and Catherine for tea, he kept scrupulously to his study. He stayed towards the other side of the salon at Mme Bonaparte's receptions. When she loitered in the corridors of the Tuileries on her way back from her weekly English lesson with Hortense, he whisked so rapidly around a corner that all she saw was the glint of a familiar golden head. Nor had there been any midnight visitations from the cloaked and masked form of the Sapphire Sphinx.

This was what she'd wanted—she thought. She only had to see him once more, one meeting to crow over her triumph, and then he'd flee back to England in embarrassment, and she would be done with him forever. No more Lord William Cabot. No more Sapphire Sphinx.

Geneviève scowled at yet another mutilated brioche.

On the day the Swiss gold was due to arrive, Geneviève paced back and forth in front of her window, watching as the streaks of sunset wended their painfully slow way across the sky. Geneviève began dressing a good hour before the time they had appointed to leave, drawing out the process as long as she possibly could.

Binding her breasts proved much more difficult than Geneviève had imagined. Geneviève scowled at the long strip of white linen that had untied itself—again. After another three tries and several cries of pain, the binding found its way onto the fire. After all, the shirt was loose and billowy, and maybe if she hunched over a bit, no one would notice.

Wriggling her nose in distaste, she shrugged into the grimy trousers—their color was indeterminate and might have been anything from black to brown originally—and pulled the coarse beige linen shirt over her head. It smelled regrettably of stableboy.

Fully garbed, down to a pair of muddy brown boots, Geneviève found herself once again without anything to do—and with an offensive stench. Next time, she resolved grimly, they would go disguised as something more glamourous. Something less smelly. Maybe they should have pretended to be ladies of the night going to meet a client.

"Ready?" Mary rapped on the door as Geneviève glowered at an infuriating streak of orange in the darkening sky.

"An hour ago."

Mary's lips quirked as she looked pointedly at the grimy men's clothes and the streaks of soot adorning Geneviève's face. "I guessed as much. I just spoke to Miss Agnes, and she says she'll meet us back here at eleven so we can all leave for the warehouse together."

"She's not going with us to leave the note?" Geneviève scraped back her hair with one hand and felt around on her dressing table for a ribbon with the other.

"No." Mary took the ribbon from her and began tightly winding the mass of dark curls so they would fit under a knit cap. "She's saving herself for the real mission. when I went in, she was skewering pillows with her parasol."

"Some chaperone."

"Fortunately for us," Mary countered wryly, knotting the ribbon. "I'm going to get dressed—are you sure you're all right?"

"Just fidgety." Geneviève demonstrated the proof of her words by resuming her pacing, scattering flecks of dried mud across the carpet. "But I'll be *perfectly* happy tomorrow once Lord Cabot is gnashing his teeth in frustration because we bested him."

"Aren't we supposed to be besting Bonaparte?" Mary inquired delicately.

"Two birds. One stone."

Mary shook her head and headed for the door. "I'll be ready to leave in five minutes," she reassured her cousin.

Geneviève glanced at the clock. Nearly half past seven.

# CHAPTER 37

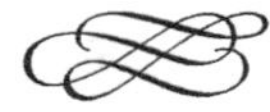

*L*ord William Cabot
Paris, France

At half past seven, in a small house across the city, Adam poked his head around the door of William's study.

"Would you like some tea?"

"You can come in, you know," William said crossly, pushing back his chair from the desk. "I'm not going to bite."

"Do you promise?" Adam pushed the door the rest of the way open. William kicked a chair in his direction. Since the floor of the study was covered by a Persian rug, the chair didn't go awfully far, but Adam took the point and the chair. "I thought you were going to skewer Michael with your butter knife tonight at dinner."

"Well… Michael." William shrugged as though that explained it. "Brandy?"

"Thank you." Adam accepted a snifter. "Why don't you just talk to her?"

William stiffened, the brandy decanter poised over Adam's glass. "To whom?"

Adam gave him a look. "The Queen of Sheba, who else?" William focused on pouring the amber liquid. "Geneviève, of course."

"Oh." William corked the brandy decanter and sat back in his chair. "Darts?" he suggested hopefully.

Adam, however, was not to be deterred. "You are going to do something about her after tonight's mission, aren't you? I don't really care what, but you've been increasingly unpleasant to live with."

"Thanks."

"Think nothing of it. Well?"

"I hadn't really thought about it," William grumbled, not meeting Adam's eye. That was the problem with friends who had known him since he was just out of the nursery. It was far too easy for them to detect lies—and they had no shame about pointing them out. William had rehearsed about twenty variants of a speech along the lines of, "Only the need to save England prevented me from revealing to you…" No, he had scrapped that one as too pompous. "By the way, thought you might like to know, I'm the Sapphire Sphinx. Will you marry me?" seemed a bit too offhand. And they just got worse from there.

*Marry.* The pause for the tenth time that day. He'd sworn off marriage but the past few days without Geneviève had felt more like purgatory than he'd like to admit. Even today, William more fully understood why Blakeney relinquished his career. William couldn't imagine leaving his wife's side for the dark alleys of France.

"I was thinking about doing a bit of reconnoitering before tonight's mission," William announced loudly. True, Adam was only two feet away, but raising his voice helped to drown out all of that silent skepticism radiating from his friend.

William hauled himself out of his chair. He hadn't really considered reconnoitering before, but now that he'd declared the intent to do so, it did seem rather a good idea. It would give him something to do, keep his mind off Geneviève, and get him in the right mood for tonight. "I might drop by Delaroche's lodgings and see if there's anything about the gold in his secret files there."

"The ones he keeps under his pillow?" Adam asked, diverted. "How such an accomplished agent chooses the most idiotic hiding places—"

"Shocking, isn't it?" William agreed heartily, seizing the change of subject and making a rapid dash towards the door before Adam could remember his initial purpose. "The desk drawer in his office and under his pillow. It takes all the challenge out of it. I'll meet you back here by ten or so."

"Anything else you need me to do?" Adam asked.

"Just dissuade my mother if she has any ideas of coming along tonight. Other than that, I can't think of anything that could go wrong," William said breezily, and exited to undertake the calming, and familiar, task of burgling Delaroche's lodgings. He glanced at the clock, just past seven thirty. He could easily be there within the next half an hour and back by ten.

By eight o'clock, the Ministry of Police's empty lodgings had become an unexpectedly lively place. Perched with one leg on the lintel of Delaroche's windowsill, William froze at the sound of a door being eased open. Trying to ignore the discomfort in his leg muscles, William watched as the door swung open in a slow semicircle and a dark-clad frame slid into the small room.

Delaroche—no. The figure, even if somewhat hard to make out in the dark room, was clearly too small to be Delaroche, weedy little man though the Frenchman was. Besides, why would Delaroche be slinking around his own bedroom? The man was odd, and probably mildly mad, but William still couldn't see him prowling around his own darkened room for fun. He preferred to prowl around other people's darkened rooms for amusement, a pastime William had to admit he rather sympathized with.

The small figure stole towards the bed, hips swaying. Hips doing what? Something about the way the prowler was moving nagged at William's memory. Heedless of caution, William leaned sharply forward. Intent on tiptoeing, the intruder didn't notice. The very *female* intruder—by Jove, it was Geneviève.

Devil take it, Geneviève was in Delaroche's bedchamber. He raised the window sash and glared at her. She turned and tripped over a leather bed slipper lying on the floor beside his bed. She hit the dusty ground, her gaze traveling up from his scuffed black boots.

"What are you doing here?" she demanded, brushing her dusty hands against her knees.

"I might ask the same of you." He stepped away from the window with a swirl of black fabric. "You don't give up easily, do you?"

"Not on the things that matter," she bit out.

"If you're looking for Delaroche's secret files"—he leaned towards Geneviève—"I'll give you a little hint. He keeps them under his pillow."

"Right," Geneviève leaned back so far her head was nearly level with her shoulders. "Thank you."

"Don't you want to look at them?" He reached over Geneviève to the pillow. She tried to lean back further, lost her balance, and toppled backwards onto the bed. It was a disaster. Not only was she sprawled flat on her back, with her bottom half off the bed and her trouser-clad legs flung apart, his hand trapped under her head.

Geneviève's wide eyes flew to William's face.

He smiled as she inhaled. His hand turned to cup her head, tangling in her hair, massaging her scalp.

"This is not happening," bleated Geneviève.

"Yes." Her face so close he could feel the gentle puff of her breath across his lips. She smelled of lavender. "This is not happening."

# CHAPTER 38

Geneviève de Bourbon
Paris, France

But it *was* happening, and worse, Geneviève wanted him. His lips reached hers, and reality disappeared in a floating mist of taste and touch and scent. Unthinking, Geneviève lifted her arms to clasp tightly about his neck. They kissed with the hunger of separated souls, lips slanting together, tongues twining, bodies pressing together. William's hand slid under Geneviève's back, molding her to him.

Geneviève gave a little cry, kissing him back hungrily. Just one last memory to story up to savor on all those long, empty nights ahead, knowing this would be the first and last time, the only time she'd feel his lips, his caress, his strong body against hers—that this wasn't supposed to be happening, but it was. The crisp brush of his hair against her sensitive fingertips, the flick of his tongue around the curves of her lips, the warm pressure of his hand along her spine.

His lips left Geneviève's to trail along her cheek, down the curve of her chin. And froze—he sniffed. "What is that smell?"

"Don't breathe, William," she said drunk with lust.

He stiffened and bit out, "What did you say?"

"I said—oh." Geneviève gulped.

William gave her a little shake. "How long have you known?"

"A little while."

"That night in the garden—you knew?"

Geneviève could barely nod.

"Damn you, Geneviève." He jumped back. "All the while I was eating my heart out—with jealousy of my own bloody self, no less. You *knew?*"

"I wanted—" Geneviève licked her swollen lips. "I wanted you to know how it felt. To be played with like that. I'm sorry."

"You're sorry? *Now* you're sorry?" He paced in a tight circle in front of her.

She hugged herself and sat on the edge of the bed. "I don't know why I should apologize. *You* repudiated *me,* if you remember correctly."

"Only because I had to." He held up a finger.

Geneviève took a step forward, hands on her hips. "And then you flirted with me the next day."

"It made sense at the time."

"For all I knew, you were just playing with me out of some… some malicious whim."

"You were never a whim."

"It certainly doesn't feel that way. For all I knew you might have been the sort of cad who enjoys driving women mad just for the sheer joy of it. You told me I was an *infatuation.*"

"I had good reasons."

"All right, then. What are they? Or do you need time to invent some?"

"It's none—" He stopped himself. With a wave of his hand, indicating the room, William whispered, "Delaroche has a list."

"Under the pillow," her tone was dark.

William's head snapped down towards Geneviève. "No. A list of prospective agents and targets."

"Targets?"

"Sir Percy Blakeney was on the list."

"And?" Geneviève sniffed.

With a grim face, William added, "Because he's married, his wife is on the list. If she were to set foot on French soil she would be followed. But it's much worse than that. There's a double agent. Someone is betraying England to Bonaparte—"

"She's not safe even in England." She nodded but the stiff posture and hard frown didn't budge. After a moment of silence, she held up a hand. "You played games with my heart because another man's wife is on a list? You made my life agony for *that*?"

"I couldn't tell you, Geneviève," William said quietly. "There were too many lives at stake."

"You could have just left me alone. Or you could have trusted me. I wouldn't have told."

"I'm sorry."

"I'm going home," she said thickly.

William immediately stepped forward. "I'll see you back."

"No." Geneviève shook her head as she flung her legs recklessly over the side of the window.

He reached for her just as she cried out—a pair hands closed around her midriff and jerked her down from the window.

William followed after her as a phalanx of military men materialized out of the darkness. The brass on their uniforms might have been somewhat dull in the dark, but it didn't take much moonlight to see that their muskets were primed and ready.

A short, bandy-legged man strutted through the semicircle of musket points. "The Sapphire Sphinx, I presume?" Delaroche sneered.

"Unhand her," William snapped.

He knew he had made a tactical error when Delaroche's smile widened. "Such a touching tete-a-tete," the little man crooned. "And so very convenient."

Fifteen men. William rapidly assessed he situation. Fifteen burly infantrymen crowded into the little alleyway behind Delaroche's lodgings. Of those fifteen, three were occupied in subduing Geneviève. She rammed into one of her captors, sending him reeling. Another darted back and forth, trying to avoid Geneviève's flailing feet as he wound a rope around her wrists. A third still held her around the waist, but his nose oozed blood onto his white cross straps from a well-placed butt of Geneviève's head.

Which only left twelve infantrymen pointing muskets at William.

"Move," cautioned Delaroche, "and my men will shoot the charming Miss de Bourbon."

Twelve muskets hastily shifted target.

"You're warring on women now, Delaroche?" William spat at the ground. "Needed to find someone smaller than you to beat up?"

"Insults will not alter your predicament, my friend." Delaroche smirked. "You fell into my trap, just as I knew you would."

"Trap?" Geneviève gasped.

"Trap," Delaroche repeated smugly. "Every man has a weakness, Monsieur Sapphire Sphinx. For some, it is drink. For others, it is cards. For—"

"Is the treatise on human nature really quite necessary?" William glanced sidelong at Geneviève. The rope had finally made its way around her arms.

"For you," Delaroche continued, as though William had never spoken, "it is a woman. That woman."

"She has nothing to do with this, Delaroche."

"Oh no, Monsieur Sapphire Sphinx? She led you to me. Just as I knew she would."

"No!" Geneviève squirmed in her captor's grasp. "I wouldn't—" Her words ended abruptly as a heavy hand clamped down over her mouth. A masculine yelp followed as the guard snatched his bitten palm away from her mouth.

William forced his body to relax, forced himself to wave a languid hand in Geneviève's direction. "Quite a fuss over a bit of fluff."

"A bit of fluff?"

William studiedly avoided Geneviève's eyes, hoping to hell that she would realize what he was trying to do. "A light-skirt," he clarified, using his best man-about-town air of bored sophistication, "a mere spot of dalliance. Don't you French know something about that sort of thing? Or did you lose your talent for amours along with your monarchy?"

"A mere spot of dalliance," Delaroche repeated, turning the unfamiliar English words scornfully on his tongue. "Or so you claim. We have ways of testing the truth of your words."

A heavy hand crashed against Geneviève's face, snapping her head back. Geneviève gasped in surprise and pain. Metal gleamed at Geneviève's throat. A knife.

"He is under orders to use it," Delaroche said softly. "A bit of fluff you say?"

A strangled yelp emerged from Geneviève's throat as the knife pressed against her skin, raising a thin red welt.

"What do you want?" William asked grimly.

"That, Monsieur Sapphire, ought to be obvious."

"Not to all of us," William snapped.

"Your confession and surrender."

"Don't!" Geneviève cried out. "Don't do it. You've made a mistake, Monsieur Delaroche. He doesn't care for me. Really. It's not worth— keep your bloody hand off my mouth."

"On one condition." William's voice rang out over Geneviève's cries. The soldiers holding her froze. "You leave the girl alone. Otherwise there's no deal. No confession. No surrender. I want your solemn word, Delaroche, that the girl will be left here. *Unharmed.*"

Delaroche nodded. "Unharmed." The knife fell away from Geneviève's throat, and the hands yanking her bound arms behind her back slackened.

The little Frenchman's eyes gleamed with triumph. "Your mask, Sapphire."

William's hands went to the lacings of his black mask.

"No!" Geneviève protested, as his gloved fingers plucked at the knot. "You mustn't."

The mask tumbled to the ground.

All eyes were riveted on William's pale face in the moonlight.

"You can still run!" Geneviève cried desperately. "You don't have to do this William."

One by one, his black gloves joined his mask on the ground. His long, slim fingers, now bare, went to the frogs holding his cloak closed. Sweeping off the garment, William sketched an ironic bow.

"Here I am, Delaroche. Unmasked, unveiled, and at your service. Now, release the girl."

With a snap of Delaroche's fingers, Geneviève tumbled, still bound, to the dirt. Delaroche wound a rope around William's outstretched wrists. Fifteen musket-bearing soldiers closed ranks around them, their high-crowned hats blocking William from Geneviève's sight.

"You won't get away with this," she railed at the row of blue-clad backs, propelling herself unevenly forward across the ground. "The Talisman will rescue him and see you hanged!"

Preoccupied with William, no one paid the slightest bit of attention, except one infantryman towards the edge of the group, who turned back and jerked a finger at Geneviève. "What about the girl, sir?"

Delaroche shrugged. "Leave her to the dogs."

As the booted feet receded into the distance, Geneviève could hear Delaroche utter, "We have much to talk about, you and I, Monsieur Cabot. And you *will* talk."

William never looked back.

# CHAPTER 39

$\mathscr{L}$ord William Cabot
Paris, France

Geneviève stared after the retreating party of soldiers, her indignant cries frozen on her lips, the enormity of the situation only gradually beginning to dawn. She half expected to hear the sounds of a fray, to see a black-garbed figure break away from the group and dart for the shadows. But he didn't.

"Geneviève." Mary bent anxiously over her. "Lean forward so I can untie you."

Geneviève stilled, shocked at both Mary's appearance and what just happened. "They have William."

"I know." Mary tugged at the tail of the roughhewn piece of rope. "I saw."

"Why didn't you do anything?" Geneviève twisted towards Mary, chafing her sore wrists as Mary pulled the rope free.

"There were *fifteen* of them." Mary thriftily coiled the rope and looped it around her arm. "I considered going for help but it seemed more prudent to wait and see what happened before charging off."

Prudent. The word tasted sour on Geneviève's tongue. "Well, now you know." Geneviève stumbled to her feet. "Let's go after them."

Mary grabbed her by the wrist, making Geneviève wince as her hand closed around skin chafed by the rope. "Not alone," Mary protested. "We'll be no use to him alone. They'll simply capture us and use us against him."

"As they already did." Geneviève's face twisted. "But we can't leave him there. We can't. Mary, the *Ministry of Police* has him. Do you know what they do to people? There's no time—"

"Stop that." Mary shook Geneviève sharply. "What good do you think you'll do him running off after him alone?"

Geneviève stared at Mary with wide, horrified eyes. "What would you have me do? Sit and wait for him to be executed? I'd rather be caught and tortured."

"We will save him." Mary took a deep breath, her own face pale and miserable in the moonlight. "We will. You wanted to be the Talisman, Geneviève? Now's your chance. You need to think like a spy. Not like the heroine of a silly horrid novel running pell-mell into disaster. Show some *sense*. We need reinforcements and we need a plan."

Geneviève drew a shuddering breath.  "His family. We can go to Lord Cabot's townhouse. There must be some members of his league there who can help us."

Geneviève didn't waste any more breath; she set off at a run. They both knew the reputation of the Ministry of Police for cruelty. Abuse, torture, even mention of the dark arts. Tales of English agents captured and never seen again. Or worse—released with minds as broken as their bodies, babbling like toddlers as they limped along on crumpled limbs.

They ran down twisted streets, past drunken carousers, through puddles of filth. Mary slipped in a patch of mud, and Geneviève yanked her upright and hauled her forward.

Hideous thoughts chased Geneviève. He'd been right in trying to end their relationship. Her involvement had been fatal for him. If he had never met her, he would still be free, not in the hands of a fanatical maniac intent on torturing him for both professional, and apparently personal, reasons. She hadn't realized that Delaroche's groom was parting with information far too freely. Even a child could have realized it was a trap. But no. She, Geneviève, in all her hubris, had assumed their instant success was due to her innate knack for espionage, not because she was an unresisting pawn in the hands of the French Ministry of Police. Rubbing salt into her emotional wound, she'd kept William there arguing and bickering while the men gathered.

Being the Talisman had seemed such a grand idea, thumbing her nose at William and a Revolutionary France all at once. She'd never thought of the consequences. She, Geneviève, had known the risks William ran as the Sapphire Sphinx, and set out deliberately to thwart him. She ought to have foreseen the dangers. She ought to have *known.*

While her lungs twisted, and her leg muscles ached, Geneviève played her painful game of *If.* If she had only told him in the garden that she knew who he was, and that she liked—no, she *loved* him anyway.

If she could only have him back, she would beg him to forgive her. She would never ever quibble with him over trivialities again. She would revel in the luxury of just gazing at his face. And it wouldn't even matter if he loved her back, just so long as he was safe and well.

Geneviève clutched a tattered image of William, his green eyes glinting with mischief, his mobile lips twisted with amusement. William with his clever turns of phrase and moments of disarming boyishness. William taking her hand and teasing her about thorns.

They had only been to Lord Cabot's house once before, for tea with Lady Asaph, and even Mary's excellent sense of direction wasn't enough to keep them from becoming hopelessly muddled in the tangled streets of Paris. A dangerously long amount of time elapsed before the two scrambled up the steps to Lord Cabot's front door. Geneviève pounded anxiously with the big metal knocker, knocking over and over until the door jerked open. Geneviève tumbled over the threshold.

The silver-haired butler sniffed as though he smelled something nasty and nudged her recumbent form with one polished toe. "Tradesmen to the back," he said with disdain.

The heavy wooden door began to close.

"Who is it, Gideon?" Lady Asaph's voice carried through the hall-way, and in the crack of the door left open, Geneviève could just see her standing at the top of the stairs, like a guardian angel in robe and ribboned nightcap.

"It's Geneviève de Bourbon and Mary Wooliston," called out Geneviève, struggling to her feet.

"We're sorry to call at such a late hour," Mary added politely.

"Do move away, Gideon, and let them in," Lady Asaph declared as she hurried down the stairs. She gasped as her eyes raked Geneviève's and Mary's outlandish attire.

"It's William." Geneviève rushed forward and reached for Lady Asaph's hand. "They've taken him. The Ministry of Police."

In the light of her candle, Lady Asaph's face went gray. She put the candle down abruptly on the newel of the stairs. Lifting her chin, she straightened her posture. "Well, we shall just have to rescue him then, shan't we?"

"Mother?" Catherine tumbled down the stairs in a flurry of white linen flounces. "Is something the matter? Oh, Geneviève."

Michael and Adam had filtered into the foyer from a door down the hall, and the form of Lord Asaph could be seen at the top of the stairs. Lady Asaph set her jaw in a way that reminded Geneviève painfully of William and looked around at the expectant faces. "William has been taken by the Ministry of Police. Asaph—"

The marquess didn't have to wait for his wife to finish the sentence. "I'll go to Whitworth at the embassy straightaway."

"Thank you." The marquess and marchioness exchanged a look that made Geneviève's throat go tight.

"What happened?" Catherine scurried across the hall to Geneviève. "Did the mission go awry—what was William doing there?"

"Mission? What mission?" As the marquess accepted his hat and coat from Gideon and hastily departed, Lady Asaph turned her attention back to Geneviève and to Catherine in her night dress. "Catherine Anne Cabot, put on a dressing gown at once."

Her words had somewhat the reverse of the desired effect. Both Michael and Adam instantly snapped to attention.

Michael's jaw plummeted. "Zounds, Kitty."

Adam had the grace to look embarrassed.

"You clearly already know about this so-called mission." Lady Asaph narrowed her eyes at her daughter.

"But—"

Lady Asaph pointed to the stairs. "Go."

Catherine went.

"There's no point to us all standing about like this," the marchioness said with a huff. "Let's all go sit down in the drawing room. Adam, dear, have Gideon bring us some tea—we're going to need something to fortify us for the evening's activities. Geneviève, would you like to explain what happened?"

Like a well-disciplined army, they all followed Lady Asaph into the drawing room while Geneviève explained the plan to beat William to the gold, leaving out her motivation and their argument.

"It was an excellent plan. I would have done the same myself." Seating herself in a large brocaded chair at the front of the room, Lady Asaph said briskly, "That's all neither here nor there. The important thing is getting William out. Adam?"

"Yes, Lady Asaph?"

"Where will they have taken him?"

With a grave nod, Adam rubbed his neck. "Delaroche has an interrogation chamber he uses for important prisoners. He'll put William in a cell for a few hours, let him stew, and then transfer him to the interrogation chamber. None of the rooms of that level of the ministry have windows, so there's no breaking in that way."

"Could we infiltrate the guards?" Geneviève wrung her hands and paced behind the sofa. "Knock them over the head, take their uniforms, that sort of thing?"

Adam shook his head. "I wouldn't recommend it. There are too many of them."

Catherine barreled through the door, hastily dressed in a dark, high necked gown with all the buttons in the wrong holes. "Have I missed anything?"

"We're trying to rescue your brother." Lady Asaph motioned to the sofa.

Catherine rushed to the furniture. "Oh, what about bashing the guards over their heads—"

"You're a bit late." Michael looked her up and down, then, as if relieved to see the old, fully-clothed Catherine back, relaxed in his chair. "Miss de Bourbon has already tried that one."

"Do you have a better idea?" Catherine reached for Geneviève.

Lady Asaph narrowed her eyes. "Now is not the time to bicker. Ah, the tea is here. Catherine, why don't you pour?"

"I do have an idea, actually," Michael said, with a lofty look at Catherine, who was scowling over the tea. "Adam and I could go to the ministry and pretend to turn ourselves in. Then we can turn on the guards and—"

"Bash them over their heads?" finished Catherine, handing him a cup of tea.

"It sounds too uncertain," Mary broke. Even wearing offensively dirty men's clothing and a penciled-on mustache, she still somehow contrived to look neat and composed. "It's too likely that they would secure you, leaving us with three people to rescue instead of one. I believe we need to move away from the whole subject of bashing and think of something a bit more subtle."

"Infiltration," blurted Geneviève. The polite trappings of the tea party grated on her nerves. "Who could we disguise ourselves as?"

Michael and Adam spoke at once, sparking Catherine to join in.

"Stop." Geneviève shouted, "Let's just think of something, for heaven's sake. Haven't you rescued people before?"

Adam shook his head. "Only from the Bastille. We've never tried to get anyone out of Delaroche's lair."

On that deflating note, Lord Asaph entered. It was plain to see from the droop of his shoulders that his own task had been equally fruitless.

"Whitworth was no help," he said wearily. "He had some sort of row with Bonaparte the other night—over Malta, he said. He was all but packing his own bags when I called. There's nothing he can do for William."

"So we are on our own," said Lady Asaph. "As we expected."

The marquess took her hand and squeezed it. "As we expected, my dear." He cast a keen look at Adam. "I suppose this Delaroche chap won't be susceptible to bribery."

"Not a chance of it, sir."

"I feared as much. There's nothing worse than an incorruptible madman."

Mary's lashes lifted over clear gray eyes. "There might be another solution, sir. Geneviève, do you remember the soot on our teeth?"

Geneviève nodded hesitantly, trying to figure out what Mary could mean by it. "Yes, of course. When we used to—oh, servants."

"Could you enlighten the rest of us?" Michael asked.

"Do you want to use servants to storm the ministry and rescue William?" Catherine looked up interested from her cup of tea. "That would be splendid."

"No." Geneviève shook her head so rapidly she knocked off her cap. "We could be the servants. Surely someone must clean the Ministry. And who would ever look at a charwoman with a bucket? Mary. You're brilliant."

"An excellent idea." Lady Asaph gripping her armchair was the only evidence of her concern. "You're quite right. Nobody ever looks closely at staff. Adam, dear, you can forge us some sort of pass, can't you?"

"I do have a copy of Delaroche's seal," Adam admitted, "but surely, you can't be thinking of going yourself?"

The room broke into an alarming hullabaloo as Lord Asaph, Adam and Michael tried to remonstrate with Lady Asaph and Geneviève— as Geneviève quickly made quite clear that the only way to prevent her going was to lock her in a tower without doors or windows, of which there were few in the vicinity. Michael kept insisting that as William's best friend, he really ought to go. The marquess thumped for his paternal privileges and Adam's usually quiet voice rose to unusual levels as he reminded them all that only he actually knew where William was being kept.

"You would all make appalling women." Lady Asaph's commanding voice cut through the babble. "And if Geneviève and I are caught—yes, I do admit the possibility—they are far more likely to deal leniently with us than with you."

"Besides." Mary said coolly, "Someone still needs to intercept the Swiss gold."

"Oh hell." Michael groaned. "The Swiss gold."

"The Talisman will steal the gold just as we planned," Mary said firmly. "With the Sapphire Sphinx incarcerated, there's all the more need for the Talisman. But if Geneviève is rescuing Lord Cabot, we need a replacement for her."

Michael nodded, hair flopping up and down over his brow. "Count me in."

"And me," Catherine chimed in.

"You." Lady Asaph stood with a snap. "Are staying home. One child in the hands of the French is more than enough for any mother to have to bear. Geneviève and I will rescue William. Adam, I believe you should come along with us as a guide. Michael, Mary and Asaph will intercept the Swiss gold. Shall we?"

The entire party surged to their feet, shoving teacups back on the tray and quibbling over details. Geneviève declared her intent to get clothes from the servants' quarters. Mary directed a footman to take a note to Miss Agnes to alert her to join them at Lord Cabot's house— and Catherine's voice rose in agitated protest.

"But Mama…"

"No buts, Catherine."

Catherine pressed her lips together. "I'm not going to waste time by teasing to come along. But you've all forgotten something. How are we going to get William out of Paris?"

Michael dropped his teacup. The point was so simple, and so essential, that Geneviève couldn't believe that none of them had thought of it. From the looks of stupefaction on the faces of William's family and friends, none of them had considered it either. Perhaps, thought Geneviève rapidly, they could secrete William in the Hotel de Bourbon till the hullabaloo quieted down and the French agents had some other poor hero to persecute.

Mary smiled. "There is a certain gentleman of our acquaintance who possesses both a carriage and a boat, which I believe he will be more than happy to place at our disposal."

"Taunton!" exclaimed Geneviève.

"The very one," agreed Mary. "If someone would be so kind as to remind him of some papers of his I hold, I have no doubt he'll be agreeable."

"Give me his direction, and I'll see to him." Lord Asaph strode across the room to Mary.

Mary held up a hand. "It might be wise to take the precaution of replacing Taunton's coachman and sending some of our own men ahead to Calais to secure the boat. I wouldn't trust Mr. Taunton's word."

Michael, for once all seriousness, yanked the bellpull. "William's coachman can take care of the carriage, and Gideon and five of the footmen can ride ahead for the boat. I'll speak to them directly."

"Can we go now?" prompted Geneviève, halfway out the door.

Following her, Lady Asaph stuck her head around the door to the drawing room one last time.

"Have the carriage brought to the Hotel de Bourbon," instructed Lady Asaph. "If these French have any sense, they'll be watching this house. I don't think they have much in the way of sense, but we can't rely on that. We'll meet you there by one. If we're not there..."

Geneviève hurried ahead of Lady Asaph towards the servants' quarters, blocking out her last words. That the plan might go awry was not to be thought of. She could not bear the thought any more than she could bear to think of what Delaroche might be doing to William at this very moment.

# CHAPTER 40

$\mathcal{L}$ord William Cabot
Paris, France

Booted feet slapped to a stop outside the door of William's cell. Levering himself on his bound wrists, he wriggled to a standing position from the floor where the guards had thrown him with unnecessary force several hours before. He had informed them that the use of that much force was a waste of their energies, but they had just grunted in response to his professional advice. They had also proved churlish in not giving him an opportunity for an escape ploy in which they bent over to untie him and he bashed them over the head with his bound wrists, then stole their clothes. A pity, that. It had worked so well in 1801. Maybe the word had spread. At any rate, they had avoided that prospect by simply declining to untie him. So William had spent the past several hours reclining, still bound, on the straw-scattered floor, his mind turning anxiously elsewhere. Not to Delaroche and the tortures the disturbed little man was arranging for him, but to Geneviève, lying bound and helpless on the cobblestones outside Delaroche's lodging.

A key squeaked in the lock. The door shuddered. "Open it, you fools," a voice thundered.

"It's stuck, sir." Someone's voice quavered.

A very loud curse from the other side of the door, and then the door shuddered again. Two sentries tumbled to the floor. Behind them stood Delaroche. Small and skinny, dressed all in black like a cut-rate Oliver Cromwell, he strutted forward in boots that could use a polish. William hopped forward on his hobbled legs and executed what he hoped was a mocking bow.

"So." Delaroche snarled. "We meet at last."

"Actually." William shrugged. "I believe we were first introduced at Mme Bonaparte's salon, if I remember correctly."

"Your powerful friends cannot help you here. You are in *my* domain." Delaroche laughed.

"You should really get that rattle in your throat looked at." William *tsked*. "It must be from this loafing about in drafty dungeons. Terrible for your health, you know."

"It is *your* health you should fear for." The evil laughter that was far too dramatic grated on William's nerves. His neck hurt from trying to keep an eye on Delaroche as the man paced in circles around him, his boots crunching on the straw and debris scattered about the floor.

Delaroche strode on bandy legs to the door, clapped his hands together, and bellowed, "Prepare the interrogation chamber."

"The regular interrogation chamber, sir?" One guard ventured kept to the other side of the stone doorframe.

"Oh no." Delaroche unleashed another of his humorless laughs. "Take him to the extra special interrogation chamber."

It didn't raise William's spirits that the guard himself blanched at the suggestion.

Down several flights of stairs, nestled in a catacomb of underground cells, Delaroche flung open the door his special interrogation chamber with pride. His guards shoved him in. He skidded across the straw on the floor. This chamber was the sort of thing whispered from agent to agent, and some had even speculated on breaking into it as part of their what-can-we-do-to-annoy-the-Ministry-of-Police campaign. But they had never gotten around to it. And William had always, in the back of his mind, assumed that the whole special interrogation chamber was most likely a rumor fabricated to terrify the enemies of the Republic.

William should have known better. He waved a hand at the skull standing in pikes around the walls. "Friends of yours?"

"No," Delaroche bit out. "But they'll soon be friends of yours."

William was also running out of dazzling wit in what looked like an increasingly bleak situation. While the skulls might be a bit dusty, the extensive collection of torture tools arrayed about the room gleamed sharp and clean. Delaroche must have scoured the dungeons of castles across the breadth of Europe to acquire his toys, which looked like they included not only the full collection of the Marquis de Sade, but a representative sampling of the best the Inquisition had to offer. In his quick sweep of the room, William noted no fewer than two iron maidens, thumbscrews in ten different sizes, and a deluxe rack. Delaroche greeted each implement of torture personally, but he stopped by each one to touch spikes and grind levers with macabre tenderness.

Across the room, Delaroche carefully eased a double-headed ax onto a specially designed stand that showed off both blades to their best advantage. "Where shall we begin?"

Strutting toward William, Delaroche crossed his arms across his chest. "Something appropriate, something tasteful. Torture is an art, you know. A skill that must be practiced with care and finesse. What is it that you use in your English prisons? The rack? Your fists?"

"We use a little thing called due process."

Delaroche shrugged. "Whatever that is, it is the work of amateurs to use the same instrument for all crimes. Here, we very carefully match the punishment to the crime."

"How very refined."

"Your compliments will not help you, Cabot. I could give you a painful poison in that tea you English love so well, nothing that will kill you—no, no—but something that will make you writhe with pain and beg to confess. Or I could cut off an appendage for every enemy of the state you stole from Mme Guillotine."

"Why not start with my head?"

While Delaroche vacillated among his toys, William once again twisted his wrists to test the slack in his bonds. There wasn't any. It could have been worse, though. At least they had bound his wrists in front of him instead of behind. If Delaroche would come close enough, he had the chance of mustering enough force to strike him a blow on the head, something the Assistant Minister of Police was clearly not expecting. He'd follow that up with a kick, but his feet were tied tightly enough that in the attempt he would more likely bowl himself over than his adversary.

"Ah, I have it." Delaroche sneered. "Since you are so fond of the company of the fairer sex, we shall start with an introduction to the lady in the corner."

He gestured towards the iron maiden, and William's eyes involuntarily followed. It was, most certainly, the most deluxe iron maiden imaginable. Like the mummy cases William had seen in Egypt, the casing had been painted to resemble a woman.

Delaroche grasped the handle cleverly concealed among the lady's skirts. Inch by inch, the façade of the iron maiden jerked open, revealing its spiky intestines.

For the first time in a long and successful career, it occurred to William that he might actually die and there was little more he could do to outwit it.

Death was, of course, a possibility he had considered in the past. Blakeney had counseled him when they joined the League of the Sphinx. Mortality hadn't seemed all that pressing at the time.

All those times he'd contemplated his potential demise—in the moments before he'd crawled through a Temple prison window or plunged into a group of armed French agents—he had consoled himself with the thought that he'd left a legacy of which he could be proud. He had done something heroic with his life. Only now that wasn't enough anymore. All he could think about was Geneviève.

When he tried to picture Henry V, plunging into the breach at

Honfleur, instead he saw Geneviève, popping out from underneath a desk. Instead of Achilles roaring beneath the walls of Troy, there was Geneviève, swinging a punch at Edward Taunton. Geneviève, Geneviève everywhere—and usually somewhere she wasn't supposed to be, William thought, with what might have turned into a grin if Delaroche hadn't tested one of the spikes of the iron maiden and sprung away, holding a handkerchief to his bleeding finger.

Devil take it, he didn't want to die. Not that he'd ever really *wanted* to die, but how in the blazes was he supposed to tell Geneviève he loved her if he was dead?

Delaroche dropped the bloody handkerchief and bore down upon William. "Cabot, meet your doom."

# CHAPTER 41

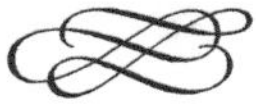

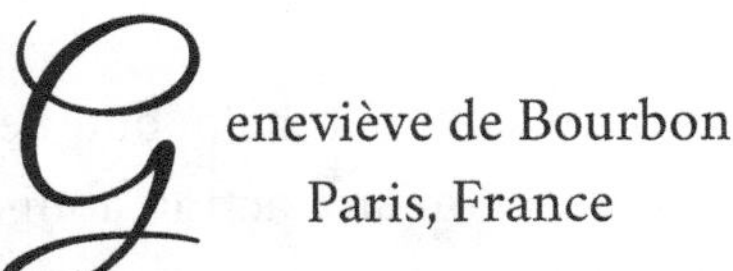

Geneviève de Bourbon
Paris, France

The uneven stones of the wall rasped against Geneviève's back as she cautiously tilted her head around the corner of the corridor for a second glance. "I didn't think there would be so many of them," whispered Geneviève.

Three sentries in dark blue coats, muskets at their sides, ranged in front of a large wooden door banded with iron. There were five other doors in the corridor, four of them mere grilles, revealing the cells within. When she craned her neck, Geneviève could see a hint of movement in one and a bony arm in another. The fifth portal was a smaller version of the guarded door, a heavy oaken affair hinged and studded with iron, with a tiny shuttered window at the height of a man's head. Geneviève's gaze darted back to the largest portal. The window was closed, the thick wood of the door and the massive stone walls muffling any sounds from within. But Geneviève had no doubts that they were finally within view of Delaroche's special interrogation chamber. And William.

And three armed sentries.

She had thought that just getting into the building had been nerve-racking. There had been that heart-stopping moment when the guard at the front entrance of the Ministry of Police had demanded their passes. He had peered at the seal Adam had stolen from Delaroche with a care that could denote either suspicion or poor eyesight. Geneviève and Lady Asaph had avoided looking at one another, lest they betray their fear in a guilty glance. But after an agonizing moment of scrutiny, the guard had shoved the papers back at Geneviève. "All in order."

He had, nonetheless, demanded to see the contents of their pails. "The minister thinks there might be trouble tonight."

Geneviève had endeavored to look nonchalant, but the unaccustomed bulk of her dagger's sheath burned against her calf. She tried to stand as a charwoman would stand, perhaps with a bit of a slump from the weight of the bucket.

Glancing over at Lady Asaph, Geneviève couldn't help but be impressed by Mary's handiwork and the older woman's acting abilities. There wasn't a hint of the English marchioness left in the woman beside her. Lady Asaph's silvering blond tresses had been liberally combed through with ashes to turn them a rough, dirty gray, and then covered with an equally sooty kerchief that looked as though it had served as both a cleaning rag and someone's handkerchief before being pressed into duty as a head covering. Her tattered brown dress hung shapelessly from her from as she slouched forward, unspeakably aged, clutching two voluminous shawls around her shoulders to warm her old bones and make up for the ripped and patched state of her sleeves. Even her face looked different. Mary had accentuated her crow's feet with a careful web of lines drawn in charcoal, but it was more than that. Something about the slack hang of the mouth, the tired droop of the eyelids.

Past the first obstacle, Lady Asaph and Geneviève had scrubbed their way down the midnight hallways of the Ministry of Police. Torches along the walls cast flickering reflections in the water in their pails. They had marched through the halls in search of the staircase that would lead them down to the dungeons and William, and had stayed in the pools of light rather than the shadows. "Less suspicious that way," Michael had advised. "Why would a washerwoman hide unless she wasn't really a washerwoman?"

The flagstones of the ministry provided an echoing warning of anyone's approach—unless that person had, like Geneviève and Lady Asaph, removed their shoes. But the only people to pass them had been soldiers, whose booted and spurred feet gave the alarm in ample time for Lady Asaph and Geneviève to fall to their knees and pretend deep absorption in grime removal.

In her daydreams of espionage, she had always been armed with an epée and a pistol, and an escort composed of well-muscled members of the League of the Sapphire Sphinx, who presumably knew how to employ both sword and firearms. Never had she imagined that she would find herself in the dungeons of the most closely guarded building in Paris, accompanied by an aging English noblewoman, with an armory consisting of one dagger strapped to her calf, one elderly dueling pistol—courtesy of Lord Asaph, who had last fired it in 1772—and a bottle of drugged brandy. Mary had insisted on the brandy, over Michael's protests that opiates had little pace in hand-to-hand combat. Geneviève supposed they could always use the bottle as a club.

A dagger, a pistol, and a bottle against three large men armed with muskets.

"Do you think he'll have more men inside with him?" Geneviève whispered to Lady Asaph, leaning over to make sure her dagger was still safely in its sheath.

"We'll face that when we get there. Or rather"—Lady Asaph patted her dueling pistol tucked beneath her voluminous shawl—"*They* will face *us*. Ready, my dearest?"

Geneviève loosened the ribbons securing her bodice and edged her neckline down to the verge of immodesty. Four weapons, she thought with a surge of optimism. After all, even Revolutionary guards were men and would make utter cakes of themselves when faced with a shapely female form. Mary had garbed her with just that prospect in mind, ransacking the wardrobes of William's maids until she had found a low-cut blouse that laced up the front and a wide woolen skirt that stopped an inch short of Geneviève's ankles and accentuated the sway of her hips.

"Ready," Geneviève whispered.

Dropping to hands and knees, the two women rounded the corner, swirling their dirty clothes over the flagstones. *Slosh, swish, slosh...*

Two yards closer to the guarded floor, another swipe of the dirty cloth and another yard disappeared under a slick film of water. Geneviève wondered if the three guards, visible to her only as three pairs of boot-tops and three pairs of black gaiters, would realize that their charwomen were scrubbing very lackadaisically and neglecting whole swaths of floor. Although, from the state of the flagstones, it didn't appear that anyone had scrubbed down in the dungeons for a very long time. Geneviève scuttled around a particularly nasty brownish stain, yanking her woolen skirts out of the way.

"You!" One set of boots detached itself from the row and tromped up to Geneviève.

Geneviève's head flew up, past black gaiters and dark blue breeches, at which point her neck refused to bend back any further. Settling back on her knees, she tilted her head up to a broad face sporting three days' worth of fair stubble. The guard who had stepped forward was the largest of the three, and clearly their leader, a hulking Goliath of a man, with jowls sagging around a beefy face, and a shock of pale hair of an indeterminate shade. He wouldn't be easily subdued. Behind him, poised on either side of the massive door, the two others looked on. If the first guard was Goliath, then the second guard, considerably shorter than his companions, had to be David. Geneviève's gaze caught him halfway through a yawn. As for the third, he was lean and dark. A thin mustache, not unlike the one Geneviève had drawn on Mary's face earlier in the evening, shadowed his lips. There was dangerous stillness about him, as though he was holding himself taut, waiting to spring. Like a slingshot, decided Geneviève. He would be one to watch carefully.

"You!" the big soldier—Goliath—barked again.

"Yes, sir."

"What do you think you're doing down here?"

Geneviève glanced down at her bucket, then over at Lady Asaph, who continued to ply her dirty cloth in slow circles, around and around the same flagstone. "Cleaning, sir?"

"I can see that." The guard rasped his hand through the stubble on his chin. "Did no one tell you you're not to clean down here?"

He sounded irritable, but not suspicious. Geneviève breathed a silent sigh of relief and feigned confusion. "No, sir," she said eagerly, making a show of stumbling to her feet and brushing off her patched skirts. "We was just told to scrub. Did you hear that, Ma?"

"Yes, yes," Lady Asaph croaked in cracked tones, the one word she could be trusted to say without alerting a listener to her English accent.

The guard visibly relaxed. "You may go."

Geneviève nodded enthusiastically. The guard didn't seem to notice as she edged a few inches closer to the door with the movement. "You don't know what a relief it is not to have to do this floor, too. Why, we thought we wouldn't see our beds before dawn, and me Ma, well, she has another job days, at a big, fancy house in the Faubourg Saint-Germain." Geneviève drawled the last name with the contempt appropriate to any good revolutionary.

"Long night," the guard agreed with a nod.

"Yes, yes," Lady Asaph smiled broadly in acknowledgement, revealing a mouthful of blackened teeth. Geneviève had always known that trick with the soot and gum would come in handy someday. "Yes, yes."

Geneviève might have been tempted to laugh had she not caught the hint of a sound from behind the door. Any potential amusement at Lady Asaph's performance drained away from Geneviève instantly. William was behind that door, being questioned and possibly—no, probably—tortured.

Geneviève flung back her shoulders and leaned forward so that her loosened bodice gaped. The shorter guard's jaw fell appreciatively open, and his musket sagged several inches. Following up on her advantage, Geneviève twined a dark curl around one finger. "Long night for you all, too, ain't it?"

"Oh, it's not all that bad," David babbled, staggering forward a few steps from the door to get a better view of Geneviève's charms. One down, she thought. Lady Asaph was nudging her bucket slowly along the flagstones, closer and closer to the door.

Geneviève took a little step back, drawing David out father from the door, and focused the force of her smile on Goliath. "Must get pretty boring just standing here all night. Don't know how I'd stay on my feet that long. But then, I'm not a big, strong man like you."

Something like a snort emerged from the shawl-covered form of Lady Asaph, but Goliath's chest puffed out. "Doesn't take much strength."

"Just staying power," put in the little one, waggling his eyebrows suggestively.

Geneviève wasn't quite sure what he meant so she grinned back at him as though she understood and waggled her eyebrows back for good measure, with an extra dip designed to show a maximum amount of cleavage.

The only one who didn't show any sign of succumbing to Geneviève's charm or her bosom was Slingshot, who stood just as firmly at his post as he had five minutes before, his hands gripping the stock of his musket. And he was eyeing Geneviève's antics with a critical eye. Either he was fanatically devoted to duty, or smarter than the others and had smelled a rat. Neither option suited Geneviève.

A rat. Geneviève grinned. She gave an agitated squeal—not loud enough to disturb the inhabitants of the room, but just shrill enough to get the attention of all three guards.

"Rat," she cried, yanking her skirt up around her ankles and hopping from one foot to the other. "Oh, there's a rat."

She flung herself straight at Slingshot. Taken by surprise, the guard staggered sideways—away from the door. Geneviève grabbed his arm and yanked him back towards the center of the corridor, squealing and hopping all the while.

"There." She pointed a quavering finger at an imaginary spot down the hall. "I saw it right there. All dark and furry with them little sharp teeth. *Oh.*" She flung both arms around Slingshot, immobilizing him in the middle of the hallway. Through the crook of his arm, she could see Lady Asaph, poised right outside the heavy oak door. But she wasn't opening it. Geneviève made little flapping motions with her hands. Lady Asaph shook her head. Drat. What was she waiting for?

Geneviève frowned. Lady Asaph mimed glugging noises—and hurriedly bent again to the floor as David glanced her way. Right. The brandy.

Goliath patted Geneviève heavily on the shoulder. "There, there, miss. It's gone now."

Geneviève whirled away from Slingshot, making sure to keep one arm linked through his, and gazed up at Goliath with big anxious eyes. "Are you sure? *That* big it were." She sketched with one hand. "I could just feel it brushing against my leg."

Geneviève yanked up her skirts and stared down at the limbs in question. Three pairs of masculine eyes followed.

"I'll keep the big, bad rat off your legs." The little one leered.

"I think…" Geneviève sagged, an arm over her forehead. "I think I need a drop of brandy." She pulled the bottle out of the large pocket in her voluminous skirt, uncorked it, and, turning her head to the side, pretending to take a big swig.

"Greedy me." She giggled ostentatiously wiping droplets off her chin. "Would any of you gentlemen like a drop?"

Goliath cast a longing glance at the flask. "We're not supposed to."

"Oh, go on. I won't tell." Geneviève thrust the bottle at him and batted her eyelashes.

David kept his eyes on the brandy. "Leave some for me."

Goliath took a long swig and passed the bottle to David, who glugged greedily, and offered it to Slingshot. The dark man shook his head. "We're on duty," he cautioned with a glower.

"What harm can it—"

Thud.

David broke off midsentence as the dungeon door swung open, banging into the wall. The ragged form of Lady Asaph darted through.

Slingshot made a belated grab for Geneviève. She yanked her arm from his, sprinting after Lady Asaph. The other two guards stood frozen with surprise as the old charwoman drew forth an elegant dueling pistol from the folds of her grimy shawl. She wielded her husband's pistol at Delaroche with the skill of an assured duelist. "Drop those thumbscrews and step away from my son."

# CHAPTER 42

*L*ord William Cabot
Paris, France

"Mother?" William gasped. Good God, Delaroche hadn't even started torturing him, and already he was hallucinating. But that certainly looked like his mother, and right behind her was—Geneviève.

William blinked. It was undeniably Geneviève—and a good deal of Geneviève was on view thanks to the unlaced state of her blouse.

"Don't even think of moving," Lady Asaph snapped at Delaroche.

Geneviève sprinted past her and made straight for William. Behind her, three guards, one fat, one short and one tall and thin, crammed through the entrance and stumbled to a stop just short of Lady Asaph and her pistol.

"Did he hurt you?" Geneviève grabbed at William's bound hands and began plucking at the complicated series of knots. "I don't see any blood."

Over Geneviève's bent head, William saw his mother carefully circle so that she could keep the guards within her sights, as well as Delaroche.

"Drop those muskets. Drop them, I said." Lady Asaph harrumphed in annoyance. Three dull thuds followed.

Lady Asaph glowered over the sights of her pistol. "If any of you so much as consider moving, I shall shoot Monsieur Delaroche. Do you understand?"

Much shifting from foot to foot and mumbling ensued from the guards.

"No talking," said Lady Asaph with a wave of her silver-handled pistol that made Delaroche flinch. "Oh, don't be such a coward, you nasty little man. I assure you, I'm a crack shot. I won't hit you unless I *intend* to hit you."

"The rope is all bunched together." Geneviève reached under her skirts and came up with a dagger. "I can't untie it."

"How in the blazes did you get in here?" William tried to keep his eyes off the blade sawing back and forth between some very vital veins. A fiber snapped and he felt the rope slacken a fraction.

"I'll explain later." Geneviève cast an anxious look at the three restless guards. She whispered, "Mary emptied well over ten doses of a sleeping draft into a brandy they drank."

William flinched as the knife nearly went into his palm. The small guard yawned, but it was well past midnight. True, both the big man's and the little man's movement seemed slower, but that might be a result of the pistol, not the drug.

"Ouch," William yelped.

"Sorry, sorry," Geneviève muttered, turning her attention back to his hands. Another fiber snapped, and another. With a determined twist of his wrists, William broke free of the rope.

Geneviève dropped to her knees and began frantically sawing on the ropes binding William's legs. He didn't like the way that the tall, suspicious guard was eyeing his mother, or the way Delaroche was edging closer to a lethal-looking double-headed ax mounted on a crimson velvet stand.

"I'll take over." William leaned over, wafting Geneviève away from his legs. Between his mother holding a gun on Delaroche and Geneviève untying him, he was beginning to feel uncomfortably peripheral to his own rescue. Michael would never let him hear the end of it. Hell, he might as well resign his memberships in his clubs and join a sewing circle. His mother, blast it, was getting far too much enjoyment out of poking Delaroche in the ribs with her pistol.

"Stop!" Lady Asaph snapped, as the little guard staggered a few paces sideways. A few steps closer to the pile of muskets. The little guard stopped, swaying on his feet.

"Sleepy," yawned the little guard, sagging against the wall.

William wrenched at the knots binding his legs, pulling a tail of rope loose with a satisfied grunt. Nearly free.

Straw and dust scattered in all directions as the large guard fell heavily to his knees and toppled over facedown on the floor. His smaller colleague gave another large yawn and tumbled on top of him, snoring. Delaroche wrenched his head around in shock. So, too, did a startled and delighted Lady Asaph. Her pistol wavered forgotten in her hand for a mere moment as she beamed at the small pile of sleeping men.

That moment was all the guard needed. Moving with a coiled energy, he knocked the pistol out of Lady Asaph's hand and grabbed her from behind, wrenching her back with such force that her feet rose off the ground. The pistol skittered across the straw-strewn dungeon floor.

Dropping the dagger with a clatter, Geneviève dove for the pistol —as did Delaroche. Hampered by her broad skirts, Geneviève pounced on the pistol just as Delaroche's bony hand swept it up off the flagstones. Her hand clutched empty air and a handful of stray straws. Geneviève gasped for air, but her breath caught in her throat as Delaroche aimed the pistol at her chest.

Geneviève scrabbled at the dirty floor, hastily scooting backwards as Delaroche followed, a self-satisfied smile on his angular face.

Kicking her legs free of the enveloping folds of her skirt, she lurched to her feet. Delaroche followed her movements with the pistol.

William tried desperately to untie his legs while Delaroche was distracted.

"You, Mlle de Bourbon"—Delaroche stepped deliberately forward, forcing Geneviève to slink backwards, her eyes fastened on the pistol —"have outlived your usefulness. You have become, how do you say in your barbaric tongue? Ah, yes. A nuisance. But not, I think"— Delaroche herded Geneviève inexorably backwards—"for much longer."

Geneviève cast a quick, panicky gaze around her. To her right, the open lid of the iron maiden blocked a sideways leap. William bounded to her side. With one fluid movement, he yanked her out of the path of the iron maiden and positioned himself between Geneviève and Delaroche. A ragged tail of rope still trailed form his left leg.

"You've had your fun for the night, Delaroche." He brandished Geneviève's dagger. "Now it's time for you to fight like a man."

Delaroche snarled.

"William," Geneviève whispered, "he still has a pistol."

"Mother." William's eyes didn't leave Delaroche. "Is that blasted thing loaded?"

"I don't—" the guard tried to clap his hand over Lady Asaph's mouth but she administered a sharp elbow to the rib. "—know, darling."

"Brilliant," muttered William, circling Delaroche to put the maximum distance between himself and the iron maiden. Trust his mother to bluff her way into the dungeons of the Ministry of Police with a possibly unloaded pistol.

"There is one way to find out," Delaroche chortled. He aimed the pistol at William's heart. "Farewell, Cabot."

Geneviève struck Delaroche's arm as his finger closed over the trigger, knocking his aim sideways. The pistol discharged, knocking a fragment of stone off the wall. The force of the recoil sent Delaroche reeling several steps backwards. Geneviève sneezed uncontrollably as acrid black smoke trailed from the pistol.

Delaroche stared in alarm at the smoking firearm. With a sudden movement, he dropped the useless pistol and darted for the double-sided ax.

"William!" Geneviève screamed. She tugged at a broadsword

mounted on the wall between two grinning skulls. The weight of the weapon sent her stumbling backwards. William raced to her side, grabbing the sword from her just as Delaroche wrenched the ax free of its mount. "Here, take this," he ordered, pressing her dagger back into her hand. "Free mother."

Delaroche swung at William, the double blade arcing in a deadly circle through the torchlight. William jumped back, leaving the edge of the ax to strike sparks against the stone of the wall. William tried to heft his sword one-handed, as he would an epée. His wrist nearly snapped under the strain. Readjusting both hands on the hilt of the weapon and raising it with an effort, William cursed softly. His childhood fencing academy had never prepared him for this. Devil take it, this was the sort of sword one of his ancestors might have wielded. It had been made for burly barbarians wearing armor and riding massive warhorses—not a civilized nineteenth-century gentleman accustomed to dealing with the niceties of epées. Hell. William swung again, a clumsy stroke that missed Delaroche by half a foot.

*Clang.* The ax clashed against the broadsword, taking a chip out of the blade. Reverberations trembled up William's arms.

Who would have thought that Delaroche would have so much strength in him?

William retreated, trying to remember everything he had read in his inquisitive boyhood about medieval warfare. It wasn't much. Just something about having to strike from above rather than stab with a broadsword, and he wasn't even sure that was right.

Delaroche's ax whistled by him again. William jumped back as the blade passed within an inch of abdomen. Delaroche staggered with the force of the swing.

Getting the feel of his weapon, William swung again at Delaroche, hoping to catch him off balance. He missed, but the weapon moved more smoothly this time, and his adversary stumbled backwards, the ax dragging visibly. William's lips curved into a predatory grin.

Lady Asaph's kerchief had been torn off and her sooty hair straggled wildly around her face. The skin around one eye was already beginning to purple and swell, but Lady Asaph fought on undaunted, kicking at her assailant's calves with her bare feet as he tried to pin down her flailing arms. Blood trickled down the guard's face from a series of nasty scratches that raked from eye to jaw.

"Unhand me, you vile, vile man." She panted. "Didn't your mother" —*kick*—"teach you any manners?"

"Don't you be saying anything about my mother." With a growl, the guard's hands shifted from Lady Asaph's arms to her throat. Lady Asaph made little choking noises as he began to squeeze.

"Noooo!" Geneviève launched herself at the guard. Her dagger tore through his sleeve, opening a long, bleeding rent along his upper arm. Roaring with pain, he dropped Lady Asaph, who stumbled, gasping, afterwards. Enraged, he turned on Geneviève. She yanked her bloodied dagger back into a ready position.

Lady Asaph rushed for the fallen muskets, grabbing one off the pile.

"I'll do it again." Geneviève's voice was shrill.

Behind the guard, Lady Asaph raised the musket. The heavy wooden stock crashed down on his head. The guard dropped to the ground.

Lady Asaph's shoulders sagged. "Finally."

In the center of the room, William and Delaroche continued to bludgeon each other with weapons that had been old when Shakespeare was young. They lurched awkwardly backwards and forwards, propelled by the sheer weight of their weapons. Both were breathing heavily; both clutched hilts slick with perspiration. William limped slightly where Delaroche's ax had nicked him just above the knee. Delaroche favored his left arm, where William had whapped him with the full force of the flat of his blade.

Delaroche lunged.

William whacked the blade away. "That wasn't very polite."

"I don't need lessons in etiquette from you, Cabot." Delaroche snarled.

"Given what I've seen of your entertainment of guests, I wouldn't be so sure."

Delaroche growled with rage and swung wildly—too wildly.

"For our first lesson"—William's blade thrust under his guard—"we'll discuss the rules of surrender." He levered his sword against the handle of the ax, sending Delaroche's weapon spiraling out of his hands.

Delaroche skidded back. "Your surrender, Cabot. Not mine."

William advanced. "Your surrender. Or next time my blade strikes home."

"Arrogant." Delaroche whirled, and ran for the door to the dungeon.

William dropped his broadsword and sprinted in pursuit.

"Gua—" Delaroche tripped over a fallen musket and plummeted to the floor.

William skidded to a stop just in time to save himself from tumbling over Delaroche. Geneviève grabbed Lady Asaph's discarded bucket and emptied the contents over Delaroche's head. A whoosh of dirty water turned his cry to an indignant splutter. A sodden rag flopped from one ear.

"Quick." Lady Asaph grabbed the rag and shoved it into Delaroche's mouth, just in case he harbored any more thoughts of calling for reinforcements.

Geneviève bound his legs, while William secured his flailing arms. With his trussed limbs, his popping eyes and the ball of fabric in his mouth, Delaroche made a particularly unappetizing suckling pig.

Lady Asaph stood back and glowered at their adversary. "I say we throw him into the iron maiden."

William whacked Delaroche's head with a musket barrel. William grabbed his mother with one hand and Geneviève with the other. "Run."

# CHAPTER 43

Geneviève de Bourbon
Paris, France

An air of suppressed excitement emanated from the small group in
the de Bourbon courtyard. Even the horses harnessed to the plain
black carriage moved restlessly back and forth, swishing their brown
manes. As three disheveled figures stole through the gates, the group
let out ragged cheer.

"You made it. I knew you could do it!" Catherine flung herself at
her mother and brother.

"What took you so long?" Michael pounded his best friend on the
back.

Geneviève hung back behind Lady Asaph, watching as Catherine
clung to William's arm, chattering and exclaiming. Adam kept shaking
his head and muttering, "Thank God." Michael bounded by William's
side like a faithful hunting dog, and Lord Asaph took William's hand
with a solemnity that was enough to make anyone tearful. Even Miss
Agnes unbent enough to announce that she was pleased to see him
return unharmed, which, for Miss Agnes, represented a great excess
of emotion.

The courtyard resounded with good cheer. Except for Geneviève, who wanted nothing more than to sit down heavily on the cobblestones. It had, after all, been a long and anxious night after all the excitement of planning the raid on the Swiss gold, and the fight with William, and the anxiety of his rescue and running across half of Paris in the dead of night.

Geneviève tried to join in the jubilant spirit. After all, they had rescued William. Huzzah. Even in Geneviève's head, the *huzzah* lacked conviction. She might have rescued William—with a great deal of help—but there was the pesky matter of why William had needed rescuing in the first place. How he must despise her. He hadn't said anything on the way back. Lady Asaph had spoken enough for all three of them. She knew what he must be thinking. She had vindicated his mistrust ten thousand times over. She had ended his career as The Sapphire Sphinx.

It was all over. Not only Delaroche, but fifteen—*fifteen*—of his men had seen William unmasked, by his own hand, as the Sapphire Sphinx. It would be all over Paris by morning and in the London illustrated papers by noon the next day. William could never return to Paris again. He might not be dead, but the Sapphire Sphinx was. Delaroche would be proud, Geneviève thought bitterly.

She wanted to crawl into the house, bury her head under a pillow and hide.

"Geneviève." Catherine darted over and dragged Geneviève into the circle. "You're such a heroine. What was the torture chamber like?"

"Torture chambers are so trite," sniffed Miss Agnes.

Catherine ignored her. "Was it truly ghastly?"

Geneviève scarcely registered the exchange because William's eyes were on her, casting her another unreadable sidelong look. The entire way back to the Hotel de Bourbon, he hadn't directed one solitary word her way. Just those *looks*.

Geneviève nodded absently. "Ghastly," she echoed. She wished he would just explode already and be done with it. Tell her he hated her. Tell her she'd ruined his life. Tell her.

"Ooh, splendid. You must tell me all about it later. But now"—

Catherine twirled in a circle in an impromptu victory dance—"guess what we have in the carriage?"

"We?" Michael waggled his sandy eyebrows at Catherine. "Just who went on this mission?"

Under cover of their bickering, William edged towards Geneviève. His father, in his own quiet way, had proved very insistent about recounting the saga of the Swiss gold in epic detail. By the time Lord Asaph got around to the bit where Miss Agnes disarmed one guard and rammed another in the stomach with her trusty parasol, William turned to Geneviève.

"I'm so sorry," Geneviève blurted. "I know I've ruined everything, and I wish there were some way I could make it up to you."

"Ruined everything?"

"The Sapphire Sphinx." Geneviève shifted on her dirty bare feet. "Your mission. Everything."

"Not quite everything," broke in Miss Agnes smugly. "We have the gold, and we'll soon have Lord Cabot safely out of Paris."

"We have a boat waiting for you," Michael called, loping around Miss Agnes.

"The boat formerly belonging to Edward Taunton." Adam joined the group.

"Don't worry," Michael added, "we sent Gideon along to clear it out for you."

"We'll pack up your things and follow in a few days," Lady Asaph contributed. "We have it all taken care of, darling. You shouldn't worry about a thing."

"You seem to have it all planned," William said levelly.

*Don't go,* Geneviève wanted to beg. But she couldn't. Delaroche knew William's identity. To stay in Paris was to flirt with the gallows, if not something far worse. Miss Agnes was right. He had to go, and quickly.

Geneviève's entire body ached with the strain of holding back tears. She tried to console herself with the prospect of carrying on the Talisman—which was, after all, what she had come to Paris to do. But, somehow, the prospect of espionage had lost its luster for her. There couldn't be a Paris for her without William. His presence would haunt her in the corners of Mme Bonaparte's yellow salon and the corridors of the Tuileries. And then there was the Seine… the boat… the carriage… even her brother's house. There wasn't a place in the city that hadn't been imprinted with the memory of William.

Even the sparkling stars in the night sky above her belonged to William

"May I come with you?" Geneviève heard herself ask.

Catherine's mouth snapped shut midsentence. Miss Agnes ceased poking Michael with her parasol. The entire courtyard went still, everyone's attention riveted on Geneviève. It was like being in Sleeping Beauty's castle, surrounded by frozen figures caught in an enchantment.

"I want to come with you," Geneviève repeated, her voice unnaturally loud in the lull. "That is," she added, as William made no response, no movement, "if you'll have me?"

"Will I have you?" William repeated incredulously. "Will *I* have *you*?"

Uncomfortably aware of the seven pairs of eyes upon her, Geneviève flushed a deep red.

"Will I have you?" William whooped. Swooping, he jerked Geneviève off her feet, and whirled her in a dizzying circle. "Oh, no, no! You have it all wrong. The question," he pronounced, lowering her very, very slowly to her feet, "is, will *you* have *me*? After all, I'm the one who made a muddle of everything by not telling you the truth—"

"But I made you reveal your secret identity." A tear fell down her cheek.

William grinned down at her. "I should have revealed it to you days ago."

Her heart was pounding so hard it was about to burst right out of her chest. The sides of her face were about to split from the smile that was spreading across them. And her head was so light it was about to float right off the rest of her body. "You don't hate me for exposing you to Delaroche?"

"Not if you don't hate me for calling you a light-skirt."

"It was the bit of fluff that hurt." Geneviève reveled in the press of William's hands on the small of her back and the way his green eyes crinkled at the corners.

"Give me a half century or so, and I'll make it up to you."

"I think he's trying to propose to you." Catherine clasped her hands together.

"Don't you have someplace else you need to be?" scowled William.

"You're going about this all wrong," Catherine said with a huff. "You're supposed to get down on one knee and—" She subsided with a muffled yelp as Lady Asaph clamped a hand over her daughter's mouth.

"Don't interrupt them or you'll spoil it," Lady Asaph hissed.

"Can't you all just go away?" William roared.

"This is all very charming," announced Miss Agnes, "but I believe *you* are the one who needs to go away, my lord, before someone from the Ministry of Police alerts the guards at the gates of the city."

William glowered at Miss Agnes before turning back to Geneviève. Taking her hand, he said softly, "Geneviève, I love you. I want to marry you. I'll get down on as many knees as you require of me—as soon as this lot *goes away.*" His voice dropped again. "Will you come with me?"

"To the wide world's end," replied Geneviève. "Or to Calais—whichever is closer."

William grinned. "Definitely Calais, then. Does this mean you love me?" he asked in a voice pitched for Geneviève's ears only.

"Yes, yes, yes."

"Ah, my excellent powers of seduction persuaded you—"

Geneviève bit her lip. "Do you really think we should be talking about seduction in front of your family?"

She looked so adorable in her embarrassment that William didn't much care whether his family was breathing over their shoulders or stranded in the farthest Antipodes. He just knew he had to kiss her. Right that very moment.

"It's all right," he murmured, leaning in. "We are going to be married."

"Oh, in *that* case…"

"Shhhh!" Through a fog, William heard Catherine hush Michael on the threshold of a snide comment. "I think he's going to kiss her."

His jaw clenched. Geneviève, meanwhile, had gone bright red again, and banged her forehead against William's chest to hide.

"Right," William said through compressed lips. "That's enough. Let's go."

"Wait, we want to see your technique." Michael jeered. "Ow!"

Miss Agnes had applied her parasol to Michael's arm with immediate effect.

"You can't just take Geneviève and go!" Lady Asaph protested, looking uncharacteristically perturbed. "I know I've been a rather permissive mother"—Catherine coughed into her hand—"but I really cannot countenance you going off along with a young lady of good family. And overnight, no less. No, William, you'll just have to wait until we bring Geneviève back with us, and then we can arrange everything properly. We'll have the wedding breakfast at Asaph House, Geneviève dear, unless you think your aunt and uncle will object? Hmm, I wonder if the dear archbishop—"

Geneviève put her arm firmly through William's. "What if someone were to chaperone us?" She looked appealingly at her cousin. "Mary?"

Mary's brow furrowed. She clasped her hands together at her waist. "Geneviève, I'm not going back."

"What do you mean?" asked Geneviève.

Little circles of pink burned in Mary's pale cheeks. "I know it was always your dream, Geneviève, but, if you don't mind terribly, I'd like to stay on as the Talisman."

"Oh. Of course I don't mind. Just, are you sure that's what you want, Mary?"

"More than anything, Evie," Mary said simply.

"What is the Talisman?" William whispered to Geneviève.

"I'll explain later," Geneviève whispered back.

"And I"—Miss Agnes thumped her parasol for attention—"am staying with her, so don't look to me for a chaperone, missy."

"Not bloody likely," muttered William.

"I'd be your chaperone," volunteered Catherine, "only Mama would never let me."

"Besides," Michael shrugged, "the more people go along, the more difficult it will be to smuggle you all out. Kiss your betrothed good-bye, old chap, and have a pleasant journey home."

"Enough!" Geneviève stamped her foot, and the sturdy boot she was wearing made a satisfying reverberation on the cobbles. It was time to take action. Grabbing William's hands, she announced. "William, I give you full permission to compromise me."

"Why aren't we all that lucky?" Michael put a hand on his chest and faced the sky in mock reverence.

"Geneviève, you don't mean that," interjected Lady Asaph.

"If anyone hears that I was alone with William, can't we just spread the rumor we were already secretly married in France? Nobody except all of us here will ever know the difference." Geneviève sent an appealing glance around the group in the courtyard. Catherine looked like she was on the verge of applauding. Miss Agnes eyed her coldly. "Please. I don't want to be separated again."

"I second that." William squeezed her shoulders.

"Who are we to stand in the way of young love, Honoria?" William's father said with a rich chuckle. "After all, if you remember—"

The marchioness shook her head, her face turning bright pink.

The marquess patted his wife's hand, smiling broadly. "I thought so, my dear."

William looked in horror from one parent to the other. "I don't want to know. I just don't want to know."

"We shall use our consequence to protect Miss de Bourbon's reputation, and no one will dare to say anything against her." Lord Asaph winked at Geneviève. "Welcome to the family, my dear. Now don't you think you ought to be going?"

# CHAPTER 44

*L*ord William Cabot
English Channel

"You do know that I didn't consider you an infatuation, a light-skirt, or a bit of fluff?" William said for at least the tenth time since they left Paris.

Geneviève snuggled into the curve of his arm. On the desperate ride from Paris to Calais, she and William had been hidden, rather uncomfortably, in large wine barrels. William would whisper through the bunghole in his barrel to hers reassuring Geneviève of his deep and sincere sentiments for her.

They were standing on the deck of Taunton's boat, watching the widening strip of water that separated them from Calais, France, and the infuriated minions of the Ministry of Police. Taunton's crew, at the sight of a few gold pieces, had happily defected to the nearby taverns and been replaced by William's staff. William only hoped that at least one or two of his men knew something about sailing, or it might be a very wet swim home...

William groaned.

"Are you all right?" Geneviève asked drowsily, her sleepless night in a barrel beginning to catch up with her.

William gritted his teeth. "Mother'll probably insist on getting the Archbishop of Canterbury. And how long does it take to prepare a wedding breakfast for five hundred people?"

"Five hundred people?" Geneviève yawned.

William seized Geneviève by the shoulders. Her eyelashes flew up. "Ship captains can perform wedding ceremonies, can't they? It's legal, isn't it?"

"Did I miss something?" Geneviève scrubbed her eyes with her fists. "I'm sorry. I must have been dozing off. Five hundred ships' captains…"

"Let's get married!"

"Wasn't that the plan already?"

"No, I mean right now. Here. We can have the captain marry us. Whoever the captain is."

"But why?" Geneviève began bemusedly. William tipped her back over the rail of the ship for a long, searing, kiss. Fortunately, Taunton's boat was in far better repair than the packet they had taken over, or they would have both been thrashing about in the waters of the Channel.

Geneviève's face looked considerably less sleepy as comprehension dawned. "What a splendid idea."

"Excellent!" William grabbed Geneviève's hand and tugged her away from the rail. "Who's acting captain?" he hollered across the deck.

It was Gideon, striding across the deck, only… William blinked. He couldn't tell whether his hair was still dyed gray, because it was covered by a bandanna of blinding red. One silver hoop swung from William's butler's ear. A white shirt billowed over breeches that had to have been deliberately frayed along the hems. And to top it all off, a parrot perched upon Gideon's shoulder.

"Arr, I be the captain," Gideon growled.

"Geneviève, you do remember my butler, Gideon, don't you?"

"There'll be no time for butlering on the high seas, me laddie,"

Gideon grumbled darkly. "I'll be busy fightin' off the sea serpents and battlin' the raging waves, waves that can bury a ship and none the wiser."

"Ah, but can you perform a wedding service?"

With a great many *arrs*, Gideon went off in search of a *Book of Common Prayer*. As Taunton's crew hadn't been much given to spontaneous religious ceremonies, the search proved fruitless. So Gideon improvised.

The midmorning sun shone down on them like a benediction. The air smelled of fish and brine. Mist was provided by the waves lapping against the keel—the wedding guests, William's footmen, staggered from side to side with the rocking of the boat. Geneviève's veil was a scrap of sailcloth, and the parson was an actor turned butler turned pirate, whose interpretation of the wedding service would have made the Archbishop of Canterbury take to his bed.

Geneviève beamed as William stood with his arm around her waist and his head resting on hers.

"I do!" croaked the parrot, who seemed to feel he had deserved a more central role in the ceremony.

Geneviève's eyelids fluttered open as the long kiss ended. "I'm not sure this is entirely legal, but I don't really care."

William grinned, and swept his new, if perhaps not entirely legal, wife up in his arms, and kissed the tip of her upturned nose. "I adore you, Geneviève, I really do."

Geneviève blew a kiss back up at him. "Despite my dubious morals, letting you compromise me like this?"

William squeezed her a little tighter as he carried her down the narrow stairs to Taunton's cabin. "I promise you," he said with an exaggerated leer, "I really don't consider that a drawback." Turning to the side, he shouldered open the door of Taunton's cabin.

Geneviève took in a brief glimpse of sunlight slanting across scarred wooden boards, a heavy table and chair, and a substantial bed. It was just like Taunton to deck his bed with red velvet draperies.

"Your threshold, my lady," William announced, carrying Geneviève over it.

Geneviève rubbed her head against his shoulder and started laughing. "Isn't it just like us?" she gasped between giggles. "We can't do anything properly. We don't even have a wedding night. We have a wedding *afternoon.*"

William maneuvered Geneviève through the door, kicking it shut behind them. "Look at it this way," he suggested, lowering her gently onto Taunton's gaudy red silk coverlet, "we get a wedding afternoon *and* a wedding night."

"Lucky us," agreed Geneviève breathlessly, as William's lips brushed across hers in an achingly tender kiss.

"It's so glorious to be able to kiss you and know it's you," said Geneviève several long kisses later, twining her arms tighter around William's neck.

"Do you miss the Sapphire Sphinx at all?" asked William, twirling one of her dark strands of hair around his finger.

Geneviève considered for a moment, leaning her head back on the pillow in a way that bared the white arch of her neck. Unable to resist, William ran a finger down the line of her throat, following it with his lips.

"Ohhh. You know, it's not at all easy to think when you do that. No. No, I don't miss him. He was a lovely romantic dream, but I much prefer—oof." The force of William's arms around her rendered finishing the thought impossible.

"Right answer."

"*True* answer. Besides," Geneviève added breathlessly, grinning up at him, "the mask could chafe."

"Do you think it ironic?" William whispered. "That a French woman was the reason Bonaparte lost out on his gold."

"Or that his beloved scholar turned out to be his Sapphire Sphinx."

"The creation and myth behind the talisman was a created of the Sapphire Sphinx." He grinned. "But you, Geneviève, turned out to be my talisman."

If he had ever taken the time to envision his wedding night—or, in this case, wedding afternoon—shouting with laughter wouldn't have been on the agenda. But that's just what he was doing. It was as if all the joy welling up within him needed an outlet. There were also other things demanding an outlet, but William wanted to keep those in check as long as possible, since Geneviève deserved the best wedding afternoon anyone had ever had.

He smoothed her hair away from her face. "I love you."

"Say it again," Geneviève begged, her blue eyes sparkling. "I can't ever hear you say it enough."

"I love you, Evie." William kissed the tip of Geneviève's nose and she giggled.

"I love you." Geneviève's giggle turned into a gasp as his lips touched the sensitive hollow above her collarbone. "As the Sapphire. As William. I love you."

# ABOUT THE AUTHOR

Clarissa Kae is a preeminent voice whose professional career began as a freelance editor in 2007. She's the former president of her local California Writers Club after spending several years as the Critique Director.

Since her first novel, she's explored different writing genres and created a loyal group of fans who eagerly await her upcoming release. With numerous awards to her name, Clarissa continues to honor the role of storyteller.

Aside from the writing community, she and her daughters founded Kind Girls Make Strong Women to help undervalued nonprofit organizations—from reuniting children with families to giving Junior Olympic athletes their shot at success.

She lives in the agricultural belly of California with her family and farm of horses, chickens, dogs and kittens aplenty.

www.clarissakae.com

# ALSO BY CLARISSA KAE

**Once Upon a Fairy Tale**

(Multi author anthology)

**Time Slip Novels**

Of Ink And Sea

**Women's Fiction**

Pieces To Mend

**Once And Future Wife Series**

Once And Future Wife

Disorder in the Veins (2023)

**Scarlet Pimpernel Spy Series**

The Sapphire Sphinx

**Victorian Retellings**

A Dark Beauty, Beauty & the Beast

Cinders Like Glass , Cinderella

A Stolen Heart, Robin Hood

Taming Christmas, Taming of the Shrew (standalone)

CPSIA information can be obtained
at www.ICGtesting.com
Printed in the USA
JSHW050526221022
31879JS00006B/147